PART I

TIME ZONES

THE SWALLOW
INHERITANCE

Laura Kalpakian

HEADLINE

First published in Great Britain in 1987 by
HEADLINE BOOK PUBLISHING PLC.

British Library Cataloguing in Publication Data

Kalpakian, Laura
    The swallow inheritance.
    I. Title
    813'.54[F]   PS3561.A4168

    ISBN: 0-7472-0006-8

HEADLINE BOOK PUBLISHING PLC.
Headline House
79 Great Titchfield Street
London W1P 7FN

Printed and bound in Great Britain by
Biddles Ltd, Guildford and King's Lynn

CHAPTER ONE

May 2, 1985

11:45 A.M.

The woman at the open window looked like any other of her class and vintage, clad to meet a conclave of like-minded, well-heeled matrons. Her taut, perfect posture reflected the cadet's rigid reflex rather than the dancer's native grace, but her makeup was modest, her blouse starched and her skirt a cool Monet blue. While her attire suggested attendance at a society luncheon, Claire Stone, in fact, had dressed for an appointment with disaster. She had a better than nodding acquaintance with disaster but preferred to meet it on her own terms, insisting on appearances, outward perfection, belying the woman crumbling within. She stood at her bedroom window and surveyed the familiar city, tiered below her like the full flounces of a crinoline, pinned with spires, threaded with wires and laced with the dull gleam of a thousand polished windows. Beyond the city lay the Pacific, obscured by gauzy banners of fog, as if someone had tried to erase the horizon and succeeded only in smudging it. Screeching gulls distantly counterpointed the finches chattering in the backyard elms as Claire rehearsed for her visit to the Emergency Ward, practicing on the elms, the finches, the Pacific, the speech she intended to use on her housekeeper. "May I borrow your car, Louise?" That would not do. "Do you mind. . ." No.

She cleared her throat and quit whispering. "I need to use your car, Louise. That phone call was the hospital. Lucky's had an accident." She squared her narrow shoulders and corrected herself. "Lucky's suddenly been taken very ill." Less than the altogether truth, this was nearer the point. "Lucky's been hospitalized for an obstruction of the gut." Yes, that's what she'd say. She need not add that the obstruction was a .22 caliber bullet and that he had got it there by virtue of having aimed at his heart and missed. Naturally, he missed.

"Matthew Mark Luke and John." Claire murmured her old childhood incantation, hopelessly inadequate to a situation that offered no sanctuary and no certainties. She glanced from the elms to the half-rumpled bed. Lucky had not come home last night. But he had shot himself only this morning. The police said so. He was not dead. Not yet. *Let him live, Lord, let him live.* Inwardly, Claire blessed her husband's incompetence, wondering if he had been drinking all night long and if the alcohol unsteadied his aim or if the alcohol itself had given him the courage for suicide. She guessed both.

She left the window and returned to the dressing table mirror, gave her loose bob one last unnecessary brush and surveyed the finished woman whose ash blond hair had considerably more ash than it used to. Still, Claire's features suggested youth retained rather than preserved. She straightened her collar; save for her jewelry, she was as ready as she would ever be. She must go now and confront Louise. *And then the catastrophe.* No, then the hospital. And after the hospital? *Let him live, Lord.* Her hand trembled as she carefully reapplied her lipstick. That her husband of nearly twenty-one years had shot himself was unthinkable, but that Claire should rush in, slatternly, unrehearsed, visibly disarrayed, was out of the question, and in that, she reflected grimly, she was still the prisoner of her mother's careful tutelage: Decency, Decorum and Dignity. The Three D's, her mother called them. These, along with good taste, good grooming, good manners, were the characteristics of nice girls. At forty-one, Claire was hardly a girl.

She went into the bathroom adjoining her bedroom and withdrew the bag of jewelry from the toilet tank. She put a pair of opal studs in her ears and then decided against them, selecting finally the sapphire solitaires to match the ring Lucky had given her in better days. That was the way they had lived: when there was money, there were sapphire solitaires and vacations in Europe and private schools for their sons. When there was money, they rented houses like this one, with manicured lawns and swimming pools, homes in newly affluent neighborhoods, living around newly affluent doctors and lawyers and computer wizards with whom they had nothing in common because when their money dried up and life changed, their boys went to public

4

school, they took their vacations at the family beach home in San Angelo and they had been known to report burglaries that never happened so that they might collect the insurance on the expendable jewelry. When there was no money, they rented homes in housing tracts where their neighbors were good-natured wage slaves with whom they also had nothing in common. Claire had learned not to make friends in either instance. She wondered where they would move now, because none of their reversals of fortune heretofore had involved the possibility of criminal proceedings or the IRS.

She scraped the jewelry back into the silk bag and stuffed the bag into a rubberized ice pack, twisting the coat hanger more firmly around the neck of the ice pack, and hung it back inside the toilet tank, replacing the lid. She did not need to flush the toilet to make sure the ice pack was above the water line. She'd done that yesterday as Treasury agents were combing her house, methodically seizing assets. Lucky had reacted stoically, sitting at the bar downstairs, staring at himself in the mirror and sipping one whiskey straight after another. Claire had responded to the emergency with the native guile of a born peasant. She fled to her bedroom, weeping loudly. She grabbed the silk bag of her jewels and retreated to the bathroom. She continued to sniffle audibly as she rifled the bathroom cabinets looking for something suitable, came upon the ice pack, shoved the bag in, ripped a robe out of the closet, twisted the neck of the hanger to fit around the top of the ice pack. She had just hung it in the toilet tank when she heard the Treasury agents coming upstairs and approaching the bedroom. As her wails rose in pitch and velocity, she took a glass from the sink and filled it with water from the tap. When she had actually heard the agents enter the bedroom, she held the glass over the toilet and retched noisily, tossing the water into the bowl in glops. She flushed the toilet, noting that the water in the tank just grazed the bottom of the ice bag. No one disturbed her.

Earrings in place, she now checked her makeup quickly and assured herself that she was ready. She picked up her purse and was about to leave the bedroom when the phone rang again. "Matthew Mark Luke and John," she whispered, lowering herself carefully to the bed. *Don't let it be the hospital. Please let Lucky live.* "Hello," she said in a hoarse voice.

"Mrs. Stone, this is Hoolihan. You might not remember me. I saw you last at Lucy Rose Cotton's wedding and that must be twenty years ago, and before that, at—"

Stop him, stop him before he "Hoolihan, of course," Claire mumbled,

5

her breath short and painful. "I remember." The past cracked open like an egg and dripped, gooey and gelatinous, into her lap. In an automatic gesture, she brushed her skirt and collected herself. "No one in my family is likely to forget you, to be that fortunate."

"No doubt your Aunt Althea sees to that."

"My aunt thinks you are a legal pimp for that whore Lucille Swallow," said Claire stiffly.

"Ungenerous, madam, but understandable. I read in the papers about your husband's bankruptcy and collision with the IRS. I am calling only to offer my services, free of charge, when he requires an attorney, as he surely will."

"Did Lucille put you up to this?"

"Your quarrel, if you have one, is with her, not with me. And in any event, Lucille has nothing to do with this. I select my own clients. I'd venture to say that if any attorney in this city could get your husband off, I can."

"Why? What is Lucky to you?"

"Nothing, madam. Your husband is nothing to me, but you were formerly Claire Swallow, were you not, the daughter of Judge Anson Swallow?"

Claire felt herself suddenly docketed in the witness stand; she mumbled in the affirmative.

"I admired your father above all men, Mrs. Stone. I offer my services as a gesture of respect to his memory—not," he added hastily, "in return for any favor or in payment for any debt. Just a gesture. You needn't decide now. I won't say call if you need me. From what I read in the papers, you need me, but you can call if you want me."

The phone went dead, and Claire dropped it like a corpse. She doubled over, momentarily undone by remembered pain, all the more brutal for its having been not simply once forgotten, but sliced from experience altogether. On the day she had married Lucky Stone, Claire resolved to inflict upon herself a selective lobotomy, and with time as her only anesthetic, she surgically, carefully, removed from memory the preceding two years of her life. She believed she could be healed by this desperate measure, and never retreated from her decision, and over the years, as necessity evolved into habit, she managed to quell memory, though she remained perpetually vulnerable to the trivial odor of oranges, the fleeting smell of woodsmoke, to wisps of music.

She rose unsteadily to her feet, reminding herself that she had quite enough pain to contend with at the present. She must, she would, put Hoolihan from her mind and concentrate first on Louise, then the hospital. And after the hospital. . . She left her bedroom and went slowly down the stairs, bracing herself with the brass rail. Gradually, she relied less on the rail and more on her mother's dictums: *stand up straight, Claire; you're never going to be a tall woman, so you might as well stand up straight and remember that Decency, Decorum and Dignity are your most precious*—"Oh shut up," she said, hugging her dignity to her like the poor rag it was and making her way toward the kitchen.

The house already had the air of a museum; dispossessed possessions stood mute as unearthed artifacts. She wandered through the living room like a lost tourist, noting the glass and chrome coffee table, the silver-framed paintings of poppies, the same pale peach shade as the rug, the floral-patterned chairs, the stereo and video equipment that Lucky's success had bought for them and that now his incompetence, or perhaps his drinking, his predilection for gambling —maybe his downright crookedness—or perhaps his simple ill luck had lost for them as well. She shrugged on her way through the living room; property was little better than illusion: she'd been nothing but a curator all along.

Claire paused regretfully only at the Steinway grand piano; she opened the keyboard and soundlessly stretched her fingers across the keys. Claire Stone was middle-aged, which is to say she had reached the time of life when nothing could happen to her only once; every face and feeling, every dream and desire, every scent and season reverberated into the past, clanged together like windchimes. In middle age any one moment can—not only coexist with the past—but co-transpire, and what is known occurs concurrently with what is being discovered and what is remains to be seen. In spreading her hand across that keyboard, she touched all the pianos she had ever played: the grand piano in her father's home, the upright at San Angelo, the practice rooms during her single year at the university, the first spinet Lucky had bought, when the children were little. She pressed the keys, and hollowly the Steinway eked out the first few bars of the "Minuet in G", and Claire could all but see herself sitting on the bench beside each of her three sons, teaching them to play, stroking their silky hair, coaxing music from the unwilling little hands. Her own hands remembered what Claire had managed to forget; she sat down and played the triumphant chords of the *allegro* from Beethoven's Eleventh sonata, the same sonata she had played on that other piano, the upright in the church in Chagrin, but the Steinway only echoed with defeat. She slammed the lid down over the keys. Nothing can happen once; if it happened once, it would go on happening because the past and present ran parallel to one another, like ledgers left in the rain, and the ink bloated with time, brushed and entangled.

She rose and blew away the pollen that had fallen from a vase full of calla lilies and turned her back on the piano, making her way resolutely toward the kitchen. She tottered slightly because she'd chosen the tallest pair of high-heeled sandals she could find, knowing she would need the added inches when she confronted Louise, who towered over her and outweighed her by a hundred pounds.

Pale light wafted through the kitchen window and gleamed on the polished chrome. Louise sat at the butcher block kitchen island, reading the newspaper. "It's here," said Louise, pointing to the inside page. "'Treasury Agents Seize Assets of Stone Imports, Inc.' Says here Mr. Stone hasn't paid his taxes in years and can't account for import duties or the withholding taxes of his employees. Says here his books are being audited and they've seen such gross—"

"Don't believe everything you read."

"Oh? I guess that was the seven dwarfs come through here yesterday."

"I need to borrow your car, Louise. That phone call was the hospital. Lucky's been taken very ill. He's in Emergency."

"That call just now?"

"No, the one before."

"That one half an hour ago?"

"It wasn't half an hour ago, and I'm losing precious time. Lucky's had a sudden obstruction of the gut, and I need your car to go to him."

"What's wrong with the Lincoln or the Cadillac?"

"You know very well they've been—they're gone."

"You could call a cab."

"I'd rather not."

Louise's eyes narrowed into slits, and a smile hovered near her fleshy lips. "You could take the bus."

"Either hand over the keys or don't, but spare me your comments and observations. You're not paid to comment and observe."

"I haven't been paid at all in six weeks," Louise grumbled, shuffling to her feet and ambling toward the pantry, where she habitually hung her purse. She made an elaborate show of digging for her keys. "You want me to tell Dan and Jason their dad's in the hospital when they come home from school?"

"Tell them nothing."

"Good thing they wasn't home yesterday when the Feds came through. Poor little lambs."

8

"They're adolescent boys, not little lambs."

"Good thing Scott's at Stanford and couldn't see them Feds pawing through his house. And poor Mr. Stone. Such a nice man. All too much for him, wasn't it? I never met a kinder man. A real gentleman, that's what he is, and when I saw him sitting at the bar yesterday when the Feds came through, drinking and staring at the mirror, I said to myself, Louise, that man's heart is breaking."

"Will you hurry?"

"It's his heart that broke, I know it."

No, Claire thought: he missed his heart. It's his gut that broke. "Give me the keys and be quick about it."

Louise dangled the keys. "You might have to put some gas in it, and it don't start too good. I need to get it fixed, but you don't pay me—"

"Yes, yes, how can you expect me to discuss your car when my husband might be lying at death's door? Just hand me the keys." True to form, Claire refused to reach; she preferred not to do things she couldn't do gracefully and this preference had, over the years, hardened into a rule. It kept her from playing bridge or backgammon; it kept her off the ski slopes and out of aerobics classes; it kept her active in fundraising for the Pacific Conservatory and away from the PTA; it kept her in the garden and out of the kitchen, and in this instance it kept her from reaching for the keys. It kept her intact.

Louise was right—her car didn't start too good. A twelve-year-old cocoa-colored Toyota, it choked and sputtered and spewed forth a grainy exhaust Claire could almost taste. It smelled, too, of Louise, of cleaning fluid and Camels. Claire pulled the seat forward so she could reach the pedals and gripped the wheel, pressing her forehead against it, grinding her teeth and the gears in unison. Now the hospital. *Now.* Slowly, she backed out of the driveway and started down the hilly street. All the houses in Claire's suburb had cathedral ceilings and tinted windows, Congoleum paved kitchens and fake Japanese lanterns in the front yards, which were full of colored rock instead of grass. The houses regarded the street impassively, not a porch amongst them, expensive shelters rather than expansive homes.

She got on the freeway and passed the city where she'd been born toward the end of the Second World War, the city she both knew and could no longer recognize, like a friend whose familiar visage has been altered by plastic surgery. A few of the old hotels retained their vaulted grace and rounded cornices, but everything new shot into the sky, lacquered and hard and sharp, the glass reflecting only more glass and girders. She passed by the old, imposing county courthouse where her father had spent his professional life: that building she knew, though not the grim glass and steel additions uneasily wedded to the old stone.

Once out of the city proper, she stopped at a gas station where she could use a credit card and found enough cash for a pack of cigarettes. Claire smoked only under duress, an understatement in these circumstances.

"Don't you want the U-pump aisle?" the attendant drawled, scrutinizing the Toyota.

"If I did, I wouldn't be waiting here," Claire retorted. She had no intention of sullying perfume that cost $65 an ounce with the smell of gas that cost $1.25 a gallon. "Fill it up," she added. She had some distance to go. Besides not mentioning the .22 caliber bullet, Claire had neglected to tell Louise that Lucky had shot himself in the parking lot of a Foodway Supermarket in a grim industrial suburb some distance from their home.

Back on the freeway, she passed through grubby towns with names that reeked of wishful thinking, Pleasant Valley and Apple Cove, suburbs connected by treeless concrete ribbons. Looking for the hospital, Claire crossed and recrossed unfamiliar streets, caught in an eddy of blinking lights and twinkling asphalt. She was utterly lost, but refused to stop and inquire. Claire Stone prided herself on her sense of direction, never mind it had failed her at every crucial turn of her life. She prayed and drove and drove and prayed to the God she had only half believed in and seldom called on in the years since she had weeded gratitude and remorse from her repertoire of acceptable emotions. *Let Lucky live. Matthew Mark Luke and John, let Lucky live.* Desperate for deliverance, she lamented and incanted, prayed and promised to be extra good, to merit the salvation of Lucky Stone, while she cursed Hoolihan for opening the fissures of the past which, like the exhaust fumes billowing up through the floorboards, threatened to overtake her. She prayed for Lucky's survival with the same breath that she cursed his gambling and then, lest it seem that he might have brought this disaster on himself, she qualified that and cursed only his drinking. The gambling had never gone badly till he began to drink. She cursed the drink and his civilized charm that so effectively masked his drinking, damned his pleasant evasions and gilded assurances that she ought not to worry about money. Well, there wasn't any money to worry about anymore, was there? *But let him live, Lord. I'll be a model wife if only you'll let him live.* What did a model wife do? She thought briefly of the model planes suspended from the ceiling in her youngest son's bedroom: glued together, held in place, perfect in every way but flightless nonetheless. Claire Stone was a model wife, but she would never soar. She was tethered to the assumptions that kept her glued together and to the marriage that held her in place.

In their nearly twenty-one years together, Claire's affection for her husband had grown and she had returned his love, even if she could not return his adoration—which was probably ill-founded anyway, the result of Lucky's blind passion for her. Claire had squandered her passion elsewhere. Her passion, her principles, had all been irretrievably lost by the time she stood in the prim Episcopal church of her youth and murmured wedding vows with Lucky Stone. She wore her mother's utterly outdated wedding gown, but not for sentimental reasons (because by June of 1964 Claire Swallow had foresworn sentiment); she wore the hastily altered gown because her widowed mother had recently lost every nickel of the family's investments, and besides, the wedding itself was hastily assembled. Claire was pregnant.

Claire's father once told her that lies are like money, useful as long as people believed in them. It would be useful if Lucky Stone believed he was the father of her child and married her. Quickly. She knew he loved her and had for as long as she could remember, so she seduced him without compunction and with only that conviction. She had known him since high school, but with the heartlessness of a born belle, she had scorned his admiration because she came by it so easily. After all, girls were supposed to flirt, to collect boys' admiration but to remain lovely and inviolate. At nineteen, Claire found herself pregnant and unwed (rather than lovely and inviolate) and marriage was not only the obvious solution to her dilemma, but perhaps the only desirable option as well. At nineteen, Claire perceived none of the perils of marriage, only the haven it offered. Safety was all Claire wanted. Just safety. She wanted to enter the institution of marriage and have its doors clang shut behind her, picket her prospects, fence promise, envelop her in the expectable. She could only enter that institution with a husband, and so she would marry Lucky Stone. Claire assumed she would be good at marriage because her mother was good at it and no doubt one could inherit a talent for marriage like dark eyes or dimples. That she did not love Lucky Stone seemed irrelevant because by June of 1964, Claire Swallow did not love anything except the tiny two centimeters of baby gathering mortal flesh inside her. By the summer of 1964, Claire Swallow was ready to be comforted by apples or anything else; she was sick of love and she was sick every morning too.

She had assumed that Lucky loved her, but she was surprised none-theless at his passion and gratitude the night she led him deftly up-stairs to her room in the house her family was about to lose. She had finally decided she would have to bring him home for the seduction because he respected her too much to park the car in a darkened street and neck.

She closed the door to her room, stepped out of her shoes and un-hooked her stockings so that (in what she imagined would be his haste and eagerness) Lucky would not ruin them. But he made no move toward her. No rough pawing. No glinty eyes and hungry lips. He stood there while his cultivated charm and diffident manner deserted him and disbelief swept the angular planes of his face. He glanced around her bedroom as if it were a shrine; the peony-flowered carpet, the white curtains at the windowseat, the chintz-covered chair, the mahogany bed and dresser all seemed to be objects of the utmost sanc-tity. He repeated her name as if it had texture, substance and ineffable sweetness.

"Are you sure, Claire?"

"I'm sure, I'm sure," she repeated as if this speech were rehearsed. "I'm sure."

"I've always loved you, Claire, but I didn't think, I never dreamed—I'd always hoped, but—I mean, I want you to love me, Claire, not just go to bed with me. I've been to bed with girls I didn't love, even girls I hardly knew, but I couldn't do that with you. I love you and I never dreamed I'd be so lucky that—"

"Lucky is your name."

"My real name is John," he said regretfully.

"I couldn't think of you as John. You're Lucky."

"Yes, but this is a miracle."

Claire turned on the lamp by her bed and paused before taking off her dress. She had reckoned only on a straightforward seduction. It would be difficult to seduce a man who wanted to put her on a pedestal and then look up her dress. She unclipped the barette from her hair and unzipped her pink and green summer dress.

"I've always loved you, Claire, but I wouldn't want to—to do this if you couldn't love me. I'd feel like I'd wronged you."

Her nipples tightened with a familiar delicious anticipatory tingle. "I love you," she said simply, and the lie was useful: as long as she be-lieved it, it heightened and intensified her simple sexual urgency. She took her dress off over her head and let the shoulder straps of her slip fall and it slid into a pool of vanilla at her feet. She stepped out of it and

12

unhooked her garter belt while Lucky gazed at her with mute, ungarnished wonder. "I love you," she repeated, freeing her breasts from the constraints of her bra. She turned down the bedclothes and slid out of her pants and sat naked at the edge of the bed, bathed in the warm, buttery light from the lamp.

Lucky knelt at her feet, running his hands over her knees as if they were all he dared to touch. "When you went away to the university, I thought you were gone forever. I was sure you'd meet some guy there and marry him."

"But I didn't." She stroked his thin, flaxen hair.

"I don't want this to be a one-night stand, Claire. I want to go on loving you."

"I know. I love you, John." She touched his cheek. "Lucky." She bent her fair head to meet his while he whispered against her knees that he would be very careful with her, that he wouldn't hurt her. Ever.

Claire did not dispel any notions he might have had regarding her intrinsic worth, her beauty or her inexperience, though if he hadn't been in love with her, Lucky might have guessed she was not a frozen, fearful virgin, that her hands had rippled over other men's bodies, that her willingness to lie back upon that bed was rooted in something other than her trust that he would not hurt her. But he was in love with her and so he lay on top of her gently, kissing her lips and neck and shoulders, tracing a perilous, unfamiliar route. He glanced up at the door. There was no lock. "What about your family?" he whispered. "Your brother—"

"Bart's not home."

"Your mother and sisters and aunt—"

"No one will bother us," Claire said huskily, confidently, and indeed she had reason to be confident: she had planned this seduction with her mother's knowledge, if not approval, closed that same door the week before and sat on this same bed and told her mother in this very room that she did not want to be disturbed with Lucky Stone and on which night. And why.

Meg Swallow wept and invoked every biblical saying, every sclerotic bit of folk wisdom, every paen to Decency, Decorum and Dignity that she could think of. Meg's very hands twitched, perhaps with rage, but more likely because she held no knitting needles, and without them, she seemed oddly naked and disarmed. Claire sat on her bed, keeping her eyes firmly on the billowing scarlet peonies worked into the carpet and absorbed her mother's abuse.

"I'm sorry, Mama. I've told you a hundred times I'm sorry."

13

"Sorry! That's more than you were when you showed up here in December looking like a lost dog, penniless, dirty, stinking and refusing to say a thing about your whereabouts for six months! How was I supposed to explain your suddenly showing up at home?"

"The same way you explained my leaving, I guess—with a lie."

"What else could I do when you left? What would people say if I told them my daughter was on social probation and then, your father not dead a week and you tell me some cock and bull story about collecting your things at the university and the next thing I know I get a one-line note that tells me you're going to some despicable place in the desert with that ridiculous name—"

"Chagrin," Claire supplied.

"And not another word!"

"I tried to write. I couldn't do it."

"You ran off with a man! Don't tell me any different. Not a grain of Decency, Decorum or Dignity, not a bit of honor or self-respect. The Gimme Girl, that's Claire Swallow. No thought for anyone else." She jabbed imaginary knitting needles at Claire. "I know you ran off with a man, disgraced the name of Swallow and your father's memory and ran off with a man you wouldn't even bring home to meet your family. Disgusting." Meg tucked a stray piece of hair back from her face and folded her hands in her lap. "A tramp, a slut, a dog has more self-respect than you do! And then—for six months we don't know if you're alive or dead until you show up at our door and expect to be welcomed back like the prodigal son. At least *he* asked his father's forgiveness, which is more than you did."

"Forgive me."

"And if that's not enough, you've spent the *last* six months playing that same sonata all day and staying out with a different boy every night! Nothing I said made the least bit of difference to you. No, Claire has to have everything all her own way. Claire can do whatever she likes. Oh, I should have listened to Althea. Althea told me—don't let Claire come back here and live, Meg. Think of the example she's setting for Jill and Marietta. If you welcome Claire back, she'll taint her little sisters with her very presence. Claire ought to be punished. That's what Althea said and she was right! I should have slammed the door in your dirty, ungrateful face! Disgrace and ruination, that's what you've brought on this family! And now you tell me that you're pregnant! I don't doubt it, the way you've been running around. Pregnant! I'm being punished for being so understanding and forgiving." Meg buried her face in her hands and wept.

"I'm the one who's pregnant, Mama."

"Do you think that only affects you, you stupid girl! Don't you know it reflects on me, on your brother and sisters, on the memory of your father and grandfather, on the very name of Swallow, which you have dishonored many times. Many, many times. And now, on top of all that, you want me to leave you in peace one night next week so you can seduce Lucky Stone so you'll have a father for your nameless brat!"

"I'm sorry, Mama."

"And Lucky Stone, of all people! Doesn't he work for his father at Stone Investments? It's his fault, it's all the fault of Stone Investments that I—that Althea, that we—lost all our money."

"I don't think so, Mama. Didn't you agree to the investments? I'm sure lots of other people lost money too—"

"What do I care about other people! What's going to happen to *us*? Your father never liked the Stones. I should have relied on Anson's judgment. Anson always said Mayor Stone was nothing but a—"

"Mayor Stone is dead, and anyway, he was only Lucky's father's second cousin or something, not his—"

"The Stones are all slimy. That's what Anson used to say. Investment counselors! Hah! What are we going to do? How will we live?"

Meg wept so bitterly Claire was tempted to leave the bed and go to her, put her arm around her mother's shoulders and offer comfort, but she was paralyzed. She cleared her throat. "I can't answer for all of that. I'm sorry about it and I don't know what you're going to do, but I need a husband. I have to think of that. I'm pregnant and I'm desperate for a husband. I can't," she added slowly, "bear the shame."

"Shame! You don't know the meaning of the word! If you had any shame, you wouldn't be pregnant! If you had any shame, you wouldn't be telling me that you're going to seduce that awful Lucky Stone so he'll marry you!"

"You don't understand. I'm desperate for a husband." Claire hung her head.

"Oh, I understand that!" Meg spat. "What I don't understand is where I went wrong with you. Anson always spoiled you. I told him, Anson, you're doing that girl no favour. You're bringing her up to think she can have the world the way she wants it. But would he listen to me? No. Oh, why couldn't you be nice like Jill and Marietta?"

"I tried."

"You never did! Never! And what did I ever ask of you? Just that you be a lady. That you follow the Three D's and show good taste and good manners. Is that so very much? How can you spit on everything I ever taught you?"

"I haven't spit on it, I—"

"You're pregnant, aren't you?"

"Virginity isn't an emotion, Mama. It's an invention."

Claire's assessment sent her mother into a screaming rage. Usually calm and modulated, the wrathful Meg searched with her hand for some invisible knitting needle with which to stab home her points as she ranged angrily over the whole swath of Claire's ravaged past, beginning in childhood. "Who is the father of this bastard brat?" she concluded. "I demand to know. I will not—absolutely will not agree to your tawdry, disgusting plan to seduce Lucky Stone. Never. You will tell me immediately who the father is and we will take steps to get him to marry you. Now, who is he?"

Claire hunched over and concentrated on the scarlet peonies in the rug. "I can't say."

Silence prickled between them. "Get off that bed!" Meg shouted at last. "I can't stand to see you sitting on the very bed where you very likely—"

"Not here," said Claire, obediently moving to the windowseat. "It was never here."

"Is that supposed to comfort me! I suppose you've been coupling in some ditch like a dog. Or in alleys. Or in the back seat of cars!" Meg closed her eyes as if the very vision were too painful to endure. "Who is the father?"

"I've told you before. I can't say."

"What do you mean?"

"I can't say."

"You must say!"

Claire raised her face. "I intend that Lucky Stone will think he is the father."

"But who is?" Meg wailed.

"I can't say."

Meg's round face and wide blue eyes lit with revulsion and alarm. *You mean you don't know? Do you know what that makes you?*

"Pregnant."

"A whore! Only whores and—whores sleep with men they're not married to! Is that what you did those six months you were gone? Whore around—"

"I didn't get this baby in Chagrin. I wasn't pregnant when I came back from Chagrin. I wasn't desperate then."

16

"A whore! Thank God your father is dead!"

"I don't want to talk about Father."

"Thank God he did not live to see you spit on his every precept and principle. Claire has such talent, that's what Anson used to say, and when I'd tell him that talent was worthless if you weren't a lady, he'd just laugh and say you were a remarkable girl. What do you think he would say if he could see you here today, pregnant like a slut."

"Everyone gets pregnant in the same way, Mama. Sluts and wives. It's all done the same—"

"Don't give me a lesson in democracy, you impertinent little slut! You have shamed this family. We give you every opportunity, we send you to the university, we give you every advantage and you repay us with ruin. Ruin, that's what you've brought down on your family."

"I had nothing to do with the investments."

"I'm not talking about money! I'm talking about honor! But I don't expect you to understand that. Not you. Oh no. Your father understood honor, but not you, and in the very hour of your father's death, you desert your family and run off with—"

"It wasn't the hour of his death. He was gone. He was buried. I never would have left if Father'd been alive!" Claire began to cry.

"And if all that weren't enough—which it certainly was—you show up at home six months later without a word of explanation and you spend the next six months playing the piano and whoring around and now you tell me that you're pregnant and you want to seduce a strange man so that—"

"Lucky's not strange," Claire wiped her eyes with her hands. "He's a good man and he'll be a good husband. He has good manners," she added in his defense, knowing how Meg treasured appearances, maintained them at all costs, kept them seamlessly groomed. Impeccable appearances. "I'm desperate, Mama. You don't understand."

"Of course I understand! I've had four children. I had three miscarriages before I had the four children, so don't tell me I don't understand, you foolish, foolish girl."

"Please don't, Mama."

"What about, Please don't, Claire? Thank God Anson did not live to see his favourite child pregnant and oh, Anson," Meg rolled her eyes heavenward, "if you are watching—"

"Stop it," Claire snapped. "I tell you I can't bear to hear about Father. I have enough trouble."

Meg collapsed in a fresh bout of weeping, snuffling into a knotted hanky.

Claire sat silently. She had won. Her mother would rail on at some length, that was to be expected, but she'd acquiesce eventually because she too could not bear the scandal, the shame of a pregnant, husbandless daughter. Shame and scandal were the same to Meg. They were not to Claire, and in that, she was very like her father. Scandal was public. Shame was private. Scandal could be avoided and appearances maintained, but shame could gnaw your heart out and leave it hollow. Lucky Stone could help Claire avert scandal, but the recognition of shame had only crept on her slowly as she saw the folly of what she had done. At the moment she had conceived this baby, she wanted it desperately, with no foretaste of shame, no thought of scandal. Now it was too late to change her mind. Now she wanted only to be safe and spared from shame and desperation forever; marriage to Lucky Stone, whom she liked but did not love, offered her that refuge. Marriage would allow her to bury the truth of her shame in a garden of lies. Once married, she could plant lies in a neat, orderly, pleasing fashion and tend that garden carefully for the rest of her life, ever vigilant against the truth that could spring up like weeds, native, ubiquitous and implacable. She need only uproot the truth, or bury it deep enough, and it would never threaten the tidy garden of lies.

In June 1964, Claire married Lucky Stone in a small wedding with only family present. Her younger brother, Bart, gave her away with a brief morsel of dissent. "He's not worthy of you," said Bart in an undertone as they waited in the foyer of the church for the wedding march to start. "He hasn't told you the truth."

"How do you know what he's told me?" Claire did not add that she hadn't told Lucky the truth either.

"Has he told you that he gambles? Oh, he's an investment counselor with his father's firm, maybe, but he makes his money gambling."

"That can't matter to me."

"It would matter to Father."

"Father's dead." Claire brought her bouquet of fleshy calla lilies up to her face and felt badly that she had been so sharp. Bart was always her unfailing ally and admirer. "I'm sorry, Bart, but you must admit that the Swallows are not in a position to poop on money. We've lost everything."

"Not we. You're getting married, remember? You're going to live with Lucky Stone." Bart lit a furtive cigarette, took a few puffs and stomped it out, kicking the butt behind the umbrella stand. "I'm leaving, too."

"You can't leave! Think of Mama and Aunt Althea and Jill and Marietta!"

"I am thinking of them. I always have. I have always been the responsible one. You're the one who just bolts whenever the notion strikes you."

"That's unkind." Not unfair, she realized, but unkind all the same. "Where are you going?"

"I got a job last week. I've arranged that my paycheck will go directly to Mama, but I have to leave."

"What about the university? I thought you wanted to be an architect."

Bart snorted. "What do you think, Claire? Can Mama go out and get a job slinging hash somewhere? Can Aunt Althea clerk at Woolworth's? You're so busy playing the piano and getting married that you don't seem to understand what it means that we've lost the money Father left us. Jill is sixteen. Marietta's fourteen. I'm the only one who can support this family. I don't say save them. No one can do that, but at least I got a job."

"Where?"

"Forget it. I'll tell you later. I shouldn't have brought it up."

"Why not?" Looking at him from under her veil, Claire thought Bart's face seemed pale and drawn, many years older than his young features attested to. "What kind of job?"

Bart frowned uncomfortably. "I'm working in the best tradition of the Swallows, Claire. Don't you remember what the Senator used to say—Give me the sea!"

"Oh no, Bart, you're not. Please tell me you're not."

"I'm a deckhand for Swallow Lines. I sail for Tokyo next week."

"No! You could have got a job anywhere. You didn't have to work for Lucille Swallow, did you?"

"Look at me, Claire. Two weeks ago I graduated from high school. I'm eighteen. I haven't got a skill in the world. I haven't got a damn dime. I have a mother and an aunt and two sisters to support, and given all that, I can make better money at sea than anywhere else, but if you're worried that I got any charity from Lucille, don't. I didn't lose my pride."

"Who gives a damn about your pride? It's the—" she started to say *principle* before she realized that she too sounded like her father, that Anson Swallow had always regarded pride and principles as irrevocably linked.

"I give a damn," Bart returned. "Swallow Lines hired me in spite of my name, not because of it."

19

"Does Lucille know you're going to swab decks and clean latrines? Oh, Bart, it makes me sick."

"Lucille didn't hire me. She saw me, though, there in the front office filling out the forms. At least I think she saw me. She didn't speak, didn't acknowledge my presence in any way. Just swept out on her way to her car. Well, I don't care." He slicked his hair down and fidgeted with the tie at his throat. "I have work. Honest work. I don't know what Lucky Stone really does, but it's not honest. Father would be ashamed of you, marrying a man like that."

"I don't give a damn," she said with more conviction that she felt. "I'm sick of men who are pure. I hate men who put their principles above everything else. It's not goodness or nobility, though they'd like everyone to think so. It's just a form of egotism and self-indulgence and stupid pride. Men like that deserve to live alone; they ought never to have families in the first place. Pride and principles." Her lips curled sourly over the words. "Men like that just get everyone into trouble and then congratulate themselves for being so saintly. I despise them."

Bart regarded her quizzically. "Who are you talking about?"

"Father, of course." She strangled the calla lilies.

"Well, all I can say is you're the granddaughter of Senator Swallow and the daughter of Judge Swallow and Lucky Stone is not worthy of you."

"I'm pregnant." That put an end to Bart's objections.

Claire's was not the first wedding in the church that afternoon, and rice from the previous wedding crunched under her feet like the castanets of disaster. The pins left in her improperly altered wedding dress nipped at her heels and jabbed at her ribs with every move. She wished the wedding march would start and put an end to all this. She grew progressively more uncomfortable with her brother's glowering silence. "I suppose the vipers are here," she said by way of breaking the tension. "I know Mama insisted we invite them."

"They're here. All three of them," Bart replied.

"Three? Three!"

"Lucille and Lucy Rose and her new husband, that rich, simpering jerk Randolph Eckdorf." Bart snorted. "It wasn't bad enough that we all got dragged to that overdone wedding, but you had to go catch the damn bouquet."

"I tried not to. I stood way at the back so I wouldn't, but it just came sailing to me. I should have let it hit the floor."

"Well, you proved it right," he said belligerently. "You're the next one to get married, aren't you? Your wedding won't be like hers."

Claire stared at the rice on the floor of the foyer and sniffed the odor of sanctimony, solemnity, implicit in the confines of the church. She wondered briefly about the wedding that had preceded hers and remembered Lucy Rose's. No close, narrow church for the Eckdorf wedding. The former Lucy Rose Cotton had been married in the Swallow Arboretum and Art Museum, the house that had once been Claire's grandfather's mansion. Claire had played there as a child, never taking note of its magnificence. When she went to Lucy Rose's wedding in March, though, she had noticed, probably for the first time, that everything in that house was ransacked from somewhere else, Europe or China or New York or colonial Virginia. Imported, they called it. Ransacked. Even the plants in the fabled garden and arboretum had been brought in from elsewhere, stuck in the California earth and commanded to grow while each spring the gardeners fought off the lowly California poppies that sprang up as if to taunt and tease the manicured roses, the tropical ferns, Japanese plums and Dutch hyacinths. The Senator's widow, Lucille, had donated the mansion to the Art League and the Garden Club, but she demanded its use for the *marriage of her daughter, Miss Lucy Rose Cotton, to Randolph Eckdorf* of the Honolulu Eckdorfs, who had settled early in Hawaii and stayed there to raise pineapple and reap profits, sell sugar and help depose the Queen in the name of democracy and dollars. The Eckdorfs flew refrigerated Hawaiian flowers to the mainland for their son's wedding, and the wicked imported antherium with their hard red hearts and extended yellow tongues reminded Claire all the more of vipers. The five hundred guests (fed on better fare than loaves and fishes) gathered in the salon for the wedding and mingled afterward on the terraces and in the dining room where, on a six-foot column of ice, the massive frozen figure of a graceful swallow melted softly into a lake of Hawaiian orchids. Everything was imported: the groom, the guests, the flowers, caviar, champagne, truffles and mushrooms; the rice thrown at Lucy Rose's wedding would have fed the entire province of Manchuria for a month and a half, and the pearls at Lucy Rose's throat were gouged out of the soft bellies of 150 oysters and the silk in her gown spun from the bodies of a million compliant worms. Worms. Worms and vipers. Claire screwed her eyes shut against the threat of tears, resolving to live through her wedding, through her marriage, through the rest of her day, without remembering that day. *Without remembering.* She lifted her hem to wipe her eyes, getting a good jab from a pin left in the bodice.

21

The clarion call of the wedding march sounded, and Bart escorted Claire down the narrow aisle. The church was empty except for the first two rows. For a moment Claire stood flanked by her brother and Lucky Stone, who beamed at her, his eyes full of love and pride. Bart relinquished her to Lucky, who lifted Claire's veil, and she smiled at him and turned toward the altar.

After the ceremony, sipping over-sweet punch in the ill-ventilated church hall, the wedding guests did not exactly concur that it was a brilliant match. They commented instead on the bride's beauty and the good weather. Lucky's family kept their distance from the Swallows; they disapproved of this marriage quite as much as Meg, though for different reasons. Claire Swallow had a reputation for being fast and loose and wild. Ordinarily, they would have chuckled to watch the fall of a girl like that, particularly now that her family had lost their money and had only the diaphanous distinction of their good name, and ordinarily, it would have doubled their delight that Claire was pregnant besides. But they were chagrined unto outraged that Lucky should be implicated in Claire's fall and manacled to her for life. They did not share Lucky's conviction that he was the father of her baby and believed instead that Claire was a nasty slut who had got herself knocked up. Their disdain for Claire and the recently impoverished Swallows did not, however, extend to Lucille Swallow, who, after all, wasn't really affiliated with the bawdy bride and who, moreover, had tons of money, which made her, at least theoretically, useful and attractive. Sitting on metal folding chairs in a corner of the church hall, Lucky's family chatted politely with Lucille and agreed unflinchingly with everything she said.

Save for Bart, Claire's family was largely a phalanx of women: her mother and aunts, all soberly dressed matrons, inconspicuously gloved, hatted and shod for the occasion. None of them deferred to fashion, or if they did, it was the fashion of forty years before. Aunt Vera wore a tight cloche hat that badly accentuated her overbite and her long nose. Vera stood on Meg's right, explaining at length the aspects of stars and the configurations of the heavens and what they foretold. Astrology was only Vera's latest addiction; since her young husband had died over thirty years before, Vera had taken refuge in a succession of dubious spiritual enthusiasms, of which astrology was the least objectionable. On Meg's left, and oblivious of Vera, Aunt Eleanor apologized profusely for the absence of her three sons and her husband. Boys, she claimed were too rowdy for a wedding. And as for

George: "His health, you know, Meg, it isn't strong."

To both of these women Meg simply nodded. She agreed that Eleanor's boys (known amongst the family as the Tenor, the Bass and the Baritone for their unrestrained shrieking) would have been restless. And as for George, Eleanor had been apologizing for George Swallow's drinking since the day she married him. Neither Eleanor nor Vera, after thirty years of nattering, had ever required more than an affirmative nod from Meg.

Claire's younger sisters, Jill and Marietta, wore clashing dresses of saffron and lilac and chatted near Aunt Althea, whose formidable bulk was swathed in interminable mourning. Althea had worn black long before Anson died, even before the Senator died, probably even before her own mother died, but Claire and Bart couldn't remember back that far. Althea's addiction to black had, amongst the children, earned her nickname of Mourning Glory and she had lived with Claire's family for ten years, ever since Lucille Swallow had evicted her from the Swallow mansion. Althea clutched her plastic punch cup with a white-knuckled grip, her eyes darting over the small assembly, coming to rest on Lucille, encircled by admiring Stones. Lucille's peach-coloured dress and pillbox hat were, by Althea's exacting standards, far too young for her, and she noted with some pleasure that an ash escaped from Lucille's cigarette and burned a hole in one of the flounces. She turned her critical gaze up to Lucy Rose and Randolph Eckdorf, a young man whose coloring suggested swedes left too long in the root cellar. Althea had not seen them since their vulgar overdone wedding, now three months before. Lucy Rose clung to her husband with the deference and dignity of a freshly minted matron, but Althea's knowing eye traveled up and down her body and she nodded to herself: pregnant. Lucy Rose was, without doubt, pregnant. Well, so was Claire for that matter, but Althea preferred not to dwell on the subject; Claire was married now and no more need be said. She studied Lucy Rose to see if she could discern just how pregnant. Lucy Rose was pretty in a plain way or plain in a pretty way, depending on your point of view. Althea never could quite decide which, but Lucy Rose's good looks were certainly vapid and she seemed—and had, even as a child—to be the instantaneous creation of whomever she'd been with for the last ten minutes. Tallow, Althea concluded with an inward sniff. Callow tallow. At least Claire had some character, Althea thought, though of course she did not approve of Claire's character and never had. She smiled to glance at Jill and Marietta; now, there were two sweet girls

23

worthy of their parents. Jill and Marietta would never break Meg's heart like that thankless Claire.

Althea's reflections were cut short because Lucille disengaged herself from the Stones and sailed over to the Swallow women like a water lily heading for a congregation of cattails. Meg, Eleanor and Althea all stiffened at her approach, but Vera was too involved with the implications of Mercury's rising to acknowledge Lucille's presence.

Lucille waited for Vera to finish and then she spoke directly to Meg, scarcely nodding to the fat, bristling Althea. Lucille said she loved weddings, and Meg nodded. She thanked Meg for inviting them, and Meg nodded; she commented that the groom clearly adored his bride, and Meg nodded once again. "Where are they going for their honeymoon?"

"I don't know," Meg replied. "That's up to John."

"John?"

"Lucky," said Meg, as if the name tasted bad. "John is his real name."

"Lucy Rose and Randolph just got back from their wedding trip to New York and what a time they had!" Lucille fluttered. "Three months in New York and Boston! Why, they've made it sound like such fun, I think I may go back East in the fall. No one goes there in the summer, of course. It just isn't done."

"Have you checked the aspects for traveling?" Vera inquired seriously. "It's very important. If the stars foretell danger, you could be in great peril. I check the charts every day, and if the stars counsel against it, I don't go out of the house."

"Well I could hardly do that," Lucille said and smiled benignly. "Duty always calls me."

"Calls you what?" Althea snarled.

Lucille ignored the barb. "Lucy Rose and Randolph leave for Honolulu next week. Randolph is going to take over Swallow Lines' operation in Honolulu. It's a big challenge for a young man, but I'm sure my son-in-law is equal to it." She glanced fondly at the bland, blue-eyed Randolph, who was patting his wife's hand.

"What about Albert Smythe?" Althea demanded.

"Who?"

"Mr. Smythe has headed Swallow Lines in Honolulu for years. My father sent him there in 1928."

"Oh him. How do I know? He quit, and I never pry into the plans of ex-employees." She gave Althea a look of consummate condescension and then glanced across the hall. "Oh, look, here comes the bride!" The

24

guests all turned to see Claire emerge from the church bathroom, her wedding gown over her arm, dressed in a loose, dark green sailor skirt and blouse with powder blue trim and collar. The colors drained her face and left her looking sallow. "Claire's grown up quite lovely, hasn't she?" Lucille said pleasantly, and Meg nodded. "Such a pity the Senator couldn't have lived to see this moment. He always said that Claire was nothing but teeth and knees, all mouth and mayhem." Lucille added, "I'm sure you're happy to see her safely married."

"I'm sure," said Meg.

Claire came up to her mother and aunts and, with an almost audible sigh of relief, dumped the wedding gown into her mother's arms, burying Meg under the satin and lace.

"Congratulations," said Lucille, offering Claire her hand. "Oh dear, you're not supposed to say that to the bride, are you? It's nice to see you again, Claire. We didn't get a chance to talk at Lucy Rose's wedding, but then I had five hundred guests to consider, after all."

"Yes," Claire replied sullenly.

"And we hardly had a chance to speak when I saw you at the university last year, Jon was being so bull-headed."

"The university?" said Meg.

"Jon?" said Althea.

"A chance encounter," Claire said coldly. "I happened to meet him once in a rare book store."

"I didn't know your son was at the university, Lucille," said Vera pleasantly. "How very nice. What's he studying?"

"He's not there anymore." Momentarily, Lucille studied Claire as if her face were a cash register that would not balance, but then she added, "In fact I'd gone to the university in one of my futile attempts to convince Jon that he ought to leave the unwashed masses alone. Lie down with dogs, get up with fleas, that's what I always say."

"You ought to know," Althea muttered.

Lucille seemed to bare fangs. Seeing appearances unravel, Meg instantly feigned the amenities. "Where is your son now, Lucille?"

"The draft board's been asking me the same question. Such a thoughtless boy. He came home for his sister's wedding and then he stole one of my cars and vanished. I thought about calling the police, but think what that would look like in the papers." Lucille toyed with her lacquered hair. "Anyway, he'll be back."

Lucky came up and touched Claire's arm. "Well, Mrs. Stone," he said affectionately. "Shall we go?"

Lucille sighed. "Oh, I just hate the departure of a bridal couple. It's all over then."

"It's just beginning," said Lucky, putting his arm around his bride.

"Here's your bouquet, Claire," said Jill, thrusting the calla lilies, wilted and leathery-looking now, at her sister. "Please throw it at me so I can catch it." Throughout Claire's wedding, sixteen-year-old Jill had been planning her own, considering all the details—except for the groom. "I want to be the next to get married."

"Keep it," said Claire. "It's yours."

She took her husband's arm, and as she stepped out of the church door and the late afternoon light gleamed in her golden hair and reflected in her dark eyes, Claire knew—belatedly—that this was her moment and it was past. If she were like most well-bred young women, this one day, her wedding day, was or would be her moment to bask in the collective admiration of the tribe who had gathered here today to witness, remember, partake of the cake and custom that preceded the social codifying of what would otherwise be mere lust. Well-bred brides like Claire were expected to be eager but untutored. They were encouraged to equate their principles with proprieties, good morals with good manners, and advised to trade their beauty and virginity (before either hardened or decayed) for a man of their choice. Shelter and respectability. The latter was as important as the former. Claire Swallow, though inculcated with all of the above, had trod on every precept she was supposed to prize. But no one would have guessed. No one, to look at the delicate, fair-haired bride, would have dreamed her to be anything but virginal and untutored. No one except for her brother, of course, who had been informed that she was pregnant. No one except her mother, who knew that she had vanished for six months in the company of a man she would not name. No one except her Aunt Althea, who knew all that and, like Meg, believed her to have conceived a child by (no doubt) still another man she would not name or could not recognize from the legion of her lovers. The groom knew her to be less than virginal. The groom's family knew that much and guessed far worse of Claire. But no one said anything of the sort, and anyone else privy to this knowledge was not there to testify.

When Mr. and Mrs. Stone left the church, the guests tossed handfuls of rice at the departing nuptial couple, and as the tiny pellets studded her back and shoulders, Claire knew indubitably what the woman taken in adultery must have felt like.

Mrs. Stone blinked in the merciless light of the Emergency Room and went straight to the desk, where nurses, hard and white as pillars of salt, tended consoles of flickering red lights and green computer terminals that reflected a briny color into their faces. They didn't quite spring to attention at Claire's approach, but they answered her questions efficiently and said they would call her husband's doctor. They asked her to have a seat in the waiting room. "I'll stand," said Claire.

The vinyl chairs in the waiting room were chained together and lined up like pews. A single framed print, badly hung, decorated the white walls: a picture of a beach with barnacled driftwood, cloudless sky and a small sailboat silhouetted against the sunshine. Bolted to the ceiling, a large TV depicted a nubile couple in the throes of (no doubt illicit) passion, but few of the people in the waiting room paid it any mind. A man held bloodied cotton rags over his hand. One family clutched together as if they were under the same tent of flesh and, like a caterpillar with many legs, could move only in unison. Several small children shrieked about the place. An old man, a drunk perhaps, slid from his chair and peed himself and everyone pretended not to notice. Two flinty old women occupied chairs on either side of the narrow solitary table, and though they each thumbed copies of *Life* and *Time*, they quarreled volubly, throwing Scripture back and forth in cannonades.

Claire pulled out a cigarette and lit it, but the nurse said she couldn't smoke there and pointed to the two old women. "That's the smoking section," she said. Claire stamped her cigarette out on the cold linoleum. The nurse punched one of the red buttons and then turned and said that Mr. Stone was in surgery at this very minute and the doctor would talk with Claire when it was all over.

"When will that be?"

"I can't say, Mrs. Stone. No one can."

"I see," replied Claire. She always said "I see" when she did not see at all, when she was defeated or confused or close to tears.

She walked unsteadily to the smoking section and took a seat beside one of the old women. They were both dressed in faded blue jeans, men's flannel shirts and tennis shoes without socks. They had long thin hair, pulled harshly from their faces in unflattering pony tails secured with rubber bands. They looked both flabby and gaunt. One offered Claire *Life*, and she declined. The other offered *Time*, and she made ready to remove herself from their ministrations, but then they each bummed a cigarette and started up a cheery conversation, as if they were steamship passengers awaiting their tickets. They were in fact sisters, Emma and Evangeline Duff, who had come up to the city for the yearly convocation of the Fellowship of the New Millenium, of which Emma at least was a devout member. They were in Emergency now because on her way up the church steps, a third sister, Wilma, had fallen and broken her hip. "And to think, Wilma and Evangeline only come up with me for the ride," Emma continued.

"Wilma come up for the ride," Evangeline corrected her. "I had to drive you, remember? Wisht I'd just said no. If I'd said no, Wilma wouldn't have broken her hip."

"Now, Evangeline, if God wanted Wilma to break her hip, it would have happened wherever we were."

"Bullshit."

Evangeline reached into Claire's pack and pulled out another cigarette, lighting it from the butt of the first as the sisters argued back and forth, scarcely listening to one another in the way of people whose quarrels have gone on for half a century. They often turned to Claire for comment, but she only replied, "I see," automatically and at appropriate intervals while she watched the clock tick off the minutes of Lucky's life. They engaged Claire's attention only when Emma mentioned San Angelo. "Excuse me," Claire interrupted. "Did you say you were from San Angelo?"

"You know San Angelo!" cried Emma delightedly.

"My family used to—we still have a house there."

"Us Duffs lived there all our lives."

"Yeah and we can't afford it no more," Evangeline grumbled. "Not with all them rich commuters moving in and—"

"Where's your house?" asked Emma.

"Jerusalem Road."

"One of them lovely new homes on the cliffs?"

Claire shook her head, regretting she'd asked at all, but Emma was not to be deflected; she kept prodding till finally Claire admitted that theirs was the oldest home on Jerusalem Road.

"Not that huge, beat-up old place that belonged to Senator Swallow!"

"Yes."

"Are you a Swallow?" Emma's inquiry held a note of reverence.

"I was. I'm Mrs. Stone now."

"Just imagine, Evangeline! Us coming all the way up here and sitting right next to a Swallow!"

"A Swallow with cigarettes." Evangeline sucked up her smoke gratefully.

"Why are you here, dear?"

"My husband," Claire replied icily: these two were really intolerable. Claire wished she hadn't bought the cigarettes.

"Accident?"

"Yes."

"Car?"

Claire snuffed out her cigarette and moistened her lips. "In a car, yes."

"Hand of God!" cried Emma as if she'd just thrown down four kings and an ace.

"Sleight of hand, you mean," grumbled Evangeline. "God don't run nothing more than a shell game. Watch this, God says, watch what I can do, watch how quick I am—and then, phht, you get snuffed out."

"The Lord giveth and the Lord taketh away."

"Why? That's what I want to know. Why do we have all the bad luck? Next time you talk to God, Emma, you ask Him. It ain't like a question He ain't heard before. What about all them Old Testament folks? You can bet they asked Him. Why was they slaughtered like flies? What did they do to deserve it?"

"No one can stand fast in Sodom," Emma replied gravely. "And anyway, death ain't the end, but the beginning. The dead will live again. When Christ comes back—"

"Who's got that kind of time?" Evangeline shot back.

"It's close at hand."

"Horseradish."

"All the signs and portents are here. The Bible says nation shall rise against nation and there will be war and famine and destruction—"

"There's always been war and famine and destruction," Evangeline grumbled. "That's no sign. That's the way people live."

"The age of the New Millenium is upon us. Trust God."

"Wisht I was a Chink or a mackerel snapper." Evangeline leaned forward and rested her bony elbows on her knees. "Wisht I could just light incense and blather chants and wasn't required to trust in nobody. 'Specially God."

"Don't be so hard on Him," said Emma, as if God were an errant schoolboy. "In God's good time—"

"You got that kind of time?" Evangeline demanded of Claire. "You got time to wait around for the millenium and your reward? Not me. I want my reward while I'm still around to enjoy it. I live a clean life. Can't afford nothing else anyway."

"You gamble," Emma chided her.

"I play bingo, Emma. That's all."

"You bet on it."

"Where's my reward for a clean life?" Evangeline returned the thrust of her argument to Claire. "What's going to happen to Emma and me when Wilma goes? Her pension goes with her. What's going to happen to us? It's the curse, I tell you."

"No, the curse is something else," Emma chided her. "You just don't take to change, Evangeline. You never have." Emma smiled at Claire. "She never has."

"I see."

"Why should I?" Evangeline took a drag off her cigarette, as if she were facing a firing squad. "Nothing ever changes for the better. Always for the worst."

"We can take comfort from the past and from the hope of a life to come," replied Emma, positively misty-eyed.

"What about now?" Evangeline demanded. "What about the present? The life to come don't comfort me in the least and the past—" she snorted smoke out of both nostrils "—you can't even count on the past. Even it don't stay the same. You'd think it would, wouldn't you?" she asked of Claire. "But it don't. The more past you have, the more it changes. Sometimes you don't even know it for your own." She turned to Claire. "Ain't that so?"

"I see," said Claire, resolving to escape these two once and for all.

"Say, you got any more smokes on you before you go?"

Claire dumped a half pack of cigarettes on the table and then, side-stepping the rambunctious children, she dashed for the safety of the phone booths, lined up like confessionals across the room. She entered one booth and closed the door, but the air was fetid with despair and she opened it again. She called the operator and asked for her son's number at Stanford. The operator demanded cash or a card Claire couldn't find. She hung up and with trembling fingers dug through her wallet, found the card and tried again. The phone rang several times; she pictured the living room of her son's fraternity house and young men lounging in the leather chairs, discussing sports or Freud; she imagined them wearing sportscoats and oxford-cloth shirts they sent out to be ironed. "Scott Stone, please," she said when someone answered at last.

"He's not here," said the boy coldly.

"When do you expect him back?"

"I don't. He dropped out of Stanford altogether."

"There must be some mistake. Scott Stone."

"No mistake, lady. Scott Stone left in the middle of the night."

"This is his mother. I must get in touch with him."

"Hey, do I look like the Missing Persons Bureau? I told you, he's gone. Packed up. Cleaned out."

"I see." Claire's throat parched. "Did he get bad news from home?"

"I thought you said this was his mother."

Claire hung up immediately and swayed against the metal upright walls of the booth. Scott must have read the papers; he must have heard about the IRS and the bankruptcy and the scandal. But not the suicide. *The suicide attempt.* He couldn't have heard of that, not yet. "Let Lucky live, Lord. Let Scott—" But she didn't quite know what she wanted for Scott, save that he should always be safe and happy and successful; she could not bear to think what all this affliction would do to Scott. She fought off tears and fastened her attention on the framed print of the beach scene just opposite her: the cloudless sky, the open water, the sailboat. Criminal to have a picture like that in the Emergency Room. Criminal. There ought to be glossy posters of funeral homes and the embalmer's art and prosthetic devices and lists of insurance rates and attorney's fees. The thought of attorneys brought Hoolihan to mind. Claire groaned and her knees weakened; she clung to the buttoned, impassive face of the phone as she searched frantically for enough change to call Bart's house. Then she banished that thought before she had even pawed through her pennies. If she called Bart's house, she'd only get Mama and Althea and what good were they? In the last five years, the family had watched, terrified and powerless, as Meg seemingly floated away from them, her mind borne prematurely, irresistibly, back on currents of the past. Her body remained healthy, but her brain rotted inside her skull. And Althea. Claire blew her nose and resumed her search for money. Althea Swallow had only one response to disaster of any sort: it was all Lucille's fault. Beyond that, Althea had nothing to offer.

Claire found her coins, buzzed the operator and asked for a number she knew all too well. "Swallow Lines," came the singsong response.

"Barton Swallow, please." Bart. Bart could be relied on. Bart had never failed her. Bart would stand between her and collapse. "Oh,

Bart," she wept when she heard his voice. "Oh, Bart."

"I just read it in the paper. Why didn't you call me yesterday?"

"It didn't happen until this morning!"

"But the paper said—"

"Oh that, the fraud, the IRS, that's nothing. Nothing!" Her voice raised to a wail she could neither suppress nor control. "Lucky's shot himself, Bart. Shot and missed and I'm in the Emergency Room and he's in surgery and Scott's vanished and I—"

"Missed what?"

"What?"

"What did Lucky miss?"

"He missed his heart and shot himself in the stomach."

She spoke those words for the first time, and they rattled like shrapnel in her mouth. When the police had called and told her that her husband had been found in a Foodway Supermart parking lot, in, as it turned out, a stolen car, stolen because his own had been impounded by Treasury agents, stolen and driven to this grim industrial suburb where he shot himself in the parking lot of the Foodway Supermart and was found by a hysterical shopper and her small daughter with his guts oozing over the seat of the borrowed (that's what Claire heard; she did not hear stolen at all; she heard borrowed) car, even then she had not said the words, not repeated them back to the police with any sort of spiraling disbelief. She said, "I see. I see." And she could and did see, pictured all too well, Lucky Stone in the parking lot of the Foodway Supermart with his guts splashed over a borrowed car. She said I see and thanked the police as if they had just quoted her the time and tide and hung up. Time and tide might just as well have stopped for Claire Stone; she never could remember quite what happened next or how it was that by some miracle compounded of reflex, synaptic obedience to the code of behaviour required of model wives, even those married to men who try to kill themselves, she found herself dressed in a skirt of Monet blue, a starched blouse, and here in this hospital, trembling with fear and anguish, crying into this phone that Lucky had tried to shoot himself in the heart and missed and shot himself in the stomach. Tears coursed down her face, turning to silt the makeup she had so carefully applied as Bart comforted her the best he could. He was leaving the office immediately. He would be at her side. Don't despair, Claire. Claire wept and nodded and wiped her nose with the back of her hand, keeping her eyes on the framed poster of the beach scene—the cold blue sea, the camomile beach, the boat; she squinted as if the glare of that sea might be real and the sailboat one she knew and had been watching for a long, long time.

CHAPTER TWO

June 1952

At the horizon a small sailboat braced into the wind, advancing steadily northward. The last of the late morning fog draped from the pine and cypress, clung to the rugged junipers and rusting madrones that covered the bluffs above a narrow slice of lemon-coloured beach. Waves crashed into pools of spent foam, nudging clumps of kelp from their torpor, pushing them toward the beach and stranding them there. Cries of gulls and marauding blue jays fell like grace notes amongst the sound of children's voices, piping and hooting as they ran out to greet the breakers, daring one another on to feats of inconceivable bravery before they scurried back to shore. Sitting in frayed wicker chairs on the beach, two women in generously brimmed straw hats faced each other over a large picnic basket they had pressed into service as a table and here one of the women placed her inkwell. She dipped her pen into ink as black as her dress and began her letter with the date, June 14, 1952, the place, San Angelo, California, and Dear George. She was fat and myopic. The other woman, knitting assiduously, looked more comfortable; she was small-boned, wearing a sleeveless sun dress frilled with cotton lace and her face was pink with contentment.

In the distance there was a house, clearly built in the last century and evincing all those certainties with its unequivocally sharp gables and single, high rounded turret. The windows were uniformly prim and narrow, curtained in white muslin, framed with smart green shutters. This was number 1 Jerusalem Road. There was no number 2; this house stood alone, low and sheltered between the bluffs. The broad porch at the front faced a garden, the Pacific and a picket fence that bounded the garden, separating it from the rocky prologue to the beach. A sea of nasturtiums bobbed between the fence and the porch, punctuated here and there by thick scarlet peonies and scrubby daisies and tall sad sunflowers. Massed like uncertain infantry, raspberry canes stood in one corner and in the other huge artichoke plants alternately lounged and lunged. Judge Anson Swallow sat rocking on the porch, smoking a pipe, leafing through the sheaf of documents from a case he was trying. There was another rocker of immense proportions beside him, empty. Anson's wife, Meg, was the woman knitting on the beach, and across from her, his sister Althea wrote a letter to their brother, George, who was having one of his periodic dry-outs in a sanatorium. The four children belonged to Anson and Meg. At least for the moment.

That's what Anson thought, looking up from the troublesome Ryan documents in his lap and refreshing himself with the sight of the distant childish figures splashing through the surf. To believe that one's children belonged to one was an illusion, albeit a necessary one. Best probably to regard oneself simply as the curator of their all too brief childhoods. He said their names to himself with pleasure: Claire and Bart and Jill and Marietta—they will grow up and have lives I cannot imagine, become very likely what I never dreamed or intended. Given his own childhood, which had been dominated by the unshakable will of his father, Anson tried not to foist his own wishes upon the lives of his children, though he could not help but envision, young as they were, Claire as a great pianist (she had the talent and, he thought, the will) and Bart as a successful architect (he had the mind for it; you could see that in the way he drew up plans for his sandcastles and then marshalled the girls into construction teams to see those plans to fruition). Anson rocked and watched Meg drop her knitting and run after two-year-old Marietta, who had probably just eaten a fistful of sand. He smiled, knowing exactly how Meg would fuss over Marietta, how she fussed over all of them, how she loved them and so wanted perfection for and from them. In the latter endeavour she was doomed, of course, but the certainty of failure didn't keep her from trying. From the time they walked, Meg instilled in her children her own virtues—those of decency, decorum and dignity, prayers and propriety—old-fashioned virtues, but useful, Anson thought, to the conduct of civilized life. Assuming one wanted a civilized life.

The floorboards on the porch squealed in a comforting tattoo as Anson puffed and watched his children cart buckets of wet sand back to the beach to lay the foundations of one of Bart's castles. Bart had even enlisted Jill and Marietta, who were as yet too young to evince anything but the tiniest glimmerings of character, but in his six-year-old son, Bart, Anson recognized his own young self: stolid, pensive, occasionally sulky. He smiled and watched Claire leave her footprint on the foundation; Meg saw it too and chided her for her thoughtlessness. It wasn't thoughtlessness at all, Anson chuckled to himself; it was deliberate. Anson regarded his eight-year-old daughter as a gift to the Swallow family. Some improbable collation of long submerged instincts surfaced in Claire: her high spirits, her impetuous will, her sassy tongue and awe-inspiring pout, the very aura of brightness around her—these were not traits ordinarily given unto Swallows, who, in Anson's judgment (and excepting his own father) were a rather sallow and dispirited clan. Meg was constantly correcting Claire, often punishing her, but Anson could not bring himself to dim, however momentarily, what he perceived as her childish luster. There would be enough later on to trim and crimp her spirits; he did not want to do it and, moreover, he did not want to imagine what would.

Anson returned his attention to the documents. The Ryan case. The death of an obscure, eccentric widow, Mrs. Sophie Goldstone, better known amongst those who had been saddled with her acquaintance as One-Strap Sophie. She died under the wheels of a car. An apparent hit-and-run. Dead and, from all appearances, unmourned. And then, as if they had neglected to bury Sophie Goldstone, the stink began to rise out of her carcass. Anson could smell the stink every time he walked into his packed courtroom to face the defendant, the spectators, the press, the jury, the prosecuting attorney, Coldwell, and the defense attorney, Hoolihan. Two men confessed to murdering Mrs. Goldstone and implicated a third, Patrick Ryan. Why should a stench arise from that? But by the time he left the courthouse every day, Anson was queasy from the smell. He tried to take it off with his clothes. He never got used to it.

Judge Anson Swallow had presided over trials involving the whole miserable range of human malice, stupidity and cruelty, but never a case that stank like this one. The sensationalism of the Ryan case bothered him, of course, but he couldn't blame the newspapers for stuffing people full of luridness at a dime a throw, and of course Patrick Ryan had doubly delighted the populace by falling from a high station. These factors complicated the case, but in and of themselves would not have admitted the sewer smell into the courtroom, would not, in and of themselves, have dogged and haunted Anson Swallow to the point that the case gnawed at his sleep, his peace of mind, eroded the attention he preferred to give his family. Even when his father had suggested this outing to San Angelo, Anson could not relinquish the Ryan case, though given the sunshine and the summer day, he regretted bringing the papers and their stench to this house, this beach. He stacked them and tied them with a string, resolving to forget Patrick Ryan and Sophie Goldstone.

He concentrated on the children playing on the beach. They were so distant that they might have been any children at all; they might even have been Anson and his brother and sisters playing in that same surf so many years ago. Anson squinted against the glare and yes, yes, he could all but see George, a timid boy, and Althea, a fat little girl, and Vera, handsome and soulful, and he, Anson, the youngest and yet the leader in their childish games and internecine struggles. He could see them in the water, but when he looked for his mother, sitting in the chair where Meg now sat, she escaped him. Though she had died only three months before, his mother, Edith Swallow, seemed so far past as to be obliterated. She had lived very quietly and died the same way and in dying seemed to have erased every aspect of her ever having lived. Even here at San Angelo, in the house that was undeniably hers (as the mansion in town was undeniably the Senator's), nothing remained of Edith Swallow, save perhaps for the funny runaway garden. Anson could remember loving his mother, but he could not remember what she looked like.

Perhaps Edith could not be expected to haunt in death; in life she had been totally eclipsed by her husband, the Senator. Fremont Ebeneezer Swallow had been a U.S. Senator for only one term many years before, and he had loathed the job. Senator Swallow was addicted to power, accustomed to praise, devoted to the deference and position that were his for the asking in his own city. In Washington these were not automatically given him, or even considered his just due. He did not know his way around Washington in any sense of the term and he despised asking direction; the Senator preferred to give directions. So when his term was up, he declined to run again and returned to California, where he could dictate rather than compromise, insist rather than inquire, and was subject to admiration rather than scrutiny. But he clung to the title and even his immediate family came to call him Senator. Even his late wife had called him Senator and Anson sometimes wondered if she had called him that in bed, but on the other hand, the Senator and his wife had not shared a bedroom in many years. Edith lived in his shadow. We all live in his shadow, and when the Senator dies, Anson thought, his body will be gone, but his shadow will still be everywhere.

His father's enormous shadow at that moment fell across the porch as Senator Fremont Ebeneezer Swallow eased his bulk into the other rocker—specially built to accommodate that bulk. At seventy-two, the Senator was an unstooped six feet tall, but he could not gracefully carry 250 pounds; he was awkward and wheezy, his heavy jowls florid and his thick hair a gun-metal gray. Like the Senator, Anson Swallow was stout and graying, though compared to the Senator, the judge was an altogether uncommanding presence.

"I won't come back to this house again," the Senator grumbled. "How can you be happy here, that's what I'd say to Edith, how can you be happy in a house like this? Damp. Never warm enough—and sand everywhere, in the beds and the food and the tub. Why can't you teach your children to wash the sand off before they come in?"

"It's probably not their sand," Anson replied, smiling. "It probably came into the house when I was a child."

"Well, I hate a house where the toilet stops up if you piss more than a pint at a time. No radio. No TV. Fuses that blow whenever you belch. You can't count on the electricity or the gas or the phone here. And the road! Hah! When do you think they'll get around to paving Jerusalem Road? After everything I've done for San Angelo, you'd think the least they could do is pave my street."

"No one else uses Jerusalem Road, Senator."

"Well, if I use it, that's enough! Anyway, I'm finished with this house. I hate it and I always have. From now on, I'm staying in the city. You and Meg can have the damn place. Just draw up whatever papers are necessary and I'll sign them."

"That's very generous of you, Senator, but—"

"I'm not the generous type. I only kept this house for Edith. She loved it for some godforsaken reason. I don't see anything quaint or refreshing about a peasant's hovel."

"It's hardly that, Senator."

"Well I had enough grubbing as a boy. Give me the city! Give me the modern world! Your mother never understood the modern world, never saw its pleasures."

Anson considered defending his mother, but to do so would demean even her dim memory. Instead, he said, "Perhaps you ought to give the house to all four of us and then we could use it together."

"There's six of you. You and Meg and the children."

"I meant me and George and Vera and Althea."

"Don't be ridiculous." The Senator lit his first massive cigar of the day. "Althea has no use for it. What would she do with it?"

"She might bring friends."

The Senator cast his son a baleful glance. "Althea doesn't have any friends, and she'll never marry. Look at her out there—a fine morning like this and she's still draped in black. Who would marry a fat woman in mourning? And Vera!" He snorted out a cloud of smoke. "You know what Vera would do with this house, don't you?"

"One never quite knows what Vera will do."

"She'd turn it into a retreat for all her homeopathic healing friends, so they could lie on the beach and lay their hands on one another and call out sickness."

"Vera's not doing that anymore."

"Oh, that's right. Now it's the toga people. Worse. Much worse. Grown people wearing togas and throwing their arms around and worshiping the sunrise. That girl should have stayed married."

"Her husband died before their second anniversary, remember?"

"Well, she should have married again. Marriage is the only thing that keeps women sane. Without marriage, they get woolly-minded like Vera or grim like Althea. Lord, I get sick of women in black. I've told Althea time after time. Don't come to my table in black, but she just starts to cry and snivel for her mother. Then she tries to coddle me. She fired the cook last week, Anson, and said she wanted to do the meals, make sure I ate properly. Hah! Pap and gruel! I had to up the damn cook's wages by ten dollars a week to get her to come back, and even at that, she wanted me to promise that Althea wouldn't meddle in the kitchen. Settle that with Althea, I told her, I have more important things to think about. I tell you, Anson, Althea drives me wild with the way she fusses over me and tries to make me stop smoking and look after my health. My health, my ass! Althea wants me to get sick like your mother so she'll have something to do, someone to look after. Althea enjoyed your mother's dying."

"That's not fair and it's not true."

"The hell you say! Althea enjoyed having to spoon-feed Edith, change her bed, bathe her, wheel her out to the terraces. Althea thought Edith was her baby and Edith thought Althea was a saint."

"Althea made Mother's last years as comfortable as they could be. She was a saint."

"Flypaper! Now that Edith's dead, Althea can't wait for me to decline. She always tells me she'll look after me in my declining years. Go look after George, I tell her. His wife don't know how to do it. Eleanor must have wrung her hands for so many years now they've turned to butter. Go look after your useless drunken brother George if you want to coddle someone."

"George may more require our pity than our censure," Anson replied evenly.

"Pity! What kind of grown man calls for pity? He's not a helpless widow, is he? He's not a stricken child. He's a drunk. I can't even tell anymore when he's sober. If he ever is. I keep him on the board of Swallow Shipping Lines because he's my son. No one else would. If George wasn't my son, he and Eleanor and their whole family of brats—the Tenor, the Bass and the Baritone, those screaming brats—would starve and well he knows it." The Senator rocked impatiently.

If George were not your son, Anson thought, he might not be a drunk; he might have been a very placid, happy, limited soul. As the son of the founding father of Swallow Lines, George more correctly resembled a sparrow pulled in the wake of an eagle. Or a vulture; that was a possibility as well.

"No, my boy." The Senator puffed and his rocking slowed. "You're the only one who's amounted to anything. You keep this house. My gift."

"Thank you." Anson's throat closed over the words uncomfortably. He could utter thanks as a formal pleasantry, but stirrings of gratitude always made him vaguely uneasy. As a judge, he endeavored always to stay clear of any entanglements that required his gratitude; over the years his professional response had become his personal one as well. He was doubly uncomfortable now because the gift of the San Angelo house would doubtlessly strew discontent and resentment amongst Vera and George and Althea and he wondered fleetingly if this too might be part of the Senator's plan. The Senator always had a plan; he was never without direction; he navigated well and he always knew exactly where he was going. In this, Anson reflected, he had the advantage over three-quarters of the rest of the world.

The silence between them was broken by the sound of their contrapuntal rockers, the circling gulls and darting jays, until Claire burst through the garden gate and flew up to the porch, flinging herself in her father's lap, sending the bundle of Ryan papers to the floor.

"What's this!" Anson cried.

"You have to help me."

"Can you say good morning to the Senator, Claire?"

"I can, but I don't want to."

"That's very rude."

"Claire is always rude," the Senator volunteered.

"I am not, but you have to help me, Father, please." She curled up in Anson's lap, her back to the Senator. "Mama says I have to have my hair washed tonight and set in pin curls."

"What's wrong with that?"

"It's not the washing, it's the pin curls I hate and you have to tell her I don't need them. I hate having my hair pinned! It hurts and I hate it and I can't sleep on the pins and I don't see why I should."

"Your mother always says that sometimes it hurts to be pretty. You want to be pretty, don't you?"

"No. I want to be a warthog."

Anson laughed and drew his arms closer around his daughter. "What do you know of warthogs?"

Claire began to root and snuffle around his clothes, snorting into his shirt and twisting while Anson laughed and laughed.

"Stop it!" he cried, setting her down on the porch. "Look, you've got me all sandy. You go back to the beach and help Bart with his sandcastle. He can't do it without you, you know."

"I won't go till you promise to tell Mama not to set my hair in pin curls."

"All right, Claire. I'll talk to your mother. I can't promise anything, but—"

"That's fine!" she called, tripping down the stairs and running back toward the beach.

"You're raising a brat in that one, Anson," said the Senator. "You better put the clamps on her while she's still young and you still can. Give her a few years and you'll have every boy in a ten-mile radius braying on your porch. You'll have your hands full unless you do something now. She'll be a wild girl."

Anson chuckled, brushed the sand from his clothes and picked up the bundle of Ryan papers. He decided not to tell his father to mind his own damn business.

"And you know what they call wild girls, eventually, anyway," the Senator added darkly.

"What?"

"Mother."

Anson quit laughing. He tidied his papers and noted his father's glance at them, the top broadly labeled RYAN. Anson covered it with his hand as if warding off a blow. "Althea says you're writing a book. Your autobiography."

Under their heavy hoods, the Senator's eyes darted from the papers to Anson and rested there. "Hmph. She said a lot more than that if I know Althea. Women have no concept of greatness. They don't think. Althea cannot understand why my book is so important to generations as yet unborn. I'm going to tell all ambitious young men how to achieve in this world. My life is a pattern of success and all of it deserved. There's been nothing like my book since the *Autobiography of Benjamin Franklin*, another poor boy who achieved riches. No spur to ambition like poverty, that's what I always say, and I ought to know. I came from a family who had failed for as long as anyone could remember. Fail and move on, that was the Swallow family motto before me."

Anson relaxed; he'd been right to bring up the book. The tide of recollection, the thrill of recounting his own glorious successes, would carry the Senator along now, far, far from the Ryan case.

"Itinerant sod busters, peasants! That's what I was born to, but no boy with courage, brains and ambition need fail in this great country, especially in these modern times. I had vision and daring! I looked around me at the land and I could see the land was already sucked up, deeded, stamped and delivered to the rich. The sea, that's the place for adventurers and explorers, for men of sinew and will! Give me the sea! That's what I said. No man can own the sea, can he? The sea belongs only to the dead who lie under it and those brave enough to venture upon it." The Senator extended his arm as if his audience included the people on the beach, the Pacific itself. "So I left the land and came to the great city by the sea. I courted opportunity and I won her. And you will reap the rewards of my success and you can bless God you never had to struggle for it."

"Struggle can be relative," Anson offered. "So can success, for that matter."

"Ha! You've never known real struggle or you wouldn't say that. None of you have. Your mother never knew struggle either, born to those namby-pamby missionaries who all died in China and never left

42

a mark on this great country. If George had to struggle, he wouldn't waste his time drinking, I can tell you that. Struggle would have made a man of him. You don't know what struggle is. None of you have known what it is to want something so bad you'd kill for it."

Anson's heart and guts and hands and tongue all seemed to shrivel; *Don't mention Ryan.* He spread his hands over the documents in his lap. *Don't mention Ryan or Nelson or Hanratty or any of those men who want so much they'd kill for it.*

"I meant that figuratively, of course. Not like Pat Ryan, who killed that poor old lady."

"How long will it take you to write your book?" Anson inquired quickly.

"The book? Oh, I don't know. Weeks. Maybe months. I have help, you know. I suppose Althea's told you all about my secretary."

Anson relit his pipe; as a judge, he was accustomed to remaining noncommital.

"I suppose Althea has filled your ears with stories of Mrs. Cotton."

"She may have."

"Ha! That's a good one. She may have." The Senator slapped one of his enormous thighs. "That girl gets more like a vulture every day."

"Althea is hardly a girl." Anson glanced toward the beach at the obese figure in black, her face pressed close to the paper. "If that's the girl you were referring to."

"Well I wasn't talking about Lucille—Mrs. Cotton. Althea thinks—well, who knows what Althea thinks, if she thinks, which I doubt. She just snarls. I mean it, Anson, that girl doesn't open her mouth, but she snarls and she snarls all the louder every time Mrs. Cotton shows up for work. Mrs. Cotton is a fine secretary. There's nothing more to be said." Having delivered this dictum, the Senator puffed and rocked and continued. "She's a widow with two little children to support. A helpless widow left alone in the world. A Christian woman. She's a member of our church."

"Mother's church, you mean."

"Well now, Anson, the church belongs to all Christians. The lowest and the highest are all equal in the sight of God. Don't be uncharitable."

"Althea seems to think you would not be so charitable if Mrs. Cotton were old and ugly."

"Is it a crime to be beautiful? I mean—" the Senator coughed "—Mrs. Cotton is a young gentlewoman in need. She works hard. She can type

43

fine. Slow but thorough. I always say, give me the slow but thorough ones. They're the ones to be trusted, that's what I always say."

"I don't ever recall hearing you say that."

"Then you never listened to me, my boy."

Anson began to protest that he was not a boy just as Althea was not a girl, but he thought better of it. "Althea says a blind, deaf and dumb man could type faster than Mrs. Cotton."

"As if Althea could judge! I wish to God that girl had married and left home."

"She could have married Albert Smythe."

"Who?"

"You remember, the man you sent to Honolulu in 1928. You sent him away because Althea wanted to marry him."

"I remember nothing of the sort. That was a business decision. Connected only with the good of Swallow Lines and nothing at all to do with Althea. I didn't even know—"

Anson rocked on as the Senator exculpated himself. He had heard it all before. It amounted to another boring family tragedy: Althea had wanted to marry the wizened shipping clerk Albert Smythe with a passion that defied anything one would have guessed of such a lethargic, inert girl as the young Althea Swallow. Albert was summarily given his choice of transferring to Honolulu or losing his job with Swallow Lines altogether. That much, Anson knew for certain. He suspected that Albert Smythe had implored his love to run away with him and that Althea hadn't the mettle to defy her father. Althea had never married and Anson suspected that Albert hadn't either. Moreover, he thought it very likely that the two had stayed in touch by letter, though his evidence there was only intuitive, not even circumstantial, and his legal training urged him to discount it altogether. Of this much there could be no doubt: the day after Albert Smythe sailed for Honolulu, God saw fit to toss the earthly rug on which the city sat. The quake leveled, killed and maimed with abandon and shook the moral fiber of those it did not destroy. Althea Swallow took the quake personally, as a sign from heaven that she had made the wrong decision, but she did not recant. She remained in her room for a week and then—Anson was there, at one of the grim, miserably long family dinners when—the eighteen-year-old Althea burst into the dining room and declared to the entire family that she would marry no one but Albert Smythe, that she would remain a spinster for the rest of her days. Then she took her place beside Vera, flicked open her napkin and the matter was never mentioned again. Looking at Althea now, bent over her letter, Anson doubted that her resolve was any longer fueled by anger; habit and inertia probably took over where anger left off, but he could not stifle a pang of pity for his sister; Althea had grown progressively more obstinate and embittered, acerbic, perpetually tense, expending whatever capacity she had for affection in the service of the sick, lavishing her love on her dying mother and looking forward only to the same prospect with her father. Anson thought she deluded herself in this: the Senator was not the sort to decline for a good many years, and he would never do so gracefully. Anson scanned the beach again, looking for the ghost of the girl Althea had been, but she eluded him.

"Althea acts as if I just thought of this book when I met Mrs. Cotton," the Senator continued. "Nothing could be further from the truth. I have considered this book for a long time, but I could hardly spend my time writing when Edith was dying, could I?"

I don't know why not, Anson thought; you never took much account of her living. "Probably not," he replied judiciously.

"Well, she's gone now. God rest her soul and I miss her, even though—well, God rest her soul." He repeated this as an injunction to the Almighty rather than a request. "All Edith ever wanted was a family to cook for and a garden to tend."

"Mother was an excellent cook. She taught Althea how to cook, and she built the most spectacular garden in the city."

"Yes, but she could have hired a dozen cooks and our garden in the city, why, that's as much my doing as hers. She wanted it to look like that—" He pointed vaguely to the sunflowers and nasturtiums. "She wouldn't even let the gardener weed out the California poppies. Weeds, I told her, they're nothing but weeds. Import! Anyone can grow a geranium. Let's import the finest and most exotic that the world has to offer. We can afford it!" The Senator shook his head. "She was a plain woman. Money meant nothing to her. She was a spiritual creature and she didn't, she couldn't, she was. . ."

Anson rocked furiously, keeping his eyes pinned to the boat seesawing on the horizon. "A fine woman," he blurted out.

"Of course. A fine woman, but she was—"

Weak. Anson suddenly realized why his mother's imprint had been so quickly effaced after her death. She was weak and prosaic and preferred the homely over the imposing, which is why she so loved this house at San Angelo. In the Swallows' palatial townhouse, with its French doors and English wainscoting, beveled mirrors, colonial sideboards and stained-glass windows, the acres of imported bulbs and banyan trees, Edith Swallow rattled like a dry kernel in a dead husk, dwarfed by the gilt frames enclosing the monumentally bad art the Senator invested in, dwarfed in fact by her own portrait, in which she was dwarfed by the heavy satin of her gown and strangled by ropes of pearls that ill became her.

". . . not the sort of girl your Meg is. Now, there's a fine woman."

Anson eased off rocking. "There's no one on earth like Meg."

"No indeed. You've done fine, my boy. You not only make me proud of your every accruing honor, but you married the finest woman God ever wrought."

"Meg's love was the only thing I ever truly sought or wanted or hungered for," Anson said candidly; he was seldom so forthright. "I never cared for the rest of it and if I didn't have Meg, none of it would matter."

"Flypaper! You've achieved. Surely you don't still hold it against me that I made you go to law school."

"I wanted to be an architect."

The Senator cleared the air of smoke and bad assumptions. "Ridiculous. Look at you. Cum laude at the university. Honours at the law school. The youngest judge in the city's history. Why, there's talk of running you for mayor when Stone retires in 'fifty-four."

"There was talk of running Patrick Ryan for mayor, too," Anson retorted, and was instantly sorry; he never should have brought Ryan up. "I have no wish to be mayor. I wouldn't run in any event."

"What about governor or senator? I've heard it said there could be two Senator Swallows in this family and I would be behind you every step of the way, my boy. Why, look at that little pissant Nixon. It looks like he might be Vice President. Think of it—a piece of spittle like that a heartbeat away from the Presidency. You owe it to the state to get into politics. You have the universal respect of your peers. Your reputation precedes you everywhere you go. Even the papers say you're the only judge who's trusted enough to try this dirty Ryan affair. I call that achievement!"

"I call it torture," he said, referring as much to the present as to the courtroom.

The Senator shifted in his rocker so he could see his son's face. "Ryan's guilty. Guilty as they come. Hang him."

"We don't hang people anymore in this state."

"Imagine, a former public defender involved in a smutty scheme to fleece widows and order the murder of a poor defenseless woman like Mrs. Goldstein."

"Goldstone."

"Ryan's worse than a murderer. He's a disgrace. He's a blemish on our city. He's an insult to the people of California."

The Senator was like gravity, a law unto himself, and Anson could feel himself pulled down, down, his own will immobilized. Struggle was relative; he struggled now. He spoke with difficulty. "Before Mrs. Goldstone's death, before Nelson and Hanratty accused Pat Ryan, he was welcomed into the best homes in the city. He was the boy wonder attorney. I've seen you throw your arms around his shoulders and tell everyone he could be President if he wasn't a mick."

"Never! I never did such a thing! Why, I wouldn't walk across the street to piss in Ryan's asshole if his guts were on fire!"

"Then why were you and every other civic worthy at a party he was giving the night Mrs. Goldstone was murdered?"

"How could we have known?" the Senator cried.

"Don't include me. I wasn't there. I am the judge. I cannot discuss it. Let's change the—"

Anson didn't have to because Claire came running up the beach, and at the gate she turned and yelled back to Meg, who followed close behind. "I'm not a bit sorry! And I won't say I am!" She slammed the gate and ran to Anson's side, laying her hand on his shoulder, as if readying herself for a formal picture of recalcitrance.

Meg hurried after her, pausing at the step to catch her breath.

"You go right back down there and tell your brother you're sorry, Claire Swallow."

"I won't."

Meg cast Anson an appealing look. "You're the judge."

"But I haven't heard the evidence."

"Oh, what does it matter?" the Senator shouted. "Get out of here, Claire. I'm trying to talk to your father. Take her away, Meg."

"Not until she agrees to tell Bart she's sorry. She kicked over his sandcastle. On purpose."

"I did not."

"She's a brat, Anson," said Meg firmly, "and I think she should be punished for willfully destroying what wasn't hers."

"It was so mine. I built it, didn't I? Doesn't that make it mine. Doesn't it, Father?"

"Bart's castles are important to him, Claire," Anson said gravely.

"He spends all night drafting the plans for them, and if they don't mean anything to you, then you shouldn't help build them."

"He makes me!"

"I doubt that. No one can make you do anything, Claire. You were helping Bart. But that doesn't make it your castle."

"If I hadn't kicked it down, he'd have made me work on it all day and I'm tired of it."

"There," said Meg, vindicated. "You see."

"How can a man relax with all these children!" the Senator cried. "Take your paltry quarrels and get out of here!"

Meg looked vaguely crestfallen. "It's the principle, Senator. Claire has to understand the principle."

Anson put his arm around Claire. "My judgment in this case is that you should go inside for a while, Claire. Dust your feet off first and go inside and practice the piano. When you calm down, you can go back to the beach."

"I'm calm."

But not contrite, thought Anson. He expected time would effect, if not contrition, at least forbearance; Bart never stayed mad at Claire too long. "You go in and practice and we'll talk about it again in a while. Go on, now. I want to hear you play. You know how much I like to hear you play the piano."

Claire shot her mother and the Senator a defiant glance and stomped into the house. Without wiping her feet. Meg scolded Anson for his leniency, and the Senator chided him for dealing with childish quarrels at all. Anson managed to mollify them both, and Meg went back down to the beach, where Bart was refashioning the ruined wall. Anson went back to rocking, his chair picking up the tempo of the mismated chords of the "Minuet in G". The Senator sulked. "They must have thrown over their anchor," said Anson, pointing to the boat at the horizon. "They haven't moved." He toyed with the string on his papers. "I always value your opinion, Senator," he said at last. "But in this case, in any case I am trying, it behooves me to consider only the evidence presented and follow no counsel but my own. Anything else would be unprincipled. Unthinkable."

"I'm not the press, Anson," the Senator said genially. "And in the bosom of your own family—"

"No."

"Everyone knows Ryan is guilty. All I'm saying is that we ought to make an example of him or people will get the idea that this city is willing to tolerate a man who would murder—" The Senator's hand shot out and squelched Anson's objection. "Of course no one is saying that he killed Mrs. Goldstein with his own fair hands. No, those jail-birds Nelson and Hanratty did it. They admitted to holding her down and running over her with a car and in my opinion—"

"The prosecuting attorney will bring all that to my attention. I don't need you to do it."

"—Nelson and Hanratty ought to hang too, but they won't now that they've turned state's evidence. They should never have got out on parole. Ryan signed for their parole. You knew that, didn't you? He represented them as public defender years ago, when they went up to the pen, and then he signed for their parole last year. Why, he gave them both jobs! Nelson was his chauffeur and Hanratty was his gardener!"

"I don't want to hear any more. You're compromising my position."

"Flypaper. I'm your father." The Senator eyed the judge shrewdly; he pointed to the papers in Anson's lap. "Surely you must have formed some opinions."

"That's my job. To form opinions. Not suspicions."

"What do you suspect?" The Senator's bushy eyebrows rose and fell across his forehead like indecisive dragonflies. "You suspect that those jailbirds Nelson and Hanratty confessed awful damn fast, don't you? Well Ed Keller himself, the chief of police, told me to assure you that they confessed of their own accord. No beatings. No bribes. Nothing of that sort. No indeed. They were treated just like any other prisoners."

"I'm going to tell Claire she can go back to the beach."

"And as for nabbing Nelson and Hanratty so fast," the Senator's words put an end to Anson's movement to uproot himself from the rocker, "that was superb police work. I commend them. None of us want you to think there's anything more here than meets the eye. That's our only concern."

Anson rolled the papers in his lap into a hard cone, a cudgel; he wanted to bring it down on the Senator's palm or his own, to smash at the flies hovering in the noon light. "Us? Our? Who, Senator? Who? What is there about this case that brings out the vultures?"

"Why, the death of an innocent widow, of course."

"No one is wholly innocent."

"We're talking about the law here, not morals."

"They're not mutually exclusive concerns. A man's life is at stake."

"So was Mrs. Goldstein's."

49

"Goldstone." Anson wilted back into his rocker and listened to Claire struggle with the "Minuet in G".

"Ryan ordered her killed so he could get her money."

"He had her money. He didn't have to kill her for that. He had power of attorney, and he was her financial adviser for the last seventeen years."

"Ryan ordered her killed," the Senator insisted. "Nelson and Hanratty did it at his bidding, but they botched the dumping of the body. It's that simple."

"It's not simple."

"Of course it is. Almighty Christ, Claire!" he bellowed. "Stop that goddamned racket! Go play with your goddamned dolls and be quiet!" He turned back to Anson. "Surely you can't feel loyalty to scum like Ryan."

"I am loyal only to my duty." Anson's tongue thickened in his mouth. The "Minuet in G" ended in mid-air. "It's up to the jury to decide Patrick Ryan's fate, and I will not have any evidence or opinion submitted to me that is not in strict accordance with court procedures, which your talking with me here certainly is not. I tell you in no uncertain terms, Senator, I will not, I cannot, I dare not, hustle Pat Ryan out of the courtroom and into the gas chamber to suit anyone. Even you." Anson faced his father squarely, searching the Senator's face for the drop of contrition or remorse that would assure him this was a casual and inconsequential conversation.

The Senator puffed on his cigar. "You misunderstand me, my boy. I'm speaking only as a concerned citizen when I say—"

"Don't! Don't say anything!"

"Let's put this whole nasty Ryan business behind us and get on with the business of life. Why loll in the muck?"

"Muck! Life and death and the law are not muck, Senator!" The papers in Anson's lap came undone and jiggled on his knees.

"It's that mick defense attorney, isn't it?" The Senator eyed him shrewdly. Behind the screen door, the Senator saw Claire, her eyes narrowed, her small face twisted with suspicion. He ignored her and pressed his advantage with his son. "It's that Hooligan, isn't it?"

"Hoolihan, Senator. Hoolihan is not getting to me. Nothing is getting to me. Not even you. If you have offered me Jerusalem Road as a bribe, if it is contingent upon anything to do with the Ryan case, then—"

"A bribe! Me offer a bribe! How dare you suggest such a thing!"

"I don't dare, Senator. I never have. None of us have ever dared. Not Mother. Not George or Althea or Vera, no one has ever dared suggest that you might conceivably be anything but unalterably correct in your judgments or your business dealings or your personal decisions regarding all our lives. Mother's dead. George, as you know, is a hopeless drunk. Vera's off wearing a toga. Althea is a nasty, embittered old maid, but I—"

"Calm yourself, my boy."

"I'm not your boy! I am the judge. Probably I am the judge not only because you insisted I go to law school, but as a result of your influence, which runs through this city, if I may say so, like a sewer connecting the very high and the very low."

"How dare you!" The Senator gasped, "How dare you? I'll cut you out of my will! I'll disinherit you!"

"I hope you do! I hope I never again have to take any of your directions, especially from the grave!"

"Damn the grave! I'll outlive you all! All my weaselly, ungrateful children! I give you everything, every opportunity, every advantage, and this is the thanks I get? I'll see you in hell before I'd let a child of mine speak to me as you have."

"I'm not a child anymore, Senator." Anson rose, so quickly that the documents in his lap spilled at his feet. He scooped some of them into his arms and left the rest as he rose to face his father, both of them fleshy, quivering combatants, outrage percolating from Anson's every pore and rage rumbling the porch beneath the Senator's feet. "I'm a grown man. We're all four of us grown and you can't use the strap on us, not even the strap of your will, or at least you can't on me. Whatever Pat Ryan is guilty of, he will get a fair hearing in my court, as far as is humanly possible. We are all human and, so, corruptible. The flesh—"

"Father?" Claire said meekly, glancing from one to the other. "Father?"

"—is corruptible, but the spirit is not. You will not corrupt my spirit!" He turned to Claire and barked, "What do you want?"

Mutely, she pushed the screen door open and stood beside him, coiled, awaiting the crack of a mythical gun that would send her off and running.

"Please," Anson begged his father, a tone he had not meant to take. "Don't you understand? I want, I must, stay within the public record. I can't bear the stench in my courtroom. It nauseates me every day.

Something in this case—I don't know what—it stinks like a corpse, it smells of rot and the more I hear, the more rot I smell and I can't—"

"Silence!" The Senator pulled his arm back as if he might strike Anson, grown man or not, but at that moment, Anson turned, yanked Claire's hand and pulled her after him as he fled down the steps, papers raining from his arms, kicking open the garden gate as he ran to the beach, to the sea, to Meg, who heard or sensed his coming and turned in her chair, astonished to see her husband shooting toward her, papers in his wake, sand flying from his feet, Claire stumbling behind him, his arms flailing as he pummeled through the ghosts that littered his path and impeded his progress.

ii

The Senator left in an uproar, demanding that Meg and Althea pack up his things, make him a lunch and phone the chauffeur, who had put up at one of the boarding houses in town. In the midst of the ensuing tumult, Meg snagged Claire and ordered her out to the beach to sit with her father. "What's happened?" Claire cried. "How can the Senator say those horrible things to Fa—"

"Just do as I say and be quick about it. Yes, Senator," she called out. "Of course I'm going to pack you something to eat on the journey. I'll be right there." She shooed Claire out the front door. "Go!"

"I'm coming too, Senator," Althea's words rang from the top of the stairs. "I'm packing up right now to come home with you."

The Senator emerged from the living room into the front hall, snorting like a bull. "You're not, by God, coming with me, Althea! You'll stay here with Meg and the children and you'll by God stay here by God all summer long, do you hear me?"

"But, Senator, you need me. Who will look after you?"

"I don't by God need looking after! I don't need anything from any of you—my weak, worthless children!"

"But, Senator!"

"I don't want to see you in town for the rest of the summer, Althea. I hate looking at women in black! I hate mourning! I hate death! I hate old maids! I hate you!"

Althea threw her hands over her face and with a wail she fled up the stairs. Meg started up after her, but the Senator ordered her into the kitchen to fix lunch because as soon as Dillard, the chauffeur, arrived, he was leaving this infernal house forever. "Burn it to the ground, that's what I'll do! I hate this house and everyone in it!" he bellowed, stalking back into the living room. "And get these goddamned children out of my way." He shoved little Jill through the doors and sent her sprawling.

Dillard drove the Senator's huge black Cadillac to the back of the house and put his bags in the trunk. The Senator pushed past Meg and Bart and Jill and Marietta on his way out the kitchen door and down the steps. He thrust aside the sheets hanging on the clothesline and smashed the peach tree branches from his path; hard green peaches thudded to the ground. He got in the car and Dillard closed the door, tipped his hat to Meg and the children, and they left in a spray of dust and gravel. Meg sadly realized she'd have to wash the sheets all over again.

Meg left her three younger children to play in the back garden and went upstairs, but the sobbing Althea had locked her door and refused to open it. Meg was just as glad. She flew out the front door, running toward her husband on the beach.

Anson sat in her chair, facing the sea with Claire at his feet. His shoulders rolled forward and he looked haggard and drawn. "You can go back to the house now, Claire," Meg said quietly.

"No. I'm going to stay with Father."

"You go back and look after your brothers and sisters."

"No."

"Go, darling girl," said Anson, patting her golden head. "Thank you for staying with me. Everything will be fine now. Your mother's here."

Reluctantly, Claire got up and shuffled back through the sand toward the house. Once she turned back to the sea, and though the sun was directly in her eyes, she saw her mother drop to her knees before her father and wrap her arms around him, his head lay against her shoulder. They pressed so close together that they looked to be a single lump of flesh. Beyond them, in the distance, a small white sailboat bobbed, its tiny mast a pin to prick the sunshine. Claire thought her father was crying, but she couldn't be certain because the tide had brought the breakers closer and their roar drowned out everything else. She walked on toward the house, humming the "Minuet in G". At the garden gate, ankle deep in nasturtiums, she turned back once again, paused and studied them: her mother and father huddled together, the sunlight flung across the ocean like a quilt of flames and the tiny sailboat retreating against the horizon.

iii

Anson Swallow returned to the city by himself on Sunday afternoon. He promised to come to Jerusalem Road every weekend, and insisted that Meg and Althea and the children enjoy themselves on the beach for the summer. He would be fine, he assured them. He kissed them all goodbye and headed north over the mountain highway and arrived as the shadows had lengthened and the city lay steeping in sunset. He drove to his own comfortable neighborhood, where everything seemed to be soothing, smoothed and softened; even the corners of the lawns were not sharp and the white stucco homes all had red tile roofs, rounded doorways and fat hydrangeas in front of arched windows. He pulled into his garage, too close to the wall as it turned out, so he put the Ford into reverse and backed up a bit and them he let the motor idle.

Presently, Anson Swallow backed down his driveway and drove out of his neighborhood and made his way downtown, deserted now in the Sunday summer twilight. He drove past the county courthouse, the city's first undertaking at the end of the war, and looked up to see the corner windows of his chambers reflecting the sun like shaken foil. Anson always felt a little thrill of pride in the courthouse, a massive structure, a stern edifice of stone and granite and the best laid brick. It occupied what seemed to be acres of land, with beautiful grounds and plenty of room left over for expansion. Its solid Corinthian pillars always seemed to Anson to embody all that was best about the law. Fleetingly, he wondered if Patrick Ryan, housed in the basement jail, thought so too.

The traffic light changed and he drove on toward the lesser parts of town, those neighborhoods that had never quite been claimed for business and were now unfit for living. The upper floors of many of the old rowhouses were boarded up and the street-level apartments had been pared into offices sheltering cheap lawyers, chiropractors and an occasional dry cleaners. Finally, he found the address he sought. Three-quarters of a century earlier, Sophie Goldstone's address might have been a respectable one, but the property around hers had been deserted, decayed, abandoned. Sophie Goldstone had lived in a dilapidated frame house set squarely in the middle of two city lots she owned. Much of this land she'd fenced off with six-foot-high planks, but Anson drove around the back and parked his Ford and got out, hoping he would not be noticed and hoping, moreover, that his being here at all did not conflict with this duty or undermine his impartiality.

He walked past the tumbledown shed-cum-garage where Nelson and Hanratty admitted to rolling the '51 Buick over Mrs. Goldstone (and then reversing the car and driving back over her again). He glanced in: cans of paint and rusting rakes and spiders' webs thick with victims. The floor was earthen, dank with oil—and blood? Anson turned and wandered toward the house, kicking litter from his path. Weeds cuddled up to the broken windows and an unstuffed chair rattled on the porch. The steps looked uncertain at best, and Anson did not risk them. The house itself was almost entirely devoured by a morning glory vine; the flowers were closed now, as if the vine were content, for the moment, with digestion. Testimony given so far at the trial suggested that Mrs. Goldstone had lived here in sloth and squalor and with some fifty-two cats and a dozen dogs, plus a number of chickens, which she kept despite civic codes prohibiting them. The chicken coops were deserted, their doors flung open. A few cats still slunk about the place and the one-time presence of many animals could be detected by the smell of urine and drying fecal matter, which Anson attempted to sidestep as he walked about the place. Probably, the local urchins had snatched the chickens, broken the windows and terrorized the cats and dogs before Sophie Goldstone was cold in her grave. Probably, they considered it just revenge for all the years she had chased them, screaming after them, swinging a mop, a rake, a pitchfork or a broom over her head like a Roman warrior. The urchins had dubbed her with the name One-Strap Sophie because she habitually wore men's overalls, which she fastened with only one strap. Anson remembered reading in the newspaper that her sister had tearfully informed the press that she had to go to Sears & Roebuck and buy a proper dress for Sophie to be buried in.

One of the mangy cats rubbed against his leg. Anson shuddered and shook it off. He went around the back of the house, where a clothesline was strung between gnarled plum trees. Doubtlessly, the urchins would get the fruit this summer too. Anson peered in the broken window of the back door. All he could see was a web-strewn washtub.

Everything stank of disuse and excrement. And something else. The same stench that assaulted him in the courtroom.

When Anson got home, he went directly to his study and poured himself a whiskey. He took his whiskey to the backyard, considered the lawn swing, but the pool shimmered in the twilight, beckoning him. He removed his shoes and turned his cuffs up to the knees and lowered his white feet into the water. The long twilight suffused the sky with a lilac glow, and until darkness overcame him completely, the judge sat there, drinking his whiskey, puffing on his pipe, watching the smoke cast insubstantial shadows across the reflective water, skimming so close to the surface he could not tell the smoke from its shadow.

That Monday, Anson Swallow began a routine that daily grew more rigid as the summer progressed. He got up very early and drove to the courthouse when only working people were abroad, on their way to or from menial jobs. He very often encountered the charwoman finishing up her tasks as he entered the marble foyer of the courthouse. Only at this early hour could he avoid the hungry spectators, the slavering press, eager to invade his courtroom. In his chambers, surrounded by the leatherbound works of Emerson, Jefferson and Thoreau (as well as lawbooks), Anson worked for a few hours until the bailiff arrived and brought the judge a cup of coffee. Inevitably, Anson drank his coffee standing at his window. Nervously, he spun the globe on its axis and, as an exercise in humility, wondered what the rest of the world was doing. More often than he might have wished, his gaze was drawn to the green swath of hillside to the south, the city cemetery far away where Sophie Goldstone was buried. Though Patrick Ryan too was in the courthouse, he could not have seen the cemetery, not from the basement. The view was not the same.

Once Anson entered the courthouse, he seemed as much a prisoner of the building as Patrick Ryan; his lunch was delivered to his chambers, and he did not leave until well past the end of the judicial day, when he could hurry to his car, avoiding everyone. He declined all evening invitations, ostensibly to assure himself that he could be kept free of taint or compromise, that his dignity and rectitude would be unquestioned, but in fact, Anson could not bear to join any gathering where he might be likely to meet people like Mayor Stone or Chief of Police Keller or any number of civic worthies who might allude to his great political future once the likes of Patrick Ryan had been ripped from the city's firmament and sent to the gas chamber. He also did not want to run the risk of running into his father.

The week after Anson returned from San Angelo, a deed reached him by the ordinary postal system, a duly signed quitclaim to the Jerusalem Road property in favor of Anson Swallow. The deed came from his father's attorney, not from his father. Throughout that summer, the Senator made not the slightest overture to end the rift between them and neither did Anson, though it grieved him—and worried him as well: he'd never before realized how implicitly he had relied on his father's sense of direction, the very direction he vowed not to take. Without his father, Anson was cast adrift on his own resources, which seemed to dwindle daily. Without Meg and his family for emotional ballast, he seemed to sink into the morass of the Ryan case. Without any sort of social contacts, he seemed to shrivel inwardly and outwardly, shrank as well from touch, small talk, from all but that contact demanded by his duty.

Had he not scorned the parties, dinners and galas of his father's friends, Anson might have heard of the Senator's marriage to Mrs. Lucille Cotton, early that July, from someone other than Hoolihan, Ryan's defense attorney. Hoolihan heard it from a drinking crony, a reporter. Anson would have preferred to have read it in the newspapers than to have heard it from Hoolihan.

"A handful of haunch and trouble," that was how Hoolihan (on the off-the-record authority of the reporter) described the new Mrs. Swallow. Anson took offense, naturally, that any lady should be so described, but he simply bristled and said nothing: Hoolihan was famed for his vulgarity and overstatement, to say nothing of his bad temper. Hoolihan was the youngest of eight children in a family that was noisy, impoverished, hard-drinking, hard-working and pious. The father had once been a stevedore at the Swallow Line docks until a labour dispute with strikebreakers permanently maimed him. Hoolihan—like his father—was as ready to engage in fisticuffs as the law; he had a reputation for settling his quarrels out of court in just that fashion, crude bare-knuckled duels. Hoolihan was the sort of attorney beloved by the downtrodden and detested by everyone else, particularly the more dignified practitioners of the law. Hoolihan had been twice decorated for his participation in the D-Day assault on Normandy, so no one questioned his bravery, though his tactics were continually suspect. Anson thought it ironic that Patrick Ryan (who, before his fall, would have cut Hoolihan in the street) chose him as defense attorney. Ryan chose well. The flamboyant Hoolihan lost no opportunity to defend his client or promote his innocence and provided a striking courtroom contrast to the prosecutor, Hugh Coldwell, whose presentations were invariably prodding and laconic. As the trial wore on, Anson came to admire Hoolihan's persistence, though he too disapproved of that attorney's freewheeling use of the press and other dubious tactics; Hoolihan was ruthless and inventive and subscribed to no principles that would stand in the way of his winning. But Anson still, begrudgingly, admired Hoolihan's toughness, his penchant for struggle. Anson had no such penchant. He was neither skilled nor schooled in struggle and so the Ryan case, with its concomitant stench, was a daily affliction to him.

Every weekday—once he dared leave his chambers—Anson drove home, poured himself a whiskey straight and took it out to the lawn swing and bolted it, noting the gay red border of strawberries around the patio; Meg would be unhappy that he'd left them to rot. Meg in fact had urged him to hire a cook in her absence, but he didn't; he let the cleaning lady go as well. He did not want to be disturbed.

After he drank the whiskey, he went upstairs and changed his clothes, got back into the Ford and drove to a small, out-of-the-way Chinese restaurant, bought the afternoon papers, went in, ordered a solitary meal and ate it while he read what had happened in his own courtroom. Then he returned to his empty house. He went into his study and poured himself another whiskey straight. This one he sipped. He seated himself at the desk, the whiskey beside him, and spread the documents from the Ryan case before him, like the pieces of a puzzle that refused to conjoin, to make any sort of pattern. The house was absolutely silent. He did not turn on the television. Dust gathered on the piano that he so loved to hear Claire play and he couldn't bear the news from the radio, so he sat in his silent study and there, surrounded by heavy leather tomes, the laws of his state and country, the precedents that ought to answer every contingency, every mutation of human nature, he dug through the documents of the Ryan case, hoping to chance on some revelation. Nightly, he was disappointed. The lineaments of the case were clear enough, but its heart remained dim, flickering and unilluminated. Anson sipped the whiskey, spread the law books, the court reports and even the evening papers with their lurid headlines before him; he turned them over and over in his hands in much the same way that a sculptor might ponder a recalcitrant piece of clay.

This much could be known for certain: Mrs. Sophie Goldstone was eccentric, grizzled, forlorn and friendless and lived as though she hadn't a nickel to her name, though in fact this was not true. At least on paper, Mrs. Goldstone was quite well-to-do. She affected her poverty, seemingly relished it, but her long-dead husband had owned great tracts of downtown property and she derived her income from the revenues of these properties. Patrick Ryan was her attorney and financial adviser. He looked after her affairs.

Anson, with due respect for the dead, endeavored always to think of her as Mrs. Goldstone, but as the trial wore on and the more he delved into the material, she emerged in his imagination as One-Strap Sophie and he could imagine that Nelson and Hanratty, both scrappy little men, had had quite a struggle before they knocked her out and dragged her to the shed, where they held her down and ran the '51 Buick over her, not once, the tire tracks suggested, but twice. Forward and reverse.

Nelson and Hanratty confessed to that. They said they'd stolen the murder car (and indeed it was found exactly where they said they'd abandoned it). They confessed to struggling with Mrs. Goldstone, knocking her unconscious with her own pitchfork and driving the car over her body, covering the blood on the dirt floor of the shed as best as they could and driving to the other side of town and dumping her body out. Moreover, they confessed that Ryan had told them to do it. Not paid them. Just told them. Hoolihan said (in effect) balderdash: *clearly, Nelson and Hanratty were in the process of burgling One-Strap's house when Sophie came upon them and they killed her to shut her up.* Privately—and particularly now that he had been to One-Strap's house—Anson could not believe anything there could have interested burglars, but circumstantial evidence aside, Nelson and Hanratty were certainly unsavory enough to have burgled and murdered; they were both former convicts, after all, and they had been represented by the former public defender Patrick Ryan when they had bungled a burglary all those years ago. Now they were paroled to Patrick Ryan and employed by him as well. These were less than auspicious circumstances, but Hoolihan was so eloquent, he all but convinced even Anson that Ryan had signed for their parole and given these convicts jobs out of a beneficent belief in the salutary effects of the California penal system, out of unstinting optimism that criminals could be happily reformed and reintegrated into the social fabric.

Hoolihan took the straw, the chaff, the circumstances that told against Patrick Ryan and turned them into gold: not only was the hapless Ryan not guilty, he was spotlessly innocent. Sitting in the courtroom, Hoolihan bathed his client in beatitude: who but a saint would have handled One-Strap's convulsed financial affairs for seventeen years? Her dreadfully disarrayed accounts? And since he had her power of attorney, Ryan had even paid her bills, often floated her loans, Hoolihan said, that he made no attempt to collect on; Ryan frequently bought her meals and saw to it that One-Strap was supplied with firewood for her stove in the winter. Who but a generous and altogether upright man would have concerned himself with the plight of a miserable, difficult woman like One-Strap Sophie? Hoolihan always referred to her as One-Strap Sophie, emphasizing her pathetic life, her friendless situation (save for the loyal Pat Ryan) and he made frequent allusion to the widow's mite.

No, thought Anson, sipping his whiskey and watching the moths flutter near his lamp. Mrs. Goldstone's was no mite, but the extent of her wealth could only be guessed at because all Ryan's records in his seventeen years of service to her—as well as her last will and testament—had vanished. (Burgled and destroyed, Hoolihan claimed, by the nefarious Nelson and Hanratty so they could implicate the noble Ryan and spare themselves the death penalty.) But Nelson and Hanratty had not confessed to that. What happened to the records could not be known with any certitude. But this much could be discerned: even during the years when Patrick Ryan was public defender and receiving a less than princely salary, he lived in some splendour, entertained lavishly and commended himself to the attention of men like Senator Swallow, Mayor Stone and other luminaries, who, upon his fall, quickly disavowed him and now seemed intent on dispatching him to the gas chamber.

But Ryan's fall—in and of itself—troubled Anson. Why had not One-Strap Sophie Goldstone died as obscurely as she lived, her death declared a hit-and-run after her body was found in the street by passersby? The question lingered in the murk of the trial; the answer beckoned to Anson and then evaporated. He stirred his whiskey and his documents, asking himself again and again what could be publicly certified and then what could be deduced from that, fathomed, construed, intimated, if not known. He shuffled through the papers. Yes, both the coroner and the insurance adjuster testified that on the day after One-Strap's death, Patrick Ryan had called them, assured them that he would take care of everything, burial and the like.

He swooped down on Mrs. Goldstone's bones like a carrion crow, Hugh Coldwell informed the jury, *eating the meat off her lifeless bones*.

Anson's skin prickled to read it.

Not at all, Hoolihan countered. *Ryan acted swiftly because he was One-Strap's sole friend in this world and he wanted to be sure she would not be relegated to the ignominy of a pauper's grave.*

Motivation aside, Ryan had indeed called the coroner and said that the papers necessary for legalizing One-Strap's untimely death should be sent to him. Ryan had indeed called the insurance company and informed them of her unfortunate demise and said the check should be sent to him as he was sole beneficiary on her policy (double indemnity in case of accidental death), her friend and financial consultant, the steward of her property, her only heir and virtual next of kin.

This was not so. One-Strap had a sister, Rebecca, from whom she had been estranged for forty years. Rebecca read of her sister's death. Rebecca knew Sophie was rich (despite the way she lived) and had no intention of letting Ryan (or anyone else for that matter) grab it all, though, Rebecca testified in court, there was less to grab than she'd imagined. Anson found Rebecca's testimony and read it, remembering the sharp-tongued harridan on the stand, barking out her statements and wagging her finger at Ryan every chance she got. She swore on the Holy Bible that all she had in mind when she requested an autopsy and inquiry into her sister's death was the proper execution (she stressed this word) of justice. Anson relit his pipe and reckoned that Hugh Coldwell had coached her on the use of these terms. Rebecca had gone to the coroner and been snubbed: hit-and-run, they told her, see the police. The police, city hall, all met Rebecca's pleas with the same indifference. Then she went to the newspapers. Here she was not snubbed. No, Anson thought, glancing at the stack of newspapers from the last three months on the floor beside his desk; the newspapers had taken up Rebecca's cause with relish, accelerating relish as the grisly facts came to light. And they came to light very quickly after that. Autopsy. Inquest. Indictments. Nelson and Hanratty seized and confess.

But so quickly? Anson leaned back, put his feet up on the desk and massaged his tired eyes. Ryan clearly hadn't counted on (or didn't know of) the existence of the sulking Rebecca, but otherwise his prompt response to One-Strap's death was not out of context with his other financial dealings. One-Strap was not the only widow in the city whom he'd served as financial adviser. He had a tidy little business extracting fees (*and then some*, Coldwell claimed) for these services to reclusive widows. More than one of these widows (*in gratitude*, Hoolihan said) had named him in their wills and on their insurance policies, but none had died from anything but natural causes. (*As far as we know*, Coldwell added grimly.) But One-Strap Sophie had been brutally murdered. Why?

Obviously, Coldwell informed the jury, *Ryan had been misusing Mrs. Goldstone's money for years and she caught on.* Coldwell brought in Ryan's secretary, who testified under duress that yes, Mrs. Goldstone came frequently to Ryan's office and had many times created terrible scenes, screaming at him, accusing him of wrongdoing, but more specific than that the secretary could not be. The secretary said they learned to ignore Mrs. Goldstone; she was mad, of course. Coldwell flinched under this unasked for admission, but inquired further what happened when Mrs. Goldstone came to the office, and the secretary said that she didn't know as inevitably, Mr. Ryan took her out of the office to buy her a decent meal; the poor thing lived on rice and prunes and was not in her right mind.

Poor One-Strap. Hoolihan lamented to the jury. *Of course she was not in her right mind. She needed the care of Patrick Ryan, relied on his sure benign hand to guide her through a world notoriously unkind to the old, the frail, the weak and friendless. Patrick Ryan was a pillar of stability in that benighted life.* Hoolihan then called in his own string of witnesses, including the urchin boys, formerly One-Strap's tormentors (but now dressed up and looking dewy-eyed), who testified that One-Strap had chased innocent little children, swinging a hoe over her head, that she'd been seen executing her chickens and squealing with delight as they ran around the yard headless, that One-Strap sometimes hung their carcasses from the porch and left them there for days. The boys further declared (*sotto voce*) that all fifty-two of One-Strap's cats and dogs defecated at will in her house, that she was plagued with senility and other ailments that impeded her judgment. *If she were sane*, Hoolihan asked the jury, *how could she have lived like that?* She had fleas and lice and ticks, and the morning glory vine over her house was infested with spiders. Cast in this light, One-Strap Sophie appeared almost as unsavoury as Nelson and Hanratty.

Anson brought his feet down off the desk, finished his whiskey and read his own words reminding Hoolihan that Mrs. Goldstone's character was not under discussion here, only Ryan's guilt or innocence.

Coldwell imputed that Hoolihan resorted to low tactics to cover up his client's guilt. Hoolihan called Coldwell a son of a bitch (the record showed this, but did not indicate that Hoolihan had doubled up his fists and taken a fighting stance as well.) Anson called them both to order, threatened Hoolihan for contempt of court and reminded them they were not there to cast aspersions on one another but to present a case to a jury of Ryan's peers.

This much was clear, though only implied and not known for certain: the avengers of One-Strap Sophie's death—the sister Rebecca, the insurance company, the prosecution and whoever else was so eager to convict Patrick Ryan—had not counted on Hoolihan.

Anson flung the papers across the desk; they floated to the floor and he further blew them about the place by slamming all the law books shut. Anson himself wished the case shut and done with. Tomorrow at least, he thought on his way slowly up the stairs, tomorrow was Saturday and he would drive to San Angelo and hold Meg in his arms and put his cheek against Claire's bright hair and his arm around Bart and play with the baby's dimpled chin. For two days at least he would not hear the cries from the courtroom harpies, would not be caught in the cross-fire between Hoolihan and Coldwell; he would not be tangled in the web of assertion and denial, of confession and repudiation. He would not have to endure the stench. He would not have to hear the gavel come down time after time, as if it smashed against his own temples.

iv

In September 1952, Althea Swallow returned to the city and her father's mansion to live with him and his bride, Lucille. Meg Swallow returned to the city to live with her husband, aghast to find the house awash in dust and rows of dirty whiskey glasses lined up in the study and by the lawn swing. She declared she would never leave him alone again and set about putting Anson's life back in order. Claire and Bart went back to school and Claire's music lessons started once again and the house filled with her (rather tidier) version of the "Minuet in G" and her attempts at "Für Elise". Anson relaxed and allowed his family to reconstitute, to revive his spirits and though the trial still took its daily toll, he no longer had the opportunity to mull over it night after night.

He would, however, almost rather have endured the murk and

63

morass of the Ryan case than to sit through his sister's visits. Thrice weekly, without fail, Althea had Dillard drive her over to Anson's to divulge some further outrage perpetrated by the new Mrs. Swallow. She snarled continually, and in that Anson had to grant that the Senator was correct: no one could snarl quite so effectively as Althea. Meg and Anson had to hold these family conferences in his study with the door closed because Althea said shocking things with no regard for the tender ears of the children and, in fact, little regard for the sensibilities of Meg and Anson themselves.

"He bedded her first. You know that's true," Althea snarled. "She seduced him. I never should have stayed in San Angelo, no matter what the Senator said to me," and here Althea gave a sniffle. "I should have come home to protect him. If I'd been here, she'd never have got to him. It's all my fault." Althea wept into the Kleenex Anson handed her.

"Now, Althea," replied Meg, her knitting needles percussively accompanying her thoughts. "You're wrong about the Senator. No honorable man has carnal knowledge of a woman not his wife. The Senator is an honorable man."

"Of course he is," she retorted, blowing her nose. "Did I say he wasn't? *She* isn't honorable. Not by a long shot. Why, she's not even what she pretends to be."

"She's Mrs. Swallow now," Anson contended. "She doesn't have to pretend to that. As the Senator's wife, she deserves our respect." Anson tried to push Althea's voice away, concentrating on the faltering chords of "Für Elise" coming from the living room, where Claire practiced on the grand piano. Claire's music always comforted him in the midst of Althea's tantrums, which, he suspected, were badly aggravated by a jealousy she could not admit to, though he did not begrudge her this: Anson too felt things for this father he would not admit to. He listened very hard to "Für Elise" until he thought he heard Althea announce she'd hired a detective. "A what!"

"A detective and he's turned up some—"

"Stop, Althea." Anson recoiled. "Not only do I not want to hear it, but you must, you will, call this detective off immediately. What good can it serve? If he uncovers some unpleasant truth about Lucille, what good can it serve? How can you allow some ferret-fingered detective to be privy to unsavory information about our family?"

"She's not our family."

"She is now. No matter what she was, she's the Senator's wife now

64

and it can only hurt the Swallows if anything unseemly were to come to light regarding her character or her past."

Althea's fat jowls shook with rage. "I told you to stop this in the beginning, Anson. Months ago, I begged you. Nip it in the bud, that's what I said, and you refused."

"I didn't refuse. I was powerless then as I am now. The best thing all around is for us to be cordial to Lucille and to welcome her into our family."

"That's easy for you to say. You don't have to live with her. Why, you haven't even met her or seen the way she struts around the house in her negligee, nibbles on the Senator's earlobes in broad daylight. Why, you haven't even talked to the Senator since that awful day last June when he left San Angelo and said all those cruel things. It's all your fault, Anson. You quarreled with him and you set him off in that foul mood and he ran back to the city and straight into her arms. It's all your—Meg! Stop that infernal knitting! The needles drive me to distraction, and tell Claire to stop that infernal playing in the next room! Can't she ever get it right? Can't she play it straight through just once? The noise here—the piano, the children, the radio, the TV—I tell you, it drives me wild!"

"Calm yourself, Althea," Anson said. Meg's knitting needles died in her hand and rested there like broken-winged birds. "You are overwrought and I will not tell Claire to quit practicing because you have worked yourself into a state. Claire has a gift for music and all gifts should be encouraged."

"Claire is a nasty little snit of a girl, spoiled and indulged and ill-mannered."

"That's not true, and even if it were, it's unkind of you to say so."

"I'm not unkind," Althea snuffled. "I'm unhappy. I'm worried about the Senator."

"There's no need to worry. Lucille will take care of him, I'm sure."

"That's what I'm worried about!" Althea wailed. "She'll take care of him, all right. She'll take care of all of us! He's rewritten his will, Anson."

Anson flinched, remembering the quarrel at San Angelo, but he answered in his most judicial manner. "That's to be expected. A newly married man would want to make provision for his bride. Besides, I'm sure there's no reason for concern. Money has never been a problem for our family."

"Never isn't always," Althea snapped. In the resounding silence,

Claire continued to stumble through "Für Elise" and slowly Meg picked up her knitting again. "Well." Althea pulled her back away from her chair as if disdaining its support. "You can judge for yourself next Friday. There's to be a reception to introduce Lucille to all the Senator's friends. Here's your invitation." She handed Anson a mauve envelope with his and Meg's names neatly engraved in silver script. "Vulgar, isn't it? Mother would never have stooped to mauve."

"Your dear mother," Meg reminded her, "never issued an engraved invitation in all her life. She was tortured by social occasions. I remember once she said to me—"

"*Open it*," Althea said to Anson. "Open the invitation. The Senator's forgiven you, I know he has. Whatever you said to him that day, he's forgiven you. When I told him I forgave him the terrible terrible things he said to me, he just looked at me as if they'd never been said, as if he'd forgotten there ever was a quarrel."

"Forgotten or denied?"

"What does it matter?"

"It matters." One was an act of will and the other, perhaps, a mere matter of time. In his professional capacity, Anson had seen the scales of justice tip one way or the other over lesser distinctions.

"What did you say to him that day, Anson, to drive him into such a rage? You might as well tell me. I'd have got it out of the Senator long ago but for that slut Lucille. She absolutely soaks up his time. Whole days go by when he doesn't even go down to the docks. Just lets Swallow Lines look after itself while he fritters away his time with Lucille. I've said to him—what do you think, Senator, you think *George* can run Swallow Lines? No indeed! You better get down there and go to work. And you know what he says to me? Althea, he says, I've worked my whole life and now it's time to play. Play! Well you can just imagine *what* they play and I can tell you *where* they play. The bedroom, that's where."

"Althea," Meg clucked.

"It's disgusting."

"I ought to decline," Anson said, regarding the invitation. "I ought not to go. Until the Ryan trial closes, I have vowed not to go anywhere that might compromise me."

"Oh pooh, Anson," Althea scoffed. "Just because Hugh Coldwell will be there doesn't compromise you. You never lived like a monk with any of your other cases."

"I wish I could live like a monk."

Meg looked up in alarm.

"Oh, I'm not referring to you, my dear. But I think it best that we decline this invitation."

"The Senator will be livid if you don't go," Althea said smugly. "He'll think you're snubbing her."

"Althea's right again. The Senator might well take offense and so might Lucille. This might be the time we've been waiting for, dear."

"I can't bear to think of it." Anson pinched the bridge of his nose. "Spending a whole evening with people who will tell me how bright my political future will be once Patrick Ryan has been gassed."

"Anson, don't be so morbid."

"I have a wonderful idea," Althea crowed. "I'll tell Lucille that she must invite Hoolihan as well. I'll say that in the interest of fairness—she's invited Coldwell, after all—she must invite Hoolihan. I'll tell her that the Senator would never forgive her if she excluded such a rising young man from her guest list. And Hoolihan will come, of course, because he never gets asked to any home in this city where they don't sleep four to a bed and drink beer out of bottles. He'll get drunk and have a fistfight and ruin the whole evening and everyone will be there to see it and Lucille will look ridiculous for having asked him! Oh, I laugh to think of it!"

"Althea Swallow." Meg jabbed her knitting needles into a ball of blue yarn. "I've heard just about enough. Ever since we got back to town, you've done nothing, nothing, but tell malicious tales about Lucille."

"Only to the two of you," Althea pouted. "I don't trust anyone else."

"Well I for one have heard enough. You shock me. You truly do. I will not hear another word about inviting that awful Hooligan—"

"Hoolihan," Anson corrected her.

"—to any reception that any member of this family would give, and that includes Lucille. You seem to forget that she is your father's wife and if you make a fool of her, you make a fool of the Senator."

"He doesn't need me to do that. He's making a fool of himself. You ought to see him. He actually whimpers with delight when she comes and sits in his lap."

"That will be quite enough."

"I hate her."

"Well, Anson and I will go to this reception, and I for one intend to welcome her into the family and there's an end to it!"

Anson smiled secretly to watch the mild-mannered Meg wax wrathful on behalf of the proprieties. It always amused him that Meg so consistently confused principle with propriety.

V

Althea, however, ignored Meg's injunction. She urged Lucille to add Hoolihan's name to the guest list with the whispered innuendo of how well regarded he was amongst the city's elite. And on the evening of the reception, dressed in her usual unrelenting black, she chuckled from her corner of the salon to see that Hoolihan was the first to arrive. Right on time. Clearly, he didn't know that punctuality betrayed a working-class background, a genetic addiction to the time card. He was more odious than Althea would have dreamed possible, and she beamed to see it. The Senator's face fell when Hoolihan entered, but nothing else suggested he might have been surprised. Hoolihan's mauve and silver invitation was clearly visible in the pocket of his evening clothes (which, Althea noted, fitted him very badly and looked quite ridiculous). Hoolihan kissed Lucille's hand with the aplomb of an Italian count and welcomed her to their fair city as if she were an exiled princess. Lucille nearly swooned.

By the time Anson and Meg arrived, the Swallow salon was awash in dignitaries and electric light. The men were all clad in stark black and white, resembling an ambulating piano keyboard, while the women in their rustling gowns provided the grace notes, the chords and crescendos. Greeting them at the door, the Senator introduced Anson to Lucille as his son in whom he was well pleased. Anson squirmed under the allusion, but at least the summer's quarrel, if not forgiven, seemed forgotten. Anson judged that true to Hoolihan's original assessment, Lucille Swallow probably was a handful of haunch and trouble. Statuesque (she towered over Meg), she wore her short burnished blond hair swept away from her face, which was lovely but older than Anson had pictured. He judged her to be about thirty-five or so; but he had imagined her some ten years younger. She wore a pebble pink evening dress, cinched so tightly at the waist Anson figured she would break if she attempted to bend. Her creamy shoulders were bare, but around her neck he recognized the pearls that had belonged to his mother. Her skirt was overlaid with elaborate amber lace embroidered in fawn motifs and the total effect underscored her high coloring and the generous lineaments of her body. Her brilliant blue eyes were framed with thick black lashes, and the voluptuous mouth suggested (even to a man of Anson's limited experience with women) a sort of promise and fulfillment at the same moment. Her voice was low and husky and her throat was supple. Lucille was charmed and charming.

The Senator beamed as Meg embraced Lucille and welcomed her into the family and said she looked forward to being great friends and knowing her well. The Senator himself, Anson noted, was far more gracious and genial than Anson could ever remember. For all his huge bulk, the Senator walked with a sprightly tread and exuded a contentment Anson had never realized he had lacked.

Meg and Anson passed into the salon, decorated everywhere with huge vases full of white spider mums, their tentacles stirred by every whispering skirt. Behind a quintet of six-foot potted palms, a small orchestra played waltzes, which Anson reflected ironically were his mother's favorite tunes. No one danced, however. The group assembled here was too stiff and full and flatulent for dancing. (Anson included himself in this ungenerous estimate.) The Persian carpets had all been rolled up and the parquet floors shone, their patterns vanishing under the shining black shoes of the men and the high heels of the women. As he and Meg crossed the floor, Anson felt a pang of regret for his mother; Edith Swallow would have been undone in a gathering like this. He glanced up at the wall: just as Althea had predicted, the portrait of Edith was gone and in its place was one of the heavy pastoral scenes from the Senator's immense art collection. (Convinced that his taste was infallible in all things, the Senator favored heavy dark canvases by German painters, usually depicting scenes with apple-cheeked and melon-breasted country girls or else serious biblical themes. Of the biblical scenes, it must be admitted that he had two of Susannah and the Elders and three of David ogling Bathsheba.)

Meg and Anson chose an inconspicuous corner from which to view the festivities, and shortly both Althea and Vera joined them. Like her sister, Vera was unconventionally dressed; she wore a toga of alarming simplicity, snapped at the shoulders with gold, and her hair drawn back severely, softened only by Roman ringlets over her ears. Her feet were bare. "Isn't it a shame Mother never gave a party like this? Why, the house just comes alive, doesn't it? I think I'll ask Lucille if she'd mind if we had one of our Dawn Convocations in the garden some

morning. How lovely it would be to rise at dawn with the pure simplicity of the truly regenerate and stand on the top tier of the rose garden and extend our arms to the sea and the dawn."

"The sun comes up the other way," Althea reminded her.

"Oh, but we could greet the dawn and then turn to the sea and
everywhere around us enjoy the beautiful handiwork of nature, manicured unto perfection. Oh, I just feel that I could lift up my arms and
ascend." She began to do just that until Althea jabbed her in the ribs
and told her not to be a silly ass.

"There's George and Eleanor," said Meg.

"Do you think George is sober?" Vera inquired, and once again
Althea shut her up.

George and his wife, Eleanor, greeted the Senator and Lucille.
Eleanor embraced Lucille tentatively, furtively, the way that Eleanor
Swallow did everything. Who could blame her? She might once have
been a pretty woman, but the furrows of worry seemed indelibly engraved in her face. She'd married George Swallow very young, urged
into the union by her ambitious society mama, who longed to see her
family connected to the Swallows. Eleanor's initial objections (even
then George drank more than was good for him) were dusted away; all
George needed, she was assured, was a loving wife. Eleanor was a
loving wife, but as the Tenor, the Bass, and the Baritone arrived in
quick succession, Eleanor found she could scarcely control her
children, much less her husband. Like his father and younger brother,
George Swallow was stout, but his floridity came not from rude well-
being, but from the broken veins littering his face. Anson shook his
head when he saw George snatch a glass of champagne from a passing
waiter, bolt it quickly and take another. In all, George consumed three
glasses of champagne before he and Eleanor crossed the floor and
joined the Swallows in their corner.

Anson turned his own champagne glass in his hand; it was molded
like a calla lily and he thought these glasses must be new, but then his
mother had a missionary's distrust of alcohol and champagne was seldom offered in her day. The waiter came by and offered them more,
but all but George declined; Meg and Althea and Vera stood, silently
staring into their bubbling glasses, uncertain of how to proceed. None
of the Swallows possessed native charm, nor had they been tutored to
it; they clung to each other like barnacles until Mayor Stone singled
Anson out, took his arm and guided him toward a group of people, the
mayor assured him, he must meet.

Anson knew all these worthies and their fleshy wives, but Stone, never relinquishing his arm, introduced Anson anyway, taking the moment to embellish upon the judge's rectitude and sterling reputation, the only man whose integrity could be counted on to give a scrupulously fair hearing even to slime like Patrick Ryan. Hugh Coldwell joined them, and Anson again heard the gavel pounding on his temples. Despite the light and the wine and the waltzes, he saw before him a twisted vision of One-Strap Sophie rotting in her grave and Patrick Ryan rotting in his cell.

Anson removed himself, not graciously but firmly, and wove his way quickly through the salon toward the library, where the smell of cigar smoke suggested a more informal gathering. The library was paneled, floor to ceiling, with unread books, set about with leather chairs and so thickly carpeted that the gong on the grandfather clock sounded like a muffled drum. A fire snapped in the hearth, and in one corner Anson noted Lucille's typewriter, shrouded now as if in mourning. Lounging in leather chairs, close to the whiskey decanter, Anson saw a group of clipped, trim young men and among them Hoolihan. Not only did Anson not recognize him at first, he could not believe his eyes when he did: Hoolihan in a tuxedo defied the imagination. The younger men stood when Anson entered the room. The gesture made Anson feel old without quite making him feel venerable.

"Ah, Your Honor." Hoolihan smiled. "I'm glad to see your stellar presence gracing us. I was just saying to the boys here that I've looked in vain for a friendly face in this glorious constellation of guests."

"Familiar maybe," Anson replied. "I'm not sure my face is usually very friendly."

"We're not to be discussing the bench here, are we, gentlemen? Here we can leave the stench of the courtroom behind us. And good riddance, I say. Here we can be men; there we must be angels." He got a good laugh out of that, even from Anson, who noted for the first time that Hoolihan had fragile, freckled skin that contrasted oddly with his shock of coarse hair, his gray eyes reflecting unassuaged hungers. "Here we are to be celebrating the marriage of the Senator to the lovely Lucille." Hoolihan raised his glass. "Gentlemen, a toast to Mrs. Swallow—a lady if there ever was one."

Anson drank with the rest, privately considering Meg to be the Mrs. Swallow under consideration. He wondered if Hoolihan remembered referring to Lucille as a handful of haunch and trouble.

"I'd offer a toast to the judge here, boys, but he'd be looking around

71

for his gavel to declare me out of order." The men laughed, but Anson's presence, however stellar, seemed to have intimidated them and they refilled their glasses and drifted away. "I must say, Your Honor," Hoolihan added in a low voice, "that in all honesty and outside the courtroom, I never expected to be included with the likes of these fine birds gathered here tonight. I feel like a rooster let loose amongst the peahens."

"Perhaps you're a peacock amongst the chickens."

"Not I, Your Honor. I'm fresh from the barnyard, I'm afraid, so you can imagine my surprise when the Senator's invitation reached me. My mother is thrilled. She's convinced that I've gone off to join the Holy Angels tonight, so I had to explain to her that I'd only be likely to get into heaven if I was dead and that's too steep a price to pay, for my taste."

"I doubt you'll get to heaven in any event, Hoolihan."

"I doubt it too, Your Honor, but a man can't tell his mother that, can he?" He refilled his glass generously. "You wouldn't happen to know how I came to be included with his Heavenly host, now would you?"

"Merit, no doubt," Anson replied, privately vowing to thrash Althea, not only for the outrage she planned for Lucille, but for humiliating the unsuspecting Hoolihan.

"Now, my father, Your Honor, he thinks I've gone off to join the devil. Which do you think it is?"

"That's not a fair question, Hoolihan. These are my family."

"And you wonder how that came to be, don't you? A man like yourself with a father like the Senator."

"I'd prefer if you didn't—"

"I spoke out of line, and if this were the courtroom, you could declare me in contempt of the Senator. And you'd be right." He sipped thoughtfully. "Ah well, I'm accustomed to being the outcast, Your Honor, and if the truth be known, I like it. I have the advantage."

"What advantage?"

"I've no expectations to live up to, have I?"

"Maybe not, but you've a lot to live down, Hoolihan."

"Up or down." Hoolihan shrugged. "It's the living that's important, isn't it?" He raised his glass. "Your health, Your Honor. May St. Peter have his arms around you before the devil knows you're dead."

Anson chuckled in spite of himself, but again there floated before his eyes the vision of One-Step in her grave and Ryan in his cell.

"Oh, Anson, here you are!" Meg burst through the library doors.

72

"My dear, this is . . . I'm afraid I've forgotten your first name, Hoolihan."

"And not surprising, Your Honor, since I keep it hid from all but my sainted mother." He turned to Meg. "Declan Hoolihan at your service, madam." He kissed her hand as he had kissed Lucille's. Meg flinched. "But swear you'll be keeping my secret, Mrs. Swallow. I'm Hoolihan to one and all, except"—he winked—"for those who call me Hooligan. Wrongly, I assure you, wrongly."

Meg recovered herself with some difficulty. "Mr. Hoolihan, yes of course. I've heard, that is, I know, I mean I've seen your picture in the papers."

"An unsavory introduction, madam. Never trust a man who gets his picture in the paper."

"Yes, I mean, no. Of course, Mr. Hoolihan. How nice to meet you at last."

"I'll leave you, then." He drank the last of his whiskey. "Madam, Your Honor, it's been a pleasure as always."

"Oh that Althea," Meg muttered when he had left the room. "She'll stop at nothing."

"She'll be stopped," Anson replied, acknowledging an inward flicker of dread. "Take my word for it. The deck is about to be re-shuffled."

Arm in arm they wandered into the dining room, where directly beneath the full-length portrait of the Senator lay a white-clad table where silver dishes and shivering soufflés and extravagant tortes stood plentifully, colorfully massed with clove-studded, fleshy hams (which oddly reminded Anson of Lucille in her pink and brown gown) interspersed with racks of oysters shining on the half shell and flaming chafing dishes, bubbling with the savory and succulent. In the center of the room, on a six-foot column of ice, a massive frozen swallow swooped gracefully, melting into a lake of white spider mums. Small tables, each fully skirted in white and bearing a vase of white chrysanthemums, swirled across the terraces that descended into the gardens, and the frail, salty September fog hovered over the hedges and trees. Anson rubbed his temples; he seemed to feel the gavel again. The overwhelming presence of white, the icy splash of silver and crystal, the electric chandelier shining on the frozen swallow effected in Anson's mind no sense of the festive and extravagant, but rather an eerie unpleasantness, a suggestion of death, white and cold, funereal and remorseless as the grave—or the prison. Or perhaps he simply suffered from the surfeit of odors, flowers and food and everything perishable, its momentary unblemished brilliance secreting the promise of decay. "Pardon me, Meg, but I think I better go out on the terrace for a bit of fresh air. I'm not used to these grand occasions. Just an old homebody, I guess."

"The best old homebody in the world," she said, squeezing his arm. "Oh, Anson, listen, they've changed the music." The waltzes ceased abruptly, as if the orchestra had decided to change horses in the middle of the "Blue Danube", and with a few ungainly fits and starts, they broke into an imperfectly timed modern piece. "Why, Anson," Meg cried. "I believe that's the tango, one of those vulgar new dances. Who could have changed the music? Let's go and see."

They moved toward the salon, but stopped short of the glittering, tittering crowd (disapproval running through it like seismic shock) and they peered around the backs and bodies to see the wellspring of commotion. Lucille Swallow danced the maxixe with Hoolihan, who held her tight across the back, and their arms were outstretched, touching from the elbow to the palm. Cheek to cheek, they looked wedded as the profiles of heads on coins. Lucille held her skirt high enough that the shimmer of her stockings was all too apparent, and cinched as she was at the waist, she did not break when she bent, but swooped, supple and graceful, and whirled away from Hoolihan and twirled back to him, her lovely mouth open, laughing. Hoolihan's face, for once, wore something other than the urge to win; he looked young, eager, athletic. Anson glanced at the glowering matrons and stiff dignitaries—so, Althea was right: Hoolihan did disgrace the Senator. He glanced at his father, who seemed oblivious to the outrage. The Senator's hands clapped in time to the music, his jowls engorged in a smile, his entire body vibrated with glee, and underneath the stiff tuxedo, his flesh rolled visibly in three-quarter time while the floor beneath him resounded and responded, and suddenly Anson was reminded of the earthquake, years and years before, the day after Albert Smythe departed for Honolulu, of the way the buildings had tottered and swayed, not like buildings at all, like frail lilies in the wind, when floors surged like angry seas and windows buckled. He was reminded of the way that the entire city, for a single moment, seemed to dance to some dreadful cantata, bricks rippling, wood snapping, doors bulging like playing cards in the hand of God, reminded how that terrible earthly music had fleetingly, rhythmically forced the entire world to dance before it all came tumbling down.

CHAPTER THREE

May 2, 1985

Like the full rigger he resembled, Barton Swallow forged through the human debris, the fleshy flotsam and jetsam clogging the Emergency waiting room. He walked with the spry athletic tread of a man younger than thirty-nine. Balding at his crown and sporting a trim beard, he emanated a brisk air of competence and authority as he cut through the crowd to rescue his sister from the interrogations of a police officer and a newspaper reporter. Claire's shoulders hunched and she toyed with her rings, spinning them on her slender fingers.

"This is a police matter," the cop said brusquely.

"Since when do the police beleaguer helpless women?" Bart took Claire's elbow.

"That car was stolen," the cop maintained. "And I have questions—"

"Then ask her husband. He's the one who stole it. If it was stolen. It might have been borrowed."

"Her husband's in surgery. He shot himself."

"My point exactly." Bart pushed the cop aside like inconvenient litter.

The reporter, however, padded after Bart and Claire, his notebook open and his pen poised. "Is it true that Lucky Stone can't account for the withholding taxes of his employees and that his gambling debts were—"

Bart doubled up his fist. "Beat it or eat it." The reporter scampered away like a crab. Bart then led his sister to a chair beside Emma and Evangeline, who had ceased their own quarrel in their fascination with Bart's. "You wait here," he said to Claire. "I'm going to find out about Lucky."

When Bart had left, Evangeline leaned forward discreetly. "Did he? Did he steal withholding taxes and the car and shoot himself?"

"He missed," said Claire quietly.

"Hand of God!" Emma slapped her knee. "God must have touched his hand at the very moment. God or one of the angels."

"Angels don't work in the morning," said Evangeline, digging into her purse and pulling out a half-empty pack of peppermint Lifesavers, gritty with bits of lint and tobacco. "Here, take one." She urged the pack on Claire. "Go on, you might need it. It's a Lifesaver." She placed one of the candies in Claire's palm, and Claire stared at it like it was a token for the last bus out of town.

Bart returned and eyed the two old women critically. "It'll be a while yet, Claire, but there's no reason to wait here. The nurse says there's a cafeteria, and they'll page us when Lucky's out of surgery. Have you had anything to eat?"

"I can't eat."

Bart sat down beside her and put his arm around her shoulders, and she buried her head against his jacket. "Lucky's going to live," he murmured. "I know it. They're going to save him."

Claire brought her dark eyes to her brother's face. "But what's going to save us, Bart? Everything's shattered, isn't it? It's my fault. I should have known."

"It's not your fault. You did everything you could."

"But I never guessed how desperate Lucky was, and I should have. If I'd been a better wife, Lucky would have confided in me, but he always just told me not to worry and so I didn't, not even this time, when I knew he was in trouble, and I thought, well, we'll probably have to move—or something, but I never suspected he was so desperate—and I should have—the phone calls, Bart."

"Lucky was always getting phone calls."

"Yes, but this time he'd come away from the phone and pour himself another drink even if he already had one and I knew he was upset or in trouble and I'd ask him—what's wrong, Lucky?—I did, Bart, I would have shared it with him, whatever it was—but he just smiled at me and said, don't you worry, Claire, and so when the IRS showed up yesterday—" Frantically, she pushed her hair away from her face. "It was such a shock! I never guessed! But it's all my fault because if I had, Lucky wouldn't have—"

"Don't, Claire. Don't. It's not your fault. You couldn't have guessed. Lucky's had other financial setbacks before, hasn't he? Who could have guessed he'd try to kill himself? Lucky Stone is the kind of man who would have caviar for dinner even if he didn't have bread to put it on." Bart took Claire's hand and pressed it. "You did what you could. You've been a good wife, loyal to him through everything. You've loved Lucky. Everyone loves Lucky."

Lucky Stone's great gift, Bart reflected, was in making people love him. He had certainly toppled the Swallows' aversion to him; within a year of his marriage to Claire, even the Mourning Glory had succumbed to the artful compound of cheer and respect that Lucky practiced on every oafish gas station attendant, surly waiter and grim salesgirl. And it worked: people thawed visibly before him, because clearly Lucky Stone recognized the sterling individual buried in them all, their shining singularity. In a sense, Lucky made a pact with the people he charmed; he gave them cheer and respect and they gave love and the readiness to forgive him anything. At first Bart had been dubious, regarded Lucky's charm as the trick of a born salesman, but even Bart's resistance crumbled, and over the years he came to like and admire Lucky, particularly as he watched the marriages of his friends fall prey to petty vanities and betrayals while the Stones' remained strong and intact. Claire could have done no better than to marry a man who had never quite recovered from his initial awe of her, and marriage to Lucky had transformed her from a wild girl into a model wife and mother. The Swallows were enormously pleased. Perhaps Bart was alone amongst the family in regretting the loss of that impetuous girl. He remembered himself as a rather phlegmatic, malleable boy who consistently admired his sister's headstrong willingness to endure punishment rather than admit she was wrong or say she was sorry. All that was lost when Claire became a model wife, lost in the translation. And something else was lost too, something more elusive, less visible. As he sat with his arm around her now, absorbing her passionate anguish, Bart wondered what that marriage had lacked that it should come to this: for twenty years, Claire and Lucky had love, loyalty and three children, but model husbands do not aim for the heart, miss and blow their guts out in supermarket parking lots. It wasn't just the money; the money was a symptom of some other lack, far more intimate, between Claire and Lucky, probably unstated, possibly unknown. But the suicide—the suicide attempt, Bart corrected himself—had made it all public, painfully implicated everyone, and now he was sorry he hadn't made more pointed comments, expressed warning and concern more vividly and frequently over the last few years, as it had become increasingly clear that Lucky's web of alcohol and indebtedness would surely undermine the entire family. On the one occasion that Bart had in fact suggested that Lucky curtail his drinking, that drinking muddied one's judgment, Lucky had only turned to Bart with his confiding smile and told him not to worry.

"Not to worry." Bart placed his cheek against Claire's hair. "His luck is going to hold. He's going to live. Everything is going to be all right," he said emphatically, belying his every instinct.

Claire wiped her eyes and stared at the sticky Lifesaver in her hand. "He's going to live," she repeated dully. "But everything is ruined. Scott—"

"Don't worry about Scott at a time like this."

"But he's left Stanford, Bart. I called and they told me he'd packed up and bolted and—"

"Scott can fend for himself. He's twenty. He's a young man."

"But that's just it, don't you see? He's a young man. He ought to have every prospect in front of him."

"He does."

"No, his future's ruined. He'll be a casualty just like you were, Bart, just like when Father lost his mind and threw all that money away and died and Mama lost what was left of it and—"

"Claire, Claire, that was all so long ago." Bart scowled at Emma and Evangeline, hoping they would decamp, but they did not budge or bother to conceal their curiosity. "How can any of that matter now?"

"What if Scott has to do what you did? What if Scott has to take some low, horrid job cleaning latrines? And those were ships you should have inherited, Bart."

"I don't clean latrines anymore," he said with a hard look at the Duff sisters. "I'm the director of Swallow Lines South American trade."

"But you're still working for Lucille Swallow, aren't you? Maybe Althea is right. Maybe everything bad that's ever happened to any of us is Lucille's fault. She cheated us, didn't she? Cheated the Swallows out of everything that should have been ours."

"Oh, Claire, even if Althea is right, how can it help Lucky?"

"What if he dies? How can I go on if he dies?"

78

Bart had no reply. Bart did not know how they would go on if Lucky lived. He unwound her closed fingers, took the sticky peppermint Lifesaver and dropped it in his pocket. "Let's get something to eat, Claire. They'll page us when Lucky's finished, I mean, when they know."

"I'll pray for your husband, honey." Emma patted Claire's knee. "Just remember that it ain't always given to us mortals to understand God's will or—"

"God didn't do this," Bart shot back.

Claire sighed heavily. "Lucky did it. Or maybe Father did it, or the Senator. Maybe Lucille, but probably not God."

"Trust God, honey. You can rely on Him."

Claire looked suddenly lost, as if her sense of direction had deserted her altogether. "I can't rely on anyone. I never could. I see that now." She gave a brittle laugh and swallowed her tears. "Now when it's too late."

Just then a young man, his blue windbreaker flying open, burst through the hospital doors and dashed to the nurse's station; he was disheveled and overwrought, but handsome, broad-shouldered and robust.

"Scott!" Claire wilted back into her chair, her hands over her face, the dry tawny shingle of her hair falling forward.

Scott crossed the waiting room quickly, knelt on the cold linoleum floor and took his mother's hands in his. "What's happened? How did Dad get sick?"

"Sick?" said Bart.

"I called your office, Uncle Bart, and your secretary said you were here and that my dad was sick. I came right away."

Claire took her son's beautiful face in her hands and smoothed his dark hair, ignoring the tiny gold hoop punched in his ear. "Oh, Scott, I'm so glad you're here, honey. I was so worried about you, and Lucky's going to live. He is. You mustn't worry about your dad. He's going to live."

"What's he got? How did he get sick? Why is he here?"

"Your dad tried to kill himself, honey." Claire spoke falteringly as if expressing herself in a foreign language. "He shot himself."

"Oh God! Why? Oh no. Why didn't you call me?"

"I did, but you'd already left Stanford."

Scott blushed.

"He missed his heart," Bart added, "and shot himself in the stomach."

"God stayed his hand," Emma Duff offered, unbidden. "God hath yet some Great Plan for your father and that's why God didn't let him die."

Bart regarded Emma and Evangeline as if they had jointly sprouted scrofula. "Let's get out of here." He took Claire's arm in his and rose. "Let's get something to eat."

The cafeteria was lit by long fluorescent tubes, thinly disguised to look like ice cube trays and casting a light very nearly as cold. The metal coffee urns and chrome counters shone dully and the crockery sounded heavy as grapeshot. Bart steered his sister and nephew to a table in a corner and dumped the dirty ashtray in a trash can nearby. "You stay here with your mother," said Bart. "I'll get us something to eat."

The hospital intercom droned in punctual intervals and, mounted in opposite corners of the room, two overhead television sets spilled forth sudsing love scenes from two different soap operas, both of them displaying lovers locked in suggestive, though not explicit embraces; one couple rolled about on a luxurious bed, and the other pawed one another in what appeared to be a bank vault. Her fingers trembling, Claire pulled a cigarette from her purse and lit it, glowering as she looked from one TV to the other. "Love," she snorted the word out with the smoke. "Everywhere you look, people are making a fuss over love. It makes me sick. Why make such a fuss over something anyone can do and everyone does? Why aren't there stories about achievement? Accomplishment?" She took another determined drag. "I ask you. Why don't they make shows about painters or poets or scientists or pianists, for that matter, why don't they make a fuss over something not everyone can do? Everyone can make love. Anyone can make money. And anyway, it's all lies. People might start out in love, but what they really want is security." She watched as the couple on the floor of the bank vault got up, not a hair or thread of clothing out of place; the man returned to a posh office and shuffled papers with seals on them. Claire puffed angrily. "And money! Money's got nothing to do with what you can buy. It's who you can buy. Only whores equate love and money. Isn't that so?" she demanded of her son.

"Please, Mom, calm down."

"Why should I?" she cried, waving her cigarette in the direction of the offending TV. "Your dad's in there fighting for his life after he tried to end it. Why should I be calm? How can I be calm?"

"What happened, Mom? Please tell me. Why would Dad want to kill himself?"

80

"You've read the papers," she replied, her bottom lip trembling. But then Claire's dark eyes hardened. "You have read the papers, haven't you? Isn't that why you left Stanford?"

Scott knotted his hands; they were small, fine-grained hands, oddly out of keeping with his bulk and frame.

Bart returned carrying a tray that held a pot of tea, three mugs and three plates precariously balanced and massed high with gooey, Chinese-looking food and scoops of clumpy rice. He put the plates before them and cast the tray on an empty table. "You must eat something, Claire. We can't do anything until Lucky is out of surgery."

"What can we do then?" She put her cigarette out and wiped her eyes with the heel of her palm, smudging her makeup further. "We're powerless."

"Can you tell me what happened yesterday?" Bart asked gently.

Claire looked from her brother to her son. "The IRS came through the house like Nazis. I stayed in the bedroom. Lucky stayed in the bar, drinking. When they left, he came upstairs and said he was sorry. I—I couldn't even reply, I was so shocked by it all. I—" She regarded her upturned palms as if they might offer some answer. "He left the house. I don't know when. And I don't know what he did between then and the time he shot himself. Shot and missed. That's all I know." Her lip trembled and she began to cry again at the inadequacy of what she knew or didn't know, of what she'd done or failed to do.

"Was he drunk, Claire?"

"How do I know? He probably sat in the parking lot of the Foodway supermart and drank all night, but how do I know if he was drunk? How did anyone know if Lucky was drunk? He was never nasty or abusive. He always kept his old charm and conducted himself like a gentleman and you never knew he was drinking at all until he fell over."

Scott and Bart exchanged glances as Claire collected herself, lifting the heavy mug of tea to her lips with two hands. Finally, Scott asked timidly, "What's this about the IRS, Mom? Is Dad in trouble with them?"

"Your dad is in trouble with everyone this time."

"Will he go to jail?"

"We'll get the best attorney there is," Bart declared.

Claire toyed with her rice. "Hoolihan called this morning."

"Hoolihan!" Bart cried. "What did he want?"

"Who's Hoolihan?" asked Scott.

"You tell him," said Claire sullenly.

Bart grimaced and decided to stick with the obvious. "He's an attorney. The best there is."

"And the worst," Claire added.

"Althea's judgment is not exactly impartial, Claire."

"He works for Lucille Swallow, doesn't he?"

"So do I! That doesn't mean—anyway, this isn't getting us anywhere. What did Hoolihan want?"

"He volunteered his services to defend Lucky free of charge. Don't look at me like that, Bart. I don't know why. He said he owed it to Father."

"To my father?" asked the bewildered Scott.

"To my father," said Bart.

Claire prodded through her chop suey as if looking for a fortune cookie amongst the cornstarch. "I can't imagine that Father would have soiled himself with scum like Hoolihan."

"Father liked him, Claire. He did. Those last few months of Father's life—"

"I don't believe it."

"It's true. He used to come to the house all the time, even though Mama hated him. Even I could tell that much. But Hoolihan was there for Father's funeral. He was loyal to Father, Claire." Bart winced when his sister grunted in reply. He sipped his tea and continued: "Hoolihan has made us a generous offer, and we'll take him up on it."

"We will not."

"There's nothing that man can't do, Claire. Hoolihan is the ablest attorney in this city and I can't think of another lawyer I'd feel as confident with—whatever you think of his morals."

"He's a swine and a hypocrite," Claire contended. "Taking on all those underdog cases, making himself out to be the great champion of the people. Every time you pick up the paper, there's a picture of Hoolihan with some wrongly accused working-class slob. Oh, the press just love to quote him on the rights of the oppressed. He's disgusting. Why, everyone knows he lives off Lucille Swallow."

"He doesn't need her money."

"He's a pimp, and she's a whore."

"You're not thinking straight, Claire. You're not thinking at all. Lucky will need Hoolihan." *If he lives to go to court*, Bart added privately.

"If he lives to go to court."

"He'll live, Claire. He will."

"He has to," said Scott. "I just can't imagine that Dad would try to kill himself. He always seemed so—" Scott's paltry imagination failed him, "so—Dad."

Claire blew her nose and then she fixed an unflinching gaze on her son. "Just tell me the truth. I've endured the worst there is today—I don't even know if your dad is going to live or die—so whatever it is you've got to say, it can't be any worse than that, but I must have the truth. You haven't seen the morning papers, have you? You didn't even know about the bankruptcy and the scandal, did you?"

"No."

"Then why did you leave Stanford?"

Scott brought his wounded eyes to his mother's face. "My checks were bouncing Mom," he said at last. "The money Dad always puts in my account—it just wasn't there. My checks started bouncing, but I thought it was just the bank's error, so I kept writing them."

"You didn't call the bank to inquire?" Bart asked.

"Well, no, not then."

"Did you ever?"

"Well, no, but I told you, I thought it was a mistake until I started getting dunned. People were calling the frat house and making scenes and—" He took a bite and chewed slowly. "It was getting real embarrassing," he added with a gulp.

Bart eyed Scott shrewdly. "Did you call my office this morning to borrow money from me?"

"Well, yes, just a little." Scott sucked on his fork. "There's this one creditor who won't let up. He said if I didn't pay him by next week—"

"How much do you owe him?"

"About five hundred dollars," Scott said to his chop suey.

"Five hundred dollars!" Claire cried.

Scott seemed to shrink into his chair; he played with his fashionable gold earring.

"It's not enough for cocaine," said Bart, "so it must be grass."

"The frat parties," Scott mumbled. "It was my turn to—"

"Grass!" Claire shrieked. "We send you to the best university in the United States and you spend your time and money smoking dope! Do you know what it cost even to get you in there? Do you know the strings your dad had to pull? Do you know what *that* cost? Do you know what a Stanford degree can mean to you? To your whole life? How! How could you waste everything we worked so hard for? If you spent your money for dope, I can imagine what you did with your time! Were your grades bouncing like your checks?"

"I was on probation," Scott admitted, "but I was working to bring my grades up."

"We give you every opportunity and this is the way you repay us! Ruined, your life is ruined! I suppose it ought to comfort me that whatever your dad has done with his money, you ruined your own life."

"I'm sorry."

"Scott's life isn't ruined," said Bart, putting his hand over Claire's reassuringly. "Just because he smoked dope and left Stanford doesn't ruin his life forever."

"Stanford was his chance at life. He's ruined that."

"Tell your mother she needn't worry about you, Scott. She has enough to worry about with your father. Tell her you won't smoke dope anymore."

"I won't smoke dope anymore," Scott answered dutifully.

"You see, Claire, Scott can take care of himself. He'll find work. He's young, he's able, he's smart," Bart added, though he didn't believe the latter. To Bart's mind, his eldest nephew was utterly undistinguished: Scott's grades were poor, his friends were musclebound mediocrities; he evinced not a shred of integrity; he hadn't an ounce of Lucky's civilized charm or a grain of Claire's spirit, nor a morsel of talent. And then there was that trouble last year with the girl. No wonder Scott had called Bart's office thinking Bart would float him the five hundred dollars. Of course. Bart had smoothed things over with that girl's irate, indeed enraged, father. Scott had appealed to his Uncle Bart, he said, to spare Claire and Lucky what would surely pain them. But Bart knew better. Bart knew that Claire would have split Scott's skull and that Lucky would have suggested simply that perhaps he ought to marry the girl. But she wasn't pregnant, after all, and they were both drunk the night Scott—what was the word her father used in that terrible conversation—ravished, yes, ravished the girl. Scott maintained he'd done no such thing: she wanted it, Scott said in his own defense, though to Bart's mind it was a weak defense, and he did not use that approach when he spoke with the girl's father. Bart said: do you want my nephew to marry your daughter? And of course the father did not. Bart was always rather ashamed of his role in this episode. After it was finished, he had vowed to Scott that he would never again take part in anything so seamy and at the same time he lectured the younger man on his lack of respect for women, his insensitivity, his shallow approach to life. All to no avail. That much was clear. Five hundred dollars indeed. Well at least Bart was glad to see that Claire was angry and not dotingly sympathetic, which was her usual response to Scott's scrapes. At least she knows now and without a doubt what a worthless, aimless, tawdry young man Scott Stone really is. Maybe she doesn't know; Bart watched as Scott poured his mother some tea and Claire accepted the cup like a vial of holy water. Bart shook his head. "Scott's life isn't at stake right now anyway. Lucky's is. I don't even care why Lucky tried to kill himself or if he was drunk or sober. Nothing matters as long as he lives."

"Matthew Mark Luke and John," murmured Claire. "Let Lucky live."

"Eat your chop suey, Claire. Please."

"I hate Chinese food. One damn bamboo shoot after another. And rice—" She made a face and plucked a few grains of rice from her plate, urged them to the edge of the table and watched them spill.

Tiny flecks of rice spilled from her hair and from the collar of her spring coat as she took it off and placed it over a chair in their hotel room, the bridal suite, they'd been assured, but it looked like an ordinary hotel room to Claire's eye, except for the champagne cooling in an ice bucket. Lucky tipped the boy who'd carried their bags, and Claire walked to the window and pushed it open. Salt air stung her nose and a dipper full of light from the unseen moon fell across the sea and the town of San Angelo, which had changed beyond recognition since 1915, when the Senator bought the old house on Jerusalem Road for his first wife. In 1915, San Angelo had to its credit only spectacular views, a one-pump gas station, a café, grocery store and a saloon. Now, forty years later, all that was gone, save for the spectacular views afforded the magnificent homes. Even those homes without views were magnificent because San Angelo flourished as a resort town, a summer mecca for the rich, who had thronged here in the wake of Fremont Ebeneezer Swallow. In recognition of the Senator's contribution, the Swallow Golf Club, on cliffs overlooking the sea, played host every year to an international tournament and Swallow Boulevard boasted baskets of pink geraniums on every corner, affluent shops, restaurants touting their chefs and splendid hotels. For their honeymoon, Lucky had chosen one of these hotels fronting the beach, and from their window Claire could see the ebony waves rise and diminish in three-quarter time, breaking ivory over the blackened beach, as if invisible exquisite fingers played some lost sonata.

Lucky closed the door, came up behind her, putting his arms around Claire: "Are you pleased, Mrs. Stone? I thought San Angelo would please you for a honeymoon." He kissed the back of her neck.

Claire shuddered deliciously, turned in his arms, stroking his handsome, angular face. "It was very sweet of you, Lucky. I used to come here every summer as a child. All summer long my brother and I played dolphins in the water and built sandcastles on the shore."

"That's why I chose it. I knew you hadn't been here in a long time."

"Years," replied Claire, telling the first lie of her married life before the rice was even out of her shoes. "Years." She bent her head forward compliantly as Lucky unzipped the back of her crêpe sailor suit. She lifted her arms, and he drew the blouse over her head.

Lucky's hand rested on her belly. "How is our baby? Our little one?"

"He's fine." Claire kissed Lucky's chin.

"How do you know it's a he?"

"I just know."

"Son or daughter, it doesn't matter to me. I love the baby because it's ours, part of us and our love. Let them think what they want. I'm proud of it, really. Claire Swallow gave herself to me before we were married. Claire Swallow loved me that much."

"I do love you, Lucky and I'm grateful."

"No, I'm grateful to you, Mrs. Stone, my wife, my beautiful wife. You'll never be sorry you married me."

Claire kissed him and smiled, graced with a moment's conviction and insight: Lucky was right; he would be a good husband and they would have a good life and this was the best way, after all—without passion. Lacking passion, that overwhelming hormonal urgency, there was less to lose, less at stake. Claire and Lucky could build a marriage based on genuine affection from the beginning; their feelings would not dwindle into affection, pale into simple regard; they would not be required to mourn or resent the passing of some vivid complex moment that could never be recaptured and would surely die as time gnawed at it. Such moments, such passion, were behind her and Claire resolved to be done with them forever. She felt as if she were not nineteen but thirty-nine, mature, reflective, calm, relishing her comfortable commitments. "You are my wonderful husband, Lucky, and I love you." She held him tight, as if she could impress his flesh on her fingers now, then and forever, as if he were her lover as well as her husband.

Claire pushed her dish away and brooded over her tea. "Mama was wrong about Lucky. He wasn't unworthy of me. I was unworthy of him."

"Oh, Claire," Bart remonstrated. "Don't say that. You've been a good wife. You've had a good marriage, and besides, Mama hasn't thought that for twenty years. Mama and Althea both, they've often said how much they all love Lucky and how glad they are you married him. They wish that Jill and Marietta had had the sense to marry men as good as Lucky Stone."

"They didn't marry at all," said Scott.

"Well, Jill has, in a manner of speaking," Bart shrugged. "She's been living with whatshisname for the last six or seven years."

"If you wanted grass—" Claire turned to her son, "—You could have called up your Aunt Jill. She might have given you a cut rate on what she grows, and you'd have known that she imported ladybugs to eat the white flies, that she would only tint her marijuana with holistic PCP. You should have gone to her instead of some pusher."

"Jill would have charged him double," said Bart. "She needs the money. She called the other night and said they were both out of work again."

"Did she ask you for money?"

"Doesn't everyone?" Bart shot a grim look at Scott, who withered under it. "I sent her a couple of hundred, but I told her that's the last of it. No more. I have enough to support with the Mourning Glory and Mama and Mama's getting so lost and rigid and irrational these days, I might have to institutionalize her."

"Oh, Bart, no."

"Althea can't always cope, Claire. She's old too, you know, and Mama has to be watched all the time. If she just rocked and knitted, it wouldn't be so bad, but you never know what she'll do. A couple of weeks ago, I woke up in the night and smelled gas and ran downstairs and found Mama standing in front of the stove, three of the four burners going full blast. The fourth hadn't been lit. It could have exploded and blown us all to hell."

"What was she doing?"

"She thought I was Father. She kept telling me I had to relax and look after myself and not worry about the Ryan case so much. No," Bart said sadly. "She needs more than Althea to look after her. But if I have to put her in a home, I don't see how I can pay for that and Marietta's treatments, too."

"I thought the doctor said Marietta could get out pretty soon."

"For yet another ill-fated assault on reality?" Bart growled. "Marietta's done so many drugs, she doesn't know how to live without them, and she hasn't got the strength of character to find out."

"Poor Marietta. I wish I could like her better, but I can't. Neither her nor Jill. I dread their visits. Marietta is always full of wild schemes, talks as if she's going to join the New York Ballet just as soon as she can struggle into her tutu. And what can I say to her—Marietta, you can't dance? So I just sit there and nod like Mama always did and feel like a fool, but talking to her is a waste of breath." Claire cupped her hands around her tea. "And Jill and whatshisname—they're worse. They come and all they do is bitch about the food. I'm not organic enough for them. They check the apples for wax, and while they're wolfing down steak and pork chops, they tell me how I ought to cook with brown rice and barley. Ugh! Then, while I'm doing the dishes, they sit around and puff themselves into oblivion. They refer to everything as groovy. They drive me wild now, but I used to envy them so much. They always seemed so free."

"They weren't. They were just imprisoned by things you couldn't see. They're still imprisoned, for that matter."

"They don't act like it."

"They don't know it. They're prisoners of the sixties, prisoners of the past. They confuse the word with the deed," said Bart soberly, as if he had thought on this a long while. "Jill says she's going to get a job, and to her mind, she's working. Marietta says she's going to lay off drugs, and to her mind, she's straight, never mind she continues to pop or snort or smoke anything she can lay her hands on. Jill and Marietta can't learn from their experience because they can't remember, not from one day to the next. They have no memory and they never recovered from the sixties. Maybe they're victims and maybe we ought to pity them, but they've strained my sympathy and my resources and I just can't feel for them any longer."

"Yes, but they had all the fun back then, didn't they?" Claire said wistfully. "All those be-ins and love-ins and peace marches, all that wonderful collective madness, none of it ever touched my life. I had a home and a husband and three little children and I missed out on everything. I remember Dan was born during Woodstock and I lay there in the hospital and I couldn't understand why everyone was making such a fuss over a typewriter. The sixties were a huge beach party that I watched from a boat, far out at sea."

Bart smiled at his sister affectionately. "I *was* at sea for most of the sixties, and every time my ship pulled back into port, my own generation seemed stranger and more foreign to me than anyone in Tokyo or Valparaiso. I always envied Jill and Marietta, too—the beads, the long hair and dope smoking and protests and freewheeling sex, but I pity them now. They shook off all the responsibilities—and they missed all the rewards."

"You sound like Father," said Claire tenderly.

"I guess I do. I probably never would have been the sort for free-wheeling sex anyway, but the older I grow, the more I see that you can't find rewards in life without undertaking responsibilities. Love is the biggest responsibility you can assume. It offers the most peril—and the most pleasure." He thought fleetingly of Scott, the devastated girl and her enraged father. He turned to his nephew gruffly. "You ought to think about that before you start bedding down with women."

"All you ever did was bed down," Scott retorted. "You never married."

"Not by choice. I like women, which is more than can be said of most men, and I loved enough women to know I'm capable of love, but I never married because I never found a woman willing to live with me and my prematurely senile mother and my Mourning Glory, Aunt Althea. I couldn't leave them. They're my responsibility."

"They shouldn't have been," Claire said sourly. "You should have had your own life, and you would have if Father hadn't—"

"Now, Claire, don't tread over that again." Bart kneaded his brow and checked his watch, mentally tallying the hours Lucky had been in surgery. "Please eat something. You'll need your strength."

"For what?" She began to cry. "For mourning if Lucky dies? And living with guilt and wondering if I couldn't have stopped him, done something to save him?"

"He'll live. You need your strength for that."

"Yes, for living with bankruptcy and poverty and scandal. For going to court and asking that vile Hoolihan to defend him."

"You don't have to ask Hoolihan for anything. Hoolihan's not demanding your pride or even your gratitude."

"What have I done to deserve this, Bart? Why has this happened to me? To us? Where did it begin? Where will it end?"

"Mrs. Claire Stone," said the watery voice over the hospital intercom. "Will Mrs. Claire Stone please come to Emergency?"

Instinctively, Claire and Bart clutched hands. "He's going to live, Claire. Everything is going to be all right."

"He is going to live," Claire repeated. "But nothing will ever be all right again."

Bart rose and offered his sister his arm. Mutely, she took that arm and the hand of her son and they walked down the long, cold corridors toward Emergency, beset, bedeviled, by the smell of decay awash in antiseptic.

CHAPTER FOUR

November 1954

Claire's response to the funeral of Senator Fremont Ebeneezer Swallow was one of pride and had nothing to do with the deceased, who had never taken pains to endear himself to his grandchildren. She wore a new maroon wool coat with a trimmed hood, black stockings and white gloves, and with the carriage of a bride, not a mourner, she led her brother, mother and father down the aisle of the Episcopal church to the front pews reserved for family. Jill and Marietta were deemed too young to attend this sad occasion, which struck Claire as rather festive, actually, given that the church she had attended all her life was filled to capacity and impacted with floral tributes massed all over the altar and the Senator's enormous white coffin. There was music, after all, and grand words and people moved to emotion. It was really quite pompous and fulfilling.

From the church, her father drove them to the city's cemetery, where the Senator was to be interred beside his first wife. The cemetery was not as much fun, although Claire enjoyed being seated on chairs, arranged on either side of the gaping hole and reserved for family. Everyone else had to stand, she noticed with great satisfaction. But the chairs were cold and the November fog and chill gnawed at Claire's coat and stockings and gloves and the hole smelled bad, of damp and decay, despite—or perhaps because of—the overwhelming presence of flowers. Claire began to clap her hands together to get them warm, but her mother told her to stop immediately and hush.

Crimping in the cold were hundreds of stiff bouquets and huge wreaths bearing sorrowful inscriptions from three dozen different lodges and philanthropic groups and every family of note in the city and well beyond, including the families of men the Senator had once corrupted, cheated, swindled or simply bested. No tribute was anonymous. The governor sent an emissary, and there was even a letter of condolence from President Dwight D. Eisenhower and a wreath from the U.S. Senate. Senator Swallow was mourned on land and sea, where flags of every vessel in the Swallow Lines flapped at half mast. Indeed, when it had occurred to him that—like other men—he was mortal and could very likely die, the Senator believed that burial at sea would be in keeping with his life as founder of Swallow Lines, those magnificent white ships all graced with a single blue swallow in flight. His wife, Lucille, however, convinced him that generations as yet unborn would wish to pay homage to his greatness and if he were buried at sea, there would be no one place where these nameless acolytes could visit in adoration, no one monument to mark his achievements.

So the Senator consented to be buried beside his first wife in the city's cemetery. An acre to the east of him lay the bones of Mrs. Sophie Goldstone, rotting in her Sears & Roebuck dress. An acre to the west of him moldered the body of the executed Patrick Ryan, but of all the people gathered to mourn the Senator, probably only Anson Swallow and Hoolihan considered these facts. Hoolihan stood now at the back of the crowd and noticed that his old adversary, Hugh Coldwell, now Mayor Coldwell and his wife had planted themselves right behind the chairs of Lucille and her two children, Jon and Lucy Rose Cotton. Glancing over the swarms of veiled women and well-upholstered men, Hoolihan figured he knew or knew of almost everyone there, but he exchanged no greetings and kept to the furthest edges. He had not approached the widow at the church and would not approach her now; he had written a brief note of condolence and thought that sufficient, though the note had extracted a good deal of time from him because Hoolihan could not bring himself to offer the usual platitudes. ("He will be much missed," "He was a great man and we shall not see his like again," etc.). Hoolihan only came to the funeral at all because he had accepted the bounty of the Senator's hospitality while he lived and it seemed just and correct to acknowledge his passing. Hoolihan shuddered in the cold and wondered, not so much if there was a heaven, but if there was a hell and it so, he reckoned, Patrick Ryan would be there to greet Senator Swallow as he approached those fiery gates.

The widow, who sat shivering between her son and her daughter, was not thinking of heaven or hell; she did not have a theoretical mind. Her beauty was strained, her face gray, her eyes red and she was hoping the eulogies could be kept brief so they could all go back to the Swallow mansion, where it was warm. Across from her and ringing the open grave sat Anson and his family, George and Eleanor Swallow, the Tenor, the Bass and the Baritone, as well as Althea and Vera, who no longer wore togas; Vera was deep in the arms of spiritualism now and that persuasion required no special uniform.

Mayor Coldwell and former Mayor Stone both delivered long eulogies (since it was the equivalent of a captive audience) and then the Reverend Dykstra, his bright ecclesiastical robes fluttering like lace curtains, began his farewell. Lucille wept copiously, as though the reverend's words moved her, as though the Senator had actually been a practicing Christian. In fact, Lucille knew the Senator had scant use for religion, privately believing that it was useful only insofar as it allowed one to make the proper contacts, present the proper face, to get on in the world. Getting in and out of the world, the Senator maintained, a man could do without the church. Lucille too was of this opinion, although she kept it to herself. Lucille had every reason to be grateful to the church, to the Reverend Dykstra's Episcopal church in particular, for it was there she had met Senator Swallow a month after the death of his first wife. What could have been more socially smiled upon? Here in the spiritual shelter of the Episcopal church, she, a friendless widow, should have approached the august Senator in April 1952, gone up to him after the morning service as the yellow tulips lining the walk nodded in the diffident sunshine, as he was shepherding his spinster daughter, Althea, to the Cadillac and asked if she might have a word with him.

The Senator was taken (not smitten, as Althea claimed, not then, just taken) with Mrs. Cotton's graceful decorum, shy dignity, her wistful manner and blue eyes. Lucille's eyes were indeed a captivating translucent blue and they contrasted nicely with her thick black lashes, fair complexion and abundant hair. As she approached him there, before the swaying yellow tulips, Lucille's doelike demeanor was not feigned: Fremont Ebeneezer Swallow was very likely the last chance she had and Lucille knew it.

For the Senator's benefit that April day, she gave her most endearing performance, but it was not her first. Lucille O'Reilly had kicked up her heels, flung up her skirt and stripped off her stockings in a New York

93

burlesque house, amid cheers and jeers and heavy smoke, in the late Depression. She had slept with the burlesque house manager to get the job, small price to pay in those grim days and, moreover, she took comfort each time she took him to bed, knowing that her job was safe. Lucille O'Reilly had fled to New York to escape her drunken, abusive father and the squalor in the family's overcrowded, ill-heated flat in Boston. In New York she shared a tiny coldwater flat with another girl in the chorus line and they took turns smoking on the landing while the other entertained men for money.

On the strength of her blue eyes, or perhaps the well-turned line of her thigh, Lucille entranced Mr. Tom Quinn of Chicago, who was in the audience one night. After the show Tom Quinn bought Lucille her first good meal in a week. (In retrospect, Lucille realized she'd consumed that meal with too much haste and eagerness, that her hunger was all too apparent.) Tom Quinn took her back to his hotel and to bed that night and for several nights thereafter and when he returned to Chicago, Lucille went with him, self-styling herself Mrs. Quinn, only to find that while Tom Quinn might have had the price of dinner and a bed in New York, he had damn little in Chicago. Their union deteriorated for a year, until the day Tom Quinn simply vanished, leaving Lucille with $9.54 and the rent on the boardinghouse room paid till the end of the week. Lucille cursed him as the son of a whore and a rapist, wished on him the degradation of penury and syphilis and then she sat on the edge of the bed and flipped a coin: heads, she would return east; tails, she would try her luck (and her blue eyes) in California. She hitched a ride west with a truck driver who picked her up contrary to company policy. She made it worth his while.

On that ride to California, Lucille reassembled her goals and prospects and decided that her fondest wish was respectability. She had watched too many well-fed matrons brush past her on the street, scuttling back to what Lucille imagined were well-run homes with reliable men who drove to regular jobs in black cars and brought home regular wages that paid for iceboxes, upright pianos and allowed the family to cluster around the radio in the evenings. Lawful marriage, that's what she needed. Once in the city by the sea, Lucille Quinn [sic] resolved to be done with the Irish forever and slept with the Italian cook at a downtown diner, which is how she secured herself a decent job as a waitress where the hours were reliable, but her meals were deducted from her paycheck. She augmented her diet by snitching scraps the customers left on their plates. She was not, however, so hungry as to lose sight of the future. Respectability, she reasoned, lay with the Protestants, and to that end she began attending a Methodist church (though, again, in retrospect she realized she could have saved herself a lot of time if she had chosen the Episcopalians to begin with). Amongst the Methodists, Lucille met the man on whom she next turned the light of her blue eyes.

Norris Cotton was a history teacher in a local high school. He had a framed degree from a normal school in Washington State and was intelligent and well read and Lucille listened to him with rapt attention. She even read a few books herself so as to cultivate her mind and demonstrate good faith. Norris, an unlovely, intense young man, was touched by her eagerness to learn and undone by the sight of her lovely body, and once he had seduced her (so to speak), he could not wait to marry her and make her his own. With the waitress job (and the Italian cook) behind her, Mrs. Norris Cotton had achieved respectability, but eventually she weighed it in the balance and found it wanting. The framed degree, intensity and reading notwithstanding, Norris's profession was ill paid and unrewarding and their life insufferably dull, hemmed in at every side by petty economies. Still, it was easier to support oneself sleeping with one man rather than many and at least Norris Cotton was able to keep his wife and their two children (Jonathan and little Lucy Rose) in a comfortable three-story walk-up, where the halls smelled of cooking cabbage and echoed with the wail of babies. By 1948 Lucille had an icebox and a radio but no car (though they lived so close to the high school that Norris could walk to work) and no piano, but then she couldn't play anyway.

Norris Cotton was run down by a runaway bus in July 1951. Mrs. Cotton was absolutely demented with grief until she learned that her late lamented husband had had the foresight to insure himself generously. Mrs. Cotton then dried her eyes and considered her next course of action: she was unwilling to continue nibbling at the stale cake of bourgeois custom but equally unwilling to risk her fate with the likes of Tom Quinn and his ilk again. Clearly, whatever she did this time, she needed to calculate everything perfectly. Life was obviously not prepared to offer her opportunity: opportunity must be manufactured.

When the insurance check arrived, Lucille took a goodly chunk of it and went to the finest department store in the city and there, despite the titters of the shopgirls, who noted her gray and fraying underclothing, she had herself outfitted from the skin up: a black suit in one of the new synthetic fabrics with a pleated basque jacket and three-quarter sleeves. The jacket was caught tight at the waist and the skirt flared out from the hips. She bought a white silk blouse and a loose-fitting swagger-back coat with fur cuffs and a smart, shallow off-the-face hat. Lucille possessed a native good taste in clothes and she could wear them well. To augment those aspects of grooming she did not come by quite so naturally, she invested in a volume of Emily Post.

While her children were in school, Lucille swilled pots of tea and poured over Emily Post in the mornings, learning the lines and appropriate mannerisms with the same savvy and aptitude she'd once brought to the routines at the burlesque house. In the afternoons she rode the city buses and inspected various Protestant churches, limiting her search this time to the Presbyterians and Episcopalians. She finally decided on the Reverend Mr. Dykstra's huge neo-Gothic edifice in the finest section of town. She reasoned that she might as well go at it whole hog, though as she plowed through Mrs. Post's dictums, she learned to drop that expression from her repertoire.

On Sunday morning that autumn of 1951, Lucille dressed in her new finery, left Jon and little Lucy Rose with the woman in the next flat (the woman, in fact, who was so extraordinarily fond of cabbage) and took the bus to Mr. Dykstra's church, where she worshipped modestly and fervently and scrutinized the congregation as if they were a citadel and she a general determined to take it by stealth rather than by storm. There were no obviously unmarried men, but in the absence of any other plan, Lucille persisted; marriage was not essential, but security was. In that regard she dismissed the corpulent Senator Swallow, certain she could not interest him in the sort of remunerative relationship she had in mind. Her prospects dwindled along with her hope until March 1952, when the Reverend Dykstra announced from the pulpit the sad news that Edith Swallow, the Senator's wife, had departed this life. Lucille glanced over to the Swallow family pew. It was empty.

As a member of the church, Lucille attended the funeral of Edith Swallow, carrying a handful of golden daffodils. She stood at the edge of the crowd and tallied up the Senator's possibilities as if he were no more than a prize pig at a state fair. She noted his four children. Both sons, Anson and George, were big men, like their father, but Anson carried his weight well, his bones seemingly supporting an integrity, a worth commensurate with his girth. George by contrast looked downright ramshackle and, moreover, clearly alcoholic; Lucille knew that look. She discounted the daughter dressed in a toga as any sort of impediment. Of the other daughter she could determine little: Althea was clad head to foot in black and so hysterical she had to be carried to and from the graveside. As the Reverend Dykstra bade Edith Swallow farewell, Lucille tried to remember what the deceased had looked like, but couldn't. She left her flowers with the rest and said not a word.

Upon leaving the cemetery, Lucille Cotton followed an impulse she could neither quite stifle nor deny. She got off the bus at the stop that would have led her to the cabbage flat, but turned and walked three blocks in the other direction to the Catholic church, the Church she had been raised in and scorned. She lit a candle and prayed to the Holy Virgin that the Senator might marry her or make some other advantageous arrangement before Norris's insurance money ran out and she would be forced to settle for waitress work or return to the informal prostitution of her youth. She was no longer that young.

Never mind. She looked young: she had lovely translucent blue eyes and a voluptuous mouth that even her newly acquired respectability could not conceal. She was a widow left alone in the world, as she told the aged, massively overweight Senator standing there that April morning beside the dancing yellow tulips and his purring black Cadillac.

"Turn that damn thing off, Dillard," the Senator barked at his chauffeur, "so I can hear what the little lady here is saying. Now then, my dear." He turned back to Lucille. "Your circumstances have altered and what—"

"I'm from a Boston family, Senator, and the doctor ordered my husband to come to California for his health. His lungs—" Here, Lucille pulled out her single starched handkerchief and daubed her blue eyes. "His lungs finally failed him last year, and I long only to return to my family, but I am too proud to ask them for money. And you must not—please, I beg of you, do not think for an instant that I am asking you for money. No, Senator, I need work and I thought perhaps a man of your stature, a Christian, might know of someone who needs a secretary. I would be most grateful for any assistance you could offer me. I can, of course, produce references."

The Senator, all 250 pounds of him, beamed at Mrs. Cotton; he would doubtless have preferred to beam down at her, but Lucille was nearly as tall as he. "In fact, Mrs. Cotton, I may require a secretary myself. You say you can type?"

"Oh, yes."

"And take dictation."

"Of course."

"And do you have any skill in the filing and arrangement of papers?"

"Lots."

"I am thinking of writing a book and your skills might be very helpful to me. Could I count on your staying, that is, not going back to Boston, until this project is completed? I believe in seeing things through to their finish, and I dislike change. I like things to stay the same."

"I do too, Senator, and if you were to offer me employment, I could do no less than to promise you I would stay until you finished your book."

"Book," Althea snarled at Anson and Meg a month later as she sat in Anson's study. "Imagine the Senator writing a book!"

"Has he said what sort of book he has in mind?" inquired Anson, swiveling in his desk chair.

"His autobiography, a book of advice for young men on how to get on in the world."

"He might yet write it," Anson ventured.

"Are you mad, too!" Althea screeched. "The Senator's gone mad with this book business and that slut in the house. First one day a week, then two and now he says she's to come three afternoons a week to help him write. Who is going to run Swallow Lines while the Senator locks himself up in the library with her? George? I ask you—George! And you should see her type." Althea snorted. "Two fingers. Why, she couldn't spell her way out of a candy wrapper. But the Senator just says very good my dear, very nice my dear. Well, I keep an eye on them. I can tell you that. I never read so much in all my life. I go into the library every half hour just to check on them." Althea drew a deep, indignant breath.

"Are they making any progress?" Meg asked. "I mean, on the book."

Althea groaned. "The book is not important. The Senator, his future—our future—that's what's important. I tell you, Anson, we must nip this in the bud. You hear me? In the bud. We must put a stop to it and we must do it now, before it's too late. If we wait—oh, if we wait—" Althea's colour drained, leaving her fat face the hue of brine. "Think what could happen if we wait."

Anson rose, walked to the whiskey decanter and poured Althea a stiff shot and gave it to her. "You might as well drink it," he counseled.

"No. Mother wouldn't approve. Mother didn't hold with spirits."

"Mother's dead. And no one can stop the Senator. You know that. There's nothing I can do."

Althea drank the whiskey in one gulp and began to blubber. "Oh, Anson, when he said that about the book there at the church, I wanted to believe him, really I did. I tried. I was surprised, of course, because the Senator had never

98

said anything about a book, before, but when we drove home, he started to rattle on about Benjamin Franklin. I wanted to believe him, but I couldn't and I didn't dare—" Althea paused uncomfortably.

"Contradict him."

"No. Yes. I didn't dare contradict him. But, Anson, he's losing his heart to her, maybe even his mind."

Anson exchanged tense looks with Meg; he returned to his chair and put his feet up on the desk. "Althea, even if the Senator went suddenly raving mad, there's nothing we could do about it. The Senator can do what he likes and no one should know that better than you."

Althea wiped her eyes, blew her nose and brushed a bit of dander from her black dress. "If you are referring to my putative engagement to Mr. Albert Smythe twenty-four years ago, I can assure you that I have since seen the wis-dom—that I have realized that the Senator had my best interests—I mean, he intended that—well, I was never really engaged to Albert anyway. It was a rumor."

"Maybe this is a rumor, too," Anson offered as a shard of comfort.

"No. No, it's not. He's raised her salary. She's got dreadful designs on him. She wants to marry him! Oh, Anson, Meg, just imagine that horrible woman sleeping in Mother's bed!"

"I doubt she would," Anson replied sadly. "Mother's bed was for many years not the Senator's bed at all."

"Oh, Anson!" Althea gnashed her teeth. "I should have ordered Dillard to drive on, right then, just as soon as I saw her coming up the walk. I should have kicked that slut in the teeth right in front of the church, smashed her face and ordered Dillard to drive on before the Senator ever said. . ."

"This book may take quite a long time, Mrs. Cotton."

"I am equal to the challenge, Senator."

"Very well then, come on Tuesday. I'll have a typewriter delivered and set up in the library and we'll begin then. In fact, Mrs. Cotton, why don't you come for lunch so we can discuss it more fully?"

"Thank you, Senator. Your generosity is matched only by your fore-sight."

The Senator and his daughter drove away. Mrs. Cotton walked to a bus stop to catch the bus that would take her to her children, the cab-bage monger and the three-story walk-up. But when she got off the bus, she once again (and without knowing quite why) went three blocks in the other direction and for the second time in fifteen years she lit a candle to the Virgin Mary, who, after all, was a mother herself and had once stood beyond the pale of society's approval and could understand these things better than the Father or the Son.

ii

At noon on April 13, 1952, a body in the city morgue with a tag around its toe was identified by Patrick Ryan as that of his erstwhile client Mrs. Sophie Goldstone, who had been found without a purse or any identification by passersby the night before, the victim of an apparent hit-and-run accident. Lucille Cotton could not have known this and would not have cared as the cabby had just quoted her the fare for her ride to the Senator's mansion. "You thieving son of a bitch," she said, counting it out in change. "I hope you get syphilis." She got out of the car and slammed the door and called after the cab, "From your wife!" But her bravado and her anger evaporated immediately after she had a good look at her surroundings, assessed them with her shrewd eye. The magnificent home, the surrounding gardens flooded with color, the tonic sunshine refracting off beveled windows and gleaming white stucco, the swaying royal palms that lined the driveway—this was more than she'd reckoned on and she gulped, feeling desperate and undone to realize suddenly the magnitude of the gamble she'd undertaken: the stakes were suddenly raised.

She knocked primly and announced herself to the butler, who led her into the library, where the new typewriter awaited her ministrations. The Senator sat at the desk amidst many papers; he rose and greeted her warmly, making small talk about the weather and the party he'd been to the night before at Patrick Ryan's, where he had mentioned the possibility of writing his autobiography. "Everyone thinks it is a wonderful idea. They are sure it will be a masterpiece and inspire young men for generations. I've promised them all signed copies," he said as he led her across the foyer (as big as Lucille's whole flat) and into the dining room, where he seated her at his left, across from his daughter Althea, whom Lucille greeted in the fashion approved by Emily Post.

Lucille was a quick study. She had learned from her experience with Quinn that it was a grave error to let one's hunger show, so she took very little and ate less of the massive lunch spread before her and declined wine in favor of soda water. The bay windows and French doors leading to descending terraces were open and sunlight splashed amongst the regal tulips, the Dutch hyacinths and Japanese plum trees. Perhaps the bounty of nature was insufficient for the Senator because a cheerful blaze crackled in the fireplace and beams from the chandelier sparkled in the mahogany wainscotting. The sounds of silver on thin china, the crisp clink of lids and serving spoons were muffled by a thick Persian carpet designed in a series of multicolored obelisks. Gently, percussively, these sounds harmonized with the Senator's description of his plans for his book. "There's been nothing like it since the *Autobiography of Benjamin Franklin*," he stated decisively. "Young men sometimes don't realize that they must groom themselves for opportunity, that our country offers its riches most fully to those men with vision and daring."

"And integrity," Althea offered, passing the dill sauce.

"Of course." The Senator helped himself to another salmon steak, finished his second glass of wine and refilled it. "The founding, growth and history of Swallow Lines and my own life testify to the necessity of developing an athletic will. The fighter who goes into the ring unprepared is knocked out and carried off by life's brutal blows, but he who exercises his will, just as if it were a muscle, who sharpens his nerve and steels his sinew. . ."

Yes, yes, Lucille nodded approvingly every time the Senator glanced at her, inwardly pleased and comforted: he was not only talking to her, but about her. Hadn't Lucille done the very things he spoke of? She was doing them even now: grooming herself for opportunity, flexing her will, sharpening her nerves and skills, though a woman could not let her sinew show, not even metaphorically, and it did not pay to be visibly clever. Lucille knew enough of the world to hide her light under her very decorative bushel; she knew that men preferred respectable women to be grave and attentive and expected the less than respectable to be indulgent and entertaining. Lucille had been both. As the Senator expanded and expounded, she glanced across the table and eyed Althea, judging her to be about forty, fat and formidable. She smiled at Althea, who did not respond.

Warmed by his meal, the wine, the coffee, all of it washed down by a tumbler of ale and a salutary beaker of mineral water, the Senator suggested that he and Lucille repair to the library, where the typewriter awaited the commencement of this great work.

Lucille begged off. (She needed to practice a little more on the Woodstock that Norris Cotton had left amongst his effects.) But instead, she told the Senator that something had come up involving the needs of her little ones and asked if she could start later. The Senator had not known she had little ones. He asked after them. Lucille described Jonathan and little Lucy Rose as dutiful, cherubic and devoted to their dear widowed mother, which was only a gross exaggeration and not a downright lie.

"Very well then, Mrs. Cotton," said the Senator, rising and extracting his great body from the chair that enveloped him like casing around an enormous sausage. "In that case, come at ten on Thursday. We'll begin then."

"Thank you, Senator."

"And if I may make a suggestion, dear lady—and with all due respect for your dead husband—would you be good enough to wear something other than widow's weeds? I am sick unto death"—he cast Althea a scalding glance—"of seeing women in black."

Lucille complied. She went that very afternoon back to the city's finest department store and spent much of what was left of Norris's insurance money on three gay frothy afternoon frocks, one in a lovely aquatic blue, one in a pale green, one in a fragile lemonade yellow, and a suit of a creamy rose colour, which heightened her skin tones and underscored the untrammeled blue of her eyes.

As Lucille sat now, clad in black between her son and her daughter, her eyes on her husband's casket and raw grave, listening to the Reverend Dykstra wax on, she wondered how long she'd have to wear mourning. Black did not become her: particularly now that grief had drained her face and nightmares stole her sleep; ever since the night the Senator died, Lucille woke, feverish and tense, from dreams where she was being buried with him, crushed under fleshy walls, smothered. Lucille peered furtively from under her eye-length veil, across the grave to Anson, Meg, their children and George and Eleanor and their children, Vera and Althea: they were genuinely grieving, but she could feel at the same time their collective anger, thinly masked while the Senator lived, exhumed now in their sorrow at losing him. And possibly losing much more.

They can damn well stew. No one can say I didn't do my duty by Eb Swallow. You couldn't do what Lucille had done with a man like that and continue to call him Senator. Even Fremont was too formal for what Lucille had done—her duty and then some. She had first made love to him on the library floor in June 1952, the very week after he had returned from San Angelo sans Althea. Even then Lucille let a few days pass until desire popped like perspiration from the Senator's pores, until his hunger rumbled audibly from his great body as he stood right beside her, dictating, and then Lucille allowed her head to droop to one side, to brush against his pants; the Senator touched her hair, pulled her close, Lucille looked adoringly into his eyes and said, "I love you," and the Senator fell to his knees before her. They made love on the library floor without either of them fully removing a single article of clothing. It was very uncomfortable, but worth it.

She married him and did her duty, respectfully, compliantly, but all in all it was like making love to a beached whale. The Senator covered her body with his great flesh; he grunted, Lucille grunted and it was done. The Senator went to sleep. Lucille did not. As a widow, of course she didn't exactly have to behave like a virgin (a condition that had never suited her in any event), but now she was a wife and expected to bear the man's weight (which was considerable), his children (who she fervently hoped would not be forthcoming) and the brunt of his moods (which were many). Lucille complied with these responsibilities, but she was bored. Discoverers, adventurers and gamblers are always bored with what's expected of them and Lucille was all of the above, but not until the night of the reception in September, when, inflamed by the slow, suggestive tango she had danced with Hoolihan and buoyed by the bubbling champagne, did she return to their connubial room, strip off her pebble pink evening gown with some of the expertise she'd learned in the burlesque house and treat the Senator to a bit of that expertise. The Senator was thrilled and, moreover, grateful.

Again, the Senator went to sleep and Lucille lay awake, half-giggling into the sheets. What a fool she'd been. She should have realized that a man who liked to eat as much as the Senator did was clearly a creature of the flesh and, far from being the needy partner in this marriage, Lucille had discovered her own power and, moreover, realized it would be very easy to consolidate, augment and glory in that power: she could reduce the founder of Swallow Lines to absolute slavering pulp.

She began the very next morning. She went into the bathroom while the Senator was in the tub, dropped her satin robe and crawled into the huge tub with him, soaping him all over, and when his every fold of flesh was clean and gleaming, she bade him rise like Neptune. Over his enormous gut, the Senator could only see the top of Lucille's bright head, but he knew that something he never guessed was humanly possible was about to happen to him and he made helpless little grunts of pleasure and pain and pleasure and pain and yet more pleasure.

Thenceforth, Lucille was endlessly inventive and each night, so as to heighten the Senator's visual sensations, Lucille insisted that the bedside lamp be left on. She scooted underneath the covers and nibbled his toes, then threw the covers off and placed the soles of his feet against her breasts, helping him to knead her breasts with his feet. Then she inched up his legs, kissing, licking as she went. She sometimes made love atop him (which, given the Senator's weight, was the position Lucille preferred), but sometimes she went further yet, daringly inched further, till she could plant her feet beneath his huge shoulders, wrap his hands around her thighs, delight him with what he might have known but had never before truly seen. She very often catered (or pandered, depending on your point of view) to the Senator's other appetites as well, ordering huge bowls of fruit and champagne delivered to their room before they retired; she sat astride him, fed him grapes and oranges while she drank champagne so carelessly that some of it splashed in delicious drops across his enormous belly. Senator Swallow may have been brilliant and ruthless and shrewd, the captain of a vast enterprise, the master of his fate and family, but he was malleable lard in the hands of a woman who could sprawl naked in the velvet chair beside the bedroom fireplace, her knees wide apart, and beckon to him.

Lucille invented endlessly and so skillfully that the Senator—Eb—came to believe that these pleasures were his own invention, that he was discovering a world denied to him all his life. His first wife had given him four children, but Lucille gave him experience, sensation he never dreamed of. And if Eb wondered at her expertise, her undulating practiced hands, he wrote it off to the tutelage of Norris Cotton. What a man he must have been!

What a woman! Who could deny a woman like that anything at all? Nothing was too good or too much or too trivial for Lucille. If the Senator ever did have fleeting thoughts of denying her, he was quickly disabused of them because the Senator too was a quick study and very early learned to dread a particularly unresponsive little pout Lucille mastered, a pout that could catapult him into despair. They quarreled first over Lucille's insistence that they invite Hoolihan to one of their festive cocktail parties; the Senator said no: Hoolihan was a mick, a thug, and he stank of the working classes from which he'd so recently sprung. Lucille pouted. And when things were so easily rectified, after all, the Senator gave in on this point and, indeed, on every other one as well.

To Althea's horror, Lucille's children—who were in and of themselves inoffensive, quiet little souls, odious only because they were hers—were instructed to call the Senator Papa when they were home. (The cabbage flat was never again referred to except once, when Jon expressed a longing for his friends in the three-story walk-up and Lucille cracked him across the jaw.) Jon, at age ten, was sent off to a posh boarding school and Lucy Rose enrolled at the Proctor School for Girls, where all the best were educated.

Lucille was educating herself. She had to acquire the Decency, Decorum and Dignity that a woman like Meg had supped on since childhood. Lucille kept her volume of Emily Post under the bathroom sink so she could open it easily and rehearse in front of the mirror. The Senator had never much relished sociability that was not directly tied in some way to certain gain, but he was so proud of his young wife that he escorted her happily to all sorts of gala affairs, and the Swallow home rang with festivity never dreamed of in the days of Edith Swallow. Lucille and her husband generously entertained the city's elite (as well as Hoolihan) with cocktail parties and dinner parties and late suppers and charitable balls because the Garden Club had asked Lucille to be their president and the Art League requested her attendance at their trustees' meetings. Lucille accepted these compliments as her just due (once she'd been assured she would not have to *do* anything at all). She was an enormous success, gloriously happy, and embraced her new life in much the way a convert might clutch his new faith, regarding everything in his past as benighted, deserving only scorn and repudiation.

Lucille had once whispered into Eb's receptive ear that she would like a little ship named after her little self. As a result, on the occasion of their first wedding anniversary, Senator and Mrs. Swallow gathered at the Swallow docks along with the rest of the Swallow family and other select dignitaries, who all watched as Lucille cracked a bottle of French champagne over the bow of the gleamingly new addition to the company fleet: the *Lucille*. She did it on the first try and then she turned and kissed the Senator, full and hard on the lips. The aging, obese Senator grinned like a schoolboy, and none other than Mayor Hugh Coldwell himself turned to Anson and remarked that he'd never seen the Senator looking so fit and healthy and happy. Dryly, Anson replied that marriage was good for people.

iii

"She's killing him," Althea announced as Anson drove them all home after the ship's christening. Althea sat in the front with Anson because she always claimed that Anson's Ford (as opposed to the Senator's Cadillac) made her car sick. Meg sat in the back with the children. "I tell you she's stuffing him into the grave. You should hear her—have another pork chop, dear, more cakes, more custard and potatoes and champagne and oysters. She has food sent up to their room so he won't get hungry in the night. I tell you, she's turning him into a—"

"I think we should continue this conversation later," said Meg.

"Into a what?" asked nine-year-old Claire.

"Nothing, dear," said Meg. "Never mind."

"I say, let's talk about it now. Why shouldn't the children know the truth of it?"

"Because there's no need to sully their sunny little world, is there?" Meg ruffled Bart's hair. "Anyway, Althea, you must admit that the Senator looks ten years younger since his marriage."

"I admit nothing of the sort."

"And I've never known him to be so cordial. Why, he's even nice to my children, especially when Jon and Lucy Rose are around."

"Vipers. That's what Jon and Lucy Rose are. Vipers in embryo."

"Now, Althea." Meg turned to Bart and Claire particularly. "Jon and Lucy Rose are nice, well-mannered little children and it's too bad they're always away at school and you can't play with your cousins more often."

"They're not cousins! Why, those children are nothing but puppets. Lucille pulls their strings and they dance. She pulls everyone's strings."

"Not yours," Anson reminded Althea as he pulled the Ford into the long driveway of their Spanish-style home, the stucco blindingly white in the summer sun. "She'll never pull yours."

The children tumbled out of the car and begged to go swimming and Meg agreed and they were already in their swimsuits and poised at the edge of the pool by the time Anson had removed his suit jacket and made a pitcher of lemonade. He put the pitcher and glasses on a tray and carried it out to the patio, relaxed into the lawn swing and smiled to watch the children plunge into the water.

Althea joined him and so did Meg, after she had changed her clothes and gathered her knitting. She began work, the needles chattering, and then she remarked on the late strawberries and wondered aloud if there might be enough for a batch of strawberry jam. Meg said this very consciously, hoping to steer the conversation from the course Althea had doubtlessly determined on.

The subject of jam, however, brought Althea back around to the Senator's eating habits. "He's twenty pounds heavier than he was two years ago. His eyes look like burnt-out coals. He's puffy."

"He always was," said Meg, knitting and purling and not looking up.

"She's killing him." Althea brushed a drop of lemonade from her black skirt. "You wouldn't make light of me if you lived there like I do."

"No one is making light of you," Anson replied.

"But you don't believe me. If you lived there, you'd know what I mean. I hear things. My room is far down the hall, but I hear things sometimes. I can't help it, and I try not to. I put the pillow over my head, but I hear things just the same. And one night last week, as I was going to bed, not late, just the usual time—the Senator always goes to bed very early these days—"

"Early to bed and early to rise makes a man healthy, wealthy and wise," said Anson.

"Don't make fun of me," Althea snarled. "I was on my way to bed and I passed their room and I could hear the Senator gasping, his breath scraping up and down his lungs. I heard it and I stopped and banged on the door and I cried out for him and you know what I got in response? Lucille laughed. I heard her giggling and she called out—your father's all right, Althea. And I said, I'm not leaving this door until I hear the Senator tell me he's all right. I want to hear it from the Senator. And then she started to giggle some more, even though the Senator was gasping—gasping, Anson. She said—go on, Eb, tell Althea. Go on Eb. Eb! Isn't that disgusting? Who could call the Senator Eb? Makes him sound like a pig farmer."

"Who's a pig farmer?" cried Claire, crawling out of the water and running into Anson.

"You're all wet," said Meg, "and you can't sit on your father's lap until you're dry. Get down, Claire."

"That's all right, Meg. But you ought to have a towel, Claire. Shall I get you a towel?"

"No." Claire took a sip of her father's lemonade and then jumped back into the pool, deliberately (so it seemed) splashing Jill, who began to cry. Meg dropped her knitting and went to the pool's edge to soothe Jill and chide Claire.

Anson turned to Althea. "Was the Senator all right?"

"I guess," said Althea grimly, "but he was still gasping. I could hear it. Him gasping and her giggling. I tell you, she's killing him."

"Maybe he was gasping from—" Anson sought a word other than the obvious. "Maybe he was having a good time. Maybe he was happy."

"Spare me." Althea all but slew Anson with her eyes. "Oh, I know what

107

everyone says, that the Senator looks younger, acts happier and more alive than ever before, but they're fools. Even George and Vera have said it." (Even Meg, but Althea did not underscore this.) "How could George know? He's a drunk."

"George may more require our pity than our censure," said Anson gravely.

"Hmph. Vera's a fool, too. She's taken up with those charlatan Spiritualists, spends her time sitting around contacting the dead. Do you know what I heard her say to the Senator? This very day, Anson, just before we had to watch that whore break the bottle of champagne over the bow of that new ship? Vera told the Senator she'd actually contacted Mother's dead spirit and that Mother gave her blessing to this union, that Mother smiled on his marriage to Lucille."

"What did the Senator do?"

"Why, he turned his back on her, of course. You know he doesn't even like to hear Mother's name mentioned anymore, especially around Lucille. Hmph. People may say what they like, but I tell you that woman is killing the Senator. He'll die and she'll giggle just like she did that night when he was gasping. Gasping and giggling—can you imagine what goes on in that bedroom?"

The Senator died much as Althea envisioned he might. In bed. Pushing. Grunting. Gasping. Straining well beyond his resources while Lucille lay beneath him, plucking at his chest hairs as though tuning a stringed instrument. "You can do it, Eb," Lucille urged him in a tiny whisper. His breath came harder and faster and what Lucille mistook for accelerated passion, for his peaking, was actually a heart attack, and when she went on in a low musky voice that a great man like him could do anything he wanted to a little woman like her, he did the unthinkable: he died.

She didn't quite realize it at first. She stroked his back, or more correctly, his sides (she couldn't reach all the way around his back). She nibbled his ears and offered all the usual applause, and when he failed to respond at all, she said, "Eb? Eb?" His head lay slackly beside hers and she could feel drool running down her shoulder; "Eb!" she shook him and lifted his hand, which then dropped to the bed with a thud; "Eb?" she tried to roll him off, but he would not budge and she could not scoot out from under his inert body. "Eb?" She began to scream, shrieks for help, cries of panic. She flailed and kicked, but she was pinned beneath his weight, buried under his flesh; she might well be entombed with or beneath the Senator's massive corpse and she began to bellow and sob all the louder, begged for help from God, the Virgin, Jesus Christ, even Althea, and she was still screeching when Althea flung open the door.

Althea stood there, rooted with rage, loathing and horror: it was the first time Althea Swallow had ever seen anything remotely resembling the act of love.

Althea was still there when Dillard, the cook and the butler pushed past her and ran to the bed. The two men, with a concerted heave ho! rolled the body off the screaming widow. Lucille scrambled out of bed, still crying and hollering for help. Dillard yanked a blanket off and handed it to Lucille, who didn't know what to do with it; her shrieking continued in metronomic blasts like a fire alarm, and finally Dillard draped the blanket around her quivering shoulders and then he pulled the sheet over the Senator's lifeless, hairless backside.

iv

On creaking pulleys, the enormous coffin was lowered into the grave. The Reverend Dykstra concluded his remarks, scooped a handful of earth and threw it into the hole. It landed with an awful thud. The widow stood, swaying slightly as she tossed her handful of hothouse daffodils into the grave. She glanced at the brass plaque denoting Edith Swallow's final resting place and then at the open wound of earth that contained the Senator. She shuddered; she would not come back to this place again.

Women snuffled, men put on their hats, children broke free of adults and mourners cascaded down the hillside to their waiting cars. Anson Swallow offered Lucille his arm, and she took it. He turned to Meg. "My dear, why don't you take Jon and Lucy Rose to the Senator's house in our car? Lucille may need a moment when she does not have to be brave in front of her children."

"Of course. Take his hand, Claire. Take the little boy's hand. Lucy Rose, come here, dear, and take my hand."

"He doesn't want me to." Claire stood with her hand outstretched toward Jon, who stared into his shoes. "Do you?"

"Take his hand anyway, dear."

"Come on." Claire pulled at Jon's coat. He remained, unbudging.

Anson knelt in front of Jon, held his shoulders and spoke to him in a low and reassuring tone. He put Jon's hand in Claire's and hugged them both and then he rose and watched the children follow Meg down the hill. He then escorted Lucille to the Cadillac, where Dillard stood at somber attention.

She made no move to get into the car. "I did my duty, Anson," she said.

"Of course you did."

"I did my duty and then some."

Vera pressed Lucille's gloved hand in her own. "The Senator's spirit will return to us," she said before she got in the car. Lucille blanched.

The Tenor, the Bass and the Baritone got in the front seat and George and Eleanor got in the back. George pulled out a small silver flask and took a sip. "Damned fog and cold," he muttered. He offered some to Vera and then to Anson and Lucille. Everyone declined.

"I was a good wife to him," Lucille said again to Anson.

"I know you were. You made him happier than he'd ever been."

Althea came down the hill, her heavy skirts tolling back and forth, making her look like a black bell. Without a word to anyone, Althea got into the car. Lucille followed her and took the window seat. Anson closed the door behind her.

Lucille rolled down the window. "Aren't you coming with us?"

"No. I'll join you there. But I want you to know, Lucille, that we are your family and you may rely on us in the difficult days to come."

"Thank you. I will. I will rely on you, on all of you." She rolled the window back up and leaned against the seat. Dillard started the car, and they pulled away from the cemetery. Lucille stared out the window and fought the smile that tugged at her lips; she had lied, of course: Lucille would rely on no one in the days to come. She had never relied on anyone or anything except her own instincts and her gambler's conviction that quick eyes, quick hands and a quick mind will render every hand just that much better than the last.

Anson walked back to his Ford, where the children were crammed in the back and Meg installed in the passenger's seat. "Will you drive them to the Senator's, Meg?" he asked. "The children need some cake and cocoa and warmth. Funerals are too much to ask of them."

"This boy needs to pee," said Claire.

Anson glanced in the back, where Jon was crouched in the corner of the car. He had not let go of Claire's hand, or more likely, Claire had not let go of his. "Take them to the house, Meg. I'll be there shortly."

"I need to pee, too," Claire added.

"It's very rude to talk about your body," said Lucy Rose in her best Miss Proctor fashion.

"I need to pee, too," said Bart.

They all laughed, even Meg and Anson. Meg scooted over to the driver's side, and Anson handed her the keys.

He saw them off, and when the car had disappeared, he turned and walked west. This newer part of the cemetery more closely resembled a golf course, with flower cups for holes and shining brass plates in the crew-cut grass. He crossed into the older section where the headstones clustered around his knees like dwarfs. A wet, chill wind blew through the old trees, which were almost wholly naked, their branches forming bare naves and wooden transepts through which Anson walked without quite knowing where he was going or, for that matter, quite why. In the distance, in another newer section of the cemetery, where the trees were mere paltry, vulnerable saplings, Anson saw a solitary hatless figure. The man's back was to him, but Anson knew who it was.

Hoolihan jumped at Anson's tread. "Your Honor, you startled me."

"I'm sorry. I didn't mean to. I didn't expect to find you here."

"I might say the same of yourself." Hoolihan held a bunch of wine red roses, already beginning to crimp in the November chill; he laid them on Patrick Ryan's grave. "I took the roses from the Senator's grave, Your Honor. I hope you don't mind."

"The Senator had many to spare," said Anson, removing his hat.

"It seemed to me only fitting that Patrick Ryan should have got something from Senator Swallow at the end."

"He was guilty, wasn't he?"

"Who?"

"Ryan."

"We're all guilty, Your Honor. The question is of what and to what degree."

"Is that your professional belief or your personal one?"

"I was called to the rail long before I was called to the bar, Your Honor. An altar boy, I was, if you can believe it, saintly as they come. My mother intended me for the priesthood, but by the time I was sixteen, I told her it would never be. I'm too quick with my fists and my tongue. I have a weakness for women. I'm not fit to deal with men's souls. The dispensation of souls I leave to the Almighty. The dispensation of property, that's more my line."

"You didn't answer my question."

"And that's why you're the judge and I'm only a mick lawyer."

"Have you ambitions to be a judge?"

"Never."

"Never isn't always," said Anson ruefully.

"I've filled my ambitions. I make plenty of money. I pick and choose my own cases. A judge can't say the same, can he? A judge has to deal with what comes across the bench."

Anson nodded sadly. "I wish I were a surgeon, Hoolihan. I wish my only responsibility was to cut the evil out of society, to help people live, not—" he gazed at the grave before them "—to condemn them to death. It is my duty, and I hate it."

"If you're referring to your duty in general, Your Honor, then you have my sympathy, but if you're wasting a bit of remorse on the likes of Patrick Ryan, don't. His heart was black as hell's own pit and he was guilty as they come."

"How could you defend him, knowing that?" Anson regarded his companion critically.

"I didn't know it at first. I suspected it, of course. I never really believed he was innocent."

"But that was your defense!"

"It was a sensational case," said Hoolihan with a shrug. "I saw the chance to win."

"You lost, though."

"It was only a chance. I took it and I lost."

"You knew he was guilty," Anson persisted. "Why are you here now?"

"I might ask the same of yourself."

Anson glanced around the shivering saplings. "I thought since I was here already, for my father, I would—" Anson faltered and they lapsed into silence, each chagrined to be on the same side of Patrick Ryan at last. Finally, Anson said, "Perhaps I do feel remorse, but it's more than that. Something—something about this case, Ryan, One-Strap—I've never washed off its stink."

"Well, stink it was, Your Honor, to be sure. There's a great sewer beneath this city, and Patrick Ryan was only a single turd floating in it. That's the only democracy in this country, the sewer. The turds of the rich and the turds of the poor alike float side by side. Ryan was a turd and he'd be there yet, bobbing with the rest of them, if he hadn't been stupid, not just guilty, mind you, but stupid and overconfident as well."

"Then why are you here?" Anson demanded.

"My mick notion of duty, Your Honor, and—if I were to be telling the truth," Hoolihan paused here as if to underscore the conditional

112

nature of his revelation, "I'd have to say as well that when I heard of the Senator's death, I thought of Patrick Ryan. I went to his execution. I saw him lean forward and inhale the gas and I heard him use his last breath to curse with."

"Who did he curse?"

"Me, of course. You too, naturally. The very Senator we buried here today."

"Why the Senator?"

Hoolihan made a face. "For disloyalty, maybe? Don't forget, he expected to be Senator Ryan himself one day. He expected to die and be buried like your old man, Your Honor. As it was, there was a half dozen of us here, his wife, his mother, a couple of brothers. Me."

"You're loyal even unto the grave, aren't you, Hoolihan? You call it duty because you're embarrassed to be loyal."

"I'm embarrassed to be shivering in this cold by the grave of a guilty man when I could be enjoying a drop of warm whiskey in a friendly tavern. What do you say, Your Honor? Let me buy you a drink."

The wind sliced between them as Anson shook his head and explained that he had to join his family at the Senator's house. Hoolihan offered to drop him there. "You're not coming to the Senator's house, Hoolihan?"

Hoolihan's old cynical smile tugged at his lips. "Now how could I go there and tell his lovely widow how much he will be missed? Not by me. I despised him. Meaning no disrespect, Your Honor, but your father didn't give a tinker's damn for the rest of the world. He'd have baled up his own mother and shipped her to Tokyo if he thought he could make a buck off it."

The two men put on their hats simultaneously and walked back through the old section of the cemetery, their feet kicking fallen leaves. Presently, Anson said, "The Senator despised you too, Hoolihan."

"Ah, you've cheered my day, Your Honor. I was miserable every time I came to that mansion, drank the Senator's champagne, ate his oysters and roast beef, thinking that he might have liked me. It was enough to drive me to the arms of remorse. But if I know he despised me, I can walk proud again. I'll tell my old man. Maybe he'll start speaking to me again."

They had reached the street and thick, misty rain began to fall. Hoolihan directed Anson toward his car. "What's your father got to do with the Senator?" asked Anson.

"Nothing, Your Honor, and there you have it. That first night I was

113

asked to the reception honoring the lovely Mrs. Swallow, I had to rent evening clothes. I was the first Hoolihan since the days of the Irish kings to wear anything but a workingman's cap and a patched vest. My mother wept to see me, thrilled she was to think a Hoolihan was about to join the elite—Irish kings being in short supply. But my father—he spat at my shoes as I left the house. Lie down with dogs, he called after me, get up with fleas." Hoolihan shrugged. "You wouldn't be remembering the dock strike of 'thirty-eight, Your Honor, but my old man was a union man. God, he loved the union, loved it better than God Himself. Every time my mother went off to church, the old man would yell after her—pray for a strong union if you want something in this world and who gives a damn for the next! He's a kicker, my old man, but after that 'thirty-eight strike, he was never the same. Your father, the dear departed Senator up there, called in the scabs and it got bloody and my old man got the worst of it. His leg's never worked right since and what's that—sixteen years? The only jobs a cripple could get were beneath my father and anyway he said he wouldn't do any work that didn't have a union. My mother went out charring to support us. God, it set my teeth on edge to see her lug around that bucket and mop, hear her come in at five and start breakfast for the family. But she wouldn't hear of me dropping out of school, and that's when I vowed, Your Honor, that I'd be rich one day. But I was just a boy then and it was the war saved our bacon, Your Honor. Ma got a job in a factory and I joined up as soon as I could and had my pay sent home and so we did all right."

"You're doing all right now, I see," said Anson as Hoolihan put his key in the lock of a gleaming new Studebaker.

"The American way. The old folks have it all now. I've bought them a house, a real house with a garden and all, a television, washing machine, vacuum cleaner. You name it, they have it. I took them back to visit the Old Sod in September. But the money's nothing, is it? The money doesn't matter. My father still thinks I'm a scab for consorting with the Swallows." Hoolihan started up the Studebaker, and it purred. "Sure I can't interest you in that drink?"

"No."

"Well, I'll just have to drink alone then."

"I can't imagine you'll drink alone for very long, Hoolihan." Anson clutched the armrest as Hoolihan darted into traffic. "Not with your acquaintance in this city."

"A man can always find someone to drink with, Your Honor. It's

114

harder to find someone to drink to. I'll drink to you, though. You're the best judge in this city, and they all know it. From the highest to the lowest."

Anson was uncomfortably reminded of the sewer Hoolihan had alluded to, of democratic turds bobbing beneath the city's streets, and as if he too recollected his own words, Hoolihan added, "Even Patrick Ryan knew it. He cursed you before they gassed him, but he knew it."

V

Anson next saw Hoolihan some three weeks later, when the adult members of the Swallow family gathered in the Senator's attorney's office to hear the will. They seated themselves around the conference table, the attorney at its head, and waited for Lucille, who was late. The elderly attorney had evidently eaten something that disagreed with him; he look bilious and stifled recurring burps and glanced nervously at the clock. Dressed in a becoming suit of pewter gray, Lucille sailed in, followed by Hoolihan whom, she said, she had retained as her personal legal counsel and as such, he had every right to be there. She put a cigarette in a holder and Hoolihan lit it for her.

Still softly burping, the attorney untied the leather folder before him and began the dreary incantation of sound mind and body while George and Eleanor clutched hands and Althea sat stonily between Vera and Meg. Anson eyed Hoolihan, who refused to meet his gaze.

When he came at last to the meat of the matter, the attorney unzipped a package full of stomach tablets and the tearing paper grated like a chain saw. He chewed up a tablet, washed it down with a glass of water and took a deep breath. Lucille was named executrix of the will and described in florid terms of praise. ". . . my dear wife . . . my dear and best beloved Lucille . . . the light of my later years. . ." Anson saw her squash a smile. The attorney added an odd provision that anyone named in the will who dared to contest it would be automatically disinherited, just as if he or she had predeceased the Senator himself, and before the family could quite digest the implications thereof, the attorney read that Vera Courtney, George Swallow and Althea Swallow were to receive $10,000 each in cash.

"That's all?" Eleanor interrupted. "You're sure that's all?"

"I'm only reading the Senator's instructions, madam," said the attorney. He then went on, reading the praise that the Senator lavished on Anson for never disappointing him and the Senator hoped (from the grave, though this was not stated) that the bequest of $100,000 in cash would not disappoint Anson, who was not so much disappointed as shocked. Anson asked if perhaps the attorney hadn't read the figure wrong, misplacing the comma. "That can't be right," said Anson as he glanced around the table and saw George's eyes flicker with loathing and Althea's small mouth cinch shut. "Why isn't it equal? Why should I get—"

"I'm only reading what's here," said the attorney, and then he came to what was given to Lucille Swallow, a widow, as her sole and separate property: the Swallow mansion and all its grounds, furniture and effects, all cars, all insurance benefits, a lump sum of cash of $100,000 for her personal use and Swallow Lines. In its entirety.

The attorney had begun to elucidate what the entirety consisted of when Vera burst into tears and Althea popped like a bubble of venom. "No! That's ours! Swallow Lines is ours! Ours!"

George slid from his chair, picked himself up with some difficulty and made a lunge across the table for Lucille. "Nasty strumpet!" he cried. "Thieving, whoring, nasty little strumpet!" He actually laid his hands around the widow's creamy throat before Hoolihan could intervene and push him back. Anson grabbed his brother's coat and pulled him away, flinging him against the wall and holding him there while George struggled and kicked. The attorney said the rest of it could probably wait, and Lucille and Hoolihan made their exit.

Eleanor flung herself on George and begged him to calm down, but frothy cocoons of spittle formed at the corners of his mouth. "A drink!" Eleanor cried. "Get him a drink! It's the only way."

Meg hastily poured some of the attorney's water, but George knocked the glass from her hands and sent it flying while Althea dug in his pocket and withdrew the silver flask, uncorked it and put it to his lips. George sucked on it and then sank down the wall, sat on the floor and wept into his hands that he was ruined, ruined, that they were all ruined, while the three women clucked over him. The attorney no longer stifled his belches, and Anson looked on, dumbfounded. "All except the judge there," George suddenly shouted. "He's not ruined, is he? What did you do for the Senator, Anson? What did you ever do for him? I gave him my life! I spent every day of my life doing anything he asked of me. I took his orders! I worked like a slave! I gave him my life! What did you ever do?"

A knock sounded at the door, and Hoolihan entered, though without Lucille. He cleared his throat and in a low tone befitting the executioner's friend he asked to speak to Miss Swallow privately.

"Say what you will!" declared Althea over the stricken form of George. "Say it here and now, you dirty, mackerel-snapping mick!"

Hoolihan glanced at Anson. "Maybe it can wait."

"No." Althea rose to her feet. "Say it now and then quit fouling the air with your foul presence."

"My client, Mrs. Swallow, has asked me to instruct—to ask if you would please leave her house as soon as you possibly can. She does not believe that the two of you can live beneath the same roof and—"

"As if I'd live there! As if I'd stay one night in a house Lucille owned! You may tell your whoring client, Mr. Hypocrite Hoolihan, that I will live with my brother! I will go directly to Anson's house and send someone to pick up my things. I will never set foot in that house or speak to Lucille again as long as I live! Now leave us!"

"I wish I could, Miss Swallow." Hoolihan's fair skin mottled with discomfort. "But Mrs. Swallow had another message as well." He looked at George, collapsed on the floor, and then met Anson's hard eyes. "It can wait." He left the Swallows to themselves.

Lucille had charged Hoolihan not only to evict Althea but to inform George that he was fired as well. She did fire George, but Hoolihan prevailed upon her to do so in writing. He also said he wouldn't carry any more messages like that again, and besides, he added, written termination would be more forceful and legal.

Anson was in court the following Monday when a bailiff tapped his shoulder and said there was an urgent call for him. Anson granted a ten-minute recess and took the call in his chambers. It was Eleanor: George had got the letter in the morning mail and had gone off on an awful bender, vowing to kill Lucille.

"Keep him home," Anson instructed her. "I don't care how you do it. Bring in three men and a little boy to sit on him if you must, but keep him home at all cost. Leave this to me."

At the lunch recess Anson left the county courthouse and drove directly to his father's home. He did not knock, but burst into the foyer and directly into the library, where he confronted Lucille sitting at the desk, beside her old typewriter, which was put to more substantive use these days (she'd written the note to George on this machine and she could type with eight of her ten fingers now). Hoolihan sat across from her. He stood when Anson entered; he walked to the fireplace and leaned against the mantle.

"A social call, Anson?" said Lucille brightly. "Hoolihan and I were about to go in to lunch."

"You know why I've come."

"Let me guess. To offer your condolences? No? To discuss the weather—which is vile by the way, is it to—"

"George."

"Have a seat, Anson."

"No."

"Can't we discuss this like gentlemen?"

Anson writhed under the pleasantries, but thought perhaps they might be put into service. He lowered himself into the chair Hoolihan had vacated. "There must be some error."

"No error. George is a hopeless drunk, and drunks are unreliable."

"Lucille, I'm sure that George can be brought to his senses. I can safely swear to you that he'll sober up."

"I hope he does, but it doesn't matter to me, except of course that I regret seeing anyone I'm related to"—and her voluptuous mouth curved into an unmistakable smile—"slaver, publicly drunk, and refer to his father's widow as a nasty little strumpet. That was his phrase, wasn't it?"

"It wasn't public, and you have to allow for circumstances. George was shocked. We were all shocked that the Senator, that is, when the attorney read that—"

"In his infinite wisdom, your father left Swallow Lines to me?"

Anson measured his words, as if they could be used like stones against her. "How could you? How did you?"

"I did nothing. It was Eb's wish." She regarded Anson almost cheerfully. "Anyway, you shouldn't complain. You certainly came out of it better than any of the others."

"I am ashamed that my father did not leave us equal portions, ashamed to have been singled out for preferential treatment. I have offered to split the excess of my portion with the other three, but they won't hear of it."

"But they hate you all the same, don't they?"

The grandfather clock struck the quarter-hour and Hoolihan bent to prod the logs in the fireplace.

"I didn't come here to discuss that," Anson continued slowly. "It was unbecoming of you to dismiss George in such a peremptory fashion."

"It was unbecoming of him to refer to me as a nasty little strumpet. I am neither a strumpet nor little nor nasty."

Anson was inclined to disagree, but he held his peace. "Lucille, I shall see to it that George writes you a full apology. I will take full responsibility for his conduct in the future."

"That's very good of you Anson, but actually, I'm not smarting over George's remark. I don't even take it personally. And I didn't dismiss him for that reason, or even necessarily that he is a drunk. He is a fool, and that's why I dismissed him." She patted a three-foot stack of ledgers on the desk beside the typewriter. "Hoolihan and I have been all over these, and we concur that George is a fool. Look at these." She snapped through the pages, and they grated on Anson's ears like rifle reports. "George might just as well have given money away. He was a puppet in the hands of people who are smarter than he is. In the last few months, George has signed away—"

"In the last few years, the Senator left the business almost wholly in George's hands. It was not fair of the Senator. George wasn't used to that much responsibility. It stands to reason that he would make some mistakes."

"Some mistakes!" she crowed.

"The Senator should have kept a closer watch on Swallow Lines."

"And paid less attention to me—that's what you mean, isn't it? Well, I don't care. Eb deserved some fun. Money, money, money." Her voice tripped and trickled over those words. "That's all Eb knew or did or thought of before he married me."

"I'm not denying that you made him happy. I'm only saying that I do not think it just that in return for those few years of happiness, he should have left Swallow Lines entirely to you, and I think you coerced him to disinherit the rest of his family."

"No. Disinheriting the rest of you wasn't my intention. I didn't give a damn what he did with the rest of you, to be perfectly frank. I was—I am—looking after myself and my own interests. And my own future. You can't really believe that I'd be content to spend the rest of my days diddling with the Garden Club and the Art League and making sure there's no tarnish on the silver in this old barn, do you? It's true that I'm inexperienced in business and legal matters, but I've hired Hoolihan to help me, and I venture to say I'll do as well or better with Swallow Lines than any of you ever dreamed. I have all the right instincts, and now I have the opportunities."

"But what about George? He is a member of this family."

"But not of this firm."

"Lucille, do not do this. I beg of you. Keep him on, even if you give him no responsibility. At least let him think he has work and something to do in the world. It will be the end of him otherwise. Do it out of respect for the Senator's memory if nothing else. On principle."

"It isn't a question of respect or principle or family. I know what you think of me, all of you. I know Althea hired a detective to find out what she could about me. I never asked that the Swallows love me, but it is you"—she leveled her finger at Anson—"all of you, who should have shown some respect. Don't talk to me about family!"

Anson looked from Lucille to Hoolihan, who stared steadfastly into the fire, as if he could not bear to witness Anson's humiliation, and Anson realized for the first time what the prisoner must feel like in the dock, what the victim must feel like as he sees the knife poised over his throat. He thought of One-Strap Sophie and Patrick Ryan. He rose slowly. "The Senator shaped and wrecked and ruined people's lives without a qualm or thought to the consequences as long as he could be certain those consequences would not include him. He was my father, but I can say this of him nonetheless: he respected nothing but money—not my mother or his sons or his daughters or such friends as he could lay claim to. He never had a friend who was not financially beneficial to him. You probably didn't notice that about my father because you don't have any respect either, Lucille, no sense of dignity or rightness or justice. My father was a man of passions, not principles. His passions were those of power. I don't know what your passions are, Lucille, but I know you haven't any principles either. You were well suited to one another."

"Get out. Throw him out, Hoolihan."

Hoolihan remained rooted, raising his gaze only from the fire to the window.

Anson continued coldly, "I will not allow my family to be ground like chaff between stones of your making, Lucille."

"Really? Does that mean that one or all of you will risk losing the pittance he left you to contest the will?"

Anson's whole body sagged and slumped. "None of us ever had the courage to contest my father's will while he lived and directed our lives. It would be unthinkable to contradict him in a courtroom. No one will do that."

"Well then, what do you want from me? Sympathy? Pity?" She lingered over the word, savoring it.

"We don't need your pity, but I assure you that we—that I at least—contest this will morally."

"Oh that, well—" She smiled benignly. "Anyway, you came out of it ninety thousand dollars richer than the rest, didn't you? Are you contesting that morally, too? For all your talk of principle, I don't see you asking where that money came from or why."

Shock twisted Anson's features. "Was it for something or from somewhere in particular?" he demanded.

"How do I know? Money talks. Shit walks."

"You're just another turd bobbing in the sewer, Lucille." Anson felt free to indulge in the vulgar, since she had. "You will be called to account for the wrong you've done. One day you will."

"One day we all will, I expect." She gave him the benefit of her beautiful blue eyes. "But in the meantime and in this deck, Your Honor, I am holding all the aces."

Anson turned on his heel and stalked to the door. The grandfather clock struck the half-hour and he paused, his hand on the knob, and waited till Hoolihan looked up. "Lie down with dogs," Anson said to Hoolihan, "get up with fleas."

CHAPTER FIVE

May 2, 1985

3:57 P.M.

Lucky Stone was punched full of tubes. He lay in a cubicle in intensive care, partitioned with a stiff white cloth, on a narrow hospital bed that more correctly resembled a slab. He was prone, groaning and groggy and connected by wires to a panel of electronically flashing lights and beeping meters. He opened his eyes very slowly, blinded by the icy overhead lights and the overwhelming whiteness. The partitions of stark white he took for angel's wings or the hem of God's robe, and he was happy to have got to heaven rather than hell. He closed his eyes and waited to see what would happen next. Whose voice. What questions. Then he itched and in trying to move his arm to scratch, he was shot through with pain and more pain: heaven and hell would both have to wait. He was alive. He began to weep with joy.

"I'm saved." The words formed with a thick mucus that coated his tongue and lips and teeth. "I'm saved. I'm alive and I'm saved. Thank you, God. Oh God, thank you." He opened his eyes, and tears ran down the sides of his face into his hair; he could hear the beeping monitors now, human voices, the ring and hum of the hospital. Once again he tried to move and was assaulted by pain; he began to blubber grateful thanks for his salvation, but the cry fell back into his throat and he swallowed it joyously, ecstatic to be reunited with his own imperfect mortality, astonished that pain could bring him so much pleasure, convinced that God had stayed his hand for some great, grave purpose he would discover in the days that were left to him.

CHAPTER SIX

September 1962

Claire Swallow had the last Victorian girlhood in America. Instilled in her by both precept and example were the elements of Decency, Decorum and Dignity, all of which collided with her character and native instincts. When she left home in the fall of 1962 and went to the university she believed that at last she could be shut of the Three D's forever and do as she liked. She did do as she liked, though she could not altogether squash these fussy Victorian maxims. The Three D's were Victorian because they were not grounded on any particular religious principles; they were predicated on and could only be vindicated in the eyes of other people. Convention masquerading as morality. Custom disguised as virtue. The Three D's had served Meg Swallow well because nothing in her experience ever called them into question. Meg had inherited them from her mother, who had doubtless got them from her mother and so on, as far back as there were young ladies whose purpose in this life was to acquire a suitable husband and keep him happy. Girls brought up on the Three D's made only one choice in this world: whom to marry. Of course they *would* marry because ambition is vulgar, after all, ability threatening, achievement suspect: men are to be cultivated, placated, and women urged to seek their satisfactions in the realm of influence, perhaps even inspiration, but gain, greed and power were all to be shunned; they sullied a girl's sweetness, imperiled her natural proclivity to niceness. To be sweet and nice—indeed, to be thought sweet and nice—did and ought to suffice. Men would recognize sweetness and reward it. Women, too, for that matter. And if Decency, Decorum and Dignity finally resulted in a woman's debility, what of it? As long as one had a good husband, what more did one need? Meg Swallow had a good husband. Others less fortunate could only hobble through life, metaphorically crippled by the Three D's, much like Chinese girls whose feet had been painfully bound since babyhood.

By 1968, of course, all that would be gloriously shot to hell. A girl of, say, Marietta's vintage could trash the Three D's with impunity, even glee, trade sweetness for swagger, throw herself headlong into destruction with the full approval of her peers, and relish her ability to say "fuck off" even (if need be) to her own mother. But in 1962, Claire Swallow, rebellious as she was, could not leap the confines of her time and had not the courage or conviction to live ahead of it. Her antics at the university earned her a pleasing notoriety, but she could not shuck off the Three D's without suffering loss and the most profound confusion.

Anson Swallow did not wholeheartedly subscribe to the Three D's. Claire had talent, Anson thought, talent and will, though not perhaps in equal measure. With talent and will, all she needed was time and he hoped that after the university, she would go to the Pacific Conservatory and train as a concert pianist. Meg concurred with Anson's dreams for Claire because she disliked contradicting him needlessly, but privately her mother believed that Claire's musical abilities would find their best expression soothing a cross, overworked husband. Indeed, Meg believed this mythical husband could be best sought and found at a private university like Stanford, but Anson refused to entertain the notion. Concomitant with his democratic vistas, the judge believed in the public schools, and so, when Claire graduated from the public high school in 1962, she went to the state university where, according to Anson, merit rather than money was rewarded.

Claire was more adept at demerits. She had the honor of being the only freshman hauled before the redoubtable housemother, Mrs. Jonah, and Whitney Hall's judiciary committee when they first convened at the end of September. In fact she was brought up on two counts: she had been caught coming through a first-floor window after curfew with a number of hickeys on her neck (and lower), though the hickeys had faded and were not mentioned in the proceedings. Five demerits and suitable punishment were pronounced, and then Claire had to back out into the hall and be called in again to face charges of having unbolfaded and were not mentioned in the proceedings. Five demerits and suitable punishment were pronounced, and then Claire had to back out into the hall and be called in again to face charges of having unbolted all the toilet seats in the bathroom on her fourth-floor hall. She denied it to the end, but the circumstantial evidence was overwhelming: one girl testified that Claire Swallow had giggled uncontrollably at the resulting splashdowns and another testified that she had seen Claire Swallow, hammer, wrench and screwdriver in hand, in the bathroom at three o'clock in the morning on the night in question. Claire got five more demerits for this escapade and the stern admonition that anything further would result in social probation.

By November 1962, Claire Swallow had garnered the praise of her music professors, a slot in a posh sorority and the respect of a bunch of fraternity boys, who had drunkenly dared her to steal the metal poster with a picture of Uncle Sam and I WANT YOU swinging from hinges in front of the Army Recruiting Center. (She stole it all by herself, though she used one of their cars to transport the sign back to her dorm room in Whitney Hall, where its presence absolutely awed her roommate, Melinda Lamott.)

Melinda was a big-boned, timid girl, a mathematics major whom Claire bullied shamelessly. Particularly after the incident with the I WANT YOU poster (never mind the number of men who called Claire up for dates), Melinda regarded her with wonder and an adoring envy. Claire, in fact, had so many dates that she could pick and choose and did so only amongst men in the top two fraternities, leaving the crumbs and parings to Melinda. However, these men usually only dated Melinda once, but then, Melinda didn't put out and Claire did.

She didn't exactly go All The Way, but she thoroughly enjoyed the fraternity parties every Friday and Saturday night, consumed her share of beer, danced to wailing surf songs, flirted shamelessly, necked and petted with abandon. Throughout all this she remained nice and sweet. Relentlessly nice, unfailingly sweet: Claire listened to her date's feats of prowess on the football field or his activities in student government, always asked after his major and where he went to high school. And indeed, men recognized her sweetness, rewarded her niceness and inevitably found her enchanting, charming; they longed to kiss her, and she let them. That and more. Claire sometimes wondered, as she felt the fraternity man tentatively exploring the rim of her breasts with his thumb, if men had feeling in their thumbs, but by the time he had grabbed her breasts like a couple of onions at the produce counter, the question was moot and the pleasure too intense

126

to be anything but savored.

However, the first boy who actually got his hand up underneath her skirt and on those three inches of flesh above her stocking—that boy, she slapped. "Royally," she informed Melinda, sitting crosslegged in front of the mirror on the closet door in their room. She was tweezing her eyebrows and flinched with every pluck.

"What did he do?" Melinda put down her slide rule and stared at Claire.

"He got angry, of course. I don't see why. He shouldn't have done it."

"But, Claire, you let him, I mean before that, you let him—"

"I probably let him go too far," Claire conceded, "but I was playing by the rules. He's the one who broke them." She tweezed and winced. "I sat there and lapped up his every word and convinced him he was the best man since Moses and that I couldn't wait to kiss him."

"Then why did you slap him?"

"Well, I had to, of course. We're *supposed* to make men want us, to touch and kiss us, aren't we? And we're *supposed* to slap them if they do anything else!"

"You ought to get yourself a boyfriend, Claire."

"I've got too many as it is."

"No, I mean just one. One boyfriend. Then you could do what you wanted with him, and it would be okay and you wouldn't look bad. You have a bad reputation," she added gravely.

"Chickenspittle. I'm in the best sorority there is, aren't I?"

"That's because your father is a judge and your grandfather was a senator," Melinda reminded her (though until she met Claire, Melinda Lamott had never heard of Senator Swallow, or indeed of Swallow Lines. Melinda was from some dreary downstate burg called St. Elmo, where her father worked for the railroad). "I've heard people talking about you, and they're not saying very nice things."

"They're just jealous. My weekends are booked up with dates by Tuesday afternoon."

"Maybe, but you're getting a bad reputation anyway. You should choose one boy and get pinned and then you could sleep with him and no one would think the worse of you. Really. My mother says you can sleep with a man if you're going to marry him."

"Your mother said that!" Claire turned from the mirror to regard Melinda with horror; she could not imagine Meg considering any such latitude, much less suggesting it.

"Hindsight, I think. I was born seven months after my parents were married."

"Well, that's not going to happen to me. Look what I've got." Claire got up off the floor and went to her top dresser drawer and withdrew a round plastic packet with blue foil inside and little white pills set in a dial. "The pill. I got them last week. Six months' supply! What do you think of that?" she demanded triumphantly. "Of course I had to tell the doctor I was getting married and let him put his clammy hand up me. But it was worth it."

"But you're a virgin, aren't you?"

"Of course." Offended, Claire put the pills back in her drawer. "But I thought I might as well be realistic. I'm not going to have anything squalid—" she rolled the word out carefully "—happen to me!"

"But, Claire, only girls who—the only girls who take these are girls who—"

"Sleep around."

"Yes!" Melinda was genuinely alarmed.

"Well I don't intend to do that, naturally, but I don't intend to get pregnant like Julie Masterson down the hall."

"Julie!"

"Haven't you heard her barfing every morning and crying her eyes out every night? It's probably her high school boyfriend, who comes up here on weekends, you know the one, the guy who looks like he keeps his brains in the vegetable drawer. God, I'd kill myself before I'd get knocked up by a jerk like that. She'll be married and out of here before Thanksgiving. You watch."

"Poor Julie. I bet she wishes she hadn't done it."

"I bet she wishes she'd been on the pill. Only fools get pregnant."

By Thanksgiving, Julie Masterson had indeed dropped out of school and Claire Swallow had parted with her virginity, donated it drunkenly during a fraternity party to a good-looking organic chemistry major who had been president of his high school and captain of their tennis team, but she couldn't quite get his name straight—was it Ted or Ned?—and she was too embarrassed to ask again after he had urged her tight green slacks down her legs and the fuzzy pink sweater over her head and Claire could feel every ounce of blood throbbing, congealing in the epicenter of her body; she arched her back slightly, kissed him and wrapped her arms around his back as the surfing sounds of the Del Tones wailed at the party downstairs. It hurt less than she thought it would.

Physically, that is. Girls brought up on the Three D's suffered mentally from the loss of virginity. And loss it was. They had no time to

128

revel in discovery because they went into mourning for that loss and calculated its implications vis-à-vis a mythical husband. In the week after the incident with Ted—or Ned—Claire was subject to spells of weeping and the making of impossible vows. She even held a midnight ceremony over the toilet, with Melinda as witness as she punched out all the little white pills and flushed them away. Melinda said she ought to hang on to at least one packet. "You never know," Melinda counseled. "You might change your mind."

"Never," Claire assured her, tucking one packet in the pocket of her robe.

To make matters worse, the Sunday after the incident with Ted (he called and this time she got his name straight; Ned was a physical chemistry major), Meg came to visit Claire for her sorority's annual mother-daughter tea. The sight of Meg—beautiful, poised, confident and so assured—threw Claire into a fit of remorse and rectitude. Thereafter, she went to every class and studied diligently every night; each afternoon for three hours she practiced the piano in the basement of the music building, furiously perfecting her sonatas. She went out but not down and only allowed her dates to kiss her good night, though she was dismayed that good night became goodbye and her phone no longer rang with its old regularity. Claire's reputation followed her, and when she did not live up to it (or down), fraternity boys were less than impressed with her and more than one let her out of his car in front of Whitney Hall without bothering to walk her in. Most poignantly, she missed the admiration she had collected from men, and even Melinda Lamott seemed to think Claire less interesting once she had resolved to be like everyone else—no longer careless, rebellious and wanton.

Her confusion was almost intolerable the first Saturday night that Claire found herself dateless. Much to her chagrin, she discovered the unwritten rule of college life: a girl could not go anywhere alone (except possibly to the library). Without a man, a girl was socially naked. In the absence of a single man, she required the company of lots of other girls to avoid looking conspicuously solitary and hopelessly undesirable. Moreover, Claire had actually enjoyed being fondled like a bunch of onions at the produce counter, and once aroused, if not satisfied, she found herself picturing the men in her classes naked, wondering how they kissed and enjoying the sticky sensations these considerations engendered. Nonetheless, she kept her knees crossed (properly crossed knees were the mark of a lady) as she imagined herself in luxurious beds with the most attractive of them. Though she kept her knees crossed, it could not be denied that Claire had once uncrossed them, admitted a man between the portals of her thighs, and having done that, a girl had to resort, in fact was compelled, to manufacture putative virginity, or at least inexperience, each time she went down, allowing each new lover to think he was the first.

This, in fact, is exactly what Claire did within a matter of weeks, whispered sweetly to her date that she was afraid because he was the first; he rewarded her sweetness and candor by being particularly quick. Thoughtful of him, considering how drunk they both were. Claire Swallow lost her virginity a number of times before Christmas vacation, but she also lost sleep, weight and confidence, and the more she lost her confidence, the more she relied on men to give it back to her. In the reflection of her dorm room mirror, Claire could see the Uncle Sam and I WANT YOU, but all her daring notwithstanding, she suspected she was vain and shallow and unconventional for all the wrong reasons.

Her situation was not made any easier when she returned home for Christmas. Before her daily was her mother's sterling example, which made Claire feel like cheap flatware. Her father, always a source of unreflected pride and unconditional love, seemed distracted, even unwell, unwilling or unable to give Claire the applause and approbation she so needed. Anson let some of her finest piano playing pass without comment.

Claire was a thoroughly confused, unhappy young woman when she returned to the university in January. Leaving the practice rooms one dank Thursday afternoon, she glanced at the music department's billboard and saw a tattered flyer announcing an appearance that very night by Nicholas Kerchiaeff. Claire was surprised that the great Russian pianist was alive at all; Kerchiaeff was so legendary, she had assumed he was dead. She enlisted Melinda to go with her because, of course, she could not go alone.

Claire was surprised to walk into the small half-filled lecture hall and see only a podium, no piano. She was disturbed to note that the man sitting on the stage (whom she assumed to be Kerchiaeff) did not look at all legendary: tall and balding, his hair hung in greasy strands too near his cadaverous mushroom-colored face; he had a weak chin and his eyes brooded behind thick glasses. She was alarmed when someone from poli sci introduced Kerchiaeff and made no reference to a concert or even a recital and moreover peppered his remarks with allusions to Soviet tyranny and the benefits of American democracy. Claire wondered what tyranny or democracy had to do with music.

"I thought you said this was a concert," Melinda whispered.

"I thought it was," Claire replied, but by then it was too late to leave, as Kerchiaeff had begun his address. Claire was at first astonished but finally simply bored when Kerchiaeff failed to mention even one of the immortal names of music; instead, speaking in sharp, harsh English, he heaped invective on the Soviet regimes and called for an end to Communism and oppression. She grew restless, doodling treble clefs and quarter-notes and trying to squelch the bass rumbling of her stomach. It would be rude to leave, but how could you care about anyone who would spurn music to wax on about a revolution that had happened long before most people were born or even thought of? Her interest in him grew only when Kerchiaeff quit heaping abuse on theoretical political systems and began the harrowing tale of his escape from Russia during the civil war, forty years ago, he explained, weeping unabashedly, to this very day.

"Revolution und civil war, those double scourges uff humanity, left the Roossian peoples starving und homeless, but the soul uff Roossia is its music! that night—forty years ago—the Roossian peoples come to my concert in rags und blankets, felt tied to their feets, they vade through the Siberian blizzard to the opera house uff a provincial city. Even before the curtain goes up, ve in the orchestra, ve hear vhispers in the audience—the Red Army haf broken through! They are at the city gates! They haf burnt everything. They haf drawn und quartered women und childrens! But vhen the lights come down und the conductor raises his baton, the Roossian peoples hush to honour music. Imagine, if you vill, if you can, *music*. Death und desolations everywhere! But the thrill uff music to ears that haf heard only screams uff anguish, cries uff mourning, shrieks uff pain." Kerchiaeff blew his nose on a yellowed handkerchief and collected himself. "In the middle uff the second movement, the doors bursted open, guns blahst und ve are all arrested by a peeg uff a Red Army captain. A peeg! Before the revolution, that captain vas a peasant, grubbing for roots to eat raw. Now, he shoots hole in the cello. He cracks the violin across the face uff the conductor."

Kerchiaeff actually throttled the podium till it shook and recounted how everyone in the theater was marched into the snow. The women were ordered home, and those who would not comply were beaten and shoved off with gun butts to the belly. The men were lined up

131

against the back of the opera house by the light of torches. The captain told them all to take off such boots and coats as they had, and the scarecrow Red Army soldiers fell on the clothing like dogs until the captain shot his pistol into the air. The captain then started at one end of the line and demanded of each man what he did for a living. Those who were not workers were dragged off and shot, a pistol to their heads, their brains splattering in the snow.

Kerchiaeff could not control himself and wept openly as he continued. "The peeg captain comes to the man beside me. That man cries—I am worker—I am worker! The peeg captain says to him, 'Let me see your hands.' The man turns his hands over und the captain spits in them. He says, 'These are not the hands of the proletariat, these are hands uff a bourgeois svine.'" Kerchiaeff pressed his fingers to his eyes. "That man, he does not march uff. He shoot him where he stands. I turn my head or his blood vill fly in my eyes. Then he comes to me. I make my peace with God—I vill die a martyr to my country und my art, but I vill not grovel before a peeg. I am Roossian, I tell him, a musician, an artist! I hold out my hands." Kerchiaeff held out his hands to the audience and Claire could see that they were fibrous and long-fingered and enormously strong. "The peeg says to me, 'A musician, eh?' He picks up a violin and a bow out uff the snow und pooshes them into my face. 'Then play,' he commands me. I am pianist, I tell him. The peeg says to me: 'You vill play this bloody violin or you vill be dead meat.'" Kerchiaeff seemed to wither before their eyes. "Und so—I play, I bless my sainted mother for making me learn the violin, und I play what little I know und I bless God I can play at all. I vant to veep, but not before this peeg. Never! At last the peeg tells me, 'Go, you haf played your last concert tonight.' Und so, with the blood uff the man beside me still staining my bare feets, I run through snow and I keep running until I escape my homeland, till I come to the Vest, vhere I live, an orphan, ever since."

A round of enthusiastic applause followed and a few people raised their hands with political and historical questions of which Claire knew little and cared nothing. She had heard quite enough from the maestro. She ditched her doodling, put on her car coat and was just about to step on feet all the way along her aisle when a voice rang out from the back of the crowd. "I have one last question for Mr. Kerchiaeff! If this Red Army captain was a swine, was it not because the old regime kept its peasants living like pigs? No, worse than pigs. Pigs at least are fattened for the kill. Did the czar fatten his serfs before he sent them off to die in the trenches by the thousands—by the millions? And is it not true that the nobility walked on the backs of the serfs for thousands of years before the Russian people rose up against them and instituted a new order?"

"Who is this man?" cried Kerchiaeff. "A Bolshevik? A—"

"I am a student of history. History teaches us that when the offices of government become temples to tyranny, they must come down. People may tolerate oppression for a thousand years, but the day will come when they will throw off their corrupt oppressors."

"Vhere are the police?" Kerchiaeff demanded. "This man is mad!"

No one called the police, but all eyes turned toward the man who stood at the back of the hall. He was young, rather scruffy looking, dressed in blue jeans and a leather flight jacket that had crumbled to the consistency of old liver, but he did not look mad. His eyes were as clear as his voice; he had a thin nose and dark hair and a mouth too voluptuous for a man. He did not sit down; he called out, "Only fascist swine call on the police to defend them, Kerchiaeff!"

"I know him," Claire whispered to Melinda. "I'm sure I do." But at the second glance, she wasn't at all certain, only aware that something had plucked at her memory, clawed through a veil of—what? Cold earth. Cold day. Cold. The smell of dank, just turned earth and wilting flowers.

The poli sci professor moved quickly to the podium and profusely thanked Kerchiaeff, who was still calling for the police and an end to Communism. People began to leave very quickly, as if he had called fire. The young man sat back down and stared, oddly, at his hands.

Take his hand Claire. Take the little boy's hand downhill awash in a sea of black with Mama and Bart and a little girl and father kneeling before the little boy before we all go downhill. Where? *To the car. Yes. The little boy holds my hand.*

The hall was emptying quickly. "Let's catch up with him," said Claire, hurrying out.

Once on the sidewalk, Claire looked for the young man, but she was caught in an eddy of unfamiliar backs and faces till she noticed people nodding toward the man in the leather flight jacket walking by himself. "That's him." She tugged at Melinda's hand and they stepped quickly into his wake, catching up with him under a street lamp, shivering in a pool of granular, foggy light. "Excuse me," she called out. "Excuse me." He turned to her but did not smile, and she wished she had not spoken. "Don't I know you? Don't we know each other?"

"I doubt it," he replied, glancing dubiously at her shiny pumps, red wool pleated skirt and smart car coat.

"I'm Claire Swallow," she said brightly. "I'm a music major."

"I don't have any music classes."

"I mean I think we met a long time ago. A funeral."

"Claire Swallow? Your father's the judge?"

"Yes."

"Your grandfather's funeral. Senator Swallow's?"

"Yes. Aren't you Lucille's boy? I held your hand in the car. Don't you remember? You were terribly upset."

A frown puckered his forehead. "Not over your grandfather's death, I wasn't. He was a capitalist pig. He was nothing to me. But I remember the funeral. You sat across from us."

"Yes, yes, we did. But I've forgotten your name. I know it isn't Swallow, though."

"Cotton. Jon Cotton. How did you recognize me now?"

"I don't know, really." Claire gave an ungainly laugh and rather wished she hadn't recognized him; he made her uncomfortable and she thought she might trot out some morsel of flattery that usually warmed men to her, but something in his demeanor dissuaded her. "This is my roommate, Melinda Lamott. We're going to the Man Bites Dog for something to eat. Would you like to come? It's not very far," she added irrelevantly.

"No, Claire," Melinda protested. "We're going home to study for our lab test tomorrow. Remember."

"Oh, damn biology!" said Claire, feeling quite unfettered and un-conventional and showing off.

"Well, I can't," said Melinda. "I have to study and so should you."

"What do I care what the insides of a fetal pig look like? Besides, they smell bad."

Melinda dutifully left them, but Jon and Claire walked to the Man Bites Dog and ordered Cokes and chili dogs in stiff paper collars. They took them on a tray to the back, where two young men were arm wres-tling and three or four others placing bets. Nearby, a young couple necked over the remains of their hot dogs. On second thoughts, Claire wished she had persuaded Melinda to stay; people would think Jon was her date and he wasn't her type at all, not well dressed and he needed a haircut. Claire was about to ask where he'd gone to high school, but she didn't really care. She was more interested in why he'd burst out at Kerchiaeff like that. "I thought he was going to shoot you," she added.

134

"I couldn't just sit there and let him milk the audience without offering a dissenting voice. These moral questions," Jon seemed to sneer visibly over the phrase, "they can't be discussed without a historical context. You can't judge Lenin by Stalin. You can't judge the revolution by the purges. Revolutions don't happen because people are nasty and ill-tempered. They happen out of historical imperative, and sometimes the historical imperative marches over people. There is no revolution without excess and the wonder of the Russian Revolution is not that it happened, but that it took as long as it did. Hundreds and hundreds of years of oppression. It would have happened without Lenin, but how often do the man and moment match? Lenin seized his moment—1917—but he'd been preparing for it his whole life, ever since the czar executed his brother. You knew that, didn't you?"

"Your hot dog's getting cold," was all Claire could think of to say.

"I did it in the interest of fairness," Jon replied in answer to her original question. "I have no feelings for Kerchiaeff one way or the other."

"He's a very great pianist, you know."

"He's a reactionary bigot. A fascist in sheep's clothing."

"But he's one of the greatest pianists who ever lived."

Jon shrugged. "What does music matter? We're talking politics, history. Nero could play the fiddle, but it doesn't attest to his worth as a human being."

As Jon talked politics and history, Claire found herself lost in a maze of many "isms", strange dates, weird places, thick German and Russian names. She wished she had asked him where he went to high school.

"I'm a committed anarchist," he explained at last, adding that he scorned communism, loathed fascism and had nothing but contempt for liberal democracy, which had had its day. "The day of the anarchist is coming. Only anarchism can unleash the human potential. I'm for the individual," he added flatly.

"But aren't anarchists, don't they—" There was something ugly about the term, but she could not think what it was.

"Don't confuse us with terrorists. Anarchism is a philosophical position just like existentialism or empiricism. Capitalism isn't the only obstacle to world peace. The old philosophies are bankrupt."

"I see." Claire watched him wolf down his hot dog and wondered what her father would say when she told him she'd met Lucille's son. Then she wondered if she would tell him.

"I haven't seen her in two years," Jon replied in answer to Claire's inquiry about Lucille. "She brings out the worst in people. No one can

135

come within a half mile of my mother and retain his integrity. I could go the rest of my life without seeing her and be happy."

"Do you hate her?"

"I scarcely know her. I was ten when I got yanked out of the apartment where I'd spent my whole life and marched off to boarding school. I've been away ever since. I don't want to know her. I steer clear. I feel sorry for my sister, though. She doesn't have that option, just because she's a girl."

Claire could picture the plump, polite little girl they'd taken in their car the day of the funeral, but she couldn't remember her name.

"Lucy Rose does whatever Mother tells her. Whatever anyone tells her, for that matter. She's been brought up to be a spineless little ornament and she'll never be able to take charge of her own life."

"What do you mean?"

"Oh, like the letter I got from her yesterday. Mother's taking her on a cruise this spring. Swallow Lines, naturally. Far be it for Mother to part with a penny she could clutch. Lucy Rose is actually excited. Can you imagine? Mother's only doing it to get her a rich husband. You watch—Lucy Rose will be married off within the year, before she can make up her own mind about anything, much less men."

"Well, couldn't Lucy Rose just refuse to get married?"

Jon snorted and crunched on his ice. "You don't know my mother." (And since this was true, Claire could hardly argue the point.) "Have you heard what she's going to do with your grandfather's house?" He leaned forward so that his intensity seemed to engulf Claire. "She's giving the whole damn thing, house, gardens, art collections, to the city. For a fat tax write-off. Don't kid yourself. She doesn't do anything without there being money in it somewhere. She'll probably get a long-term lease on the penthouse apartment of some fancy hotel. She likes lots of people fawning over her publicly. Privately too," he added, "if Hoolihan is any example."

"Hoolihan?" asked Claire, feeling vaguely that, like Marx and Engels, it was a name she ought to know.

"Mother's lawyer and lover. He's been fucking her for years."

Claire backed off, shocked at the use of the word to describe the actual act and ascribed to his own mother. She hoped the people around her hadn't heard it, but the arm wrestlers and the lovers were gone and the Man Bites Dog was all but empty. "How can you say that about your own mother?"

"Why shouldn't I? It's the truth."

"But it's—"

"Vulgar?" a light twinkled in his dark eyes. "I can't help being vulgar. I enjoy it. Anyway, I probably come by it naturally. Mother's vulgar. She tries not to be, but she can't help it and all her friends are vulgar, rich, sniveling and hypocritical. Hoolihan's the worst of them. The great guardian of the oppressed! The only attorney who'll battle the establishment on behalf of the little guy and not charge him a cent! Bullshit. He's a dog at my mother's feet. He's a pimp, and he lives off her money. A hypocrite. He's been corrupted to his core. I despise him and I despise her."

"But you let her send you to the university."

"Who says? I'm here on my own steam. I burn her checks. She's not getting my soul. I work. I wash dishes in the Chinese restaurant across the street from where I live. For the time being. I'm thinking about leaving the university altogether."

"Are you on probation?"

"I get straight A's," he said with unintentional pride. "But while I'm here studying history, history is being made somewhere else. I'd rather be where it's being made. I'd like to live in the forge of history."

"The forge of history," Claire repeated as if it were a geographically knowable place.

They flicked the lights twice in the Man Bites Dog and the few remaining patrons ambled out. "What time is it?" Claire asked.

He glanced at his watch. "Ten of eleven."

"Oh, I'll never make it!" She grabbed her coat and thrust her arms in. "I have to hurry. Curfew. I'll be locked out."

They flew up Union Street in the direction of Whitney Hall and they were halfway there when the big clock at the University Presbyterian Church began its tolling. "My watch says you still have a couple of minutes. You want to make a run for it?"

"I'm done for. If I get there late and they see me—I've already got ten demerits. They'll put me on social pro. It will kill my mother." The big clock struck its eleventh hour. "I'll be thrown out of school, and my family will be humiliated and never forgive me," Claire moaned.

"Do they do a bed check in the dorms?"

"Only if there's a fire drill. If there's a drill and you're out, you're dead."

"Do they have fire drills often?"

"They haven't had one yet."

"Well, chances are they won't have one tonight either. You're safe, without a fire drill, aren't you? I mean if you just come in tomorrow like nothing happened, they'll never know you stayed out all night."

Claire shivered, enviously eyeing groups of college boys, some of them drunk, roistering down the street. "Why do girls have curfew? Boys don't."

"Do you have a friend who lives off campus? I'll walk you there."

She shook her head. "Only my sorority sisters, and even they have a curfew."

"You could stay with me if you wanted. I have a small apartment not far from here. It's not very comfortable, but it's better than nothing. Come on, you might as well."

Embarrassed and angry with herself, Claire reluctantly followed him down Union toward Western; she figured her chances would be better with a confirmed anarchist than Mrs. Jonah and the judiciary committee.

Jon Cotton lived in an old house that had been carved into a great many tiny apartments let to men only. On the ground floor there was a rare book and map store, its windows grilled and darkened. He told Claire to wait there while he checked to make sure his landlady, Mrs. Schripp, was asleep. He came back out the front door and beckoned to her.

Jon put his fingers to his lips, and she followed him into a narrow vestibule with a door fronting it that had the word MANAGER scrawled at eye level. They tiptoed up two flights of stairs lit by naked bulbs. The place smelled of men; Claire had never before quite realized that men had their own smell. Jon put his key in the lock of number four and ushered her into a small room and pulled the chain on the bulb overhead; the fixture swung and momentarily the room seemed to rock. The walls were lined with orange crates stacked to make bookshelves; a single iron bedstead stood in the corner, and beside it, an overstuffed chair on a braided rug. Where there had once been a fireplace, there was a heater; Jon bent and switched it on. "It'll warm up in a few minutes," he assured her. "Mrs. Schripp is very strict about leaving the furnace going."

Claire could see why: the room, the entire building, seemed dry, rickety, little better than kindling. She noted a sink, drainingboard, tiny cupboard, a refrigerator and a hotplate. Jon took her coat and hung it on a peg at the back of the door beside his own jacket. Claire smoothed the white angora of her sweater as if it were a kitten that had suddenly jumped on her shoulder. She sat—careful to cross her knees—in the overstuffed chair. "This is very—" She sought some pleasantry, but it eluded her, as they had all evening.

"It's a roach-infested, rat-ridden slum, but the rent is the cheapest I could find—short of a basement apartment. I can't stand to live without a window."

The much prized window was hung with frayed gingham curtains. It was long and narrow, betraying the age of the building and afforded a view of Western Avenue's small shops, including a flashing green neon sign that read JADE SEA. "Is that where you work? The Jade Sea?"

He nodded. "Would you like a beer?"

Claire declined; she'd never been in a situation with a man—a strange man at that—that she couldn't get out of, just waltz on back to Whitney Hall if the notion so took her. "I have to go to the bathroom," she said. "Where is it?"

"Down the hall. Just a minute. I'll check to make sure the coast is clear. Here, I'll get you a clean towel." He reached in the bottom of the dresser and drew out a thin cotton towel and handed it to her with a bar of harsh-smelling soap. He stuck his head out the door and bade her follow him down the hall to the bathroom. "Just make sure you lock the door," he cautioned her.

Needlessly, Claire thought. The bathroom was wretched unto grisly: the plumbing wept incessantly and a grim ring encircled the tub; the whole placed smelled of bleach and urine, and Claire did not sit on the toilet. She washed her hands at the sink and stared at her reflection in the badly cracked mirror. "What am I doing here? I set out tonight to listen to a pianist and I've ended up—" *You haven't ended up yet*, the reflection seemed to say. *The evening isn't over.* She checked the red bow on the barrette holding her hair in place and peered down the hall. Seeing no one (save for a mouse, which darted back into the woodwork), she bolted to number four. She had forgotten the towel and soap.

"That's all right," said Jon. "I'll get them later." The room had warmed and cheered. Jon was rolling a cigarette, and the kettle on the hot plate hissed. "I thought you might like a cup of tea to warm up. Jasmine tea, just like we have at the Jade Sea."

Claire took her seat again and glanced around the room; over the desk there was pinned a black flag, which Jon told her was the anarchists' symbol, and below it an old Woodstock typewriter, which he said had belonged to his father. There were no other adornments save for a framed formal portrait on the dresser, a girl whose hair was lacquered in a bouffant French roll and who held a fur stole about her shoulders, and beside it, a rather jauntier snapshot of the same girl in a tennis dress.

"My sister, Lucy Rose," he said, noting Claire's curiosity.

"She's very pretty."

"She's doomed for all that." He lit the cigarette and held the smoke in his lungs. He offered it to Claire.

"I don't smoke, thanks."

"This is a reefer. Marijuana. Ever tried it?"

"No. What do you do?"

"You take a deep drag and then you let it out slowly." Which is what he did.

Claire took the reefer gingerly, pulled on it and coughed.

"That's okay. Just go gently at it. You'll get used to it."

Claire did, but the smoke filled her brain and she thought she would faint. She sat down on the chair and they passed it back and forth several times. When her brain began to pucker and recede from her skull, Claire said she'd had enough. She realized her knees weren't properly crossed and went to move them, but they wouldn't obey; she was absolutely paralyzed and amazed to see Jon move quickly and gracefully to the hot plate, retrieve the kettle, make the tea, bring it and two small Chinese cups to the orange crate beside the chair. The odor of the tea wafted over Claire like the promise of spring. Jon got two oranges off the top of the refrigerator and sat on the braided rug at her feet peeling them. Each time he stripped the peel off, little sprays of orange flew from his fingers and the smell of orange and jasmine encircled Claire, enveloped her, washed over her like a benign tide, and as that tide ebbed, it bore away the threat of the judiciary committee, all thoughts of the lab test and any apprehensions she might have harbored: she was perfectly happy.

Claire did not know it then, but for the rest of her life she was to be victimized by oranges. She could never see one peeled, never sniff, however fleetingly, that sweet fragrance without being manacled to memory, to a tiny room over a rare-book store, to smoke and tea, to the man sitting cross-legged before her separating one section at a time and handing them to Claire and occasionally their fingers touched over the firm, moist slices. She would remember the oranges and the thin cups of hot tea, the comfort of the overstuffed chair, but never quite what they had talked about, their conversation being elliptical and non-sequitur and yet perfectly understandable and very funny. For all the men of her acquaintance, indeed of the men she had known in every sense of that term, Claire had not felt so intimate and at ease since the last time she and Bart had sat up late and toasted marshmallows in the fireplace of her father's study. Jon rolled another joint, thin as a needle, and Claire smiled at him, accepted it and inhaled gratefully.

The church clock tower tolled three times and then Jon got up and said he was going to the bathroom. He rummaged in the dresser and brought out a T-shirt and said she could sleep in that, but when he came back from the bathroom, it still lay across her lap. "I'm not sure I can move," she said sheepishly.

Jon took the pumps from her feet and placed them side by side beneath the chair. He took her hand and pulled her to her feet as she swayed slightly. He undid the tiny buttons at the back of her neck and asked if she could lift her arms. She said she could. She did, and he pulled the white angora sweater over her head. Claire tensed slightly. "It's all right," he said, folding the sweater and placing it over the back of the chair. "I don't believe in seduction. It's against my principles." He unfastened the waistband of her pleated skirt; it fell to the floor and, balancing herself on his shoulder, she stepped out of it. The skirt, too, he placed on the chair and then he pulled the T-shirt over her head; it floated on her. "Can you get your own stockings?"

She nodded and sat on the bed, unhooked her stockings, drew them down her legs, left them where they fell. She put her head on the pillow, and Jon covered her up. She was asleep before he turned out the lights.

Early morning light, pale as lemonade, filtered through the faded gingham curtains, and noises floated up from the street: the chug of buses, the rumble of cars, the sounds of the windowgrills being rolled back at the rare-book store downstairs. Claire woke up, uncertain of where she was or how she'd come there; she rolled over and saw Jon Cotton asleep on the floor. A shadow of beard dusted his cheeks and his dark lashes lay against pale skin; she hadn't thought him at all attractive last night, but now he seemed quite beautiful. He yawned and stretched and a tuft of dark hair showed over the rim of his T-shirt. He smiled at her, then he looked at the clock on the dresser, jumped up and pulled on his jeans hastily. "We have to hurry if you want to use the bathroom before you go. I'll run down and make sure the coast is clear."

While he was gone, Claire quickly put on her clothes. He came back and put the soap and towel in her arms. "I don't have an extra tooth-brush, but you can use mine if you want."

"Thank you." Claire Swallow had never in all her life used anyone else's toothbrush; it seemed the height of intimacy.

"Be extra careful this morning. If Mrs. Schripp finds out, she'll evict me. No women allowed in the rooms." He winked.

"You didn't tell me that before."

"Well, you didn't have anywhere else to go, did you? The hall's clear."

Claire dashed for the bathroom, and when she came back to number four, he had her coat ready for her. He walked out first. "Good morning Charley," she heard him say. "You're up awfully early, aren't you?" Charley answered with a resounding belch, and the bathroom door slammed shut. "Now, quick!" said Jon, and she followed him into the hall and down the two flights of stairs. He left her on the landing and went into the vestibule alone. "Morning, Mrs. Schripp. Need help taking those milk bottles in?"

"Do I look like I need help?" Mrs. Schripp grumbled, and closed the door behind her with a thud. Jon gave a quick whistle and the two of them were on the street in front of the rare-book store, its grill rolled back, tattered books and aged maps displayed in the window and the smell of coffee percolating out of the transom over the door.

Claire and Jon laughed. "I guess we're both safe," she said.

"This time."

"Let's hope there won't be a next time." Then she regretted saying that; she rather hoped there would.

"Yes, let's hope so," he replied as though he did not believe it either. They said goodbye, and Jon went back up the steps and Claire trotted in the direction of Whitney Hall, hoping she could scoot in un-obtrusively, change her clothes and get down to breakfast in the cafe-teria. She was famished; at least she was light-headed and euphoric, and she was certain it was due to hunger.

ii

Claire saw quite a lot of Jon Cotton after that. Although the university was huge, she wondered that she'd never noticed him before, so often did his path cross hers: in the throngs between classes, in the library, walking along Western Avenue, she looked for him and was continually rewarded. She even dragged Melinda to the Jade Sea for dinner one night with the promise of treating her. The waiter informed her in fractured English that Jon went to an anarchists' meeting every Thursday night and that the hot and sour was very good.

Jon and Claire often met informally for coffee, sipping it out of thick paper cups in the university coffeeshops, or sometimes in the shadowy espresso places along University Avenue. Occasionally, they walked along the dry creek bed that wound through campus which in the spring was a favourite haunt of lovers, but they had it to themselves while the weather remained cold and the trees leafless, scrawny branches scratching at the leaden sky. On one of their walks, Claire remembered that she had a letter from her Aunt Althea in her purse. She did not show Jon the letter (which was full of unflattering references to his mother), but she did show him the clipping and picture Althea had enclosed: Lucille Swallow handing over the keys to the Swallow mansion to the president of the Art League and the Garden Club, which would now conjoin to form the Swallow Foundation. Behind Lucille stood a young girl Claire recognized as Lucy Rose and a man she didn't know at all. "Hoolihan," said Jon, knotting the clipping in his fist and thrusting it into his pocket. "Hoolihan the hypocrite."

Claire hurried to catch up with him. "My mother says that sometimes you have to be a hypocrite. It's expected of you. You can't go around saying what you truly think. You have to lie now and then in the interest of good manners."

"I don't believe in bourgeois morality."

"That isn't what I said."

"It's the same thing."

"I suppose you're going to tell me that you are always honest."

"I try to be."

She followed him across a log with some difficulty, getting her red patent leather shoes muddy. "I guess I'm usually dishonest. It's easier

143

that way. People expect you to be polite."

"If you spend your life living up to what people expect of you, your life won't be your own. You tell enough lies, and pretty soon you don't know the difference. You'll never know the truth."

"Oh, you're just exaggerating. What difference does it make to tell a few white lies?"

"There's no such thing. Lies are either black, if they're told for malicious reasons, or pink—if they're prettified and dandered up to flatter the assholes of the world."

"Where do you get off knowing everything?"

"I don't claim to know everything."

"But you do! You judge everything and everyone very harshly and you won't admit to compromise."

"Compromise is not in my nature. I work hard, I have principles and beliefs and I try to live up to them. I don't believe in pragmatism; it's just another word for opportunism."

Claire hated the way he threw "isms" around, confounded and inevitably bested her. "You're the devil to talk to, Jon Cotton. Why can't I ever win an argument with you?"

"Because I don't argue. I never ramble. I never get distracted, and I always know exactly where I'm going. I never quarrel. I convert."

"Well, you haven't converted me."

"Not yet." He gave her his hand and pulled her up the hill. "We have a long time yet."

Claire smiled to herself, secretly flattered, though she followed him in silence. When they came to the intersection of Western and University, he said he had to meet his anarchist friend Kharabian and then go on to work at the Jade Sea. "I'll probably see you Monday, after your English class."

"I don't have a date for Saturday night," she burst out, kicking herself; she'd intended to bring it up more gracefully and in fact she had declined two offers for dates in order to do just that.

"That's too bad. I'm sure something will turn up." He darted into the traffic, turned and waved.

Jon was right; something did. A Phi O man asked her out on Friday afternoon, amazed that she said yes, so Claire did have a date for that Saturday night as she had for all the others and often for the weeknights as well. Indeed, after she met Jon Cotton, Claire's life remained outwardly the same, only she inwardly ceased to take such pleasure in any of it—the attention, the flattery, the beer and giggling sorority girls and wailing Del Tones, the boys who were eager to go out with her and even more eager to go down with her. The pattern repeated itself endlessly, and before curfew each night, she returned to Whitney Hall to face the expectant gaze of Melinda Lamott, whose silent slide rule was always reproachfully at work. "Did you have a good time?" Melinda invariably asked, and though Claire always replied affirmatively, there wasn't much to tell, less and less as time went on because the interval between when her date met her in the dorm lounge and the time he began pawing her seemed to shrink. Short of confessing that she couldn't keep her clothes on, Claire hadn't much to say.

Instead, she always took her soap and robe and towel and went down to the showers and spent thirty minutes washing off the touch of whoever she'd been out with and wondering what Jon Cotton did with his Saturday nights and wondering why Jon Cotton did not ask her out and wondering why she cared at all, since she had absolutely nothing in common with Jon Cotton or his insufferable principles.

Jon Cotton spent his Saturday nights at the Jade Sea washing dishes. The green neon sign was flashing, but the door said CLOSED. Claire banged on it anyway, and the waiter came and shook his head and pointed to the sign and began to turn away. Claire banged again. "Jon Cotton," she shouted, as though he were deaf as well as foreign. "I want to see Jon Cotton." Reluctantly, the waiter opened the door and pointed toward the back of the restaurant.

The waiter went back to vacuuming the red carpet, pocked everywhere with cigarette holes. The Jade Sea was small, with plastic-topped tables, each with a small vase of plastic roses. Dotting the walls were colorful Chinese fans, their ribs thick with dust, and the booths had been artfully mended with black tape where the plastic was ripped. Drunk as she was, Claire feigned equilibrium for the waiter's benefit and made her way unsteadily through the tables to the kitchen, where she found Jon, sleeves rolled up, hair plastered damp against his forehead, enveloped in steam, soap bubbles frothing out of the sink before him.

She leaned against the doorframe and watched him until he finally turned to her, his face registering curiosity rather than surprise or pleasure. He studied her entire figure: the rumpled navy blue skirt, disheveled oxford-cloth blouse, the red sweater buttoned up all wrong, the stockings hanging out of her purse and her bare feet thrust into red patent leather shoes. Her tawny hair came loose from its barrette and tumbled into her face.

He dried his hands deliberately and took his watch off a hook. "It's almost midnight."

"Do I look like a pumpkin?"

"Do I look like the prince?" He returned to the dishes.

"Oh, my error. Forgive me. I guess you're the pauper. The prince and the pauper all rolled into one."

"You look like someone has rolled you."

"I have not been rolled, thank you. I have been laid. Lay, lie, lain," she sang. "The King of France, the Queen of Spain, Matthew Mark Luke and John, take it off and put it on. So." She drew herself up stiffly. "You see I'm quite in control."

"I've seen winos in better shape than you."

"Well, you know what they say." Claire shrugged and burped indelicately. "Win a win, lose a few."

"I'll walk you back to the dorm when I finish up here."

She lolled against the door and caught herself before she fell. "I don't need to be walked anywhere. And if I did, I wouldn't have come here. I'd have asked my date to take me home. I'm sure he would have. He was a prince. Charming. A sorority man. Efficient. Doesn't waste a minute of your time."

Jon scoured the sink and rinsed it with a final blast of scalding water. He took off his apron; the front of his shirt was damp. "What's his name?"

"I can't remember. I do, but it doesn't matter. Now my name matters. I'm Claire Swallow and my father is a judge and my grandfather was a senator and the founder of Swallow Lines."

"Your grandfather was a capitalist pig and a befuddled old fart."

"That's not polite. You must not have been brought up properly. You must not have been brought up with the Three D's."

"Diarrhoea, dysentery and diptheria?"

"Decency, Decorum and Dignity," reported Claire coldly. "The mark of a lady. You can always tell a lady by the Three D's."

Jon scoffed, put on his jacket and switched out the kitchen light. "You want to come across the street? Is that what you want?"

Claire mumbled something deprecating, and he took her arm and said good night to Chen Yu, the waiter, and led her from the Jade Sea into the April night, where the air was damp and gritty with bus fumes and the sidewalks littered with quartets of exuberant college boys. They crossed the street and he left her in front of the rare books and maps while he checked the vestibule. Then he nodded and she followed him in, stopping briefly to curtsy in front of the door marked MANAGER. He yanked her up the stairs, and at the second landing they encountered Charley, who snickered, made an obscene gesture and wished Jon luck.

"Fuck yourself," Jon muttered as he led Claire to number four and leaned her against the wall while he unlocked the door. She rolled into the dark apartment and he closed the door after her; she fell against the coats hanging on the back and began to cry.

"Don't blubber," he said, turning on the light. "You're not the crying type."

"What do you know?"

"You better sit down, and I'll make you some coffee."

"Don't want any."

"Tea?"

"No."

"What do you want?"

"Don't know." She flopped into the chair, kicked off her shoes and rubbed her feet, but the effort made her dizzy.

Jon turned on the furnace and the hot plate and then removed his jacket. He sat across from her on the bed, his fingertips together. "What do you want from me, Claire? Why are you here?"

Claire started to say something flip and sassy, but bit it back. She drew her knees up under her skirt and hugged them. She might have cried if she could believe Jon would comfort her, but he was cruel and judgmental and didn't seem to care that she needed comforting and Claire herself didn't quite know why she should be comforted: what had happened tonight was not all that different from any other Saturday night—Claire had gone to a fraternity party and drunk a lot of something with gin and fruit punch and couldn't really think of a good excuse for not going upstairs with her date, who had closed the door, pushed her back on the bed and climbed on top of her. Invaded her. Claire hadn't even had time to ask him where he went to high school. She turned her face away from his lips and tried to be sweet about declining, but he kept her pinned beneath his weight until she began to protest that she didn't want—she hadn't intended—she didn't think he should— But her protests dwindled into whimpers and her arguments were weak, worthless, because Claire didn't really know what she wanted or intended or thought. She only knew she loathed being invaded, that this man had turned her body against her; she became her own enemy territory.

147

Jon got up and made a pot of jasmine tea and asked again why she'd come, but his tone was so dry and clinical, Claire couldn't answer. How could she tell him that when her date was finished with her, he laughed to watch her cry and grab her clothes and race out of the frat house, that his laughter rang in her ears as she ran to the Jade Sea and Jon Cotton. And why? "I wanted to be with someone who thinks I'm special," she said in a small voice. She sniffed and continued with more conviction. "I am special, you know. I'm a very talented pianist, and just because you have a tin ear—"

"I don't give a damn for music."

"Well I do and my father does, too. I think I'll just go home to him and never leave."

"You're free to do as you like."

"I'll be like Emily Dickinson and stay at home my whole life and never come out. I'll be like my Aunt Althea." Claire slid her sticky un-willing feet back into her shoes and stood. "Except I refuse to get fat, and I can't go back to being a virgin again."

"They wouldn't need to know that," Jon offered. "Virginity's not like some sort of diamond brooch that's noticeable when it's gone."

"It is in my family."

"Then your family is stupid and bourgeois and you look like a fool, weeping over something like that."

"How do you know what I'm weeping over?" she demanded. "How do you know what I feel like?"

"I don't, but I know virginity's not an emotion. It's an invention. It has to do with property, not with love or good or evil or any of those words that get weighted to it like stones and tied to girls to sink them into marriage, which also has to do with property and not love. Vir-ginity is ridiculous."

"Are you a virgin?"

"Of course not. No one with a grain of sense is a virgin."

"You wouldn't say that about your own sister."

"Lucy Rose hasn't a grain of sense. No, Claire." He carried the pot and the cups to the overturned crate by the chair. "You can stay or leave just as you please, but if you're upset because you're not a virgin, I haven't a lick of sympathy. If you just got up from the bed of someone you despise, then that's different."

"Why?"

"Because it's supposed to be an act of love." He poured two cups of tea. "I don't guess you loved this guy."

148

"No. He was brutal and when he was finished, he said—"

"I don't want to hear it."

"It does bother you, doesn't it?"

"I don't care who you sleep with," he said sternly. "I don't believe in tribal codes or property or bourgeois morality or marriage or any of that shit. I don't believe in seduction, either. I'm not going to seduce you."

"But you'd like to, wouldn't you?" Claire sounded rather more hopeful than she'd intended.

"Seduction implies trickery—that I should coerce you into doing something you didn't want to do."

A philosophical discussion was too much for Claire. "You better have a look down the hall," she said through clenched teeth. "I think I'm going to be sick."

Claire vomited the remains of the fruit punch and gin into the toilet at the end of the corridor; the toilet would have been enough to make her barf even if she hadn't already been nauseated. When she was done, she washed her face carefully and, on second thoughts, stripped off her clothes and turned on the rusted shower and climbed in. She had to dry off with paper towels.

Damp, dressed, her hair still dripping at the ends, she peered around the bathroom door, then sprinted, carrying her shoes, back to number four. Jon was sitting on the bed, tea cup in hand, reefer lit, the smoke wafting around him like a shadow. "I feel better," she announced.

"I was just about to come after you. You were gone a long time."

"I took a shower."

He rose and turned off the furnace; the room was suddenly over-warm, thick with smoke and steam and heat. "You can have the bed again." He placed the reefer to her lips and she puffed and then he put it in a saucer.

In her bare feet, Claire barely came to Jon's shoulder; she stood before him without touching. "How is it done without trickery?" she said at last. "Do anarchists hold hands and denounce property? Take vows of everlasting allegiance to the leaderless state?"

Tentatively, he brushed the damp hair behind her ear. "If it's an act of love, the vows are implicit." Jon touched her cheek, her chin, her shoulder. He kissed her.

He went to the narrow bed and turned back the scratchy blanket and Claire went with him, lay full length on top of him, and the strands of her wet hair brushed his cheek and she smiled into his eyes and lips and hands and her clothes seemingly departed of their own accord and Claire began to feel like Christopher Columbus, embarking on a voyage of discovery as well as exploration, and if her own body was no longer virgin territory, neither was it alien or inimical.

For that night and the following three days and nights, Claire and Jon stayed in that room, except for jaunts down the hall to the bathroom (when she sometimes encountered the understanding Charley) or when Jon went across the street to the Jade Sea to bring them back food in waxy little cartons and extra fortune cookies, which he said Chen Yu included for luck. The world fell away from them; they might have been Adam and Eve, at least that's what Claire thought when she found herself naked and created; she wondered, much as Eve must have wondered of Adam, what he would do with her now that she had been created from and of—if not by—him, consumed and consummated by a love she did not altogether understand and knew intuitively she could never duplicate. Each time she fell asleep beside him—day or night—Claire dreamed of Jon and Jerusalem Road, saw Jon in the old house by the sea, in the crazy garden with its sunflowers and nasturtiums and clashing scarlet peonies again, dreamed with her body; her body became that fulsome flower, each of its many petals united to a tender vortex that sucked them all together, held, until that moment when Jon reached that vortex and only then did it burst, sending everything centrifugally billowing through her. Claire herself burst with pleasure and, oddly, with loss, certain she could never again recover those petals. But they miraculously reconstructed. Every time. She seemed to herself an inexhaustible garden of delight.

On Wednesday morning, by common consent, they vowed to get dressed and return to their classes and the rest of the world. Claire hadn't been fully dressed for three days, and as she slid her clothes back on, she felt as if she had a brand new body. "I don't know what's happened to me," she whispered against his chest as they stood at the door before making their lunge through the halls and past Mrs. Schripp. "I can't bear to let you go."

"We're not letting go of one another, Claire. We never will." He kissed the rim of her hair. "I'll never leave you."

"No matter what happens."

"No matter what."

On their way out the door, they met Charley, clad in his underwear and clutching his toothbrush. Charley smiled at them. They made it past Mrs. Schripp without incident and had a last passionate embrace in front of the rare-book store while the grizzled proprietor, arranging his wares in the window, beamed at them.

The entire world seemed to beam at Claire. She caught a quick bus to Whitney Hall and the bus driver commented on the lovely weather and Claire agreed and people seemed to smile at her and she embraced them with her eyes. Had the world always been this lovely? How could she not have noticed? Was it Jon or love or some strange alchemy of both that peeled the old ungainly lacquer from her eyes, left them shining and able to see the world afresh.

She entered Whitney Hall through the side door and took the stairs two at a time up to her room, where she found Melinda pulling curlers from her hair. Melinda threw her arms around Claire and burst with a volley of concern and apology. "Oh, Claire, I'm so glad you're back! Where have you been? I'm so sorry. I've been so worried. I did the best I could. I tried everything, but what else could I say? And I didn't know where to reach you or how. Are you all right? They all think—I don't know what they think—that you've been kidnapped or something."

"Kidnapped?"

"Oh, Claire. It's been so awful! There was a fire drill Sunday night and Mrs. Jonah did a bed check and you weren't there and you hadn't signed out and she asked me where you were and I lied the best I could for you and said you'd gone home, but there was no way I could reach you and I didn't know what else to say. And then I was sorry I said that because she called your house and told your parents and she said she'd call the police if you didn't come back today and she hauled me on the carpet for lying and now I've got to go before the judiciary committee too, but I don't care about that. At least you're safe. You are safe, aren't you?"

Claire had thought so until that moment. "Oh Lord." She sank down on the bed. "Oh, Matthew Mark Luke and John! What next?"

That question was answered within the hour. Claire showered and changed and was ruffling her hair dry when a knock sounded at the door and the great gray edifice of Mrs. Jonah appeared, her upper lip quivering spasmodically. "You will be in my office in twenty minutes, Claire Swallow," she announced, and then she left.

Mrs. Jonah's lip was still quivering when Claire knocked at her office door. "You wanted to see me?"

"I wanted to see you last Sunday night, when we had a fire drill. And Monday. And Tuesday. And I demand to know where you were."

Mrs. Jonah pointed to the chair in front of her desk, but Claire remained standing.

"I don't think I'm under any obligation to tell you that, Mrs. Jonah," she replied, deciding in that instant on bravado rather than contrition.

Mrs. Jonah heaved her enormous bosoms and they seemed to flop on the desk. "Maybe you will feel some small shred of obligation to the judiciary committee. Or the dean of women, who has instructed me to send you to her when I am finished with you. Maybe you'll see your way clear to tell your mother, whom I called after Melinda told me you'd gone home. You did not go home, did you?"

Claire remained obdurately silent.

"Your mother was none too pleased, but then, I can't imagine that any mother would be. Neither was your sorority, I might add. I called them. I also got in touch with that nice young man you went out with Saturday night and he didn't know where you were, but he gave me the names of twenty or thirty others who might have known your whereabouts." Mrs. Jonah lingered hatefully over the implications. "So where were you?"

"I was all right. You needn't have worried."

"You can tell that to your mother, Miss. I am not at all worried. But you have disgraced Whitney Hall, you have disgraced your sorority sisters and you have disgraced this university."

"I don't believe that. I'm in trouble, that's all."

"That's all!" Mrs. Jonah then lowered her tone to conform with her duties. "That's enough, or it would be for most girls. Yours will be the first case the judiciary committee considers when they convene, and it's social probation for you, young lady. I will recommend expulsion Now, you'd better get to the dean's office. She is expecting you. I've called her and told her you're back. At last." Mrs. Jonah rose, indicating that their interview was terminated, but she closed with a few more injunctions and the wagging admonition to call her mother immediately.

"Old hag," Claire muttered on her way out the door. Mrs. Jonah she could endure; her mother was quite another question. She checked her mailbox before going to her room to get the dreary dime that would allow her to call Meg. She found the box stuffed with the usual flyers and a letter from her brother, Bart, which she tore open.

Dear Claire—
I think I better write and tell you because no one will admit what's

152

happening here. Father is sick, Claire, and I think he's sicker than he or anyone else will let on. He can't seem to eat anything or keep anything down once he does eat. He hasn't even been to work or out of the house in over two weeks. He just sits at his desk and doesn't talk, just keeps breaking pencil leads and looking at the walls. Everyone's tried to keep it from me and Jill and Marietta, but I know he's really sick just from the way Mama and the Mourning Glory fuss over him, but all they'll say is that Father has a cold even though he hasn't sneezed once. They must think we're stupid.

Could you come home? Even for a weekend. I think you could do Father a lot of good. You are his favorite and he always says isn't it too bad Claire isn't here to play the piano. He misses you. If you can't come, at least write Father a letter or call him, but don't let on that you know he's sick or that you heard from me. Mama will sling me to Kingdom Come, but I had to write. I can't stand to watch him sink. It's like he's just drifting and not caring where he's going and I can't stand to see it.

Love,
Bart

"To hell with the dean of women." Claire flew to her room and packed an overnight bag and asked Melinda to go down and call the bus station and find out the schedule.

Melinda came back, breathless from having run up the stairs. "There's a bus at twelve-thirty, Claire. An express."

"Good." She snapped her purse shut and hugged Melinda quickly. "I'll see you soon. I hope."

"You're not angry with me, are you, Claire? I lied the best I could for you."

"Of course not. I hope you're not angry with me for getting you into trouble."

"Oh, I don't think the judiciary committee will do too much to me. But it's social pro for you, Claire."

"Well, what do I care? The judiciary committee is full of prigs and perverts."

On her way out of Whitney Hall, Claire met with titters and the stares of other girls. Unfortunately, Mrs. Jonah was manning the desk when she dutifully went to sign out.

"Have you been to see the dean of women?" Mrs. Jonah asked.

"To hell with her. To hell with all of you!" And then in a moment of literary inspiration, Claire cried, "You're nothing but a pack of cards!" And bolted.

Before she went to the bus station, Claire went to the Jade Sea. "Not here," said Chen Yu, who knew what she wanted before she even spoke. "Not till tonight."

"Can I leave him a message?"

"Sure—sure, paper back there." He nodded toward the cash register.

Claire couldn't find anything but a paper napkin, on which she scrawled:

> *My love my love my love*
> *I have to go home. My father is sick. Can you call me? No, don't. Bad idea. I'll write here. At the Jade Sea. Okay? I am in lots of trouble, Jon, but it was all worth it and I love you I love you I love you and I am yours and always will be*
>
> > *All my love*
> > *Claire*

She folded the note and gave it to Chen Yu, who tucked it in his apron pocket. He handed her a fortune cookie. "For luck," he said. "Nothing but good fortunes here."

iii

In this ignominious fashion Claire Swallow left the university, forever as it turned out. She rode the bus home, alternately drenched in happiness thinking about Jon or clenched with fear thinking about Anson and desperately trying on one lie after another, like clothes that refused to conform to her body or the circumstances. She hailed a cab and gave him her parents' address, and when he stopped in front of the white stucco house, she still didn't know how she could account for those three glorious days, short of the truth, which was inadmissible and, given that Jon was Lucille's son, unthinkable.

She felt like a foreigner the minute she stepped into the tiled hallway. To her left, the door to her father's study was closed and she could hear the low murmur of voices. She peered around to her right, through the arch that opened into the living room, where the grand piano stood, closed up now and silent. She was about to dart through the dining room, hoping to find Bart in the kitchen, when her Aunt Althea appeared on the landing, still clad in all her mourning glory. "Meg!" Althea cried. "Meg! Come see who's here." She fixed a hard glare on Claire. "The prodigal returneth, I see."

Claire put her overnight bag on the floor and stood straight as if tied to the stake; at last she could put her girlhood admiration of Joan of Arc to use.

Meg came down the stairs, pushing past Althea. "You! What are you doing here?" Since Claire could not answer without implicating Bart, she remained silent, and Meg rushed on. "I gather you weren't kidnapped and that we needn't have called the university police! Althea, you better go up and call them back and tell them she's here. Call Mrs. Jonah and the dean of women, too."

"They know I'm back."

"Do they know where you're back from?" Meg said icily.

Claire fervently wished she could turn into a butterfly or a moth, flutter away, impale herself on an electric bulb and be done with it. "There was no cause to worry."

"No cause to worry," Althea snarled. "They call us up and tell us you've been missing for days and you tell us not to worry!"

"I'm here now. I'm fine."

"But where have you been?" Meg demanded.

"How's Father?" Claire parried.

"Where were you?"

"I'd rather not say." Then she added, "I can't say." Wasn't there some legal name for this stance? "I have to take the Fifth Amendment."

Meg clutched her daughter's arm like Claire was five and caught with her fingers in the cream cheese. "You will tell me where you were and you will do so immediately."

Just then the wooden door to her father's study opened and a man came out. He was neither young nor old, but well dressed, with fair, close-cropped hair and intense gray eyes. He closed the door behind him.

Meg pushed Claire aside and confronted him in an ostentatious manner that ill became her. "Goodbye, Mr. Hoolihan, and I'll thank you not to come again. Never, never to come again. Whatever your business with my husband, it can wait. Your visits do nothing but upset and unnerve him."

"Mrs. Swallow, I'm trying my best. I want to help. I—"

"You're not helping, Hoolihan. You're hurting him, and I won't have it. I mean it, don't come back."

"I'm as concerned about the judge as you are."

"I doubt that."

He looked weakened, even defeated. "Goodbye then, Mrs. Swallow," he said, stepping out.

"And good riddance, Mr. Hoolihan." She closed the door and locked it with a definitive snap.

"That was *Hoolihan*?" asked Claire, incredulous.

Meg ignored her. She took Claire's arm and dragged her through the dining room and the kitchen to the service porch, where the washer chugged and the dryer hummed and the air was tinged with the smell of soap. "Listen to me because I won't have time to repeat myself. Your father knows nothing of this—this awful business with you, so don't you go sniveling and taking any damn Fifth Amendment with him, you understand?"

"What's wrong with him, Mama, is he—"

"Just listen. You can give any reason you like for coming home, but he doesn't know you were missing. I kept it from him and I want it kept that way. I won't have you upsetting him."

Bart bounded through the back door carrying athletic shoes, a sweatshirt and school books; he reeked of the locker room and surprise. "Claire!"

"You ask her," Meg said, her lower lip suddenly thrust out. "You ask her where she's been. Maybe she'll tell you. You always keep secrets from me, you two." She took Claire's arm again and shoved her back through the kitchen. "Now, you go into that study and say hello to your father and remember what I said." Meg loaded the words as if they were bullets into a pistol and the gun leveled at Claire's gut. "He doesn't know a thing about your little escapade and he had better not find out."

April 20, 1963

My love my love my love

    How brilliant you were to use Melinda's name for the return address! I was happy to have a letter from her, but when I opened it and saw it was from you, I nearly burst with joy and read it a hundred times and took it to bed with me wishing it was you. But I got some bad news today too. Same mail. A letter from the dean. Social pro. Unless I tell them where I was, they will throw me out of school.

156

But I'm only worried about my father now. He is grayer and dryer and saggier than I remember him and he's lost a lot of weight so his skin just sort of hangs from him and he looks like he is being eaten up from the inside. My brother and I think he's got cancer, but no one will tell us and to be fair, maybe they don't even know because he refuses to see a doctor. Mama and Althea are always after him to eat and Althea makes him gruesome rice dishes and he always thanks her, but sends the trays back. The only good thing about it is that they are so worried and so taken up with fussing after Father, they haven't had time to try to pump the truth out of me. Mama and Mourning Glory just give me dirty looks and make snide remarks, but nothing—ever—in front of Father. In the week I've been home, I've been practicing eight and ten hours a day, learning Beethoven's Eleventh Sonata for my father. He asked me to learn it. I wanted to play things I already knew well, but he said he wanted to hear me learn something and he sits in the living room rocker with one of Mama's knitted shawls over him and listens to me like I am Nicholas Kerchiaeff. Actually I'm glad to have a piece that grand and passionate to play. I don't think I could have played it before—before you—because I might have had the skill, but I didn't have the passion and control. That's what you need for the Eleventh Sonata, passion and control. (I know you don't care about music, my love, but if you could hear the Eleventh Sonata, you would.) And if I can't spend my passion with you, at least I can spend it on the piano and it's as close as I can come to being with you, to making love with you, my love, I carry you with me, on me, in me (but you'll be happy to know I got my period so we don't have to worry about that) but oh my love I'm so glad you love me and miss me and can't wait for me to come back. I will. I'll think of something. I'll come back when my father gets well.

I get frightened though sometimes, Jon, thinking about what we did and created and shared in those three days. I'm frightened to belong to you so totally, but I've never felt so free. Is this what happens to people who get religion and start babbling in tongues? This kind of joy and freedom and obligation that you could not live without? I never felt anything like this in church. I like the music in church and the words and knowing everything they're going to say, like going to the same play every week. You can recite the lines and you get to go up on stage to get communion, but I never felt anything. And I'm sure that what I feel now is what I'm supposed to feel in church which is holy. (I know you don't believe that and hate religion, but it's true just the same.) Sometimes I wish I could deny what I feel but it's all too physical and viseral (sp?) and I love you and need you and miss you so much I could cry, but I am not *sad, my love, because I can always feel you still with me, underneath and on top of me. One of us is the ocean and the other the boat and as long as we're always touching, I don't care which I am. Do you?*

I have to go now. My father wants me to go downtown with him. I think Mama's a little hurt because he specifically asked me to go and not her, but it's his first time out of the house in weeks, so we all think this is a good sign. I'll mail this when I'm out with him. I love you I love you I love you

All my love,
Claire

Once they pulled around the corner and out of sight of Meg, who had remained at the living room window, Anson asked Claire to drive. "Where to?"

"To the bank. I have some business there."

Claire took the wheel and rolled her window down and a fresh breeze blew in, replete with salt air and exhaust; the city looked new and bright to her, the steel cords of bridges reflecting sunlight, the glass and girders of new construction shining. Claire felt very grown-up; she'd never before driven her father anywhere.

"Have you flunked out of school, Claire?" Anson asked after a time.

"Not exactly."

"What exactly happened?"

Claire could not say because she hadn't the words to describe that she was madly in love and happier than she ever dreamed of being, so instead she replied, "I feel I'm needed at home."

"Home has got on very well without you since September."

"You weren't sick in September. You haven't done very well without me at all." She tried to laugh, but it died feebly between them.

"I can't believe that you would fail. You're a very smart girl and you're immensely talented and you could have a wonderful future, but you must act on it while you're young. You have every opportunity."

"I get confused sometimes."

"I don't imagine you are talking about English 1A."

"I get confused," she said stubbornly, taking a left turn and pulling into view of the bank.

"If you do your best and fail, there's no shame in that, but anything less than your best effort shows a lack of principle and fortitude, a kind of moral cowardice that is unforgivable in people who are fundamentally brave. It's cowardly to run away, and I can only assume that's what you're doing now."

"Only in a manner of speaking, Father."

"With evasion like that, maybe you should give up the piano and study law."

The bank was done in fake gilt and real marble; the crack and natter of a thousand typewriters resounded in the vaulted ceiling like target practice on some distant range. The place smelled of money; Claire recognized the smell at once and wondered why she hadn't done so before: it was the way her grandfather's house had always smelled—not so much of the pleasures or comforts that money could buy, but the raw green stuff itself.

When the manager saw Anson, he came out of his office and greeted him effusively. Anson asked Claire to wait and she took a seat on one of the hard benches with a view of the manager's glassed-in office. She could only see her father's back, but she watched the manager's face express cordiality and then in succession (and over about a twenty-minute period): disbelief, horror, pleading and finally, resignation. The manager left the office and vanished into the bowels of the bank. Her father did not turn around. The manager returned with a paper portfolio and spent another twenty minutes with Anson, who bent over the desk, finally, as if signing something. When Anson emerged from the office, he was carrying the portfolio.

He asked her to drive down the hills toward the sea, down one seemingly sheer cliff after another, till Claire eased the car at last along the boulevard fronting the harbor. He told her to go to the Swallow docks. "Are you going to see Lucille?" she asked.

"No. It has nothing to do with Lucille. Don't go to the Swallow building, just drive as close as you can to the dock and then stop."

Claire turned the engine off, and they got out. For all the sunshine, the wind was stiff and chill, redolent with the odor of pitch and pine, sea and ships and engines. The huge *Lucille* was at the dock, tied to the pilings; the holds were all open, the gangways down, looking like the tongues of a many-mouthed monster. Anson clutched the portfolio, and they started down the dock. Stevedores emptying the cargo holds of the *Lucille* eyed them dubiously but said nothing. At the end of the dock, Anson stood and looked out to sea. Then he turned to the east, where the city crested, higher, ever higher at the tops of successive hills, as if in waves that could not bear to break. He pointed to the office of Swallow Lines before them, three flags snapping from the roof: the American flag, the Bear Flag of California and in between them (and higher than either) the white flag of Swallow Lines, with its brilliant blue swallow in flight.

"Lucille was probably right," Anson said slowly. "She probably has done better with Swallow Lines than any of us could have. She has the right instincts, the same sort of instincts that the Senator had."

"Did she really cheat us, Father, like Aunt Althea always says? Did she really take everything that ought to have been ours?"

"She did, but we should have expected it. She was desperate. We should have known that. Besides, she had lived in great poverty, which, contrary to popular opinion, does not have a salutary effect on people. Poverty of choice and imagination and prospect, more than money, these are the things which contribute to bitterness. Bitterness makes people sour up long before they should. Look at the Mourning Glory."

"I didn't know you called her that!"

"I don't, but I know you and Bart do. She probably deserves it, but I pity her all the same. She'll go to her grave all twisted and bitter. I don't intend to go to my grave like that."

"Please, Father, don't talk like that."

"Well, dear girl, it's not only a possibility, it's a likelihood isn't it? I'm not just speaking of myself. But"—he regarded her fondly—"you're only eighteen and I don't expect you to think of death as inevitable." He untied the portfolio and walked to the side of the dock, where the ocean washed around barnacle-encrusted pilings. "No, you never know these things till you're too old and it's too late."

"What things?"

"Pattern and scheme, orders and importance. When you're young, it all looks random, but when you get old, you look back and you say, yes, that's what happened and that's why it happened and you realize that you either failed altogether to read the past or misread it badly. You wake up one day to find the present blacked up like a boot, but you think you might yet, perhaps, salvage the future."

"I see."

"You realize that you have not only believed the lies that people have told you, but believed the lies you've told yourself. But the trouble with lies"—Anson reached into the portfolio and grabbed a handful of hundred-dollar bills—"is that they're perishable. They rot. They decay and finally because of the stench, if nothing else, you know them for what they are." He flung the money into the ocean.

"What are you doing!" Claire cried. "That's money!"

"No, it's lies." He took another handful and tossed them; they fluttered to the rainbow-hued oil slick and floated there, buoyed up by the colorful grease. "And anyway, lies are exactly like money. Lies and money are only useful, only have currency, as long as people believe in them. When people no longer believe in them, they're valueless. I no longer believe." He pulled out another sheaf, flung it to the wind; they fell into the sea and the current pushed them inexorably forward.

"Maybe that's enough. You ought to stop, Father. Does Mama know? Why are you—" Claire couldn't bring herself to scream or cry out for help or snatch the portfolio from him.

"You have to regard this money—these lies—the lies and money the Senator willed me—like something dead that's been cremated and now we're burying it at sea. Dust unto dust. Ashes to ashes. Rot and decay into the only ocean that's big enough to absorb them." He cast another handful of bills seaward.

Claire watched the money flutter, and bits of biblical phrase rolled around in her mind, unbidden. *Cast your bread upon the waters and thou shalt find it after many days.* Anson grabbed one handful of bills after another, a few slipped from his grasp and the breeze scooted them along the dock toward the *Lucille*; stevedores and longshoremen dropped their loads and pranced after the hundred-dollar bills until they saw that Anson was throwing the money into the sea, and then they ran toward the rocky shore, like fat, tattooed marionettes, and Claire could only wonder if everyone running after money looked that ridiculous.

"I wanted a witness," said Anson, flinging another handful. "You only need one witness, some one person to testify in your behalf. Will you do that for me, Claire?"

"Testify to what?" she asked, still rooted with shock and chagrin.

"To my good intentions. I am of sound mind. I am, Claire. Don't doubt it."

"Yes, but—please stop, Father. Oh, I wish you'd brought Mama! She'd know what to say."

"I could not bring your mother because Meg does not believe in gestures and that's her strength. One of them. She doesn't make gestures. Only desperate people do, and all gestures are futile and serve only to underscore their own futility. But this gesture—" he threw another handful down "—will free you, you and your brother and sisters. It doesn't free me, but at least I'm no longer contaminated, no longer bought off, after the fact, but bought off nonetheless." He stopped for a moment and faced the gray Pacific, where in the distance sturdy tugboats steamed and jostled around the great ships, prodding them like gnats. "Promise me you'll never curse me for this."

"Never! I could never curse you for anything! You're my father. I love you. I admire you!"

"Don't admire me. I don't deserve it. But don't curse me, and don't let the others. Tell them I did it for you, all of you. I wanted to leave you free from contamination, free to live your own lives." He finished, turned the portfolio upside down over the water and watched the final bills drift down, turned to the east and saw the soggy money being nudged ever closer to shore by the current. "Because you're young you think your lives are your own anyway, but it's not true. There's pattern and order, all there before you were ever born and you never see—I never saw till it was too late. You get bound up, Claire, connected, constricted by cords so silky that you don't see them for the fetters they really are. That's what that money was—a silken cord. Now it's broken. You're free of the Senator's money and free of his lies." He dropped the portfolio on the dock. "All that went into the sea. But don't worry. There's plenty of money, honest money, for all of you and your education. Money will not be a problem for you, whatever happens to me."

"Please don't talk like that, Father. Nothing's going to happen to you."

"It already has, but you're safe."

Claire longed to pat his shoulder, but that sort of maternal gesture, once made, would alter their relations forever and so she refrained. She offered him her arm and he took it, his great frame leaning on her narrow one.

"I never really thought of myself as a judge, you know," he said as they started slowly back up the dock. "I really thought of myself as a surgeon. The law was my scalpel and I thought it could be used to peel back the human heart and see what lies there. I thought it could be used to cut the evil out of society. But the law fails. It's not a scalpel. It's more like a crude butcher knife, dull and stabbed uncertainly, isn't it?"

"I don't know, Father. I'm not a judge."

"Neither was I. I had the gavel and the robes, but I failed in my judgments. Everyone is guilty. It's a matter of degree, that's all. But you'll testify for me, won't you, Claire? You won't let them curse me. You'll never curse me, will you?"

"Never."

"I was a poor judge. Of character, if nothing else."

He leaned on her more heavily and she was suddenly afraid that having referred to himself in the past tense, Anson would crumble to dust beside her. As they walked toward the Swallow building with its three flags flying, Claire frantically assembled every assurance she could think of and offered them to him: Anson was a great judge, a wonderful father, a sterling man. He seemed neither to notice nor to care and finally she fell silent, praying inwardly only to get him back to the car and home so he could rest. As they passed the hulking, gaping *Lucille*, Claire was suddenly seized with a hatred for her grandfather and Lucille, who between them had somehow brought her father to this awful impasse, this wanton deed, this unimpeachable misery.

"Hey, mister," one of the stevedores called out. "Got any more money you don't need? Got any more?"

Anson did not seem to hear him at all, but as they traversed the long wharf, the question rang in Claire's ears and she knew that there was more, not more money perhaps, but something more, and she fought off the urge to confess all to her father, to tell him she'd fallen in love with Jon Cotton, that Jon Cotton was and always would be her lover. The feeling was insubstantial as smoke, frail as the shadow of smoke on water, but as she watched the bills bob onto the beach, spin and tumble in the scummy yellow foam, she fathomed that in loving Jon Cotton, she was, in some ineffable way, bound to the very thing from which Anson had hoped to free her. She ushered her father into the car and closed his door, but stood then, watching, helplessly transfixed before the awful sight of a dozen derelicts, foragers, garbage pickers, wretched old men and stooped women who emerged from their crevices, ran out on the rocky beach and danced to discover money, soggy bills, in the lisping surf; they hooted with pleasure and crowed with delight as they kissed Benjamin Franklin's impassive smile.

iv

"Six weeks later, he was dead."

Jon and Claire lay side by side, naked and holding hands on the narrow bed. An oblong patch of sunlight fell through the gingham curtains and across the braided rug. "It was cancer, but it was something else too. Something ate him up inside, even his mind. He lost his mind.

Why else would he have thrown all that money away? My mother got the doctor to come to our house, but Father only saw the doctor to please her. It must have been too late even by then because when the doctor left, my mother went to the bathroom and flushed the toilet and turned on the sink and the tub full blast and cried her eyes out. At the end, Father couldn't bear to see anyone and he even said the funeral was to be family only. Not anything like you expect for a judge." She nestled closer to Jon and pressed her head against his shoulder. "Hoolihan was there, though. He came. I saw him standing in the distance. He never spoke to us, though, just put on his hat and left when it was over."

"Why would Hoolihan come to your father's funeral?"

"I don't know. My father was perfect, and Hoolihan is a slug. My mother threw him out of the house."

"What was he doing at your house?"

"I don't know, but he was there, talking with my father the day I got home and I've never in my life heard my mother talk that way to anyone. She told him off, and he never came back."

Jon rolled on his side and put his arm around her, pulled Claire's hand to his lips and kissed it tenderly as if he could remove her grief like splinters from her palm.

Claire was touched, moved and assured that she had done the right thing, even though she'd felt wretchedly guilty, a mere three days after her father's funeral, lying to Meg, saying she was coming to the university to get her things and see about her final withdrawal. She had done no such thing. She had gone directly to the Jade Sea and Jon Cotton. Only Jon could mend the rent in her life. And yet—once they had got past Mrs. Schripp and to this small familiar room—as Jon unzipped her summer dress and freed her small breasts from the heavy strapless bra, Claire felt horribly disloyal to her father's memory: she ought not to have come to her lover; she ought to have dealt with Anson's death in some more decent, decorous, dignified way and, as if sensing this, Jon had murmured to her, "There is no other way, Claire. I love you and I want to make love to you so you'll know you're alive and as long as you're alive, your father will never die, not as long as you go on loving him. This is the only antidote to grief, believe me."

Claire had begun to cry then and he led her to the bed and she wept into his lap; he parted the hair at the back of her neck and kissed her there, stroked her back, held her until her sobs diminished and she lay back on the bed. His hands explored her as if she were a mortal boulder, an incline he wanted to scale, as if he need only find some cleft, some safe place he could cling to, brace himself and inch by inch ascend. And when they touched that last mutual chord, Claire found she had sloughed off destructive grief. Mourn she might, but the worst of her grief was past.

Only now, after they had sunk back refreshed and exhausted in each other's arms, could Claire speak of her father. "I should have noticed at Christmastime how sick he was, but I didn't."

"You can't blame yourself for that."

"Bart saw it. Bart saw it coming."

"Bart lived with him all the time, you didn't."

"Bart's not self-centered and I am. Bart always notices when people are hurt or sad or unwell. Bart always takes care of things. Now he's got more than even he can handle with Mama. She's devastated. I never realized it before, but Father always managed the day-to-days, the money, the bills, all that, and Mama's undone by the responsibility. Bart's told her if she doesn't quit crying, she'll get sick too, but she won't listen to him. She's gone mad. The day after the funeral, Bart found her in Father's study lighting a fire and he said to her, Mama, it's June, we don't need a fire. But she just squatted there like a squaw—you'd have to know my mother to know how unthinkable that is—burning Father's papers. She swept his desk clean, and she wouldn't get up until every scrap was ash. The whole world's gone mad."

Jon patted her haunch. "Not the whole world. There's still you and me. Come on, let's brave Mrs. Schripp and go to the Jade Sea and get something to eat. You need your strength, Claire. You've lost weight in all this and you don't look well."

"I'm fine now. With you. I'm always fine with you, but what about tomorrow, Jon? I'll have to go back home tomorrow, and how will we see each other after that? How will we—"

He sat up and placed his fingers over her lips. "Let's not talk about that now. We're going to be together. We must. We'll think of something."

"We could get married."

He frowned. "I don't believe in bourgeois marriage. I love you and I always will, but I won't allow the state to enter into my private life."

"But if we were married, we could live together."

"We could live together anyway."

"I couldn't. My mother—"

"Not now. Later. Get dressed, babe." He rose off the rumpled bed and pointed to his penis, coming visibly to life. "Or it will be too late and we'll die of love and starvation."

"Matthew Mark Luke and John," said Claire. "Bless the bed that we lie on."

"I keep telling you, it doesn't go like that."

They scooted skillfully through the halls and past the MANAGER and into the street and the Jade Sea, where they ate and lingered over jasmine tea and fortune cookies. Hunger assuaged for the moment, they relaxed, but like all hungers, theirs were recurrent, and in that sense no single meal, no single golden afternoon would sustain their lives unless they could be content to nibble on the dry cake of memory, and they were too young for that, too eager and impulsive.

"Let's go back and bless the bed that we lie on." Jon winked at her and bussed their dishes to the back and thanked Chen Yu for the extra fortune cookies.

Claire waited, as she always did, in front of the rare-book shop while Jon went into the vestibule to check for Mrs. Schripp. She stared into the window where ancient maps were spread, their corners held down by fat leatherbound volumes, and watched her own reflection ripple across the strange configurations of land and sea, the errors men had made when they confused desire and delusion. Jon popped his head out and beckoned. Claire hurried up the steps and into the front hall, where Mrs. Schripp's door was open, and warbling from the record player, someone crooned "Moon River". Mrs. Schripp was nowhere in sight.

Jon got his key and they made their way quickly upstairs, but when they came to number four, they found the door ajar and excited voices tumbled into the hall. To their open-mouthed amazement, they beheld Lucille Swallow.

She stood in the dead center of the braided rug, brilliantly plumed in a dress of lilac-flowered crepe, the sunlight snagging on her jeweled rings and refracting wildly around the room. Mrs. Schripp—squat, drab and barefoot, her hair wired for sound with hundreds of little metal rollers—squawked at Lucille, maundering on about the rules of the house. Behind Lucille stood a soberly-clad man with intense gray eyes whom Claire had last seen, hatless and somber, some distance from her father's grave.

Lucille regarded her son with neither relief nor eagerness, and when she caught sight of Claire, mild curiosity crossed her face, but did not linger there. She turned to Hoolihan and with the flick of her hand said, "Shut her up, will you?" She nodded to the flapping Mrs. Schripp.

Hoolihan reached in his pocket and took out a sheaf of bills. He pared off the top three and thrust them at Mrs. Schripp, who snatched the money and pushed past Jon and Claire with a few parting epithets about rules and order and the announcement that Jon was evicted. As of now.

"I suppose," said Lucille in a peppery tone, "that under the circumstances, Jon, I should invite you in, rather than the other way around. As you can see, we weren't exactly welcomed here."

"Hello, Mother." Jon went to her and she offered him her cheek, which he dutifully kissed. "I can't say this is an unexpected pleasure. Only unexpected. You remember—" he flushed and stammered, as if torn between the urge to lie and his anarchist's commitment to the difficult truth "—Claire Swallow, don't you."

"I remember her, but I wouldn't have recognized her. So that's you, Claire? You're not big enough to be a Swallow."

Unencumbered by morality or political principles, Claire lied instinctively. "I was just, just—uh—downstairs, buying a book in the rare-book shop downstairs and I happened to see, to meet Jon and he—"

Before she could finish, Hoolihan crossed the room and took both her hands in his. "I'm so very sorry about your father, Miss Swallow. He was a great man. A very great man."

"Yes, Claire," Lucille offered. "Such a tragedy about Anson."

"Your father," Hoolihan continued, "was the only fundamentally just, inherently honest person I've ever known and his loss will be felt in this world as long as there are men who value honor and truth."

Lucille smirked. "At least you're not one of that dreary tribe, Hoolihan." She turned her attention to Claire. "I would have thought you'd stay with your mother awhile before coming back to the university, Claire. I'm sure she needs you now."

"I was just buying a rare book," Claire repeated stupidly, noting that Hoolihan cast a glance to the rumpled bed.

Lucille didn't even regard this circumstantial evidence. "I came as soon as I got your note," she said to her son.

"It was a note," he replied. "Not an invitation."

"It was nice to see you again, Jon," said Claire quickly, "after all these years, but I'll be going now."

"No. Mother isn't going to be here very long."

"Neither are you," Lucille retorted, "judging from your landlady. Do you mind if I sit down, or do we need to fumigate first?" Lucille sat in an overstuffed chair, crossed her knees demurely and lit up a cigarette. Hoolihan retreated to the window. "Let's get down to it, Jon. What is all this crap about going off to live in the forge of history?"

"I'm leaving the university. I told you. My friend Kharabian has started an anarchists' commune and I'm going to join him."

"What!" cried Claire. "You're going to what?"

Jon refused to look at her or Lucille, keeping his eyes pinned to the anarchists' flag pinned above the Woodstock.

"And where is this commune?" Lucille demanded. "Some godawful place. What was the name, Hoolihan? It took you thirty minutes to find it on the map."

"Chagrin," Hoolihan replied without inflection.

"Chagrin, California. How quaint. Tell me, how do you intend to live there? The last I heard, bread baked on principle alone is not very nourishing."

"My work is preparing people for the revolution. My job will be in the date groves with Kharabian and the others. They grow dates in Chagrin."

"Oh, the simple life! The sweat of one's brow! The curse of Adam! Oh, it just sounds idyllic as hell."

"I'm going, regardless of what you think."

"Go! By all means! Far be it from me to stop the march of history. Why, I'm a mere woman, what can I do against Marx and Angles?"

"Engels. I don't believe in Marx and Engels. I believe in Bakunin and Kropotkin."

"Radical politics!" she sniffed. "They're as old as money and mint, as old as religion and just as ridiculous."

"I don't believe in religion. I don't believe in Christ or sin or redemption or any of that."

"My, my, you don't believe in very much, do you? Well, neither do I, but I can tell you this: I forbid it."

"You can't forbid me anything, Mother."

"I won't allow it. You don't approve of me and I don't approve of you, nonetheless I am still your mother and I will not allow you to ruin your life. You've systematically snubbed every chance in life I have offered you, Jon, but I won't allow you to go off into the desert and convert heathen date pickers to some sort of radical religion."

"I don't believe in religion," Jon repeated.

"Oh, it's all the same thing. Some rigid view of rightness that tolerates no compromise, detests anything to the contrary, hates comfort and security and won't rest till everyone thinks just the way you do. Excuse me, Jon, but you might as well be a Holy Roller. I don't see a damn bit of difference."

"I hope you didn't come here thinking to make a Christian of me."

"I can't make head or tails of you! I never could. I work my whole life to give you and your sister the best of everything, and this is how you repay me."

"What you call work is not what I'd call work."

Contempt twitched at the corners of Lucille's mouth. "Not honorable, eh?"

"I don't discuss honor. It has no basis in the material world."

"The material world! What do you know of the material world? What do you know of the world at all? What about all my sacrifices for you?"

"Can it, Mother. Whatever you did, you did for yourself. You've never considered anyone else."

"You rotten little bastard!" Lucille shrieked, and then she began to rage in earnest and Claire, feeling faint, made her way to the bed, sat there, eyes closed. Lucille seemed to be absorbing all the oxygen in the room—her smoke, her screams, her words, thick as cotton wadding pressed against the walls and window.

"What your mother means, Jon—" Hoolihan began.

"I don't need a pimp like you to tell me what she means!"

The veins on Hoolihan's forehead engorged with blood and anger.

"I'm leaving for Chagrin, Mother. I wrote you as a courtesy, not as application for a visa. I'm going to make a dent in history, however minute. I'm not going to spend my life paying bills and get shoveled into some bourgeois living grave. I'm not going to have my life dictated to me by other people's expectations. I have no interest in property, so feel free to disinherit me. I don't care about a university degree—what would that do? Suck me into the bourgeois world, the known world. I want to explore what is unknown, I want to—"

"When are you leaving?" Claire asked, each word wrapped in a thick paste, delivered up to her tongue like dumplings.

"Soon." He turned to her miserably. "I was going to tell you when—"

"And where is it, Chagrin?" she said weakly.

"Down south. In the desert. In St. Elmo County. You know, the same county Melinda's from—"

"Ha! I see it all!" Lucille crowed. "Melinda! You're going to leave the university and take after some girl. Anarchism, my ass! Melinda who? Some little whore who thinks she can marry you and get her hands on my money!"

"You've got it all wrong," Jon cried, half appealing to Claire and half to his mother. "It's got nothing to do with—"

"Well, I wash my hands of you in that case. You're worse than I thought." Lucille stood and flipped her cigarette expertly into the sink. "Led by your prick! That's the worst sort of man there is. I can't believe that a son of mine—"

"Mother, please, that's not the case. I—"

"Well, I hope you knock Melinda up and have a whole tribe full of brats, but don't come crawling to me. Not ever. I'm finished with you. I've had enough of your insults and your pious perversions. Let's go, Hoolihan."

Hoolihan's flush had retreated and the skeptical twist returned to his lips. He ignored Jon altogether, but nodded to Claire. "Again, Miss Swallow, my condolences on the loss of your father."

As though she just remembered Claire was there at all, Lucille said indignantly, "And as for you, Claire Swallow! I don't suppose your mother would be any too pleased to know you're visiting boys who live in degrading squalor—and your poor father not even cold in his grave."

"Don't you dare mention my father," snapped Claire, remembering the open maws of the *Lucille*, the lies and money—and whatever else Lucille and the Senator had done to Anson—cast into the sea, carried shoreward on the tidal scum. "Don't you even say his name!"

Hoolihan took Lucille's arm with the grip of a man who might have been pulling teeth. "Let's go. There's nothing more to be done or said here." They got as far as the door when Lucille freed herself and barked at Hoolihan to give her the money. "What money?' he asked.

"Are you a fool, too?" She reached into his pants pocket and pulled out a sheaf of bills. She threw them into the air and they fluttered like drab green, wingless birds. "That's the last you'll get from me! Lie down with dogs, Jon Cotton, get up with fleas!" And with that, they left.

Neither Jon nor Claire moved. They waited for Lucille's smoke and perfume to follow her down the hall. Claire sat with her hands pressed between her knees. Without looking at the money, Jon went to the window and pulled the curtain aside; he watched his mother elbow aside pedestrians on her way to the car, which was parked somewhere out of sight. "I'm going to the toilet," he announced. He closed the door behind him.

Claire commanded her body to rise, but just like the night she had first met Jon, nothing obeyed. She was not stoned now, but she was paralyzed all the same. Her breath came in short, sharp stabs, alternating currents of loss and shame electrified her body, but still she could not move. She would not cry. Not now. Later, she promised herself. She had just wobbled to her feet when Jon returned. He leaned against the door heavily.

"Well, I guess I'll be going then," she said uncertainly. "I guess there's nothing more here."

"Don't leave me, Claire."

"Don't leave you!" she shrieked, realizing vaguely that she sounded like Lucille. "Don't leave you! You were going to leave me! You're going to some hole in the desert! You didn't even tell me you were going and then you have the nerve to ask me not to leave you! You'd never have told me at all if your mother hadn't come here."

"I would have. I was going to. I tried to write you when I made the decision, but it wasn't a thing I could write, and then, when you came here you were so undone about your father, how could I say anything then?"

"Let me out of here. Get away from that door and let me go."

"I won't. Not that easily, anyway. I love you. Oh, Claire—you've known—from the beginning—that I intended to leave the university. Don't you remember that first night, after Kerchiaeff, I said to you then—"

"Get out of my way."

"I can't go on living like this, Claire, getting my life pruned down so I'll fit the same mold as everyone else. The revolution's coming, I know it. I want to be where the revolution is, not studying what's happened in the past. I want to act, not read!"

"Let me out of here." She advanced on him, her fingers curling into fists and she hurled them against his chest, his gut, his shoulders and then she kicked him, but he held her until she began to sob and the kicking stopped and she fell against him. "Liar," she wept. "Liar."

"Oh, babe, oh, Claire, I love you so much," he whispered in her hair. "When you left here, I felt like I was suddenly dead and I'd only just been brought to life those three days here with you. I was dead without you, babe."

"How can I lose you?" she sobbed. "I've just lost my father."

171

"You're not losing me. You'll never lose me." He held her tighter. "Come with me, Claire. Come to Chagrin with me. You can have a life there."

"In Chagrin!" she laughed, an odd, gasping laugh. "What kind of name is that?"

"I don't know. I don't care. Just come with me, please. I'm begging you, babe. Let's go somewhere fresh and have a life together. Live together and sleep together and eat together and be crazy and free together for the rest of our lives."

"Is that a proposal of marriage?"

"Oh, Claire, don't. Don't ask me to be expedient and marry you for the sake of convention or because I can get out of the draft if I'm a married man or—"

"I didn't say that! I said, If you love me, you'll marry me!"

"I do love you, but you know I hate religion and all that—"

"How can I go off with you? What would my mother say?"

Jon almost said, Fuck your mother, but thought better of it. Instead, he offered the obvious, "You think your mother would let you marry Lucille Swallow's son? You think for one minute she'd give us her blessing? What do you really want, Claire? What matters to you? A real marriage, a real alliance of people who love each other or some stupid fucking white wedding day, with bells and flowers, a preacher who'll allow you to go to bed with a man? We've been to bed, Claire. We know that about each other. We know what we want."

"We don't. You. You know what you want."

"I want you. I want to have a life with you."

"Then marry me."

"Even if I said yes, do you think you could marry me? Do you think they'd let you? Do you really think you could dress up in some white satin and have your family grin and throw rice at Claire Swallow and Jon Cotton? I say, Damn the Swallows, Claire. Let's damn all of them and go away together."

"To some horrible hole in the desert?"

"What else can we do? What kind of future do we have otherwise? How can I stay here and live for those weekends or once a month or once every three or four months when you can escape from home? Think of all the sneaking and the lying. They've thrown you out of school, Claire—the hypocrites—but it means you can't come back here and I'm not going to write you letters with Melinda Lamott's name on the envelope for the rest of my life. What are you going to do with the rest of your life? Think of it. We have a future. Come with me or you'll end up living at home and looking after your mother for the rest of your life. She can't ask that of you."

"She hasn't."

"But she will," he said passionately. "Don't you see? She won't mean to, but she will. She'll mourn your father for the rest of her life."

"So will I." Claire began to cry again. "He was the best man who ever lived."

"Are you going to give your life over to his memory? Are you? God! You're too young to live on memories. Memories are nothing but sand-castles, Claire. You build them up and then the tide of everyday life washes over them and they're gone, vanished, and you stare at the spot where you built them and you've got nothing. Do you think your father would want you to live like that?"

"My father wouldn't want me to run off with you, either."

"Would your father have wanted you to marry me?"

"Probably not," she admitted.

"Then I say, To hell with the Swallows—living and dead—to hell with the Senator and his money and the past. It can't have any power over us, Claire, we can't let it. If we do, we're defeated and they've got us. I'm not going to end up like my mother—manacled to money. Are you going to end up like your mother—manacled to the goddam Three D's and what everyone expects of you? Claire, we love each other—do you know how really rare that is?"

"Oh, everyone falls in love. Don't they?" she added quizzically.

"Everyone thinks they do and then they get married and they end up hemmed in, jailed behind all the conventions. That's what institutions do to people. Marriage is as much an institution as the jail or the mad-house—you go in docilely enough and you get sent to a clean padded room where you can't hurt yourself and you stay there for the rest of your life. Not me, Claire. Not us. Without you, I'll be an empty man, but I won't live like that."

"I want to get married," she said stubbornly.

"Is that all you want? Just to get married? To anyone? If that's what you really want, then why don't you marry one of those stupid frater-nity boys you were fucking?"

"I was not," she said defensively. "I was—I was—" But in truth Claire had only the dimmest recollection of what she was before Jon; Anson's death had obliterated that girl and the dreams he had for her. In the week since her father died, Claire found herself sitting in front of the piano like a neophyte, utterly bereft of the skill and drive required of a professional. Perhaps that was never her own dream at all; perhaps she had simply, consistently lived up to Anson's bright expectations. Without Anson there were no expectations, no visions of the future, nothing save for love and Jon Cotton, who offered her love and a life that could be shared indefinitely, forever, always. She had lost Anson and if she rejected Jon, what would Claire Swallow be? A dreamless vessel bobbing on an empty sea. Without Jon, her heart, her future, her very life would go dry and hard and brittle, and she thought, oddly, of the Mourning Glory, dry and hard and brittle.

"Don't leave me, Claire. I'll be yours for the rest of my life. I promise. We'll have a wonderful life together and it's here and it's ours and all we need to do is take it."

"Promise?"

"I promise. For the rest of my life."

"For the rest of my life," Claire repeated as his eloquent, persuasive hands moved over her back and shoulders and hair and hips. "Promise," she said as they moved backward toward the bed, pulled in its lunar tug. She left her summer dress in the middle of the floor and the half slip where it slid from her hips and she sat at the edge of the bed and unfastened his cotton shirt with fumbling fingers and the belt and the snaps on his jeans and placed her cheek against his thigh and parted her lips and closed her eyes. Claire lay back slowly and Jon stroked her face and his words and hands and body enveloped her. She wanted him everywhere at once and as the late sunlight retreated from the room, she floated on the physical currents they engendered, a body without volition, so translucent, simple and fulfilled she did not recognize the moment for what it was: the first decision of her life for which she was wholly accountable. She lay beneath Jon and let him flow over and through her; on that narrow bed she gave herself to him, just as she had given herself to the vast Pacific when she was a child at San Angelo, when she let the slow waves turn her in their hands, when the foam prickled along her back and legs, when the breakers continually nudged her toward the beach and she resisted because she never never wanted to reach that shore; like a dolphin, she wanted to stay in the waves and slow water, but for all her struggle she found she couldn't hold on to the tide. A man, of course, was different; a man you could hold on to.

PART II

SANDCASTLES

CHAPTER ONE

September 1985

Claire eyed the wave about to crash over her, dove down and then plied forward, graceful as a gray dolphin, till she came at last to that point just beyond the breakers where the water was taut and smooth, where she could float, arching her back and tilting her head so the water framed her face in a huge oceanic bonnet and the sun beat on her belly. She tried to find time every afternoon to swim, to float here, so that when she went to bed at night, her body could remember the rocking sea, recapitulate the undulating transport, effortlessly recapture the Pacific's pitch and toss—court sleep—because without this watery interval, Claire herself pitched and tossed, sleepless in her bed. She began to tread water, facing west, where the sun hung in the cloudless sky like an enormous brass pocketwatch. The current nudged her shoreward, but she resisted until at last her arms and legs tired and then she relinquished herself unwillingly and one wave after another wafted her back to the beach. Foam and sand blurred, golden-green underwater light whirled in tiny points before her eyes till at last she staggered to her feet and made her way dripping to her towel, spread out like a hundred others on the beach that was no longer the—more or less—private property of the Swallows.

In the mid-seventies, a freeway had cut through the coastal hills of San Angelo County and though the town retained its posh reputation, it no longer catered solely to the needs of resort seekers; shopping malls and light industrial parks now shingled the land, and housing developments sheltered the lives of commuters, who daily drove distances that would have been impossible without the freeway. Amongst the pine- and cypress-clad cliffs overlooking the ocean, these commuters had built lavish hillside homes with redwood decks perched on stilts. Senator Swallow's wish to see Jerusalem Road paved had long since been granted, but he probably would not have been pleased to know that it had also been enlarged and extended up the bluffs to accommodate those glass-and-wood testaments to upward mobility. Indeed, San Angelo itself would not have pleased the Senator. His fame had receded in the wake of time, and Swallow Golf Course had been rechristened Ocean Pines; his old Victorian home, rather than being number one Jerusalem Road, now bore the undistinguished address of 3246. Nestled below and between the gleaming new homes and condos, the Swallow house no longer commanded the beach and bluffs, no longer commanded at all, but seemingly sulked, a dated, dilapitated eyesore, the rain gutters falling off, paint peeling, shutters awry, hemmed off from public pathways to the beach by a fence of unembellished chicken wire.

Claire threw herself down on her towel and quickly put on a pair of dark glasses and a sunhat. She liked to look at the world with the sun slatting through the straw interstices, and from behind the shelter of the glasses, she felt quite invisible and not at all obliged to speak to others, however close their towels and children and dogs might be. Behind her, a group of teenagers lay stretched out, their limbs twitching in time to the jackhammer rhythms of the popular song blasting out of their radio. Claire determined to ignore it, oiled herself with suntan lotion, picked up her novel and reached into her bag to check her watch. She had half an hour yet before her last piano student of the day, Justin Moffat, arrived. She hoped that Lucky and his friends from the Fellowship of the New Millenium would finish in the living room by then. Thrice weekly they met to ask each other if Adam had a belly button. Where might Cain's wife have come from? Did AIDS qualify as one of the scourges mentioned in the Bible? Oh, there was no end to their tiresome discussion and Claire could have ignored them altogether, except they insisted on meeting in the living room, where the upright piano sat, and though Claire objected continually, they met her every complaint with unshakably nodding beatitude.

She settled down on her towel, ostensibly reading, but from beneath her hat she watched a group of nearby children carrying buckets of water to shore up their sandcastles. Mediocre sandcastles, she thought, but then Claire's judgment was based on a nostalgic assessment of Bart's grand designs during those sweetly stagnant childhood summers. Claire turned her attention to the children's mothers: how pleasant their lives looked, how simple and safe and certain—feminine camaraderie amongst the ice chests and beach buckets and then home to soothe their occasionally cross, overworked husbands in houses with chromium kitchens where they made pastry in their food processors by day and made love in their waterbeds at night.

Claire had not made love in a long time. Lucky's health forbade it, though he was recuperating nicely, making excellent progress, his doctor said. True, Lucky stooped a bit, as if the stitches in his gut made it difficult for him to stand altogether upright, but Lucky's eyes had lost their alcoholic puffiness, his face had lost its pallor and his voice no longer quavered. He was cheerful and helpful around the house (if overly absorbed by the Fellowship of the New Millenium) and soon he would be well enough to begin doing the community service imposed by his sentence. No doubt, then he could make love. Perhaps he could even get a job, though the family tacitly avoided the question of who, exactly, might hire a man with Lucky's record. At least it was only a record. At least Lucky was not rotting in some minimum-security prison, where he almost certainly would have gone if not for Hoolihan. Hoolihan had saved them.

As Claire had sat in court those early awful days of the summer, she blessed Bart for insisting they accept Hoolihan's offer. There was nothing Hoolihan couldn't do—turn water into wine, stones to butter, straw to gold, a stolen car into a borrowed one (after the front seat had been replaced). Daily, Claire had tensed on the edge of the courtroom bench and watched the sixty-year-old Hoolihan cast things in a certain light. Throughout the trial, Claire had the sensation of Hoolihan guiding them—one and all—round and round a still, deep pool in a forest where shafts of his created light pierced the trees and, though fractured, that light retained its blade-sharp intent until it plunged into the water, where it shattered, sliced at oblique angles and distorted: what was straight became swirled and what was firm, gelatinous. Hoolihan rendered Lucky's labyrinthine business dealings into a simple formula, which he applied again and again: Lucky Stone was the victim of nasty criminal elements; he was more sinned against than sinning. Hoolihan trotted out Lucky's general unblemished record at every interval, never mentioned his drinking (and when the prosecutor did,

Hoolihan turned it to the defense's advantage), reduced Lucky's penchant for high-stakes gambling to the equivalent of social bingo, portrayed his suicide attempt as the act of a man who preferred death to dishonor. Moreover, Hoolihan treated the Stone family as bit players in a drama of his own devising: no detail escaped him. Hoolihan insisted that Bart push Lucky into court in a wheelchair, allowing him to walk with canes only toward the end. Hoolihan suggested Claire's wardrobe and even stooped to pressing Althea and the ailing Meg into service, probably guessing the ordeal would prove too much for Meg, who missed her knitting and occasionally cried out for Anson, which allowed Hoolihan to make the point that the immortal Judge Anson Swallow (father-in-law to the wrongly accused) would never have omitted those weightier matters of the law, mercy and faith.

When Claire could tear her eyes from Hoolihan's masterful performance, she watched the judge. (The prosecuting attorney didn't bear watching; he was a young man, clearly—and correctly—undone by the prospects of facing the great Hoolihan in court.) This judge was middle-aged, sleepy, and nonchalant. Claire remembered the rectitude redolent in Anson's office—the works of Emerson, Thoreau and Jefferson amongst the law books, the globe spinning by the window. Surely a judge of Anson's stature would never have succumbed to Hoolihan's magic. She hoped this judge had no such resistance.

In the end, her hope was rewarded: Lucky got off with a fat fine, his wrists slapped publicly, and the penalty of six hundred hours of community service, to be rendered when his health returned. Hoolihan, however, never once relaxed. On the trial's last day, he explained to the family outside the courtroom that they should not display too much relief at the sentence (did he already know what it was?); relief implies guilt, he warned them, no weeping or embracing: save all that for outside the courtroom.

But once outside the courtroom, as Bart and Hoolihan flanked Lucky on their way to the car, Claire hung back. She felt not the slightest twinge of relief, only wild unreasoning fear: Hoolihan was leaving them. Hoolihan would no longer be there to direct them. They could no longer simply obey his injunctions, but must now act, think, judge for themselves. What would become of them now?

Hoolihan shook hands with Bart and Lucky and dusted away their protestations of gratitude with kind words about Anson Swallow. Hoolihan turned to Claire, who took his hand, clutched it, held him while she searched his gray eyes. "What will we do now?" she asked, half realizing how childish and frightened she sounded. "What will happen to us? Where will we go? What can we do?"

"Whatever you like, Claire. Within the confines of his community service, Lucky is a free man."

"But we can't—" her voice spiraled upwards, "we haven't—we aren't—we've lost everything."

"That's not true," Lucky said gently. "We have each other. We have our family, and God will watch over us."

"God watched over us in there." Claire nodded toward the hulking federal courthouse. "But now we have to—to—"

"Cope," Hoolihan supplied, not unpleasantly. "I have every faith in you. You're Anson Swallow's daughter, after all."

Bart held Lucky's canes while he lowered himself into the back seat. "We'll manage," Bart said cheerfully. "There's always Jerusalem Road. The Swallows have always returned there, haven't we, Claire?" He smiled at his sister. "Whatever our migrations, we always come home to roost."

Claire and Lucky and their three sons had done just that, and despite the humbling circumstances of their return and the old home's obvious decay, Claire found a warmth and pleasure and permanence here she had never felt anywhere else. Every room (save for the turret bedroom, which now served as an attic) succumbed to an onslaught of cleaning; cobwebs festooning the furniture uprooted, windows creaked open, the old plumbing tourniqueted with new rags, the impacted dust reduced to motes glowing in the afternoon sunshine that poured through the tall windows. All those changes that could be effected with simple soap and water were undertaken; there wasn't money for anything more thoroughgoing, but as she assaulted each room with the brush, mop and broom, Claire listened as the old house whispered to her of a happier past, her lost childhood, her long-dead father, her once-gracious mother.

Meg was more than a spiritual presence. Meg and Althea also moved back to Jerusalem Road with the Stone family. Meg required more care, caution and watching than the aging Althea could provide alone, and they all agreed that the return to Jerusalem Road was the happiest alternative to an institution; Meg could be comfortable here, loved and cared for. Claire was happy to have her, relieving Bart of the responsibility for Meg and the Mourning Glory was the least she could do for the brother who had not only stood by them throughout their ordeal, but made the requisite gesture of thanks as well. Bart sent Hoolihan a case of fine Bordeaux with a note swearing the family's undying thanks. Claire thought this a bit much, but then she hadn't Bart's generosity of spirit. She loathed feeling grateful and in this, though she could not have known it, she was very like the Senator himself; like him, she preferred the clean crackle of crisp bills, to pay and be done with things and not have them mucked up with gratitude. But in this instance, she hadn't that comfortable option as she hadn't any crisp bills to crackle.

Money. Claire worried about money. Day and night. She figured expenses down to the last quarter and then refigured them down to the last dime. Rent was free and Bart paid the now-exorbitant taxes on Jerusalem Road, but the Stones had to pool their every resource to live at all. Althea wrested a thriving garden from the nasturtiums, and Claire began giving piano lessons (surprised, actually, at how much she enjoyed her work) and gradually her students increased. Her youngest son, Dan, got a job in a gas station, and Jason got a job hanging dry wall, and Scott worked the night shift at the Hole in One, a doughnut shop near the golf course. Claire's heart broke every morning when Scott came in, surly and reeking of grease. When he wasn't sleeping off the doughnut shop, Scott sat in the kitchen with Meg and watched soap operas and drank beer and toyed nervously with his earring. Claire longed to comfort him, but all she could muster were assurances that his tenure in the doughnut shop was finite, that she would find a way to send him back to Stanford. "I'll think of something," she promised continually, but now it was September and Scott assuredly would not be returning to Stanford this term.

Claire made a futile swipe at the hovering sand flies, covered her face with her book and dozed, grateful for the beckoning rest, because night after night she lay sleepless, tense and beleaguered. Money. Money. She could have better borne her burdens had she been able to share them, but she didn't want to alarm the younger boys and Scott was too preoccupied with his own unhappiness. Meg always confused her with Jill or Marietta, and Althea simply answered Claire's anxieties with variations on her thirty-year-old refrain against Lucille Swallow, who was the author of their every affliction. True, perhaps, but hardly helpful. And Lucky? Oh, Lucky.

Claire rolled over, the book slid from her eyes and she buried her face in her arms, as if she might weep. Claire now realized how much of their marriage had rested on physical intimacy, how eloquent and communicative they had been with their bodies. Denied sex, they grew daily more distant, and as Lucky retreated from her, Claire felt increasingly stranded, staggering under the responsibilities he left with her. Everything changed. In the past, Lucky had always insisted that he would worry over money, not Claire. Claire was not to worry. Now he embraced that role as his own and showed not the slightest interest in their worldly circumstances. God's will, he assured her gently, God's will, he intoned, God's will would become known to them in God's good time. Claire did not have that kind of time. Good or otherwise. And she told him so, but the past and future held no appeal for Lucky Stone: he lived in a static, beatific present.

Since his suicide attempt, Lucky Stone had undergone what could only be described as a sea change. When the family first came to San Angelo, he went to a different church every Sunday and spent the weekdays closeted with various pastors, seeking a faith to accommodate his new fervor. He did not rest until he found the Fellowship of the New Millenium, one of those mellow collations of no particular persuasion who subscribed to the New Testament literally and to the Old Testament when it suited them. They cultivated heaven and clucked over hell; they took their religion personally and Jesus was their best chum.

Claire groaned to remember the first—and only—time she had succumbed to Lucky's entreaties to accompany him to a Sunday service. The Fellowship of the New Millenium met in the gym of the YMCA. As if inspired by the basketball hoops, the young pastor spoke extemporaneously of Jesus's abilities as a team player and a spiritual coach. The small congregation sang hymns from dog-eared mimeographed sheets. Sweltering in the airless gym, Claire fanned herself with the hymn sheet and regarded the worshipers, men and women dressed very much alike, in tank tops and jeans, not at all the gloved and hatted Episcopalian Sundays of Claire's youth. This congregation (save for an occasional enthusiastic Praise Be!) exuded a contentment Claire found downright soporific and she had in fact very nearly nodded off when her attention was caught by a woman who rose to lead them in prayer once the young pastor had finished. Her iron gray hair was pulled back severely from a genial face and her tennis shoes squealed on the gym floor. She was big, with sagging breasts and skinny flanks, and Claire somehow connected her with the odor of peppermint Lifesavers. *Matthew Mark Luke and John, I don't believe it! The weird sisters from the Emergency Room. Yes, some religious meeting had brought them up from San Angelo. It's her, all right, the Scripture-spouting busybody. Oh Lord, let us get out of here before she recognizes me.*

But Emma caught sight of her from the podium and Claire might just as well have tried to outrun destiny as Emma Duff. Delighted with Lucky's conversion to the Fellowship, Emma personally inducted him into the heart of their small body—Sunday worship, proselytizing in parking lots and thrice weekly biblical discussion groups held in members' homes, more often than not, in the Swallow home. Her sister Evangeline usually drove Emma over for the meetings and stayed to chat in the kitchen with Althea. Lucky often asked Emma and Evangeline to stay to supper—much to Althea's chagrin and Claire's dismay. Evangeline grumbled incessantly and Emma never stopped talking. Emma's favorite topic of conversation (other than the Second Coming) was the old days in San Angelo, where her mother had ironed sheets in the basement of one of the big hotels for thirty years. Emma saw the house on Jerusalem Road in a fog of remembered glory, never noting the buckling lineoleum, the cracked ceilings or the little mounds of termite dust. Emma said she'd never dreamed she'd be a guest one day in the home of Senator Swallow, but then God worked in mysterious ways. Claire once retorted that her presence there better testified to how the mighty are fallen, but Emma's good humor was absolutely imperturbable. Claire could never decide which was the more intolerable: Emma's mindless, happy faith or her untrammeled adoration of Lucky Stone.

The children nearby flipped sand on Claire; she jumped, and the matrons apologized. She dug in her bag and found her watch. Damn. Justin Moffat would be here any minute. She'd have to give him his lesson still reeking of suntan oil. Unprofessional, but she saw no help for it. Claire pulled on a pair of shorts and a T-shirt, gathered her towel and bag and scampered toward the house, where she washed her feet and hands with the garden hose.

Althea had tamed but by no means eradicated the nasturtiums, which still dominated the area from the porch to the gate and turned up where they weren't wanted besides. Nasturtiums blinked in between the fat tomatoes and glowed under the low-canopied squashes. Althea tended her garden with the diligence of a Danton (as opposed, say, to a Bonaparte), exterminating white flies as certifiable enemies of the vegetable state, stripping the silk from corn, snapping the crowned heads of lettuce and today loading tomatoes in tumbrils. She was assisted by a triumvirate of ducks, who wandered the garden at will and whose small pond (which Althea had constructed from a child's pool) continually stank. "Close that garden gate, Claire, unless you want to chase the ducks all over the beach. Again." Althea no longer wore strict mourning but contented herself with sober grays, neutral beiges and the occasionally festive lavender. In the garden, she worked in a pair of overalls and an embattled hat. "Your student's here," she called out. "That snotty little Justin is waiting in the hall."

"Are Lucky and the rest of them out of the living room yet?"

"They're praying goodbye in the kitchen. With any sort of luck, they won't be there when Christ comes again—or when Bart gets here."

"Bart's coming down?"

"He called a while ago and I told him I'd have something extra special for him for dinner."

Claire hurried into the front hall, where she found Justin clutching his music books and looking pleased to have caught her in a frazzled state. "I'll take just a moment to change," she promised. "You go in and start on your scales." His face fell.

"Jesus H. Christ! Can't you leave a guy in peace!" rang out from the kitchen, and Claire hurriedly urged Justin into the living room, closed the door and then went down the hall, where she found Scott lounging in Meg's rocker, beer in hand, watching the five-inch tummy TV set on the kitchen table. Ringed around the table, eyes closed, hands held, Lucky and Emma, the young pastor and five other Fellowshippers conducted their closing ceremonies. ". . . give us Thy blessings and protection, Lord as we. . ."

"Can't you do that somewhere else?" Scott barked. "How can I watch TV?"

Claire unplugged the TV and wound up the cord. "Take the TV upstairs."

"You know damn well Grandma's having her nap up there and she bitches if anyone so much as burps on the stairs. Anyway, I have more right to be here than they do. I have to go to the goddamned doughnut shop in a few hours and I want to—"

"You're being very rude, Scott."

". . . united in thy holy peace which surpasseth. . ."

"Me! What about them?"

"Amen," said the seven voices in unison.

"Well, Claire." Emma turned, embraced and enveloped her in an aura of menthol cigarettes and good intentions. "The Great Work goes on, don't it? Every day I know my Lord better and I stand all amazed at

His sacrifice. He was god, but chose to be human. Don't it just grab you, Claire?"

"He wasn't so human that He'd have a temper tantrum!" snapped one of the Fellowshippers.

"He did so, Enid." Emma bestowed on Enid her sweet but utterly obstinate smile and then turned to Claire, oblivious to the younger woman's impatience. "What you think, Claire? I say the Lord lost His temper. He threw them wicked scribes and Pharisees and hypocrites out of the temple in Jerusalem, scattered them like bowling pins and lost His temper. I like Him better for it. It just proves He was human and had failings."

"He was human, but perfect," retorted Enid.

"Well now, Enid, that ain't possible, is it? Human and perfect just ain't a possible combination. Claire knows I'm right, don't you, Claire?"

"Oh, Emma," Claire cried, helplessly pushing her hair from her face. "What do I know of it? What do I care?"

"Well, you certainly ought to care! He was your Saviour, too. Besides that," Emma proceeded, unwilling to relinquish her monopoly on correctness, "Jesus felt bad He'd lost his temper, just like an ordinary mortal would. He was sorry for His tantrum and sorry for Jerusalem. He come out of that temple and beheld that wicked city and cursed it—cursed it, Enid, and wept for it too. He knew how Jerusalem would be desolated and it just ate His poor heart out." As Emma began to crown her arguments with appropriate biblical quotations, Claire pulled away from her, telling Scott in no uncertain terms to take the TV upstairs.

"Scott can stay in the kitchen," Lucky offered. "We're leaving now."

"O Jerusalem, Jerusalem!" Emma continued triumphantly. "There shall come a day when these great buildings will be leveled unto dust! When there shall not be one stone left upon another! O, the things ye ought to have done, Jerusalem! Your temples are nothing but whited sepulchers beautiful without, but within full of dead men's bones and—"

Caught between the babbling Fellowshippers and the glowering Scott, Claire clenched her fists and shouted, "Where's Evangeline! Doesn't she usually take Emma and the others home?"

"Not on Tuesday." Emma sighed; compared to biblical invocation, matters of transportation were unspeakably trivial. "Tuesday's Evangeline's bingo day. She gambles, you know."

"Begin with bingo, end with bankruptcy," Lucky added gravely, ever ready to draw a moral from circumstances.

"Did you begin with bingo, Dad?" Scott sneered.

"You hush!" Claire admonished him. He sulked over the TV clasped in his arms.

Lucky held out his hand. "Can I have the keys, Scott? I have to take Emma and a few others home."

"It's my car and I need it to get to work."

"It's our only car now, Scott," Claire reminded him.

"Let Emma take the bus."

"I don't mind at all." Emma patted Scott's arm, and he recoiled. "Just the other day I brought another soul to Jesus on the bus."

Claire swept Emma and the Fellowshippers through the back door. Then she turned to her eldest son. "Now, give your father the keys and be quick about it. I can't stand here all day."

"I have to go to the goddamned doughnut shop."

"Not for hours yet. He's only going to drop them off, aren't you Lucky? He's not going to stay at anyone's house, are you? Your dad will be back in half an hour, won't you?"

"That's what he said the last time. Oh shit." Scott flung the keys across the table and with the TV under his arm, he stalked out.

"He gets worse every day," said Lucky, reaching for the keys. "More profane, more godless, more cynical."

"Don't be so harsh, Lucky. He's just at loose ends. He'll be fine once he goes back to Stanford."

"That's in God's hands," said Lucky, rebuffing as he always did any discussion of their finances or their future.

"No, it's in our hands, Lucky. It's up to us to see he goes back to Stanford. We have to think of something," Claire implored. "Dan's still in high school and Jason can go to San Angelo Community College, but Scott has wonderful gifts and he can't let them rot at the goddamned doughnut shop!"

"Don't blaspheme, Claire."

"I'm sorry, but you don't seem to understand how important this is. It's Scott's whole future. His whole life! We have to think of something. Scott needs money for Stanford."

"Scott needs moral guidance. I wish he'd join me at the Fellowship. I wish you would too, Claire. You'd find comfort there. Really. You should rely on God. He will answer all our queries in His time."

"I don't have that kind of time."

Lucky patted her hand and then began to whistle "Onward Christian Soldiers" on his way out of the door and the tune jangled alongside the uncertain measures of "Minuet in G" wafting from the living room and bits of leftover Scripture rattling, echoing amongst the potted herbs and mismatched crockery, and together these sounds rang discordantly in Claire's skull. Alone in the kitchen, she sank down at the table, her hands over her face, and in that moment snatched between her neverending obligations, Claire wept, like Jesus, and wondered if the destruction He promised and visited upon the ancient stones of Jerusalem might not be the same fate awaiting the Stones of Jerusalem Road.

ii

Althea Swallow sat drumming her fingers on the kitchen table as she leafed through a pile of cookbooks and made notes in her prim hand. Sometimes she chewed her pencil. On the floor beside her, a basket bulged with tomatoes. She glanced at the windowsills crowded with pots of leafy herbs: enough cilantro for salsa and enough basil for spaghetti sauce, but Althea really wanted to can these tomatoes. The thought of them glowing and rubicund in jars lined on the shelf pleased her, but that was a project to begin in the morning, not this late in the afternoon. "And besides, there's more where these came from, right Meg? Meg? What do you think?" she shouted across the invisible chasm where her sister-in-law lived largely in the past. Personally, Althea was of the opinion that Meg's affliction could be cured by careful attention to diet, but nothing proved particularly efficacious. Althea looked after Meg with the same untiring devotion she'd once given to Edith Swallow and would have donated to the Senator if he hadn't married that whore Lucille Swallow and been spared his declining years. "You have to help me, Meg. Bart's coming to dinner and I have to use up these tomatoes or they'll all rot."

"Let them all rot," replied Meg, rocking furiously over the uneven linoleum. "All of them. They're not worth a hair on your head, Anson. Not even the Senator, and how can you believe Hoolihan anyway, Anson? Hoolihan is odious and vulgar and low, you can't let someone like that. . ."

Althea rose, crossed the kitchen and pressed Meg's hand. The fleshly contact seemed to stir her, she smiled, her rocking slowed its pace and her knitting needles picked up theirs. "Damn Hoolihan all to hell," Althea muttered, returning to her tomatoes. Such a brute. Oh sure, he saved Lucky, but to bring Meg into court! She hadn't yet recovered. Well, you won't find me slavering after Hoolihan, dripping gratitude. He's an insufferable hypocrite, and the only person worse is Lucille herself. "Meg dear, I have to go out back to get some peaches for dessert tonight. Would you like that, Meg? Peaches Althea? They're Bart's favorite. I'll be right back. You sit tight."

Althea quickly picked the few remaining peaches, bright as royal orbs, and hurried back into the house. It didn't do to leave Meg alone for long. Last week she'd got up in the middle of the night, donned her shoes, hat, gloves and stockings (which she forgot to attach to anything), and in the morning, after a frantic search, they had found her sitting in the car, waiting to be taken to church. About an hour after breakfast, Meg had removed her own gloves so she could knit. She no longer knitted anything in particular, neither shawls nor blankets nor socks nor sweaters, she just knitted until the work grew so immense and unwieldy that Althea unhooked it from the needles after Meg had gone to bed. Painstakingly (and always out of Meg's sight), Althea undid her efforts and rolled the yarn back into balls so that, without knowing it, Meg used the same yarn over and over—her favorite colors, starfish mauve, barnacle green, mussel gray and sea urchin blue. Re-using the yarn was a necessary economy in the family's current circumstances, and Meg seemed none the wiser.

A great tragedy, Meg, Althea reflected as she scrubbed and split the peaches, readying them for their transformation into namesakes. Perhaps the tragedy was the family's rather than Meg's own. Meg, after all, seemed generally placid, even happy except when her voyages into the past foundered on Hoolihan's name or Lucille's or the Senator's or a few odd, incongruous others including someone called (of all things!) One-Strap. When one of those names came up, Althea never failed to go to Meg's side, rouse or comfort her, whichever seemed the most expedient. She glanced at her now; Meg's face was still smooth and pink, but her mouth hung slack and loose, her tongue continually running over her teeth.

"Where is that nice lady who lives here?" Meg asked at length.

"That's your daughter, Claire. She's just finishing up a music lesson in the living room. Can't you hear them? I wish that child would get that piece right, just once. There, you hear that car in the driveway? That'll be Justin's mother."

Justin Moffat executed a facsimile of the final chord of the "Minuet in G" and presently he came into the kitchen on his way out the back door.

"Little boy." Meg crooked her finger. "Come here."

"Now, Meg, Justin has to leave." Althea took the boy's shoulder, but he squirmed free and trotted over to Meg.

"Have you got candy for me?"

"Candy!" Althea's eyebrows ricocheted upward. Her dietary principles for Meg did not include candy.

"She always gives me a peppermint Lifesaver if I answer right."

"Answer what?"

"Little boy, what is the capital of Anza Borrego?"

Justin considered carefully. "Portland."

"Very good." Meg dug in her pocket and brought out a sticky Lifesaver and Justin left with it bulging in his jaw.

"It's that Emma Duff, isn't it?" Althea snarled. "I've told her a hundred times not to give you candy. That woman is a pest."

"Emma is very nice."

"Hmph. I detest nice people."

"I'm nice."

"Of course you are, dear Meg, I didn't mean you. You're a lady, though, and Emma Duff is coarse and common, but she's not as bad as that awful sister of hers. Evangeline sits here and guzzles beer and takes up my time and—criticize! Evangeline Duff never has a kind word for anyone. And swear!" Althea gave the peach halves each fat belly buttons of amaretto biscuits, sprinkled them with brown sugar and put them in the fridge. "No lady swears. I tell you, Meg, if the Senator had ever heard the names Lucille called that typewriter, he'd have known her for the whore she is, but no, around the Senator she all but gargled sugar water. Makes you barf."

"Barf is very vulgar, Jill."

"Yes, you're a lady, Meg, and it's a pity your daughters didn't take after you. Claire's not too bad, though, but you never would have guessed it would turn out that way, would you? Always the wild one, that Claire, Jill and Marietta, such sweet little angels they were. Always so polite and nice and sweet. But just look at them now. They should have got married. Marriage is what saved Claire. Shaped her right up, marriage and motherhood. Well, I guess she's finding out now how a mother's heart gets broken and how sharper than a serpent's tooth.

Hmph. Twenty years too late to do *you* any good, Meg." Althea decided on the salsa because Bart liked tacos; she put a pot of water on to boil and hoisted the tomatoes to the sink. "Scott and Stanford, that's all Claire talks about. Stanford, hah! Scott was lucky to get a job at the Hole in One, and even then he had to wash the green streak out of his hair, didn't he? Children are a curse, Meg. After everything you did for yours, just look at them. Jill living in sin with whatshisname and Marietta always breaking down, though Bart told me on the phone he got a letter from her and she's got a job. She's a drug counselor in L.A. A drug counselor! Well, I said to Bart, that's like the blind leading the deaf, dumb and lame, isn't it? But Bart said I ought to show some charity. What for? No Swallow ever took charity, so why should we give it? But Bart's a gentleman, all right. Just like Anson."

"I can't bear what this is doing to your health, oh, Anson."

"Now now, dear." Althea smoothed Meg's soft cheek. "Tacos for dinner. How does that sound? Tacos and fresh salsa just for you and Bart. There's not a Mexican in San Angelo who makes a better taco than I do. Of course there aren't any Mexicans in San Angelo anymore. They can't afford it. Who can? All those nouveaux riches types with their BMWs and Mercedes, they've turned this town into a—"

"He was guilty, Anson, you said so," Meg pleaded with the irrevocable past. "He was guilty—"

"Oh listen, Meg. There's Claire playing that awful old Mozart. Or someone like him."

"Does someone like Mozart?" Meg looked up quizzically and her needles hushed. "Is he coming for dinner? You better tell Althea."

"No, dear, only Bart's coming for dinner." Briskly, Althea cut a handful of cilantro from the pots lining the windowsills and its peppery odor filled the kitchen. The water started to boil and she popped the tomatoes in a few at a time and brought them out with a slotted spoon, their skins crackling and peeling like the paint on the front of the house. She chopped her cilantro with an executioner's aplomb as the music from the living room beat its way to a glowing crescendo. "What's Claire got against Jerome Kern? I ask you? Why does she have to play that awful old seventeenth-century stuff?" Althea punched a couple of onions into her Cuisinart and over its roar outlined a few more of Claire's shortcomings and by the time the onions were sliced, Claire had finished at the piano and returned to the kitchen. "You look terrible," Althea commented. "You have dark circles under your eyes. I keep telling you to drink hot chicken soup with lemon juice before you go to bed."

"I need a beer." Claire went to the fridge.

"You'll look in vain in there. Your dear son swilled every drop. In one afternoon, I might add."

Claire glanced up at the kitchen clock. "When will dinner be ready? Scott has to eat before he goes to the doughnut shop."

"Let him eat cake." Althea began chopping tomatoes, and seeds spurted everywhere.

Claire poured herself a glass of cold white wine and frowned to see the price tag on the bottle; she wouldn't trust Althea with the shopping anymore. "Is Lucky back with the car yet?"

"Do pigs have wings?"

"I hope Scott doesn't have to take the bus to work."

"You could carry him piggy-back, Claire. You could stand there at the Hole in One and hold his hand while he fries doughnuts."

"Quit ragging on Scott! You never say mean things about the other boys."

"And with good reason." Althea dumped the onions in with the tomatoes. "Dan and Jason, those boys are Swallows. They know how to manufacture opportunity. The Senator would have been proud of Dan and Jason. They have brains and energy."

"So does Scott."

"Scott's pretty and he has charm. I'll say that for him. But brains? Really, Claire. He flunked out of Stanford, didn't he?"

"He left because there wasn't any money. He'll do wonderfully at Stanford now. He has more maturity."

"Hmph. Send him to the community college, where Jason's going. You don't hear Jason weeping in his beer because he can't go to Stanford."

Claire started to say that Scott didn't weep over Stanford either, but she could not let Althea guess that Stanford was her own dream. She could scarcely admit to herself that she had pinned her every hope of victory on Scott's returning to Stanford. Claire had only to close her eyes to see Scott's life—a series of undiminished successes—unfurl from a framed, cream-colored degree she had hung on the wall of her mind.

"It's not the money Scott lacks," Althea continued mercilessly. "It's initiative. Why, look at Bart. He was younger than Scott when he went to work and now he's director of the South American trade."

"Scott's not Bart."

"Don't I know it! Bart never wore an earring. Bart never dyed a green streak in his hair. Bart never lay around and watched soap operas and drank beer. Bart went out and got a job."

"I don't want Scott to do low work. He has a brilliant future. He's going back to Stanford," she said firmly.

"Maybe Scott could get a scholarship." Althea got out a frying pan and poured oil in it and heated it up. "You should call up Hoolihan and ask if Lucille has endowed a scholarship with all the money she stole from us. The Lucille Swallow Fund for Brainless Boys."

"Scott's not brainless."

"Or maybe you could get her to loan you the money."

"Very funny, Althea."

"You could say, Look here, Lucille, you cheated us and it's all your fault we don't have any money to send this brainless boy to Stanford, so why don't you just cough it up?"

"Lucille would die first."

"Yes, of course. You could say, Lucille, you're old and you're going to die and go to hell and burn there for the rest of eternity." Althea smiled at the vision of Lucille wriggling over a hellish pit. "But if you sent the Senator's great-grandson to Stanford, maybe God would forgive you. You have buckets of money, more than you know what to do with."

"Isn't that the truth," Claire said sourly. "If only she would give us a loan for Stanford."

"You could say to her, Lucille, after everything you did, disinheriting a whole family—"

"Scott could pay the loan back after he graduates," Claire added.

"Yes, with the money he gets when he wins the Nobel Prize. Here." Althea tossed Claire an orange and the grater. "Grate the peel off that and make yourself useful. Orange peel—that's the secret of my salsa, and I leave it out whenever I give anyone the recipe. And even if Lucille didn't believe Scott would win the Nobel Prize, you could always remind her how she didn't have any luck with her own son—what was his name, the one who became a terrorist?"

"He wasn't a terrorist." Reluctantly, Claire dragged the body of the orange over the grater and brilliant bits of moisture and memory flew into her face; she sniffed the ageless orange like cocaine, dangerous, exhilarating, addictive, that rare moment of smoke, shadow and jasmine tea in the room above the rare books and wrong maps. "He was an anarchist."

"Same thing. His picture's probably up in the post office somewhere. I always laugh to think how that boy broke Lucille's heart, but then I remember that she didn't have a heart. She never did give a damn about that boy, or the girl either, that little twit, Lucy Rose."

"Such a lovely bride, Lucy Rose," Meg interjected wistfully. "And such a grand wedding, Vera. Did you ever see such food and wine and all those flowers. They came from Hawaii, and look! Look, Vera, Claire caught the bouquet!"

Claire thrust the orange and grater away from her and went to her mother and smoothed Meg's short hair. "Yes, Mama, I caught the bouquet."

"It was an expensive wedding, Meg," Althea corrected her. "But it certainly wasn't grand. For grand you need taste, which Lucille hasn't got. For expensive you just need money. But, oh, that wedding just burned me up."

"Why?" asked Claire, taking her wine glass to the fridge and refilling it. "What was it to you?"

"Not the wedding so much, but the aftermath."

Claire stopped pouring with her glass one-third full. "The what?"

"Oh, you know, when Lucy Rose and Randolph went back to Honolulu and Lucille just gave Albert's job to that worthless Randolph. Randolph didn't even need that job, and Albert did."

"Albert? Who's Albert?"

"Mr. Albert Smyth," Althea returned coldly, "is a loyal, trusted employee of the Senator's. He quit Swallow Lines before Lucille could fire him and found employment elsewhere, but it was hard for a man his age, very hard, but at least he didn't have a family to support. He never married, you see." Althea flipped a corn tortilla into the hot oil and watched it bubble and burn. "Worms. Worms and vipers, all of them. Lucille and Lucy Rose and Randolph and what was that boy's name? The terrorist."

Claire kicked open the screen door on the back porch. "He was not a terrorist. He participated in a few marches protesting the Vietnam War." The screen door squealed shut behind her. "His name was Jon."

Claire had a chromium kitchen herself in those days. A chromium kitchen and a waterbed and an occasionally cross, overworked husband who was mowing the lawn that Saturday morning. She had three children, too. Her baby, Dan, fretted in his crib; Scotty watched cartoons in the living room, and squawks and squeals floated into the kitchen where the toddler Jason spilled blocks across the floor while

Claire made lunch. Flickering in black and white across the TV screen, Claire watched a peace march in Washington, D.C., as she deviled eggs. She was having company for lunch—her mother, Althea and Vera—and she reminded herself to turn the TV off before they arrived or there was sure to be a nasty quarrel between Vera and Althea that would ruin the afternoon. Althea had grown rabidly pro-Nixon and chanted his praises loudly, all the more partisan every time she saw Vera, who, in the two years since 1968, had taken to wearing love beads and bell-bottomed pants and workshirts embroidered with the peace symbol and the motif from Zig Zag cigarette papers.

Claire put the eggs on a plate and began slathering mayonnaise across slices of bread as she listened to the commentators natter about the lack of violence so far, as if describing a sporting event that would soon heat up and provide viewers with vicarious thrills. TV cameras panned through the crowd of young people, who embraced and held hands and gave the peace sign and sang "Give Peace a Chance", who wept and laughed and cheered and jeered with equal fervor as they were admonished from the podium to make love not war. The camera swooped and fastened on a young mother sitting on a picnic blanket. She had three children. Just like Claire. She was slathering mayonnaise on bread. Just like Claire. She wore a long tie-dyed skirt and her work-shirt was adorned with buttons protesting the war and she had flowers in her hair. Claire pushed her own long hair behind her ear, as if feeling for phantom flowers. *Might I just as easily be making sandwiches on the grass at a peace march surrounded by the army and the police? Can her life be so very different from mine? Aren't we the same generation?* The young mother caught sight of the camera and gave a peace sign and a smile. *What is it like to be that passionately committed to principle that you could bring your children to do battle for peace, that you could make sandwiches while soldiers behind sandbags trained their guns on your whole generation. My generation. Mine?*

Certainly it was Jill's generation. Claire looked amongst the crowd for her sister's face. Jill had been at a peace rally in New York some months before and wrote enthusiastically of her arrest and overnight stint in jail. And certainly it was Marietta's generation, but Claire did not bother to look for Marietta. Marietta was living in a commune in New Mexico. The last they heard.

Claire sliced the sandwiches and stacked them, arranged them on a plate, the lettuce curling out like crinoline. Then she went to Dan's room and got him out of his crib, changed him and kissed his tummy.

She heard Lucky ushering her mother and aunts into the kitchen and offering them each a glass of sherry. Damn. She'd left the TV on, and she could hear Althea and Vera begin to quarrel almost immediately.

Claire brought Dan into the kitchen and put him in Meg's arms, where he fussed and cried. Jason kicked his blocks over for the last time and left them where they lay, flinging himself into his grandmother's lap as well. Lucky poured Claire a glass of sherry, which she downed in one gulp.

"They ought to pack up every last hippie there and send them all to Russia," Althea snarled.

"I think those protesters are very brave," Vera countered over the baby's squall and Jason's demands for attention.

"What do you think of the weather, Lucky?" asked Meg.

"Just jiggle the baby please, Mama," Claire said, peeling a banana. "I'm going to fix him something to eat right now." She had the fork poised over the banana when, counterpointing the baby's cries, she heard a voice on the television, clarion as a coronet, cool and assured, so unlike the hectoring of the previous speakers. *Matthew Mark Luke* anyone but Jon.

His hair was shoulder length, his beard longer, his face thinner and more gaunt and he wore wire-rimmed glasses, which she did not remember. He gripped the podium with a white-knuckled intensity that she oddly did remember, though she had never seen him address more than a dozen people gathered casually around an outdoor fire. He was Jon Cotton, all right, but he reminded her of someone else, someone equally strange and foreign. Of Nicholas Kerchiaeff. Jon had Kerchiaeff's same lean, hungry look, as if he had supped too long on hope alone, confused dream with desire and passion with complex, volatile conviction. Seeing him there, exhorting the crowd to revolution, Claire felt a pang of envy: Jon had got what he wanted. But at the same moment, she could not stifle the pang of pity: *he's become the thing he hated.* Like Kerchiaeff, Jon Cotton percolated searing rage, the ruthless urge to convert. Claire fought to catch his words over the baby's screams.

"We who are gathered here today represent a petition in boots. We petition this government, that pig Nixon and all his swine to stop the war in Vietnam. We the people will not tolerate oppression, whether in this country or any other."

"Right on, brother," said Vera.

"I think it's going to rain, Meg," said Lucky. "That's why I'm mowing—"

196

"I come here today not to preach to the converted, but to reach the ears, the minds, of the corrupt. Power in this country is in the hands of swine." Cheers broke through and clouded his following words. When they subsided, he continued. "I want the swine to look up from their troughs long enough to hear the cries of babies they have napalmed, of women they have widowed, of men they have tortured. I want them to smell the rot in villages they have defoliated and lives they have ruined. I want them to listen, not simply to me or to this, our petition in boots, but to hear the voice of history, to attend to the words of Thomas Jefferson, who once said: 'I tremble for my country when I reflect that God is just!'"

"Calling our President a pig! Who does he think he is?"

Don't you know who that is? Claire nearly cried.

"He looks like Jesus," said Meg vaguely, dandling the angry baby.

"They all look like Jesus," Lucky added. "Except for their eyes."

The crowd chanted. The baby howled. The toddler whined. The speaker continued. "Look at the White House. Look at it, comrades. However pale and elegant its facade, the White House is full of filth and death. It is a tomb! The government buildings around us here in our nation's capital are temples to tyranny! Those temples will come down. We will bring them down. The revolution is coming! The revolution is here!"

"It won't be a revolution," said Vera sadly over the clamoring of the crowd and the baby's hungry cries. "It will be civil war. That's what I'm afraid of. Brother against brother. Sister against sister."

"Listen to us, Nixon! This petition in boots is brought to you by the people, for the people and of the people."

"Don't count me, you dirty hippie," Althea snorted.

"All power to the people!"

"Claire dear—" Meg pleaded. "Lucky, won't someone take this baby and do something with Jason? I can't stand the screaming. I thought you were going to feed him, Claire. Claire? Why are you just standing there? Do something!"

Claire tore her eyes from the television as the camera left the podium and meandered through the exulting crowd; she glanced at the ring of faces in her quiet California kitchen; she fastened on them individually, as if seeing each for the first time, and then she snatched Dan from her mother's arms and ran with him into her own room, where she slammed the door and leaned against it, breathing hard, pressing that baby so close that his cries ceased in amazement. She buried her face into the sweetness of Dan's neck and wept until she heard Lucky's tepid knock at the bedroom door. "Go away," she cried. "Just go away."

Lucky pushed the door open slowly and enveloped Claire and Dan in his arms. "I've turned the TV off, Claire," he murmured after a time. "I've told Vera and Althea they can't quarrel anymore and we won't talk about the war or peace or politics. I didn't know it upset you so." He patted her heaving shoulders. "Don't cry, please, Claire. It will be all right. Everything will be fine." He kissed the rim of her hair. "We'll get away from everything tomorrow. Would you like that? We'll go on a picnic. We'll take the kids and a blanket and go on a picnic far away from everything."

How far away could you travel? Wasn't time enough? Wouldn't three thousand miles of distance suffice? Claire choked back her sobs and nodded, agreed that tomorrow they would go on a picnic, promised herself that tomorrow Jon would once again be buried in the past, swallowed back into the maw of history or the mass of protestors, the fight for peace or the struggle for revolution. These things had no connection to Claire Stone. None. Tomorrow Claire Stone would go with her husband and three children, spread a picnic blanket on the grass, slather mayonnaise over bread and pick some flowers and put them in her hair.

Barton Swallow drove up Jerusalem Road and pulled into the narrow driveway. He found Claire sitting on the back stoop; her wineglass was drained and so was her face, but he greeted her cheerfully and sat down beside her. "How are the piano lessons going? Any more new students?"

"Two this week," she said without enthusiasm.

"You see, your fame is spreading."

"So are my debts."

He took her hand. "I wouldn't worry about that."

"Of course you wouldn't," she snapped, withdrawing her hand. "They're not your debts." She knew Bart didn't deserve her ill will, and to conceal the need for apology, she added quickly, "Anyway, I'm glad you're here, Bart. Lucky took the car to drive Emma and some others home and he's not back yet and Scott needs to get to the doughnut shop pretty soon. Will you drive him?"

"Lucky will be back in time. You can't always be providing for Scott, Claire. It's time he took some responsibility, at least for himself, if not for others."

Claire stiffened and regarded him dubiously. "Why do you hate Scott? Tell me."

"I don't hate him."

"But you're forever criticizing him."

"And you're forever idolizing him. Maybe the truth falls somewhere in between." Bart wanted to mollify his sister, but steer clear of an outright lie. "This entire family has pulled together under these—these unlooked-for circumstances—"

"Catastrophe. Say it."

"Unfortunate circumstances. Everyone but Scott. He is the only one who continually bitches and sulks. I'm disappointed in him, that's all, surprised he hasn't accepted all this with better grace."

"I suppose you think Lucky's being graceful! Praying and hibernating and not caring about the rest of us."

"You know what I meant."

"Well I'm glad Scott hasn't accepted it gracefully. I'm glad he knows he's cut out for better things than the doughnut shop. Grace is not a requirement for frying doughnuts."

"If he wants something better, then he should do something about it. Why doesn't he sign up at the community college like Jason?"

"He wants to go to Stanford, of course."

"Of course," Bart repeated uncomfortably.

Anything further he might have said was cut short by the swirl of dust and exhaust as Lucky pulled into the driveway, and the car continued to splutter even as he got out, exhaling its dying breath only when Lucky had ambled to the porch. Bart commented on how well and fit he looked. "God has healed me," Lucky replied, "body and soul."

"That's great, Lucky." Bart put his arm around Claire's shoulders and gave her an affectionate squeeze. "You see, Claire. First things first. Lucky's health is back and now he can get a job."

Claire scrutinized her husband. *Can he make love?*

Bart rose and dusted off the bottom of his sports coat. "Guess I'll go in and say hello to Mama and see what Althea cooked up."

"You look terrible, Claire," said Lucky as the screen door closed behind Bart. "Are you sick?"

"Nothing that a hundred thousand dollars wouldn't cure."

"You worry too much."

"And you don't worry enough."

"The Lord is my shepherd. I shall not want. He is your shepherd too, Claire."

"I thought the Lord helped those who helped themselves. At least I'm giving piano lessons." Following an urge to wound, she added coldly, "I don't see you looking for a job."

"When God wants me to have a job, He will send one."

"Well, with all your experience juggling books, maybe God will let you balance the ledgers of heaven."

"You're just tired, Claire." Lucky sighed and went inside.

"Of course I'm tired! You'd be tired too if you did anything but talk to God and Emma Duff. I'm tired of her, too! And don't you walk out on me, Lucky Stone." Claire scrambled to her feet and followed him into the kitchen, where Althea busied herself at the stove and Bart knelt beside Meg's rocker. "This is all your fault, Lucky," Claire continued recklessly. "You brought this on us with your drinking and your gambling and you—"

"I renounce my unconverted past. I've humbled myself before God. I've repented. I'm saved."

"What about the rest of us! Are we saved? Are we? No, we're lost, but I guess that's not cosmic enough for Lucky Stone to care about."

Lucky sniffed the air. "Tacos tonight, Althea? There's not a Mexican in San Angelo who makes a better taco than you do."

"There aren't any Mexicans left in San Angelo!" Claire cried. "They can't afford to live here. We can't afford it! We haven't got any money."

Lucky opened the refrigerator. "And peaches, Althea. What a treat."

"We haven't got any money," Claire pleaded again. "We can't go on like this. I can't. I won't."

Lucky kept his back to his wife, taking some plates from the cupboard and a handful of silverware; without looking up, he began setting the table. Into the seething silence, Bart interjected the observation that they had endured bad times before.

"But it's not the same now," Claire wailed. "You know it's not. There isn't any hope this time. There aren't any prospects of any kind of life except worry and want, pinching every damned nickel, squeezing the life out of every dime. And he—" she waved an angry finger at Lucky's back, "he doesn't give a damn! Lucky doesn't even care if he gets a job! He isn't even trying. Are you? Admit it. You're not doing a thing to get us out of this mess."

"In God's time, He will—"

"I don't have that kind of time," she shrieked. Alarmed, Meg looked up from her knitting and Althea stopped with a spoonful of salsa halfway to her lips. "I can't wait for *God*!" Claire spat the Almighty's name out contemptuously. "Scott can't wait for God! He doesn't have that kind of time, either. He's a young man. He's got to have a future. He's got to have a Stanford degree, something he can rely on."

"Lower your voice, Marietta," said Meg testily. "I shouldn't have to remind you again and again that nice girls don't raise their voices."

Her narrow shoulders quaking, Claire crossed the floor to her mother's rocker. "It's me, Mama. Claire. It's not Marietta—Marietta's pithed her brains with drugs—and it's not Jill. Jill's living in sin and growing dope with whatshisname."

Althea flung her spoon into the pot. "How can you say such dreadful things to her?"

"Come on, Claire," Bart interceded. "You don't want to upset Mama."

"Oh yes I do," she replied defiantly. "It's about time we got upset, all of us. It's about time we did something besides wipe our noses on linen hankies and remark pleasantly on what it's like to be dirt poor."

"You have a home," Bart shot back. "It doesn't even cost you anything. You have food. No one is hungry here. No one—"

"You think that's enough! I'm not talking about food and shelter—though don't get me wrong, Bart, I know if you didn't pay the taxes on this hulk of a house, we'd be living under the viaduct, so don't think I'm not grateful." She sneered out this last remark and let it linger in the air. "But I'm not talking about food and shelter—I'm talking about life. I'm talking about a future—and I don't give a damn for the past, Althea, so don't say anything about the glorious Senator or one word about Lucille. Maybe that's enough for you, but it's not for me. The past is a trap. I want a future—and not when God gets around to it, Lucky, but now, when it counts!" Her voice was thick with menace, and she seemed to stalk them individually, "And I don't give a damn how I get it!"

Meg put down her needles emphatically. She would have risen from her chair but for Bart's hand on her shoulder. "Such fool language, Jill. How do you expect to get a husband with talk like that?"

"Oh God." Claire flung her hands over her face and alternately laughed and sobbed. "It's me, Claire, Mama—don't you recognize me? I have a husband. That's him, over there, Mama, the one who goes out every day jogging for Jesus. I'm the one who grew up to be everything you wanted, Mama. Not Jill. Not Marietta. For twenty years I'm the one who's lived up to the Three D's. For twenty years I've done everything that was expected of me, and I'm sick of it!"

201

"Claire," Bart remonstrated softly. "Can't this wait till after Mama goes to bed? Can't we talk about this some other time?"

"I haven't got time! How clear can I make it? You want me to spare Mama's feelings, Bart? You want me to be polite, Althea? You want me to pretend that I haven't noticed you don't give a damn about getting a job, Lucky? Is that what all of you want? Well, to hell with you! All of you!" Her voice crescendoed with conviction. "I'm giving you notice right now. I'm through. Sick unto death of the Three D's. I hate them, and they can go to hell too!"

"Claire," Althea bristled. "Please!"

"You really don't understand, do you?" She pushed her loose bob back from her face and drew a deep breath, exhaling in short, hot monosyllables. "No. No. No. I've learned. One thing. Money counts. Nothing but money. The rest of it is fiction, Althea, lies, don't you see? The lies that powerless people tell themselves, the varnish they put on abject helplessness. The Three D's condone helplessness, and make it into a downright virtue. Lies." Her voice took on a flinty, sarcastic edge, as if to mince those lies to powder. "I haven't the power to change anything, so I'll be sweet, nice and polite and maybe the world will admire my good manners—grace, isn't that what you called it, Bart—while they pity my situation. It's not only false, it's stupid! Real people don't believe that. Ladies believe it. Crippled up, hamstrung ladies. Well, not me. I'm ready to struggle for what I want, and if I get dirty doing it, then that's just too goddamned bad!"

Bart glanced beseechingly at Lucky, who assumed an expression he must have adopted from the Holy Martyrs. Only Althea could collect herself sufficiently to parry Claire's assault with the weak observation that maybe she ought to stop there.

"I'm not going to stop! I'm going to start. And I'm going to win. I'm going to make certain my son goes back to Stanford and has the future he deserves and I won't be ladylike about it. A lady can't work or want or sweat or feel passion for anything except a man. Well, I'm through with men, too. You hear me, Lucky? I'm through with men who make grand gestures and leave the rest of us to rot. I'm through relying on men."

"Rely on God," Lucky offered.

"I'm sick of Him, too. And the next time you're talking with the Almighty, Lucky, why don't you just skip the conversion of the Jews and the end of worldly time, why not ask for something that can do us some good here and now and on earth while we need it? Ask Him for money. We need money. We need hope. We need to send Scott to Stanford." Claire kicked a kitchen chair and it clattered to the floor. "The rest of you can live any old way you want—rot in this tumble-down rotten house till you die, live in the past or commune with the angels, but not me." And then she added passionately, "And not Scott."

Bart placed himself effectively between Claire and Meg, whose hushed needles trembled in her hands and whose bottom lip quivered. He faced his sister levelly and his voice was crisp and flat. "So you want Scott to go back to Stanford. This is not news, Claire. Are you quite finished with your tantrum?"

"No." She flung them each an unrepentant glance. "I want more. I want a future. I'm going to think of a way to give that boy a future."

Althea folded her arms across her breast with the gravity of a cigar store Indian. "How?"

It came to Claire. Just like that. So appealing and fortuitous, so obvi-ous, that she actually laughed before she turned to her aunt and lilted, "Well maybe I'll just get the money from Lucille. That was your idea, wasn't it, Althea? Maybe Lucille will take the Swallow good name for collateral on the loan, and if she won't, I'll give her this house. I'd give her my soul. I'd give her your precious soul, Lucky. I'd do anything," she snarled at them. "And if I have to part with my last stick of morality or strip off every shred of sweetness, I don't care. I want that money, and I'll get it from her. You watch me." Pleased with herself and her revelation, she walked to the kitchen door and kicked it open. "You can do whatever you like, but you'd better not judge or natter or scold me. Don't say a word. You can all of you just sit tight and zip your lips and clutch the Three D's all the way to hell!"

And with that, Claire marched out of the kitchen, through the front hall, slamming every door in her wake till she came to the porch and the garden, where the ducks scattered before her like buckshot. She left her sandals at the garden gate and slogged through the cool sand. The beach was nearly empty, save for a few fires and families waving hot dogs on the ends of coat hangers. In the cruel light of sunset, they looked like dancing demons. Claire moved beyond them, out to where the beach was hard beneath her feet and the foam washed over her ankles. She willed her breath to calm and her heart to stop pounding as she squinted due west into the sunset. Along a broad, watery path, the sun gleamed like a burnished, bloody, upside down exclamation point. Claire herself was rather surprised, shaken, tense and, oddly, free. Over the ocean's melodic roar, she could all but hear the manacles unsnap as she stepped from her girlhood prison into the liberty of middle age.

Without pausing to relish that liberty, however, she considered quickly how best to use it. She rewrote Althea's jesting scenario, fondled, shaped, rehearsed what she would say when she called Hoolihan to arrange a meeting with Lucille. Soon. Before her bubbling resolve went flat. This week. She would not tell Hoolihan, not precisely, why she wanted to talk to Lucille, whom she had not seen since the day she had married Lucky Stone. Twenty-one years ago. More. Age mellows everyone, she reasoned. Even Lucille Swallow. The burden of want, the mantle of worry, slid from Claire's shoulders like Lazarus's shroud as she heard herself suggesting a gift, but asking for a loan, at say, five percent, to be repaid once Scott graduated from Stanford. Lucille would probably be dead by then anyway. The money was nothing to Lucille, but it could assure Scott's whole future—the cream-colored degree, everything. Claire began to tally up the costs of a Stanford education, but her math skills weren't equal to it. She'd figure it all out later, and whatever it came to, maybe she'd even tack on a little extra, ask for a bit more money so she could build a studio adjacent to the house and move the piano out of the living room and give lessons beyond the reach of the Fellowship of the New Millenium. Her students could have recitals in the studio, too, until, of course, their numbers grew too many. Claire began to hum the "Minuet in G". Girls in organdy dresses, boys in suits that nipped their armpits, parents dewy with pride. Lemonade afterward.

iii

The sight of Alfredo's Mexican Café, squeezed as it was between a bicycle repair shop and a pornographic video rental, did not augur greatness. Claire checked the address on her scrap of paper: 212 Pacific Coast Highway, Esperanza Point.

"Here, Mom? This sleazy joint in this dumpy burg?"

"This is where Lucille insisted we meet. This is it."

Scott drove to the back, down an alley and stopped where cats prowled the dumpsters and the odor of grease and cumin hung heavy on the air. He parked between a battered pick-up and a stationwagon full of grass cuttings. "There's Hoolihan's car," said Claire. "I recognize it."

They got out, and Scott walked across the blacktop to peer into Hoolihan's white Mercedes. "Thirty thousand on the hoof," he said, fingering the chrome. "Maybe more."

"Come on." Claire smoothed the collar of the shirt she'd ironed for him that morning. Scott towered over his mother and submitted to her ministrations restlessly. "There, you look fine. Thank you for taking your earring out." She smiled to listen to him grumble. Originally, Claire had planned to go alone, but careful consideration suggested that Scott's pleasing face and personality, his winsome charm, might make a decided difference. Still, she had left him ignorant of the true nature of this errand, saying simply she wanted him to drive her to Esperanza Point, a drab, dusty beach town in the north end of San Angelo County. She had admonished Scott only to be (in Meg's vague lexicon) nice. "Let me do the talking," she added now.

"Hey, I'm just the chauffeur."

"Remember that." She brushed the wrinkles from her rose-colored skirt. Claire wore makeup and stockings, matching shoes and purse; she exuded an air of practiced poise, as well she should, having relentlessly rehearsed the entire three days prior to this meeting. Take command immediately, she reminded herself.

They entered Alfredo's from the back, walking through the kitchen, where the sweating cook smoked and eyed them dubiously. An unpleasant odor (not altogether masked by Pine Sol) wafted out of the bathrooms as they passed these doors. Alfredo's itself was dim, and Claire took off her sunglasses to peer into the mote-speckled light; glowing beer signs dotted the walls, along with pictures of Mexican maidens swooning before dusky gods. Cobwebbed pinatas hung from the ceiling, and Claire was slightly unhinged to hear a twenty-year-old tune, "It's My Party and I'll Cry if I Want To", warbling out of the jukeboxes, lined up, one to a table. At the long counter, a couple of bearded, tattooed working men sipped beer and read the sports pages. Most of the booths were empty, but Claire could see the back of a wide-brimmed hat swathed in turquoise tulle and from this booth Hoolihan emerged and greeted them, but Lucille did not turn around.

"Hello, Claire," Hoolihan said. "Where's Lucky?"

"Lucky didn't come. You remember my son Scott."

Hoolihan shook Scott's hand firmly, but his brow puckered and he looked like a man who longs for a change of venue.

Claire slid into the booth after Scott and stared at Lucille Swallow. Time had never been so cruel. Lucille hunched over her coffee cup, pulling it so close that the steam wafted up to the hairs on her chin. Her face furrowed into wrinkled ridges, her skin tanned to the color of turmeric. Her once abundant hair had thinned, permed into frizzy corkscrew curls that stuck out beneath her floppy hat. Her eyes were still blue and agate hard. Claire drew a deep breath and dropped the idea of asking for more money. Her dream of the girls in their organdy dresses faded along with her vision of the frail, pale powdered old lady who could be bullied.

"Hello, Claire." Lucille offered one thin clawlike hand across the table. Every one of Lucille's fingers bore a dazzling ring, sometimes two, huge stones encrusted with smaller ones, and her wrist clanked under the weight of myriad gold bracelets. Tucked inside the collar of what Claire recognized as a cheap polyester print dress, ropes of pearls and glinting gold chains, a spray of emeralds, a wreath of rubies, bulged against Lucille's thin chest. "Who's your young friend?"

"This is my eldest son, Scott. This is Lucille, the Senator's widow."

"He's a Swallow, all right," Lucille cackled. "Big and good-looking, aren't you? I bet you break their hearts. I bet the girls come running for it."

"I guess." Scott played with the dish of hot sauce.

"You should see my granddaughter Christine if you want to meet a heartbreaker. I've got some pictures here somewhere." Lucille pushed her coffee away and pulled her huge bag up on the table and began rifling through it. Claire's eyes widened to see Lucille tug at gold chains, gem studded charms and amulets, earrings and medallions, to see hundred-dollar bills burble to the surface like onions bobbing at the top of a great stew. When the waitress came to their table, Lucille ceased her search and hugged her purse to her chest.

The Chicana waitress was young and plump and surly, with a ponytail sticking out behind one ear. "More coffee?"

"I'll have an iced tea with lemon," said Claire.

"What's good here?" Scott gave the girl an ingratiating grin and she thawed and said they made a nice bean burrito.

"Overcooked, oversauced and overpriced like everything else," muttered Lucille.

"I'll take a bean burrito," Scott said.

"You'll regret it," Lucille warned. "Mexicans don't wash their hands after they pee. I wouldn't eat anything they made, them or the chinks or wops or frogs either."

Hoolihan shot an apologetic look to the waitress, who departed in a snit. "Weren't you going to show them Christine's picture, Lucille?"

Lucille drew forth a folding album and pointed to each picture in turn. "Here's Christine's baptismal picture and here she is at two and here's her first day at the Manoa Montessori and here's second grade and this is from her hula class, that's her, second to the left, and this is the ballet she was in when she was eight. She's been in one every year since. See, here she is in "The Nutcracker" when she was twelve. She's had ballet lessons since she could walk. This is the day she got her first bicycle and here's the Porsche I bought her for her sixteenth birthday and. . ." By the time Scott's burrito arrived, they were privy to every glorious moment in Christine Eckdorf's nearly twenty-one years.

Claire doubted Christine was much of a heartbreaker; she looked a demure girl who greeted the world from behind braces and glasses, prim and bland and pleasant-looking, like Claire's recollection of both her parents.

"Here's Christine's high school graduation," Lucille concluded, pulling forth a studio photograph of a young woman (without braces or glasses) who had short, fair hair and beautifully brushed brows. "Oh, and here she is in her dorm room at the University of Hawaii. I begged Lucy Rose to send her to Vassar or Radcliffe. I said I'd pay for it, but Christine didn't want to come to the mainland. She's had a very protected life. She even insisted on living at home last year, but this year I talked her into living in the dorm. She can't decide if she ought to be an English major or art history. Lucy Rose took her to Florence this summer, but Christine had diarrhoea the whole time. How could she help it, with all that wop food? I don't think she wore her retainer in Italy either." Lucille pulled the picture closer and inspected Christine's teeth. "Just think, all that expensive orthodontic work might go for nothing."

"I see," said Claire.

"She's a very dear and loving child. The light of my life." Lucille handed the University of Hawaii photo to Scott, who heaped more hot sauce over his burrito. "Do you have any daughters, Claire?"

"No. Two more sons."

"Too bad for you. Sons are nasty and thankless and will leave you stranded in your old age. Sons don't care about their mothers."

"And your son?" asked Claire, defying her own injunctions, rebelling against her own rehearsals, strangling slightly on the question she had vowed not to ask.

207

"Lucille does not mention his name," Hoolihan interjected. "It pains her."

Lucille snorted. "It does not pain me. It enrages me! I gave Jon every opportunity in life, and he turned out to be a turd."

"I see."

"I haven't seen him since the day of Lucy Rose's wedding, when he stole one of my cars. He could have asked. I'd have given him the car, but no, he had to steal it."

"He returned it, Lucille." Hoolihan glanced nervously at Claire. "He called and told me I could find it at the bus station and that's where it was."

"And the next time I see him," Lucille continued obliviously, "he's on TV—inciting a bunch of drug addicts to riot and calling the President of the United States a pig. He's got a jail record as long as your arm, Claire, protesting this, picketing that, and I've told Hoolihan all along, not a penny of my money to get him out."

"He's never asked for money, Lucille, he—"

"Let him rot in jail, that's what I say." Lucille's eyes and bracelets flashed in the dim light. "Let him rot rot rot."

"Who are they talking about, Mom?"

As if the past were suddenly exhumed in Alfredo's trailing decay, shroud and memory mulched together, composted, crawling toward Claire, accusing her and, unwillingly, she recreated that frail net of flesh in which she had cast her finest love, her best hopes and the life she had buried with Jon Cotton; the stone rolled away and she looked into the awful sepulcher of the past, saw his beautiful body, the body she had mingled with her own, with dream begotten of desire and delusion. She confused the overpowering stench of the burrito with that of unendurable loss and feared that her resolve would wither before she could recover herself, or the dream that was beyond recovery, feared that she would crumble before her son, who would witness her humiliation and judge her harshly. But Scott stuffed another bite of burrito into his jaws, and cheese dangled from his lips.

". . . and when that hospital in Kentucky called me a couple of years ago and said he was dying of hepatitis, I said, it will save me disinheriting him. What little I have is going to Christine and not to another soul. I won't give a dime to a drug addict. Only drug addicts die from hepatitis." Lucille slurped her coffee. "Where's that girl? I want some more coffee."

"You shouldn't drink coffee," Hoolihan reproached her. "Have a glass of milk, please."

"What! Pay seventy-five cents for a glass of milk when I can get a half gallon for a dollar fifteen?"

"I'll buy."

"No you won't. You're such a fool with money, Hoolihan. You let yourself get cheated all the time. Coffee's the cheapest thing here. And that's robbery," she called out.

"And did he"—Claire coughed, *Matthew Mark Luke and Jon can't*—"die?"

"If he had, I'd have put a stone over him that says here lies Jon Cotton, a jerk, a turd and a doped-up drug fiend."

"He was not a drug addict." Hoolihan spoke as if marshalling evidence before a hostile jury. "The hospital told me he had not contracted hepatitis through drug use. He did not die. We paid his bills at the hospital, but he changed his name again and left before I could contact him."

"You paid his bills, Hoolihan." Lucille snapped. "I say, let the state take care of indigents. I pay my taxes. I haven't got money to throw away, and as one mother to another, Claire, you should have had daughters."

"More coffee?" The waitress stood poised with her pot.

"Only if it's free."

"I'll take a Coke," said Scott, mopping up the last of his burrito and pushing his plate away. He grinned at the girl. "That was the best burrito I ever ate." He took note of her sassy behind as she left them. "If you like swill. The beans in the burrito came over with Cortez." He flipped through the tunes on the jukebox. "So did every song in here. Who ever heard of the Del Tones? How did you ever find this place?"

"It's cheap," Lucille retorted.

Claire sat dazed and immobilized as Hoolihan skillfully deflected the conversation away from Jon. He asked Scott what he had done with his summer vacation, and Scott lathered on a bit about the goddamned doughnut shop until Hoolihan remarked cordially that probably Scott would be happy to have school start again and return to "Stanford!" cried Claire, seizing the command that had thus far eluded her. "Scott was at Stanford last year and he has a brilliant future there. And after graduation too, but right now, well, we, our, he—" Command dribbled away from Claire; she burbled and heaved, rattled in a fashion she never intended that she'd come to offer Lucille an investment and incoherent words to the effect that Scott's Stanford degree was a thing Lucille could take pride in and the money was nothing to her anyway.

"You're asking me for money?" Lucille's wrinkled face lit with alarm. "I thought you wanted to see me to give Lucky a job with Swallow Lines."

"That was my impression," Hoolihan said hastily. "I thought that's what you wanted, Claire."

"I never said a thing about Lucky. I said I wanted to meet with Lucille and that it was important."

Lucille waggled a bejeweled finger at Scott and laughed shrilly. "You want me to loan this meatball money for Stanford!"

"Five percent," Claire said firmly. "To be repaid when—"

"Everyone thinks I'm rich and old and they can take advantage of me," Lucille whimpered, and clutched her bag closer; her bracelets clanked with the effort. "People try to cheat me. I'm poor. I haven't got any money."

"Then what's all that cash and jewelry popping out of your bag?"

"I have to carry it with me. Everyone tries to rob me."

"Oh, God," Hoolihan moaned. "First Jon, now money."

"I have to protect myself. I'm poor. The shipping business is going downhill and the board of directors ties my hands all the time and the Japs are ruining me and the government gouges me with taxes. I haven't got any money." Lucille's eyes narrowed into angry little slits. "And if I did, what makes you think I'd loan it to him?"

"Mom, I don't even want to go to—"

"Shut up." Claire leaned forward and spoke very carefully. "This is your last chance, Lucille, to right a great wrong. An injustice you did to my family."

"Oh Christ," Hoolihan groaned.

"You're old, Lucille, and you're going to die."

"I'll outlive you all."

"But you'll die just the same and you'll go to hell and you'll burn in hell forever," Claire added, savagely plagiarizing Althea, "unless you give my son this one chance he needs. This is an investment, Lucille, and if you don't take it, God is going to flick you into hell. You disinherited a whole family and—"

"Your father had a hundred thousand dollars!" Lucille wailed. "Can I help it if your mother was a dolt and lost it all!"

"My mother is not a dolt, and she did not lose it," Claire retorted, and, without thinking, added, "My father threw it away."

Lucille's expression perked with curiosity, but Claire did not see it. In that moment Claire saw, pictured all too well, the lies and money, bread cast upon the waters, hundred-dollar bills floating on the scummy foam, washing up on the rocky beach. *Lies and money are only good as long as people believe in them.* Claire believed in lies and money and as a result she saw as well the silvery hologram of her eighteen-year-old self, and moreover, there, amongst the foragers and garbage pickers, hunching along the beach, she saw herself, the forty-one-year-old desperate mother, bent over, scrambling to rescue those soggy bills, hoarding them against this moment, when her son's future glowed phosphorescent from every greenback. That woman looked up and cursed Anson Swallow as the eighteen-year-old Claire looked speechlessly on.

Claire pulled tattered aplomb over her unwonted admission. "The money the Senator left my father was tainted. Somehow. And I'm sure you had something to do with it, Lucille. You are treacherous and cruel and deceitful, and you'll die and go to hell unless you take this chance I'm giving you."

"You giving me!" Lucille hooted.

"A chance to make it up. Just give—loan—Scott—"

"I wouldn't give Scott the snot from my nose."

"Ladies, please. Claire. Perhaps Lucille could not in conscience pay for Scott's education, but—"

"Lucille hasn't got a conscience!"

Hoolihan restrained the quivering Lucille. "Please. Calm down. Let's talk it over. Maybe we could arrange a job for Scott with Swallow Lines if he's unhappy in the doughnut shop."

For a moment they all three stared at Scott, who sat bewildered, clutching his Coke, and then Lucille swore she'd never hire another Swallow and Claire vowed she'd never allow her son to suffer the same demeaning fate as his Uncle Bart because of want, because of poverty, because of money. She wrung that last out as if she expected to hear coins clatter on the table.

"Mom—I don't—"

"He's going to have a future that isn't blighted!"

"If you're his mother, that's blight enough," Lucille sniffed.

"You owe it to him, Lucille. He's got as much claim on that money as—look at your twit granddaughter! You'd send her to Vassar if she had the brains. My son has everything except the money, and the reason he doesn't have the money is all your fault. Everything's your fault."

"Did you hear that, Hoolihan?" Lucille cackled. "You should have used that for Lucky's defense. My fault. Hah! Let me tell you, Claire, the Swallows didn't deserve that money. They'd have made a mess of Swallow Lines. Think of George Swallow. I ask you. Or Vera? I puke to think of it. Or that fat, foolish virgin Althea. Do you think she could have done with Swallow Lines what I have? Never! And Anson—he was the worst. The great, moral Anson Swallow, the pillar of—"

"Lucille, please."

"Oh shut up, Hoolihan. I know you always admired him, though I never could figure out why. You have more sense than to go about mucking things up with principle. Principle." She pulled the word from her sinuses. "Anson Swallow didn't have the—"

"That's it." Claire brought both palms down hard on the table and the spoons danced and rang. "I won't hear my father slandered, not by the person who killed him, and you did it, Lucille. He died of shame and anguish for what you did to our family. His death had something to do with the Senator's will and I know it."

"He choked on principle, dearie. Now let me out of here, Hoolihan." Lucille's jeweled fingers flailed at Hoolihan's back as she shoved him out of the booth.

"You lost your own son, Lucille," Claire cried. "He hated you! He despised you. Giving Scott this money is your last chance before God."

"Screw God." Lucille scooted out of the booth, her beads and chains rattling like Marley's ghost. She rose and her cheap dress clung to her bottom and wasted flanks. "If I wanted to give to beggars, I'd find some eyeless reprobate with his hand stuck out."

"I wouldn't beg from you if you had the last nickel on earth," Claire shouted.

"I intend to have the last nickel on earth," Lucille shouted back as she pushed Hoolihan in front of her and fled Alfredo's, her huge purse bouncing in her arms.

Claire and Scott slumped in the booth, cringing at the ungarnished delight of Alfredo's few patrons and the waitress, who ambled over to their table and slammed down the check. They stared at the check and not at each other.

"Are you out of your mind, Mom? What made you think that old hag—"

"That vulture." Claire's breath scraped audibly up and down her lungs. "That viper."

"Quit hyperventilating, will you? Listen, Mom. It's all right. What I mean is, I don't care, I—"

"How can you not care?"

"I mean, well, maybe I should have said something earlier. I know you've been talking all summer about me going back to Stanford, but there wasn't a hope in hell of getting the money, so I didn't, well, Mom, what I mean is, I couldn't—look. Stanford's just not for me."

"I suppose you want to stay in the doughnut shop."

"No."

"Well? What do you want? What are you going to do with your life?"

"I want to make money. I want to be rich," he said crisply, quickly, emphatically.

Claire shook her head. "You have all these wonderful gifts, Scott, and that's all you can say? You disappoint me. I don't believe it. Let me have that bill. Just like Lucille to stick me with the bill. Let's see. Seven and five are thirteen, carry the one—"

Hoolihan snatched the check from her fingers, slammed it on the table with a ten-dollar bill. "If I'd had any inkling, Claire, what you were up to, I'd never have agreed to this. If I knew you were going to bring up Jon and money, the two things that upset her most. I thought you wanted to bring Lucky along and we'd find him some undemanding job. I thought the rift in this family could be healed. I thought I was doing both you and Lucille a favor."

"You're just full of favors, aren't you, Mr. Magnanimous?"

"You should have come to me first."

"Spare me your advice, Hoolihan."

"I know how you feel, Claire, but—"

"You don't! No one does!" She heard in her own middle-aged voice the defeated whimper of a lost child and writhed under the last deprecating glance Hoolihan gave them both before he turned and left Alfredo's. Claire hurt. As though she'd been beat up, bruised. Ludicrous, horrible and humiliated in her own eyes, she slowly moved her bones out of the booth, following Lucille and Hoolihan's path past the counter toward Alfredo's back door. She hunched over, eyes cast down at the floor until she spied a hundred-dollar bill lying there, the benign grin of Benjamin Franklin beaming up at her, and right beside him lay Lucille's folding picture album with the photos of Christine. Claire saw the moment for what it was: if she stooped to pick up that hundred-dollar bill, she would remain forever groveling and gleaning, hunched over like a peasant picking through an already plowed field. She paused for a moment and gingerly plucked the picture album off the floor. Then she picked up the hundred-dollar bill.

Silently, Claire stared out the window as they zipped along the freeway heading south, past fields of artichokes and alfalfa, many of which were being bulldozed for housing developments with names reminiscent of antebellum plantations, utterly unindigenous to the California earth. Dust flew into the car and she choked on it, choked as well on the dust blowing about her mind, as if the graves she'd tended for more than twenty years were bulldozed, unearthed and left gaping, desolate, and raw. Claire rolled up the window.

"It was a fool's errand, Mom," Scott said at last. "A failed fool's errand at that."

Reluctantly, Claire brought her gaze to her son's handsome profile. "If anyone at home, Althea or anyone, asks you one thing about what happened at Alfredo's, you just say we met with less than success. That's all you have to say."

Scott snorted and mumbled inaudibly.

Claire bit her lip against tears and rummaged in her handbag for Kleenex. She came upon the photos of Christine and turned them over in her hand; accordion-like, they rippled into her lap. Claire wiped her nose and stared at them. "Look at this girl. She's never known a moment's unhappiness."

"She has zits and braces in some of those pictures."

"I'm not talking about zits and braces—I mean she's never lost a moment's sleep worrying about the future or the past—or the present for that matter. Look at her. This calm, lovely untroubled young face. Can you imagine what it cost to bring her up? All those braces and ballet lessons and contact lenses and whatever else? Silly little twit. She has everything money can buy and to think—when Lucille dies, she'll get all that too." Claire found the picture of Christine Eckdorf sitting at the desk in her dorm room at the University of Hawaii wearing a pink muu muu and a lei of orchids. "Only a twit would go to the local school when she could have gone to Vassar." Or Stanford. If Scott had one-tenth of Christine's opportunities. Her securities. Her assurances. Just think of all the wonderful things Scott could do with his life—if it weren't for money. What Scott could do with Christine's money.

Claire turned to look at her beautiful son again just as they passed a water-treatment plant and a foul odor accosted them. Scott rolled up his window automatically, cutting them off from all distracting sounds save for the car's asthmatic wheeze. Claire found the picture of the red Porsche and the sixteen-year-old Christine smiling beside it. Scott had every bit as much right to his grandmother's largesse as Christine. If only Claire could demand that right without the necessity of telling Lucille or Hoolihan, without telling Lucky or Bart—without, dear God, telling Scott—who his father was and what his mother had done to get him. The lies. Oh Lord, there they are again, lies and money. But that secret—not only maintained, but manicured for over twenty years—was Claire's last weapon and it was utterly worthless to her. If she used it, she would, in effect, be granting easements over her past, paths for dirty feet to tread, and it would never be her own domain again. Claire flipped through Christine's childhood photos and shook her head. She might be returning from a failed fool's errand, but Claire was not such a consummate fool as to tell the irreversible truth. She put the thought from her firmly. Well then, what next? What now? She drew herself up and tried to look her failure in the eye, perhaps to see beyond it, but that failure seemed to wink at Claire, to suggest that failure could be relative. Relative, as opposed, say, to absolute. Relatives could be failures too, but they were always absolute; one could never quite undo the knot of family: deny, dismiss, revile, but not undo. Relatives, family. And what constituted relative family? Marriage, of course. Families were made by marriage. And the man who married Christine Eckdorf . . . Claire buried the thought, but it sprang up again like an indigenous weed in an imported garden . . . that man would have opportunities, security, assurances. And Lucille's money when she died. Relatively speaking. *If Scott were married to Christine. . .*

Claire shut the pictures back up and thrust them in her purse. Too gross and vile and clammy even to consider. Christine and Scott were already relatives. *But no one knows that*, and besides, they were only cousins, nothing closer. Cousins could marry. Often did. What if Scott and Christine had known each other as children? Loved each other since babyhood? They might marry and keep all that lovely money in the family.

Claire's happy picture of the infant Scott and Christine cooing in the same crib was cut short by the announcement that they were running out of gas. Scott said it twice. Then he added, "Give me that hundred you found and I'll pull off at the next station."

"She's pretty, though, isn't she?" Claire inquired dreamily.

"Who?"

"Christine. You can just look at her and tell she's pretty and pleasant. A very appealing young lady."

"I think there's a Shell station up ahead, or maybe we should just get a few dollars' worth at the Upumpm."

"It could have happened like that. Why couldn't it still happen?" Star-crossed lovers..Romeo and Juliet. "It could happen."

"It will if we don't get some gas."

"Don't be small-minded, Scott."

"There's a Shell station."

"I don't have a Shell credit card."

"You don't have any credit cards, Mom, remember? Bankruptcy does that to you."

"Then get two dollars' worth at the Upumpm, and use your own money. I'm saving this hundred." She found the bill and frowned at Benjamin Franklin.

"What for?"

"For your trip to Honolulu."

Scott missed the offramp.

"Look," Claire added quickly, her reverie evaporating. "Lucille didn't loan us the money for Stanford, that's true, but maybe she gave us something just as good. Maybe better."

"Whatever it is, we'll need that and two dollars to get home on."

"Use your imagination, Scott. You can still go to Stanford. Your whole future can be secure. All you need is money and it doesn't matter where it comes from, does it? Lucille owes it to you, I mean, she could give it to you, in a kind of roundabout fashion. If, say, you were to go to Honolulu and fall in love with Christine Eckdorf. She's pretty. She hasn't got any more zits or braces. You could marry her."

"Marry her!" The car swerved over the line and thumped on the lane markers.

"You'd have to marry her, though. It wouldn't be enough to live with her or any of that. You'd have to be legally and lawfully married." Having actually uttered this proposition, Claire's mouth went dry with vestigial disgust, but she licked her lips, closed her eyes and commanded the vision of the cream-colored degree, billowing under a full sail of success. "You could go to Honolulu and stay with that friend of Althea's. He was a friend of the Senator's too, and Althea could call him and—"

"What if she hated me?" Scott asked dubiously.

"She wouldn't! Girls have never hated you. You've never had trouble with girls."

Scott changed lanes, and they drove a mile in silence. "Anyway, what would I use for money? Honolulu costs money."

"I have money."

"Give me a break, Mom. What were we doing in Alfredo's today?"

"Not that kind of money, not enough to send you to Stanford, but I have, well, not money exactly, but jewelry. I have some jewelry I saved from the IRS and I could sell it and it would be enough to get you to Honolulu and keep you there for a bit, until, well, for a bit."

Silence and the hum of the car hung between them as they each turned the idea over like rising yeast dough awaiting formation by the proper pan. "Well," Scott said with a chuckle. "I guess if it's a choice between Honolulu and the doughnut shop—"

"That's the choice. Don't you see? I mean, if it doesn't work, then it doesn't work, but it's your only chance, so it's worth a try. You're young, Scott, and you've got to have your opportunities when you're young, you have to get a first-rate education and make something of yourself when you're young. I can't bear to think of your life wasted and it *will* be—people always screw up their lives when they're young and then spend years and years trying to remake their opportunities, or just groaning and gnashing their teeth. It's too late when you're my age to say, oh, if only I'd finished college, if only I'd taken that chance when I had it! It's too late. Why, you can't even get into medical school after you're thirty."

"Medical school! Who said anything about medical school!"

Claire didn't hear him. She began to hum "It's My Party and I'll Cry If I Want To", a lilting little refrain despite its lugubrious title. She hummed and watched Scott's future spread out like the freeway before her: straight, assured, unimpeded. She hummed and successfully stifled her whimpering conscience with the practiced ease of a woman who has spent twenty years burying the things she loved best. Claire confidently entombed that whimper under the rubble of time and desire, but it refused to be altogether stilled, and in the ensuing weeks, on those nights when she heard the continued cry of conscience, like an earthquake survivor crushed under brick and mortar, she rolled over in her sleep and retorted in her dreams that she could not come to its aid, that she did not have that kind of time.

CHAPTER TWO

September 1963

Chagrin may not have been the forge of history, but it was certainly hotter than hell. A small oasis in the lap of the white desert, Chagrin Springs lay at the eastern edge of St. Elmo County, surrounded by ash-colored hills, as if the devil had mounded soot from his every inferno right there in the California desert. Incessant winds incinerated everything they touched and the only surcease from this furnace could be found in the air-conditioned all-night diners that clustered beside the single freeway offramp, like Petey's, where Claire worked, or in the canopied acres of date palms, where Jon worked. These groves spread over the desert floor, the date palms lined up in feathered regiments, and through their dark, stiff fronds, the sun dappled only intermittently, rendering the ground so thick with shadow one could swim there, perhaps drown. The local Indians had called this place Gorongo Springs. In 1908, a USDA agronomist brought the first Arabian date suckers there, gave the streets colorful thematic names and called the oasis after himself, Pringle Springs. However, his attempt at immortality was ground away by dust and wind and the chagrin of everyone else who came there, appalled to find the desert so unrelentingly poor, hot and unforgiving.

Claire Swallow came to recognize that chagrin on the faces of travelers who crawled into Petey's Coffee Shop. One man walked into the frigid confines of Petey's and literally fell over. Claire bolted around the counter and screamed for Coralee, who came running with Petey and the busboy close behind. The customers for the most part kept chomping on their cheeseburgers; they were truckers accustomed to the perils of desert travel: you kept jugs of water in your cab, you doused yourself with water every twenty minutes or you died. It was as simple as that.

"Put his head in your lap, Claire," commanded Coralee. "And, Petey, bring me some towels." She snatched a glass of water off the counter and threw it full in the man's face; it splattered over Claire, who jumped, but the man did not rouse. "Shit." Coralee pushed the man's shirt up, exposing his hairless white belly, and laid a cold wet towel there and one over his forehead; she chafed his hands and when he did not respond, she gave his face a sharp slap and slowly his color returned.

"I thought I died and went to hell," he mumbled as he opened his eyes to see Claire and Coralee bent over him. "You saved my life."

"Don't take it personally," said Coralee, wandering back to her iced tea and half-smoked Camel behind the counter. Like Claire, Coralee was dressed in an unflattering brown uniform that ended well above her thick knees and began well below her neck, the ensemble topped off with a frilly, once-white apron and a name tag. She was about thirty-five, with Shinola-black hair, close set eyes and wide spaces between her teeth. "Just another dumb sucker," she confided to Claire, who was rinsing out a gallon tub to make thousand-island dressing. "They oughta stop easterners at the state line and make them leave the name of their next of kin." One of the truckers beckoned, and Coralee ambled to the cash register to ring up his tab.

"I'druther it was Melinda," he said with a wink at Claire.

"Don't get no funny ideas, Earl." Coralee took his money and punched it in the drawer and then returned to her cigarette and Claire. "Truckers come in here and they see a pretty face like yours and you're nice to them 'cause that's your job." She nodded toward Earl, whose rig they could hear firing up in the parking lot. "And the next thing you know, they get ideas. It gives the place a bad rep. Carney's down the road, you know? A whorehouse. They call themselves a coffee shop, but every trucker from Albuquerque to San Pedro knows they're a whorehouse."

"I see," said Claire, dumping a load of relish on the mayo.

"Me and Petey, we don't need that. We run a respectable place. We had one girl run off with a Seatrain driver just 'fore you come here and that's why Petey said, Don't hire her."

"Who?"

"You, of course." Coralee gave Claire an affectionate jab in the shoulder. "Petey said you was too pretty and you wasn't married and you'd probably be off humping in the tumbleweed if you didn't get enough in tips."

"I told you, I am married. Sort of."

Coralee clucked and lowered her voice, stomping her Camel out on the floor. "How old are you, Claire? Eighteen?"

"Nineteen."

"Well, I been around a lot longer than you, and let me give you a little advice, honey. You get him to marry you before he gets too used to things like they are. I kick myself, Claire, that I didn't make Petey stand up in front of the judge before I let him into my pants. You think I can get him to marry me now, after nine years of living with him? Not on your life. But what can I do, Claire? I love the guy." They both glanced over the grill at the stout, tattooed Petey, his crew cut stiff with butch wax. "You get your boy to marry you soon. Or he never will."

Another trucker came in and sat down at the counter. Coralee sauntered over to him and flipped open her pad. "What'll it be, Frank?"

"Whatever you got and wherever you got it, Coralee."

"Burger, fries, date banana pie and a Coke," she called out.

Claire poured a gallon of ketchup into the vat of mayo and relish and stirred it. She delivered a cheeseburger to the man who had fainted on the floor and he said he would give her a big tip for saving his life. As she walked away, she could feel his eyes boring into her backside. Someone put a quarter into the jukebox and "It's My Party and I'll Cry If I Want To" wailed over the coffee shop, effectively squashing the strains of Beethoven's Eleventh Sonata, whose splendid melody Claire heard playing at the back of her brain when she got up this morning, every morning in fact, but by the end of the day, it was silenced, seemingly drowned in grease and thousand-island dressing and juke box tunes. Quickly and before "It's My Party" could altogether extinguish the Eleventh Sonata, Claire executed the first half-dozen chords on the counter, trying to release the tension in her fingers, which ached to touch a keyboard. Claire had not played the piano since the day she left her mother's house, ostensibly to collect her things from the university. *I am going to Chagrin Springs*, Claire wrote Meg on her way out of town. She did not say who with or quite why. *I will write again when I have an address.*

She had had an address from the day she arrived. (At least the brush-strewn lot at the edge of town was designated 1629 W. Damascus; there was no East Damascus.) But all the many letters Claire began to her mother (more to Bart) ended in the fire. Claire was a pianist, not a poet; she endured insight the way others suffer indignity, stumbling upon it unwillingly, ungracefully. She had no facility with words, and even if she had, how could she write without mentioning Jon Cotton? Her life in Chagrin defied description, so alien was it from anything the Swallows could have imagined. Indeed, Claire herself could not have imagined it: she had to live it.

Her job at Petey's occupied her hands and body, but in her mind Claire drafted long letters to her mother and brother, circling around the unspeakable with the merely unsayable. Dear Mama, I am well and happy. I am living with anarchists on a commune in a converted schoolbus. Not converted to any faith, Mama, but parked, and its inn-ards torn out and a kitchen, a bed and bathroom installed and with sunflowers lined up in front of the windows and a clothesline tied to the back. The schoolbus is flanked on either side by old trailers with a fire ring in the middle of all three. No, Bart, not a fire ring, but the tub section of an old washer, where the anarchists burn scrap and wood and brush and trash (and these letters I start to you and Mama) at night while they sit around on overturned milk crates and talk about a lot of dead Russians and the leaderless state and historical imperative and what's going to happen After the Revolution. By day the bus and the trailers are like infernos and by night they are ovens, but no one can sleep outside because of the tarantulas.

There are nine of us, Mama. No. There are seven of them and two of us. The Schoolbus Seven, I call them, but sometimes I think there are eight of them and one of me, Bart, because I have tried to love the revolution and read the books the anarchists say are essential for an under-standing of the historical imperative, but I don't really care about the past and anyway, how can you love something you can't feel or see or hear? Just hope for. I don't quite understand it, Mama, but to hear Kharabian and the rest of them talk, the revolution is going to be glorious and they make it sound like coming attractions at the movies while we sit around the washtub at night, smoking marijuana and drinking beer and watching the flames jump up and dance. Kharabian is the only one here with a last name. The rest of us just have first names like Mark's dog, Squat. Kharabian is older than the rest of us, maybe twenty-six, and the only one without a girlfriend (though personally, Bart, I think he and Kathleen do the Dirty Deed whenever Bob's not

221

around. Or is it Art?). It's hard to keep the names of the Schoolbus Seven straight unless I think of them like animals on the Ark, marching two by two into the Bus. Kathleen and Bob. Art and Ilse. Mark and Maggot. (Margot is her real name, but I slip sometimes because Maggot actually suits her.) Nobody has a last name or any past or family, or if they mention their parents at all, they call them bourgeois or snobs or fascists. Except Kharabian. He doesn't belittle his family and he writes his mother once a week. I wonder what he says to her. I am well? I am happy? I am living in Chagrin with some anarchists on a commune?

They call it a commune, Mama, because everything's shared. We pool a percentage of all our wages and share the beer and marijuana and food and take turns with the laundry and shopping and cleaning and cooking. I'm not much good at any of it, but then neither is anyone else. Maggot tosses hamburger over Chef Boy Ar Dee and calls it spaghetti, and Ilse thinks Chow Mein is a good address. Sometimes I think I'd sign my life away for one of the Mourning Glory's roasted chickens or her apple tarts bubbling in the oven. But I take my turn like everyone else and I don't complain. I'm pretty used to it, Bart, but I can't get used to sharing the bathroom and I do complain about that. There's only one bathroom and that's in the bus, which is where we—I—sleep and everyone has to walk through our—my—bedroom to get to the bathroom. They never knock. They say they don't believe in bourgeois notions of privacy. Art doesn't even close the door when he pees, and when I asked him to, he called me a snob.

There are only three real curse words on the commune, Bart. Snob. Bourgeois. And fascist. Nothing else counts as cursing, no matter what you say or how you say it. And I have got used to that too, Bart, and honestly, I sort of like it. Every time I say shit (and worse!), I feel like I am scraping the Three D's off my mind, prying them off my life, but even way down here in the desert I can still hear Mama scolding. Mama and the Mourning Glory would just die here. For instance, at night, when they're not talking about the revolution, the guys sit around and make jokes about their job. Tree fucking they call it. Tree fucking! Can you imagine what Mama would say to hear people talk like that? The guys all work in the date groves, where they pollinate female date palms, which is a necessity I guess nature overlooked.

Girls can't work in the date groves, so Ilse and Maggot are maids in the Travelodge on Scheherazade Avenue (wouldn't you rather just starve, Bart, than change other people's spermy sheets?) and Kathleen does something for a chiropractor (probably the Dirty Deed) and I wait tables here at Petey's, where it's cool anyway and the pay is good, $200 a month, more really, since I get to keep my tips. Coralee is the other daytime waitress and I like her, but you wouldn't, Mama. Coralee never heard of the Three D's either, but she's a good, generous person, though I can't understand what she sees in Petey. She lives out back of Petey's. With Petey.

Coralee lets me take a shower at her place because the bathroom at the Bus doesn't have a shower. I don't know where the rest of the anarchists shower (and maybe they don't; maybe that's too bourgeois), but every day on my break, I go out back to Coralee's and shower and wash my hair and then I sit on their back stoop and listen to the trucks roar by on the freeway. It's so hot here my hair dries before my break is over and I have to go back to work. I never curl my hair anymore, Mama, I just pull it back from my face and clip it and let it fall on my shoulders. I haven't used nail polish or lipstick or a smidge of powder either, come to think of it, Mama, and I never wear dresses (unless you count this damned uniform, which I don't). I have a couple of pairs of shorts and a couple of pairs of jeans and I share T-shirts with. . .

Look how much I have been able to tell you without mentioning Jon. Maybe I really could write this letter. But if I could talk about Jon, a letter would be so much easier. Would it matter so much if he weren't Lucille's son? The Mourning Glory and Mama would never forgive me, but you would, Bart. I can count on you to forgive me.

Sometimes I wonder if I can ever come home again at all. Sometimes the worry keeps me awake nights, but most nights I'm too tired to think at all. Some nights we don't go to bed till real late. Those are the nights when the anarchists invite the other workers from the date groves to come and sit around the washtub fire and smoke marijuana and drink beer and listen to talk about the revolution and historical imperative and the leaderless state. There's a mimeograph machine in one of the trailers, and it's the girls' job to run off flyers and hand them out to the workers. I'm sure those workers use the flyers for toilet paper, Bart, because Jon says the bathrooms at the groves are worse, smellier and back up more often than the bathroom at the Bus.

The workers are mostly Mexican. The white and Indian workers are local guys who have families, but the Mexicans are braceros and they come up here for the money and leave their families behind. They are horny and make dirty remarks, which I can recognize even though they're not in English. After working at Petey's, Bart, you get so you know that kind of talk, whatever language they use. Personally, I think the workers come to the Bus for the beer and marijuana and don't give a damn for the revolution, but you can't tell the anarchists that. Oh no. Jon refuses to believe me when I tell him: they don't understand a word of what you're saying—you'd be better off putting your ideas into a song than mimeographing those stupid flyers. Music is the only universal language, but Jon says, No, math is too. No, I told him, you have to *learn* how to do math, but anyone can hum a tune—put your idea into a song and teach them the song and then they could hum ideas all day long, just like I hear the Eleventh Sonata in my head. At night I dream I'm playing the Eleventh Sonata, Mama, and when I wake up, I still have it in my head, but not in my hands any longer. My hands ache for music. Here at Petey's I use my hands to make disgusto thousand-island dressing and wipe up water rings and sink frozen french fries into tubs of boiling grease, but my hands long for the piano, my fingers twitch to play the grand piano at home or the upright at Jerusalem Road.

Jerusalem Road. You'd just be leaving San Angelo now, wouldn't you? Packing up in September and going back to the city. Bart and Jill and Marietta and the Mourning Glory and you, Mama. Not Father this summer. Not Father ever again—but do you remember how Father used to love to hear me play? He was dying and I wanted to play for him, something I knew really well, but he used to say to me, no Claire, the Eleventh Sonata is truly glorious, practice that piece Claire, learn it *before I die.* He didn't say that, though, did he? He didn't have to. He just sat there with the shawl you knitted him, Mama, draped over his knees and listened to me by the hour and I did learn it for him before he died and sometimes I think if Father hadn't died, I never, never would have gone away with Jon, but I had to be loved, Mama, unconditionally loved, don't you see? That's the way Jon loves me. That's the way Jon loves everyone. He doesn't reserve his love only for anarchists. He doesn't care if I don't convert to anarchism. He loves me because I'm Claire, and I rely on that love, just like I relied on Father's. Father's love for me never depended on how well I lived up to the Three D's or if I were nice or sweet or cute or any of that. Father just loved *me.* Maybe it's just as well I'm in Chagrin. I don't think I could bear San Angelo without Father, but oh, Bart, what I wouldn't give to make a sandcastle with you or hear the ocean crash or taste the salt on the air or see some fog, anything to soften this ghastly, killing heat. What I wouldn't give to see a runaway nasturtium. The closest I come are the sunflowers lined up in front of the Bus. I water them every morning before I go to

Petey's. Petey always makes dirty cracks because I come to work in a car full of guys. So what? None of the other anarchists has a car, so everyone uses our Falcon.

The Falcon is used, Bart, badly used, but it got us down here. Jon bought it with the money Lucille threw at him. Jon wanted to burn that money because it came from his mother, but I told him I'd seen enough of men throwing money away. Besides, I told Jon, we need a car to get downstate. So we drove the Falcon off the lot and directly to Chagrin, barring the number of times we had to stop to let it rest its radiator. In fact, every morning Jon has to put more water in the radiator, and then me and the guys get in the Falcon and he drives us all to work. The Swallow in the Falcon. Funny, don't you think, Mama? Only I don't have a last name here either; I'm just Claire, except at work, where I'm Melinda. That's what I put on my name tag because I don't like being ordered around by a bunch of dumb truckers. If they order Melinda around, it's not too bad, but sometimes I forget I'm Melinda. Sometimes I can't hear the truckers no matter what they call me because I've got the Eleventh Sonata washing around in my head, but it fades, too. By the end of the day, it's gone.

But in the morning, Mama, in the early morning, I wake up at dawn and the Eleventh Sonata is still grand and clear and fresh from my dreams and I get up and put on a T-shirt and brew the coffee and while it's perk-perk-perking on the stove, I go out front and water the sunflowers and then I pour myself a cup and I take my coffee to the front of the Bus, Bart, and I sit in the driver's seat and I play with the steering wheel and with the key that's frozen into the ignition, just as if someone parked the Bus here and might be back at any moment. I turn that key and pull that throttle, I choke that Bus till it strangles to a start. I punch my foot down on the gas pedal and turn the Bus toward West Damascus, yanking out the clothesline tied to the back, where my uniform is always hanging, and pulling up the sunflowers and I aim the Bus right for the washtub and the milk crates and I plow through them and send them flying and I drive out of this tumbleweed lot, down Damascus toward Scheherazade and I go right past Petey's and I get on the freeway going north.

I come home with my lover, Mama and I do love him. I love him so much it makes me ache all over sometimes, ache to feel his body in and on and around me, like I'm empty, Mama, unless he fills me up. Can't you remember what it was like to love Father like that? Can't you remember what it's like to love a man that way? Jon is my flesh and blood, he's a cool spring I go to every night to get refreshed. He's everything to me and maybe I'm not quite everything to him, but we're absolutely essential to one another and I know that everything would be better, Bart, everything would be just fine if I could get this Bus to move and drive away before Jon wakes up, everything would be perfect if I could roar out of here, away from the washtub fires and the trailers and the mimeograph machine and the Schoolbus Seven and the dog and the date groves and the leaderless state and this hellish heat. I'd drive this bus north, up along the cool foggy coast, and people would smile to see the sunflowers and clothesline and the Eleventh Sonata flying out behind us.

ii

At six o'clock Claire went through the kitchen, collected her purse, said good night to Petey and then out the back door to wait for Jon. She did not like to be picked up in front, in full view of the truckers, because dressed in the skimpy uniform with its stiff short skirt, she felt half naked, as if she were wearing a lampshade that left all her switches accessible. Heat billowed up off the blacktop, seared through her shoes and scorched her legs until Jon pulled up in the steaming Falcon. He was alone tonight, and she got in the car and kissed him and asked where all the others were.

"I took them home first."

Claire put her hand on his knee. "There's a Chinese restaurant on Schcherazade, right beside the five and dime, you know. Let's go there for dinner, just the two of us."

"We have responsibilities, Claire. It's our turn to cook tonight. I bought a couple of cans of beans and some rice at the store before I picked you up."

She withdrew her hand and sulked as he drove down Chagrin's main drag, Scheherazade Avenue, and past the Chinese restaurant. Jon broke the silence as he turned on West Damascus. "Bad day at Petey's?" Jon stroked the full dark beard he had grown.

"Just the usual dog meat hamburgers. We had a guy nearly die in there today, though."

"From the food?"

"From the heat." Claire lapsed into a sullen silence. "I hope there's no one using the bathroom when we get back to the Bus. I'm not in the mood to put up with it."

Jon pulled the Falcon into the diminishing shade cast by one of the trailers, and they found Kharabian camped on the front step of the Bus, patting Squat and waiting, he explained, for Ilse to get done in the bathroom.

Claire pushed past them, into the kitchen area. All the windows were open, but the blast of wind cooled nothing, served only to shudder the cobwebs rimmed with grit. She washed her face and hands but did not bother to dry them; the wind would do that more quickly than a towel.

"Hey, Claire," Kharabian shouted from the step. "Tell Ilse if she doesn't hurry up, I'm going to shit on the stairs."

"Do that, Kharabian, and you can clean them with your own toothbrush," Claire called back as she took the four necessary steps back to her bedroom—the bed on one side of the Bus with a black flag pinned above it, a narrow chest of drawers and a pencil-slim path between them leading to the bathroom. She chuckled to hear Kharabian's laugh. Overweight, swarthy, weak-eyed and intense, Kharabian's convictions were nonetheless not so fragile as to be threatened by a breath of humor. Kharabian could even joke about the revolution, which the others (Jon included) held sacred.

"Fascist swine," said Ilse, coming out of the bathroom with a newspaper in her fist. "Did you see this article, Claire?"

"Do you mind, Ilse? I want to change."

"Modesty is bourgeois," said Ilse on her way out.

"Can I come in and use the bathroom now, Claire?" Kharabian called.

"Hold it."

"Till when?"

"Till you pop." Claire heard Kharabian whistle for Squat as he left the steps, and she wished she'd been kinder. Kharabian, after all, was the only one who ever bothered to ask.

Jon came into the bedroom and handed her a cold beer.

"Unzip this damned tutu, will you?" Claire always breathed easier once she stepped out of her uniform.

"Everyone has to pee, you know, Claire."

"Not a foot away from my head, they don't. Let them water the

227

cactus. Let them fertilize the desert. This is my bedroom, isn't it? Our bedroom?"

"But it's the communal bathroom."

Claire took a long draught of the beer, but it did nothing to cool her smoldering temper. "Why not teach Squat to pee in the pot, and maybe we could housebreak the jackrabbits while we're at it. Why not post a sign in the men's room at the bus station: for a really good pee, come to the Bus on Damascus."

"There's no talking to you when you're like this." He turned to leave, but Claire caught him and pulled him into her arms, rubbing the top of her head against his thick beard, kissing his neck where the hair from the beard and the hairs from his chest curled together.

"Lock the door, Jon, let's make love right now. I need you now."

"There is no lock. We'll have to wait till tonight, but tonight. . ." He ran his hands down her back and held her cheeks. "I know it's hard to get used to a new way of living, babe," he murmured, "but after the revolution, everyone will live like this and you have to remember, we have work here."

Claire let go of him and struggled into her shorts and T-shirt. "You might have work, Jon, I have a job. I didn't come down here to work at Petey's. I came to live with you and I've ended up living with all of them—them and that damned dog."

"Oh, babe, I know it's hard. It's hard for me sometimes." Jon sat on the bed. "It's a new way of living, and you have to let go of your old notions. You have to try harder, Claire. You have to learn to live with others."

"But do I have to love them? That's what you're asking of me. You know it is. I love you, but that's not good enough for you, is it? No. You want me to love Kharabian and Squat and Bob and Kathleen and Art and Ilse and Mark and Maggot."

"I've told you not to call her that."

"Maggot. Maggot. Maggot."

"Keep it down, Claire. They can hear you."

"Matthew Mark Luke and John! Is this the great anarchist talking? You sound like my mother: quarrel if you like, dear," Claire twittered over the words, "but don't let anyone hear you, don't let anyone guess how you truly feel, don't hurt anyone's feelings." Claire kicked her uniform across the floor. "Do they ever ask how I feel when they walk right in when we're in bed together. No—that's bourgeois, isn't it? Well, keeping your voice down is bourgeois too!"

228

"It's the heat that's getting to you, isn't it? The heat and Petey's and the uniform."

"No, Jon. Jon." Claire knelt between his knees and put her arms around his waist and kissed his inner thigh. "I can stand the 109-degree heat. I can stand the job and the uniform. I can stand anything just to live with you, but don't you see, you and I, we don't live together at all. We live with the seven of them and the Mexicans three times a week and—"

"The revolution doesn't happen in a day. People have to be led to see its wisdom. The revolution is a field you have to plow one clod at a time."

"That's fine for you, but what about me? After you're done with the date groves and the washtub politics and the anarchists, what's left over for me? What's left over for us?"

"We make love every night," he whispered against her hair.

"I love you, Jon, I'd die without you, but the only time we have together is when we're in bed." She rested her head on his leg and unbidden, the Eleventh Sonata's soft adagio crept into her head. "I want us to have a home together, a home and a life together that's just ours."

"You know I don't believe in bourgeois life—secret horrible private little lives without an ounce of political conviction."

"Would a bit of privacy, a little time for us alone, compromise your precious principles?"

"Don't make fun of me, Claire."

"I'm not. I don't mean to, but you've had it all your way, haven't you? I've done all the compromising. I wanted to get married and you said it was against your principles and I said all right and I haven't said a word about it since, have I? Have I?" If Jon answered, Claire could scarcely hear him because the adagio crescendoed and she had to speak over the music to hear herself. "Now it's your turn to compromise. I don't say leave the revolution or your principles. All I want is to quit living with the seven of them and Squat. Kharabian is the only one I can endure at all, and I hated his guts last night when we were in bed making love and he and Art and Maggot were out there at the washtub quarreling about the leaderless state. You were more interested in their argument than you were in making love to me—don't deny it."

"I do deny it."

"Then why did you get out of bed and pull on your pants and go out and jump into the fight?" Claire got off her knees and sat beside him on the bed, which was so soft it nearly swallowed her up. "I don't want to live in this bus anymore, Jon, or spend my nights sitting around an old washtub while you spout revolutionary slogans to Mexicans who can't understand English anyway."

"You hate my politics, don't you? You always have."

"I don't hate them! They're part of you and I love you. But I'm not asking you to give them up! I'm not saying, Jon, go put on a suit and work in an office while I sit at home in the suburbs and eat bon bons. I don't ask that of you, but what you ask of me is impossible. You want me to love you and anarchism and the revolution and Prokotpin—"

"Kropotkin."

"And the historical imperative and the Schoolbus Seven besides and if you ever looked at them honestly, you'd admit that you and Kharabian, you're the only ones who are committed to all that. The rest of them just don't want to end up like their parents. This commune is nothing but summer camp for them, and pretty soon they'll pack up and go home."

"Is it summer camp for you, Claire? Will you pack up and go home?"

Three months before, Claire would have answered unequivocally no, but that uncritical moment in their love had passed. Indeed, it seemed to die before Claire's eyes and perhaps it deserved to be mourned, but there wasn't time, not if they were to move beyond it. She took a long drink from her beer. "You are my home," she said finally, "but I can't live with them any longer. I want us to have a home that's just ours."

"What about my work here?"

"What about it?"

"How can I do my part for the revolution if I sit at home with you at night and watch TV?"

"Matthew Mark Luke and John! Don't you ever think in anything but absolutes?" She got off the bed and snatched her uniform from the kitchen floor and stuck it into the sink, where she poured soap and hot water over it, scrubbed at the grease and sweat and stench while the steam flew in her face. She wrung the uniform so fiercely the very threads gasped from the strength in her hands. She washed that uniform allegro con brio and in four-four time.

In the next month and a half, the heat abated, the scorching sun cooled, but everything else deteriorated. Petey sliced the top off his index finger with the tomato knife. Coralee caught the busboy pilfering canned goods and fired him, so Petey had to bus the dishes, which made him nasty and ill-tempered, and he threatened to fire Claire after she slapped a customer for goosing her. Coralee took Claire's part in the matter, but privately told her, if she was going to react so violently to a little goosing, she was in the wrong business.

"It's not my business. It's my job and nothing more," Claire retorted with the Eleventh Sonata ricocheting through her skull, louder and louder all the time. She no longer needed to nurse the melody or coax it to the fore of her mind. From the time she woke till she fell asleep, exhausted in Jon's arms, the music pounded in exuberant contrast to her squalid life. She brandished it as one might a sword against the leering truck drivers, the smell of grease, the medley of ketchup and mayo and relish. She found that with very little effort, she could turn up her internal volume and hear the Eleventh Sonata even when the jukebox blared. Unfortunately, this meant she heard nothing else as well and her tips dwindled accordingly.

At the bus, the Eleventh Sonata deafened her to the chafe and scraping of eight ill-suited people, to the political arguments, the tri-weekly meetings of would-be converts. She sat around the flaming washtub and smoked a reefer and smiled to watch the fire dance in time to the exquisite rondo in her head; gradually, the music engulfed her body and her hands began to twitch and she played at an imaginative keyboard in her lap, discreetly at first, but then reaching further afield to touch the notes and chords, laughing to see the curious faces of Jon and the Schoolbus Seven and amazed they could not hear the music or feel its passion or profundity. She heard the sonata's most grandiose chords when she reached the orgiastic moment of love with Jon and its tender, ineffably sweet passages when she held his head between her breasts or followed a pattern of notes across his chest, arpeggios that disappeared into his curly beard. The allegro, adagio, minuetto and rondo, endlessly repeating, enhanced Claire's nights like a drug and rendered her days bearable.

Jon had no such shelter. He got moody and uncommunicative after the foreman at the date grove told him he'd lose his job if he didn't quit bringing his Commie political tracts to work. Jon declared he was not a Communist, called the foreman a fascist and described (graphically) what would happen to him After the Revolution and got fired anyway. Right after that, the mimeograph machine broke down because Maggot used it when she was stoned and poured fluid into the wrong hole. Jon spent a week fixing the machine and writing furious manifestos until Kharabian got him on with another grower. Kharabian advised him not to burn the carpet to get rid of fleas.

Squat tore Claire's uniform from the clothesline and chewed it up and she ceased speaking to Mark after the incident and Maggot quit speaking to her in retaliation. Kathleen borrowed the Falcon and backed into a fire hydrant, forever locking shut the trunk, and when Claire found out, she flew into a fury and accused Kathleen of screwing Kharabian and the chiropractor and Kathleen retorted better a whore than a snob and Claire said only a whore would think so.

The kitchen drain backed up and had to be reamed out with a coat hanger. The sunflowers died. Claire's period was late. The sonata's sorrow and triumph so totally absorbed Claire's entire being that she sometimes forgot to take her pill—or any other precautions—and now her period was late. She was pregnant and she would have to kill herself. Jon's principles would never allow him to marry her for anything so bourgeois as pregnancy, and if she went home to her mother, Meg would die of the shame and scandal, and Claire could not bear the thought of an abortionist reaming her out with a coat hanger like she was the kitchen drain. She'd have to kill herself. She decided to wait, however, because her period was only two days late and might yet come. When she finally got it, she was so relieved, she picked a terrible fight with Jon, who moved out to the Falcon to sleep.

Kharabian found him out there the next morning when he went to pee in the brush. "She's on the rag," said Jon by way of explaining his presence in the Falcon.

"No," said Kharabian, zipping up his pants. "You're spitting into the wind, Jon."

Jon rubbed his beard and squinted into the hard morning light. "What?"

"I mean, she won't take much more. You'll wake up one morning and Claire will be gone. Even anarchists don't live by revolution alone."

"You do."

"Not by choice. You have the choice."

iii

Claire and Jon rented half of a furnished duplex on Cairo Street for sixty dollars a month. Their landlords lived in the other half, an old British couple, Roy and Etta, who had left Blackpool for Roy's health some fifteen years before. They clung to their customs of tea and toast despite the 115-degree heat, they gossiped about the royal family and clucked over wartime rationing and the Blitz as if it were still raging. They cut pictures of Westminster and Stratford-on-Avon out of magazines and taped them to their walls. They claimed to hate England and love Chagrin. Claire got on with them famously.

The little clapboarded duplex offered scant protection against the sun and desert wind, but the house was shaded by a coterie of congenial palms and the porch (which they shared with Roy and Etta) furnished with a card table and fraying wicker chairs. Like the other small, odd homes on Cairo Street, the duplex even had a tiny scrap of lawn, to be prized and nurtured in Chagrin the way a bed of orchids would be anywhere else. Claire still rose at dawn, but now she drank her coffee outside, and since the Eleventh Sonata had subsided, she could hear the birds quarreling high in the palms, the jackrabbits marauding nearby and the crunch of dry grass under her feet.

Without the deafening music, Claire could once again enjoy a few laughs with Coralee, tap her feet and fingers to "It's My Party", tolerate the truckers, and she even offered a bit of cordiality to Maggot, who stopped by Petey's one afternoon for a Coke. "Next you'll be getting married," scoffed Maggot.

"Why should we?" Claire wiped up the water ring on the counter. "I have everything I want. Everything I've ever wanted."

And she did. The time. The man. The home. Each day seemed to Claire a voyage of discovery to a new world and yet these days were only extraordinarily ordinary. Occasionally, Claire and Jon went to the Chinese restaurant; they saw *Lawrence of Arabia* in Chagrin's sole movie theater; they lay in the claw-footed tub and passed cold beers and slender reefers back and forth, exchanged words and dreams on sheets that smelled of love and bleach and burning sun. While Claire played Scrabble on the porch with Roy and Etta, Jon attended washtub political meetings at the Bus three times a week. (Claire explained to Roy and Etta that her husband was a student of history, and they seemed very impressed.) Claire avoided the Bus at all costs, returning only for

Thanksgiving and then not at all surprised to find that Art and Ilse and Bob had bolted, that Kathleen was living with Kharabian and the anarchists had been joined by two new women.

In order to drain Thanksgiving of its banal bourgeois associations, the anarchists decided to celebrate it communally and to that end invited (pot luck) the workers from the date groves, the other maids from the Travelodge and Kathleen's chiropractor, who didn't come, but everyone else gathered that afternoon at the Bus on West Damascus. The Mexican men brought jugs of wine and quart bottles of Dutch Lunch beer; the wives of those workers with families brought dishes of beans and rice and potatoes and yams. Some came only with loaves of bread and cubes of margarine. One woman made oatmeal cookies, which disappeared immediately.

The late afternoon sky was the color of sassafras as the sun inched its way toward the ash gray mountains, the queer light intensified by flames shooting out of the washtub. Wind teased plumes of smoke and blew tumbleweeds past them like careless pedestrians. Claire clutched her sweater against the chill and put her store-bought fruitcake on the long trestles supported by sawhorses with all the rest of the food and a radio blaring "Sally Go Round the Roses". She got a paper cup and some wine, but lost Jon in the crowd and ended up talking to Beth Hepplewhite, the pale, plain wife of a date grove worker, a woman not much older than Claire, with three dirty children under the age of six. Beth jiggled the baby in her arms and yelled at the other two while she talked with Claire.

"Tiffy, you go get Tami right this minute. You're Miz Cotton, aren't you?"

"Yes, I am," said Claire modestly.

"Well, I just want you to know how grateful we are."

"For what?"

"Didn't your husband tell you how he saved Chuck's job? Chuck got the sunstroke, got it bad, and the foreman was going to fire him, but Jon said he'd do Chuck's work too while he was out if only the foreman wouldn't fire him. This job means a lot to us, Miz Cotton, and we're real grateful. Tiffy, I thought I told you—'scuse me, Miz Cotton."

Beth ran after Tami, while Squat came to have a sniff at Claire. She brushed him away and joined Jon and Mark and the two women new to the commune. She came in on Mark's joke about this being just like the first Thanksgiving. "We even have the Indians!" Mark added. Jon grimaced and introduced the two women to Claire as Barbara and

Sherry. They introduced themselves as lesbians, which Claire figured must be some sort of weird nationality like Armenian.

"Admit it," said Barbara, who was solid and sallow. "Lesbians are the only true anarchists, the only ones committed in their everyday lives to the overthrow of the patriarchy and all it stands for."

"All it stands for," echoed Sherry, who had the droopy eyes and slack jaw of a hound.

Kharabian burst into the discussion and threw his insights into the political stew and then led Claire back to the trestle table, saying she must try the dish he had made. He pointed to a pan of what looked like fat green cigars swathed in tomato sauce. "Grape leaves," he told her proudly. "I had to call my mother for the recipe, and it took me all night."

Claire tasted one and took several. She put some rice and potatoes and yams on her plate and sat on the step of the Bus. Barbara and Sherry joined her, balancing their plates on their knees.

"If I was ever to go to bed with a man, it would be him," said Barbara, nodding in the direction of Jon, who squatted by the trailer in the enclave of womenless braceros. "Your man isn't like the rest of these bimbos. You need balls to be a real anarchist, and Jon Cotton has them."

"I see," said Claire, uncomfortable discussing Jon's endowments, even politically.

"The rest of these guys might as well be trade unionists, they're so narrow," Barbara went on, her mouth full of mashed potatoes. "They wouldn't know Bakunin from Bull Durham and they haven't got any moxie. Why, you put most men, even anarchists, within twenty feet of a lesbian and they jerk off just to prove they have dicks. Not Jon Cotton."

"Not Jon," repeated Sherry.

"He has compassion and vision, too. Jon understands that the patriarchy has to be overthrown along with capitalism. The working class will never triumph without the solidarity of women, who are the really oppressed. We have to get rid of men."

"Get rid of men?" asked Claire. Maybe lesbian was not like Armenian at all.

"Well, get rid of marriage and men's power over women or—"

Barbara's soliloquy was cut short by singing as Jon and Kharabian stood, their arms draped around each other, booming out the "Marseillaise" and drowning out the "Louie Louie" from the radio. They laughed and floundered over the verses, but their valor and enthusiasm was so contagious that one by one, the others rose, even the children, joined hands and sang as best they could, the refrain, though none of them spoke French and some didn't have much English; they rose to the moment and to the men, stirred by song and a vision of a more just world. Barbara stood up and so did Sherry, leaving their plates on the step beside Claire, who was the only person still sitting.

In the deepening twilight, Claire stared at the surrounding faces, lit by flames from the washtub. A caul of wind-spun smoke enveloped Jon and Kharabian, blew into Claire's eyes, but even through the smoke, she could see that Jon Cotton was as happy as he had ever been. She took a drink of wine to wash away the taste of soot accumulating on her tongue, the smoky premonition of defeat: Claire thought these people dirty, disheveled and ignorant, at best objectionable, at worst odious, but Jon loved them as he loved her, unconditionally. His love for her was personal and his love for them political, but for Jon the differences were not of kind but degree. These people were her competitors, her enemies. They didn't understand Jon, but neither did Claire. Most of them didn't give a hang for the revolution, but neither did Claire. They responded to the same qualities that had drawn Claire to Jon; they too wanted some part of his unimpeachable integrity, his thirst for work, his gravity of purpose, his dauntless energy and unswerving loyalty. They loved him. She could see that love in their faces, the Mexicans and Indians and lesbians, the whites and wives and Travelodge maids and Mark and Maggot and Kathleen and all the rest of them. *This is the enemies' camp; these people are my enemies.* And there were not, as she had first supposed, merely six or seven or eight of them, but hundreds. And hundreds more where they came from.

iv

In early December 1963, Chagrin Springs made the national news. No less than Walter Cronkite himself told the nation that an outbreak of typhoid, unheard of in these modern times, had flattened this tiny desert oasis, filled the small hospital to overflowing, and that three local churches had been turned into makeshift infirmaries to accommodate the stricken. Ten deaths were so far attributed to the disease, mostly elderly and infants. He added that the bacillus had first manifested itself amongst the migrant workers in the date palm groves and seemed to have got into the water supply from the wholly unsatisfactory sanitation provided for those workers. County inspectors ordered the grove owners to raze the shacks and outhouses and build new ones with plumbing that met the current codes. Residents of Chagrin, Cronkite added, were being urged to have the anti-typhoid vaccine and to stay away from tap water. Shipments of uncontaminated water as well as hospital supplies were being trucked into Chagrin daily, from as far away as St. Elmo.

Cronkite did not know the extent of the catastrophe. Chagrin died. The date palm industry toppled at its peak season, laying off even those men who could work. Truckers drove right through the afflicted town, even though the next stop was seventy-five miles in either direction. Petey's and Carney's and all the other diners shut down for the duration. The motel signs on Scheherazade Boulevard blinked VACANCY for about a week and then went off altogether. No one was likely to sleep in Chagrin who had the money or strength to get out.

In the middle of the night, Kharabian walked all the way to Cairo Street and banged on the wrong door, rousing first Roy and Etta, apologized and went to Jon and Claire's. "Can you come over and drive them to the hospital or one of the churches, Jon? I'm the only one not shitting my guts out."

Jon went back into the bedroom and pulled on his jeans. "I have to go to the Bus."

Claire sat up and rubbed her eyes. "Why?"

"They're sick. They need me."

"Even Squat died," Kharabian called. "I buried him this afternoon, and I thought if I don't get some help, I'll be burying Mark and Sherry too. They've got it the worst."

Claire got up, dressed in jeans, sneakers and a blue turtle neck sweater of Jon's, wrapped up in her coat, and the three of them drove through a town that was silent as death, dark except for those homes where people kept bedside vigils.

A dry cold wind slapped Claire's face when she got out of the Falcon. Lights blazed in the trailers, and in the ring of darkness just outside the encampment, Claire could hear someone vomiting into the brush. She followed Jon and Kharabian into the Bus, where they found Sherry lying in Barbara's arms, her droopy eyes sagging over her cheekbones and her breath rattling in her chest as she muttered incoherently. Barbara bathed her forehead and muttered endearments. A terrible noise emitted from the bathroom and then the toilet flushed and Mark stumbled out. Jon took off his own coat and wrapped it around Mark's shoulders, and Claire found Sherry's coat and some socks to keep her feet warm. She held Sherry while Barbara dug for her own jacket.

"Where'll I take them, Kharabian?" Jon asked.

"Well, the hospital's filled and I think the Methodists and Catholics are, too. Try the Mormons."

"If they ask Sherry her religion, I'll kill them," Barbara vowed.

The tired Mormon matron behind the desk at the doors of the Latter-day Saints' church hall asked only Sherry's name, age, address and how long she'd had the symptoms. Behind the matron, a stiff hospital partition separated the admission desk from the church hall, but it could not screen the sight of some three dozen cots filled with moaning men nor stifle the smell of the chemical toilets lined up in front of the stage like tall, odiferous footlights before a green curtain pinned with Christmas decorations. The few fluorescent lights winked and shorted as volunteers and nurses scurried amongst the cots.

The matron asked the same questions of Mark. "He'll stay in the hall," she said, "but the women and children are in the Sunday School classrooms, through those doors and to your left." Barbara picked Sherry up in her arms and carried her out.

"We've got more coming," said Jon.

"Well, you better get them here fast. We only have so many beds." The matron frowned over her roster. "Oh, here's Dr. Adamson. How many more can we take, Doctor?"

"How the hell do I know? Can't someone else count? I've got my hands full. Where are those Red Cross people with the hospital supplies? They told me they'd be here at nine and it's two-thirty. And get on the phone and get us some more fresh water and someone in here in the morning—eight, sharp—to empty those chemical pots."

"I've been trying, Doctor, but they don't answer."

The young doctor scraped his stubbly chin with hands that were gray from disinfectant. "I've got an old man here so dehydrated he'll die by morning if we don't get some more IV's, and a dozen women and children delirious with fever. I need more enemas, too. Either they're constipated or they've got diarrhoea so bad they can't make it to the toilet. Open your mouth," he said to Mark. "You have a rash?" Mark nodded numbly. "You'll find a bed there at the back. There's no clean sheets, though. Call the hospital," he ordered the matron. "Get some more sheets. We've got enough blankets, though, I think." He patted Mark's shoulder. "You'll live. It's only the very old and the very young who can't take it."

"I don't want to live," Mark replied thickly. "I just want to quit shitting blood."

Claire put her arm around Mark's shivering shoulders. "You go back and get the others, Jon. I'll stay here and help. I'm not sick."

"Not yet," said Dr. Adamson. "Get the nurse to give you an anti-typhoid vaccine if you haven't already had one and keep your hands disinfected, don't drink tap water, and you might stay that way."

Jon returned to the commune to collect the rest of the ailing anarchists, and Claire found a cot for Mark. As she wrapped the blanket around him, she watched other volunteers remove soiled pads and bedpans and help men puke into buckets beside their cots. Those who could walk were assisted to the chemical toilets. Mark began to retch, and a pale, plain woman handed Claire a bedpan. Claire held it for him, nearly retching herself in revulsion. "What'll I do with this?" she asked the woman when Mark had finished.

"Dump it in one of the toilets," the woman replied. "Doctor says don't dump nothing you don't have to in them porto-pots. Then take it to the tub of disinfectant in the kitchen and just leave it sit there. They all got to be—why, it's you, Miz Cotton! You don't remember me, do you? Thanksgiving. Beth Hepplewhite. My Chuck's got it bad, and Tiffy too. I'm going in to my girl right now. That's not Jon, is it?" she asked, nodding to the stricken Mark.

"No."

"People all look the same when they're sick, don't they."

Claire soothed Mark and told him she'd be back. She picked up the bedpan gingerly and wandered through the double doors in search of a bathroom and the kitchen, where the disinfectant was. She passed classrooms full of groaning women and a room of children, where she saw Beth Hepplewhite on her knees beside a cot, singing softly to Tiffy. Down the hall, Claire found the men's room. A streaked, stinking nightgown lay outside the door and a cry sounded from within. Claire opened the door and found a naked middle-aged woman, her distended abdomen spotted with a rash, her teeth and lips covered with brown sores, bent double in pain. Claire put the bedpan down and held the woman's shoulders till the worst passed and then got a blanket and wrapped her in it and led her back to her cot. "I'll find you a new nightgown," Claire promised, "and whatever else you need."

It was dawn before Claire dumped the bedpan she'd left in the men's room. By that time Jon and Kharabian had brought the rest of the sick anarchists. Jon, Claire and Kharabian submitted to anti-typhoid vaccines and then Jon made a run to the hospital for sheets and gowns and IV's and enemas. At ten the next morning, Claire collapsed into sleep on a church pew.

They lived at the Mormon church for days. With the other volunteers, the few nurses, Dr. Adamson and the St. Elmo doctor who occasionally relieved him, Jon and Claire and Kharabian slept on hard pews, ate dry toast and strong tea brewed from such fresh water as could be spared, doused themselves with Lysol and waded back in amongst the suffering.

The plight of the Mexican workers was the most poignant because although they shared pain and fear with the other victims, they could not make themselves understood, cried out in Spanish and for families that were far away. Some of the volunteers treated the Mexican men less than generously, as though they had willfully brought this plague to Chagrin, but Jon Cotton sponged their bodies, changed their bedding, emptied their bedpans, checked their pulses and respiration with the untiring diligence of a mother. He donated the same tenderness and dedication to them and his anarchist friends that he gave to the foreman who had fired him from the date grove. Men, women, children—Jon carried them all to and from the toilets, swabbed their fissured tongues, bathed their feverish limbs, massaged and dressed their incipient bedsores and sat for ten straight hours beside the bed of a woman who threatened to sink into a coma. The glazed eyes of the sick lit to see Jon Cotton, and he seemed to carry assurance like an electric current in his very touch.

Claire Swallow had no such magic. She barfed into the bedpans and her own bowels weakened when she gathered up fetid sheets and blankets or tossed foul cotton pads into the church's incinerator. Claire winced at the sight of lips and teeth encrusted with sores. Her head rattled along with the cart full of urine specimens she pushed to the makeshift lab in the kitchen and she held her own breath every time she heard the bronchial gurgle of others. She fed patients dilute milk preparations, placing the spoon on their white-furred tongues, and then she retched. Claire's sneakers stained with the haemorrhages she cleaned off the church floor and her eyelids dried with fatigue and her hands grayed and puckered from Lysol. She checked pulses and administered such comfort as she could, but that was damned little because fighting off collapse came to absorb most of her strength. She refused to succumb, to admit that her own fleshly fabric was as prone to decay and death as others. Claire never before realized how ugly and ungainly and vulnerable the human body could be, how hairy and splayed and saggy, how foul the flesh, how prey to pain, how tawdry and weak and pitiful the body's defenses. She watched the Mormon elders going from cot to cot, laying their hands on feverish brows, and wondered how anyone, in the midst of this physical carnage, could believe in an ethereal soul.

In five days, Beth Hepplewhite went home with her husband and Tiffy. Claire leaned on the doorway of the classroom and watched as Beth wept into Jon's arms, thanking him for all he'd done. He gave Beth the keys to the Falcon and told her to drive her family home and bring the car back whenever she could. As Beth left, the matron called Claire to the front to help an old couple to their beds.

"Roy! Etta! Not you too!"

"Oh, I'm not too bad, Claire," replied Etta, belying the anguish in her eyes. "But it's Roy, the old dear. He hasn't got any fight left and I couldn't—"

Claire put an arm around each of them and led Roy to an empty bed in the men's ward. Etta said she would wait till Roy got comfortable and then Claire led her to the Sunday School classrooms. "Roy doesn't think he's going to live, Claire," said Etta, leaning heavily on her. "You tell him he's got to live. Who'll get my tea in the morning if—"

"He'll live, Etta."

"Just point me to a bed and go look after Roy. There's a good girl. He was always so fond of you, Claire. Maybe you can get him well."

But Claire couldn't. No one could. Claire gave Roy such time and care and infusions of strength as she could, but she was there with Jon and Dr. Adamson when he haemorrhaged and died. Dr. Adamson pulled the stethoscope from Roy's chest and announced that it was finished, but Claire shook Roy's old shoulders and cried out his name. His lifeless head lolled as she wept over him, sobbed as though he were Anson Swallow, as though she were watching Anson die all over again. Dr. Adamson told Jon to take her outside and then beckoned to Kharabian to call the morgue.

As Jon led her out of the church doors to the parking lot, Claire buried her head against his shirt, though he too reeked of Lysol and what it could not conceal. Outside, the desert wind grazed her cheek and she was blinded by the cold hard sunlight twinkling off asphalt and chrome. She wept uncontrollably and Jon tried to quiet her.

"Don't tell me to stop!" she blazed out at him. "I hate it! I hate the sickness and death and misery. I can't—"

"Hush, Claire. Hush, babe. You're overworked. You're overtired."

"Even you stink of death. Me, too. Death and blood and disease— disease and—"

"You should go home, Claire." He led her to a bench and made her sit beside him while she shivered in paroxyms. "You go home and—"

"Home? Home to a ghost house? Roy dead and Etta sick and who's going to tell Etta? Not me."

"I'll tell her. You go home."

"I'm not leaving you." She clutched his shirt. "I'll come back and you'll be dead, too."

"No I won't. We're not going to get sick, Claire. We've been spared so we could help the others."

"But I *hate* the others! Don't you understand. I hate their diarrhoea and vomit and blood and rashes and distended bellies! I hate them! I want out of here. I want to go home."

"That's what I said, babe, you go—"

"That's not home! That's a slum in the middle of this stinking desert. I want to go *home*. I want to hear the ocean and feel the fog and—"

"Claire, the worst of it is over, babe. It is."

"You tell Roy that. Tell Etta."

"But it is. We've only had four new cases since Roy and Etta. It's clearing out. All the anarchists are well. Pretty soon we can all clean up and go home."

"Cairo Street isn't my home and it isn't yours, either. You'd rather live in that stinking bus, that's your real home, with those filthy anarchists."

"Please, Claire, don't say things you'll regret."

"I don't regret it! I mean it! You love them better than you'll ever love me."

He took her face in his hands and brushed her lips. "I love you, Claire. You are my resurrection and my life and I love you, but I'm needed here." He stroked her hair and pushed it back from her streaked, dirty face, and she hid her eyes against his shoulders and listened to his hands as well as his lullaby voice, tap out a message, a telegram with his palms and fingers as he kneaded her back and neck and shoulders, and gradually her sobs eased and ceased and she believed him: the plague was almost over. The worst had passed. The vaccine protected those who were not sick, and those who were seemed to be recovering. Everything would be all right and they would go back to Cairo Street and their house with its claw-footed tub and its friendly palms. Everything would be fine. He told her he had to return to the patients but that she should go around back of the church and get a cup of tea, that she should rest, and the worst was over, and she believed him and did what he said.

When Claire finally returned to the church hall, Roy's bed was empty, as were half a dozen others, their thin mattresses rolled up, testifying to Jon's correctness: it was coming to an end. Dr. Adamson moved amongst the cots at a less frenetic pace and the matron at the admittance desk was gone and two volunteers chatted together, resting. Claire had not seen anyone (who could walk) rest in a week. Here and there a groan, a grunt, a retch sounded, but most of the men could stumble unaided to the chemical toilets and the hall no longer resounded with the cacophony of human misery. Jon sat beside the bed of an old man who lay with his knees drawn up to his chin, his body writhing with the misery in his gut. "Pray for me," the old man pleaded.

"I don't know any prayers." Jon replied. "I'm sorry."

The man put his hand in Jon's. "Pray for me. Please."

Jon pressed his forehead against their united hands. He remained thus until finally he said, "Matthew Mark Luke and John, bless the bed this man lies on. Make him whole. Make him well. Make him. . ."

"Go on. Please."

"Take this affliction from his body and grant him peace of spirit."

Claire bit her lip against the tears welling in her eyes, wept to hear her childhood chant from Jon's lips. She marveled at his reservoirs of strength, wondered at the compassion that allowed him to part with his principles to spare another person pain: she was moved to see him put aside his anarchist's convictions, his hatred of religion, to soothe a nameless old man's misery. She felt suddenly humbled, diminished in the light of Jon's moral stature; by comparison she was puny and small-minded, her recent outburst weak and unworthy of his love. She never loved Jon Cotton as much as she did that moment.

"Will you get a few more chairs, Claire?" She jumped at the sound of Dr. Adamson's voice. "Some of our people are ambulatory and we'll need more chairs as they begin to move around. You'll find them behind the curtains on the stage."

Claire climbed the few steps to the stage, pushed aside the thick green curtain and as it closed behind her, breathed in the musty stillness. She stumbled over some tables and a blackboard before her eyes grew accustomed to the dim light, groping her way toward the back of the stage, where she could perceive folding chairs stacked like firewood. As she reached out for them, her fingers brushed soft felt and she squinted into the darkness, leading with her hands, trying to see as well as feel the lineaments of the large object under a baize covering; she ran her hands over its hulk and recognized its shape in the same way a sailor, castaway at sea, would recognize a piece of greenwood floating between him and an unseen shore.

Claire pushed a path through the chairs and they clattered to the floor as she grabbed hold of the baize and yanked at it, twice, three times, before it fell away and she could actually touch the piano, the wood embellished, ornate, dustless, upright, the only dustless upright thing Claire Swallow had touched in months. She opened one of the folding chairs and sat down, lifted the wooden lip covering the keyboard and spread her fingers over the keys. She executed a brief run and smiled to hear that the piano was perfectly in tune, utterly unspoiled. Claire struck a few bass chords and a tinkling trill on the upper keys and she laughed aloud. She could not clearly see the keyboard in the darkness, but didn't need to; her hands followed a behest she did not consciously will as she quietly wrung the Eleventh Sonata's second movement, the gentle adagio, from the piano. Her fingers hesitated, stumbled, but the right note always followed the wrong one, and softly, the music spilled, inexpert but eloquent. She stirred more than music from that piano—balm, and more than that—memory: she evoked from those keys the words of Nicholas Kerchiaeff and understood them: what music can mean in the midst of death and desolation; how profoundly music can speak to ears that have heard only screams of anguish, cries of mourning, shrieks of pain. Music: born afresh each time new hands compel it from a piano. She had come upon the adagio's gentlest passages with an almost maternal love when the dimness was shattered by a crack of light. Jon thrust the curtain aside and Claire turned to see him, framed in fluorescence.

"What are you doing?" he asked.

"Oh, Jon, look what I found! And listen—I can still play! Isn't that wonderful? Do you know how long it's been? It's like I was starving for the piano and here it is! I've dreamed about this piano, Jon, and here it is! Oh, Jon, listen—of course I don't play well anymore, I haven't played it since my father died, so I'm rusty, but, listen—"

"Goddamnit, Claire! Have you lost your mind? Have you forgotten the typhoid?"

"No, but—"

"We've got patients here, Claire. Sick people. People who need rest and quiet."

"But I need to play. Listen, just for a moment. I'll just play the opening. The Eleventh Sonata is so beautiful, Jon, you'll—"

"I don't give a good goddamn if it's the Mormon Tabernacle Choir, close that damned thing up and get out here where you can do some good. You can't play the piano now just because you feel like it. Shut that thing up. I mean it. Get out here and empty a bedpan, for Christ's sake. Do something useful."

Claire's hands fell from the keyboard as if they'd been shot off. Jon dropped the curtain and left her in the suffocating silent darkness, but he had admitted to her sanctuary the smell from the chemical pots and the scrape of retching and the ring of bedpans and glassware. Defeated, Claire wept into her disinfected hands, powerless against Jon's betrayal: he loved these sick and helpless, putrid people more than he loved her. She could not command his loyalty or compassion, but they could. Claire pulled her damp hands away from her face and stared at them, the fingers trembling with suppressed strength, vibrating with longing, taut as weapons, tingling with the music she had forgotten but they had not.

Claire Swallow wiped her hands on her jeans. This time she began at the beginning of the Eleventh Sonata, the allegro con brio; the jubilant opening spurted from her fingers and she played with a mastery she had no right to. With a precision born of passion, she hit one joyous chord after another, rippled along the keyboard, her fingers running in pursuit of simple melody, counterpointing in increasing, almost mathematical complexity, the bass and treble, the runs tripping and traveling over keys that sang at her slightest invitation. She had never before—and would never again—play with such clarity or miraculous grace because at that moment Claire Swallow was simply a vessel that needed to be emptied of its music. The Eleventh Sonata rumbled against the reverberating metal of the stacked chairs; the wooden flooring of the stage beneath her quaked with the sonata's seismic shock; the allegro, in a glorious, inexorable tidal wave of triumph, flowed over the stage and underneath the green curtain, rumbled down the steps, washed over the chemical toilets and into the church hall, floated the pain, death and disease, the fleshly debris out of the church, out of Chagrin, out of Claire's life forever.

She hit the allegro's last ecstatic chord and with her hands still poised over the piano, she looked up and saw Jon Cotton. She had no

245

idea how long he had been there. Their eyes locked in wordless combat. Claire slammed down the keyboard cover, rose and kicked the chairs out of her path. Defiantly, she walked past Jon, past his resentment and unspoken rebuke, past his passion for people he did not know, past his principles and the prayers he was willing to say to ease a stranger's suffering, past his inability to understand hers. Past him and out of the Latter-day Saint church.

She stepped into the winter sunlight and walked quickly, following the sonata's dictates, up the street and out to Scheherazade Boulevard, where the motel signs blinked once again and the Chinese restaurant and five and dime tentatively reopened as people cautiously took up the threads of their old lives. Fortissimo chords so filled her skull, they probably would have spilled from her lips had she opened them, but she kept her mouth cinched shut against the desert wind and walked on, in four-four time. As the sonata spiraled toward the resounding crescendo of its finale, Claire opened the door of the bus station. "When's the next bus north?" she asked. The music in her mind shattered into a million grace notes.

"You've got an hour's wait, miss."

"Give me a one-way ticket."

"To where?"

Claire looked for her purse, but that and the rest of her life were still in the duplex on Cairo Street. She rummaged in her pockets and laid out $5.67 on the counter. "How far can I get on that?"

"A ticket to St. Elmo is $5.05."

"Give me a ticket to St. Elmo." She'd get to St. Elmo and borrow or beg the money off Melinda Lamott, off Melinda's family if she wasn't there. She'd wire Bart or Mama if need be. She'd get the rest of the fare somehow, but she needed to get out of Chagrin now, before she had a chance to remember or regret.

Claire took her ticket and found a seat in the crowded bus station. She was the only solitary person there, the rest were couples or families or the broken off shards of families, hovering around suitcases and roped boxes. Frazzled parents quarreled with their children, a mother and her middle-aged daughter comforted one another, husbands shuffled through lunch bags and wives soothed squalling babies. Their noises all melded into another kind of music, which Claire also recognized: the discord and harmony, adagio and allegro contingent only upon those same conduits of blood and sinew Claire had so recently seen spilled over the church floor. Like Claire, these people were dirty, disheveled, tired and eager to escape Chagrin. Refugees. Fleeing the plague or the revolution. What did it matter? Fleeing.

The bus pulled into the station, and inhaling its exhaust gratefully, Claire shuffled after the other refugees and got on. She found a window seat near the front and an old woman sat beside her after stuffing her three grandsons into the seat across the aisle. The woman passed out peppermint Lifesavers to the boys and offered one to Claire. Claire took it, but nothing could save her life, nothing could save Claire Swallow until at last the bus doors closed with a pneumatic hiss and— trailing the Eleventh Sonata like a banner of audible freedom—the bus lumbered out of the station, past the intersection of Cairo and Scheherazade, past the Chinese restaurant and the single movie theater, the motels and the Mormon church, past West Damascus, past Petey's Diner and onto the freeway heading north, out toward the timeless, silent groves of date palms and past them, too. Past. All of that past.

CHAPTER THREE

October 1985

April may be the cruelest month, but September is the sadist. Autumn—this autumn in particular—tortured Claire Stone more poignantly with every passing day; the parallel past accosted her at every turn. September: the family ought to be closing down the house on Jerusalem Road, returning to the city, to school and piano lessons, the Episcopal church on Sundays, the days drawing in under lamplight and Anson's benevolent gaze. Cradled in September's dry arms, jagged endings and beginnings juxtaposed, memory rasped against loss: the unrepentant Claire defies the judiciary committee in that, her first and only autumn at the university, that last autumn of Anson's life. Now, Anson's confidence in Claire's future seemed to be relentlessly mocked by the metronome on top of the upright piano, tapping out time as Claire directed small, unwilling hands toward melody. While the western sun squandered itself on the living room, Mrs. Stone sat beside her pupils, smiled, applauded their mismatched chords, but in her mind she heard the Eleventh Sonata, rolling through that sunflower September in the schoolbus, the cooling of Chagrin and love. The death of summer affected Claire with a lunar tug, sucking her back into currents she had forsworn and casting her upon shores she had renounced.

October was easier. Nothing began or ended; October brought only fog that softened even regret and blunted the dagger of memory. All

September Claire had lain beside Lucky and hoped, expecting that with his returned health he would resume their intimate life anew, take her in his arms, hold her head against his shoulder and love her. Lucky began his community service in September, donned an orange fluorescent vest and picked up trash along the highways along with people convicted of lewd conduct, drunk driving and shoplifting. His health was equal to that task—and to proselytizing amongst his co-workers. He came home glowing with tales of the conversions he'd effected, or if not quite conversions, at least people who had agreed to attend Sunday worship of the Fellowship of the New Millenium. The outdoor work, the opportunities for Christ, proved a tonic to Lucky and he seemed more relaxed and happy than Claire could ever quite remember. But she waited all September for him to make love to her and he did not.

Perhaps, Claire reasoned, it was not a question of mere physical health. Perhaps Lucky needed to be reassured that she wanted him. Perhaps their long abstinence acted upon him as it had upon her, making her more self-conscious, wary and mute, as if abstinence opened a chasm in their marriage that one or the other of them must leap across. Perhaps Lucky's health was not equal to that effort, but Claire's was and so she kissed the hollow of his shoulder and toyed with the scanty chest hair she knew so well. "I love you, Lucky," she whispered.

He patted her head. "I love you, Claire."

Across him, she could see the digital clock, its eerie blue light giving off an underwater glow. She watched the minutes tick inexorably by and then she slid her hands down his body and he leaped to life in her fingers.

"I'm still trying to find the ways of the spirit, Claire. I don't want to be confused by the flesh. Please move your hand."

"The Fellowship doesn't believe in celibacy! Do they?"

"Our bodies are instruments of God and we must have reverence for that instrument and use it only when such acts accord with the spirit."

"What?"

"I can't make love to you tonight. My love for you remains unchanged, though," he added.

"Don't tell me you're screwing Emma Duff!"

Lucky turned away, leaving her with the empty vista of his back.

Claire changed her tactic. "Human beings need affection, Lucky, even God would grant you that. People can't live without affection, without intimacy, without closeness. We've always had that. Even in the worst of times. We've always had each other even when—"

"I don't care to retread the unsanctified past. We have to answer for more than our bodies, we have to answer for our spirits and my spirit is no longer in accord with yours. I would belie my spirit and my Christian principles if I made love to your body." He spoke sadly, but his words had the air of having been rehearsed, as if he knew this moment would come and he was not unprepared. "You are still beautiful without, Claire."

"Without what?"

"Outside. You are a beautiful woman and I have hungered for you, longed to know you in the biblical sense."

"Why didn't you let me know, honey? I wouldn't have hurt you. I'd have done anything you asked. We could have—"

"But inside you're not beautiful anymore. You know what I'm talking about."

Claire tensed in the ensuing silence.

Finally, Lucky continued. "I know why you sent Scott to Honolulu. You tried to keep it from me, but I know." Lucky paused as if picking his words like plums, or thorns. "I know what you used for money, and I know you weaseled Albert Smythe's number out of Althea and made her call him."

"I didn't make her do anything. She agreed."

"Althea does not have a beautiful spirit either. I am ashamed of both of you and ashamed that a son of mine would agree to such a cruel and loathsome plan." Lucky pulled away from Claire; the chasm between them was slender but real, physical and no longer simply imagined. "But then, Scott is not my son, is he?"

"Religion's rattled your brains, Lucky."

"The thought occurred to me before, now and then, but I know now for certain that no son of mine would, could possibly be party to anything so despicable."

"You did plenty of despicable things before you got so holy. Why do you think you're out picking up trash?"

"I am prepared to pay for my sins, both to society and whatever atonement God may ask of me. We're not talking about my transgressions, which I freely admit to. We're talking about Scott. Scott is not of the flesh of my flesh."

"Don't you remember, Lucky? That night in my room? We made love and I got pregnant and we got married."

"We made love and we got married, but someone else begat Scott on you."

250

"He's yours! You're his father!"

"Yes, in every meaningful way I am Scott's father, and he is my son. But not physically. I love him like a son. That does not and will not change, but he is not the flesh of my flesh, the bone of my bone."

Lies are like money, useful as long as people go on believing in them, please believe, Lucky, don't make me admit that our marriage is counterfeit, not now, after all these years of need and belief and I need you, Lucky.

"I don't bring this up to inflict pain on you, Claire, and I don't regret our life together and I hope you don't."

"You've been a good husband," she said to the ceiling. "I've loved you."

"You've been a good wife, Claire, and I know you've been faithful to me for twenty-one years, and even now I can look back and remember the way I felt about you then. I probably would have married you anyway, even if you had told me the truth."

"I did tell you the truth."

"The truth that you were pregnant, but not the truth of who begat the child on you. I don't suppose it matters now. I'm not asking you to tell me who was the man who was Scott's father, I won't—"

"You! You are Scott's father!"

"—bring it up again. I just want you to know that I am not a fool. I know what you did in the past, that you made love with me, lied about loving me, so I would marry you and I can forgive you that because we've had a good life together and a rewarding marriage and I love you and I think you do love me, even if you didn't then."

"I do! I did!"

"I can forgive the past, Claire, but not the present. I can't forgive you for sending Scott to Honolulu. It was an abomination, malicious and abominable. If I didn't love Scott, I wouldn't be so ashamed of him. If I didn't love you, I wouldn't be so ashamed of you."

"You mean you won't make love to me until you can forgive me?"

"Forgiveness is between you and God. You have to repent first, but you are cursed with pride, Claire, and God requires humility of us. You must humble yourself before you can repent, before God can offer you forgiveness or salvation. It's not up to me to forgive you. All I'm saying is that my making love with you must accord with my Christian principles and until you have humbled yourself before God and discovered those principles for your—"

"God! I hate it when you get so sanctimonious!"

"I'm not sanctimonious. I'm not making love, either. Good night."

Claire rolled over and began to cry silently, not tears of remorse, but anger; she was hungry and humbled and angry and angry because she was hungry and humbled. She craved reassurance and wept into her hands, but Lucky seemed to have drifted immediately into sleep and the very peace of his breath offended her. She was startled by the blast of the phone and snatched it up with the first ring.

"Claire?"

"Hoolihan? Is that you? What do you want?"

"I need to talk to you, Claire. I haven't slept right in a month. Not since that day at Alfredo's."

"What do I care if you sleep or not? Go have a brandy. Don't call me in the middle of the night. I have nothing to say to you."

"I just want you to listen. Look, I'll come to San Angelo. Tomorrow. Just tell me a time that's convenient. Sometime tomorrow afternoon. It's important."

"Not to me, it's not."

"Consider that I am calling in the favor you owe me for Lucky's defense," he said dryly.

"Oh, all right. I'm finished giving piano lessons at four. You can come then, but park down the street and come to the front door. My mother will be in the kitchen, and if she gets sight of you, it'll set her back a month and a half."

Claire hung up and hugged her knees, waiting for Lucky to say something, but he did not stir. She bounced on the bedsprings while she sought her slippers and the voluminous shawl Meg had made her as a wedding present. She hoped Lucky would wake, put his arms around her and ask her to come back to bed. But he did not. She walked disconsolately to the window, parted the curtains and watched the moonlight swim in long lapidary strokes across the sea.

ii

Hoolihan was already on the front porch, sitting in the Senator's enormous, fraying rocker, when Claire finished giving her lesson and came out. He wore a maroon sweater and a tweed jacket and he looked casual but not comfortable. Claire could not miss his appraising gaze running over the ramshackle house, peeling paint and sagging steps, the garden they grew of necessity, and she wished she'd met him in

252

some more neutral public place.

"If it's about the hundred dollars, you can save your breath, Hoolihan," she said by way of greeting.

"What hundred dollars?"

If it was about Scott and Honolulu, he could save his breath too, but Claire decided not to say so; she had suffered quite enough rebuke last night.

They left the garden, turned south on the beach as if by mutual consent. Claire had to quicken her pace to keep up with his athletic stride and wondered fleetingly if Hoolihan had ever relaxed in his sixty years or if he brought the same coiled tension to the courtroom that he brought to the squash court or a walk on the beach. The beach was empty now, matrons back in their chromium kitchens, children back in their schools. The few people here this overcast October afternoon were solitary, scantily-clad runners and a woman with a Peke on a leash. Claire zipped up her short jacket as the damp invaded her bones and the sky seemed to scowl. "What is it, Hoolihan? What's so important?"

"All I ask is that you hear me out."

"This isn't the courtroom, you know. You can't manipulate me like—"

"I'm begging your indulgence, Claire. That's all."

But once he had obtained her indulgence, Hoolihan seemed oddly constipated and at a loss. Usually so certain, pointed and direct, Hoolihan waffled about with the pleasantries, inquiring how she liked giving piano lessons, to which Claire flatly replied that it was a living. More or less.

"A pity you didn't keep up your music, Claire. Your father always had such belief in your abilities. He used to say to me, those last months before he died, that he thought you had the stuff of a concert pianist."

"Well, I don't."

"No, getting married, having children so young finished that dream, didn't it?"

"What business is it of yours?"

"The law is my business, but I can't help thinking that if Anson was right, your gifts are going to waste teaching pre-pubers their scales. Maybe you should think about picking up your old dream."

"In case it's escaped your notice, Hoolihan—I know how busy you are—you can't become a concert pianist at forty-one."

"Maybe not. But you could commute up there a few days a week and still give lessons here at home. Their new president, Dr. Julian, is a client of mine and I'd be happy to say something to him on your behalf."

"When I need your help, I'll ask for it, Hoolihan."

"You needed my help last month and you didn't ask for it. There was no need for you to upset Lucille and endure that humiliation at Alfredo's. I could more easily do something for you with the conservatory, but if you still want to discuss your son's future—"

"I don't," she said tersely. "And if that's why you came down here, then save your breath. Anyway, I loathe being indebted."

"Then you must be a very unhappy woman," he observed. When Claire retorted with a flip response, he added, "Desperate women are always unhappy. Look at Lucille."

"I'll pass on that, thanks."

"Don't misjudge her. She looks like that on the outside because of what's happened to her on the inside. She's all soured up inside, Claire, undone finally by the thing she wanted most when she was a desperate young woman. She was even more desperate than you."

"I'm not desperate."

"You were in Alfredo's."

"Unkind," said Claire, bringing down an invisible gavel.

"I ask you to understand her position. Not now. Then."

"Why should I? What do I care? You said you wanted to see me about something important. Why don't you just get to it?"

"I am. But in my own way. Any lawyer knows you can't understand the present unless you look at the past. Precedent. There's always a precedent, and none of the Swallows—Anson included—made any effort to consider Lucille's precedents. Here was a young woman who had robust good health, a smashing body, a face the angels envied and brains—Lucille is the smartest, shrewdest, the most remarkable person I know. She had all that and what did it get her? Nothing. What had life dealt her? If she'd been born a man, all this would have been different."

"I'm sure it would have," said Claire, with malice aforethought. "I doubt a man would have seduced the Senator."

"Oh that." Hoolihan gave a derisive laugh. "If she'd been a man, Lucille would have run rings around the Senator, beat him out of his money fair and square, but a woman can't work that way, couldn't then, can't now. I don't give a damn what they say about equal opportunities or how many women get Harvard MBA's. Men have the power, and women rely on them. Women who want access to power have to court them. A man with Lucille's gifts would have been called a leader. A woman with those gifts is called a bitch."

"She is a bitch."

"Maybe. But she was one of ten children and her father held a bottle far better than he held a job. He beat whoever was handy when he was drunk, which was most of the time, and as soon as she could, Lucille left. She used what God gave her—her gorgeous body—and got a job dancing in a burlesque house."

"Althea always said she was a whore."

"I'll be frank with you, Claire, as long as you'll give me your oath—on your father's grave—that whatever we say here today will go no further than you and me and these gulls over our heads."

"I swear. Was she really a whore?"

"Maybe. Maybe she did sell her body. It would be hard for a woman to sell her brains in that position."

"You don't need brains for the missionary position," sniffed Claire, disappointed at his evasion.

Hoolihan chuckled in spite of himself. "In those days Lucille was hungry all the time, figuratively and literally hungry until she finally retreated or stumbled or took refuge in marriage. Marriage was the only safe place she could find and if it wasn't comfortable, well, marriage is never comfortable."

"How would you know, Hoolihan? Have you ever been married?"

"My marital status has no bearing here, Claire. You agreed to listen." He let Claire glower before continuing. "Lucille was a good wife to Norris Cotton—who wasn't her equal in any way, I might add, but never mind. She was faithful. She bore him two children and then he died. Lucille was desperate, but no more desperate than you were last month in Alfredo's. I'm not casting aspersions, Claire, I'm asking for your hypothetical understanding. Think of a widow alone in the world with two little children."

"Oh, go gag a maggot, Hoolihan. She didn't give a damn for those children."

"Perhaps I overstated her case. I admit she's not exactly the Madonna type, but if Joseph had walked out on the Virgin, could she have stayed at home with the baby Jesus and tiddled his toes? No. She had to work, to support those children. She had to get a job. You might have a little more understanding of Lucille if you think of the Senator as her job. She didn't love him, but you don't have to love your job. You just have to do it. You know whereof I speak, Claire." He scooped up a handful of small stones and cast them, one by one, into the sea. "You've had that kind of job. At Petey's. In Chagrin."

Beneath the sand, Claire thought she could hear the earth's plates colliding, as if great fissures were about to gape open and swallow her whole. Wasn't it enough that Lucky had beat her with the past? Must she now endure Hoolihan's abuse as well?

"Don't worry, I never told Lucille."

"Told her what?" said Claire defiantly.

"That for six months you lived with Jon Cotton and worked at Petey's. I had reliable sources in those days. I expected to find you there too when I went to Chagrin to get him to come up for his sister's wedding. But you were gone by then, and Jon was living with that tribe of crazy anarchists. My sources aren't as good these days. I haven't been able to track him down since that hepatitis attack in Kentucky in, I think, 'eighty-two, as I told you in Alfredo's."

"Will you quit mentioning Alfredo's!"

"But I'm still looking. If I find him, would you be interested?"

"No."

"Well, I'll keep my own counsel then. I'm no priest, but a lawyer hears a lot of confessions."

"Not from me, you won't."

"Anson should have sent you to law school, Claire. You'd have made a hell of an attorney."

"Get back to the point, Hoolihan. If you have one."

"Spoken like a judge's daughter." He tossed his last stone and picked up a few more, rolling them in his fingers. "To put it bluntly, sleeping with the Senator was Lucille's job and she did it well and faithfully. As long as the Senator lived, there wasn't another man in her life. I never laid a hand on her until after the funeral."

"You and everyone else money could buy."

"I'll let that pass, but I don't want you to misunderstand the relationship, Claire, not for any moral reason, but because it bears directly on why I'm here today. I loved Lucille. I truly did. I still do, at least I remain loyal, and at my age that's as good as love. Maybe better," he said, as though the thought had just occurred to him.

Claire stopped and turned to him fiercely. "Why, Hoolihan? If you're loyal to Lucille, then why are you here and why did you defend Lucky and why—"

"I told you that day I called—I defended Lucky for Anson, though you must admit your father would not have been as generous with your husband. Your father would have been quite revolted by all that mess. It would have sullied him and Anson could not bear taint, but I'm not like that, Claire, not that noble or sensitive or pure." Hoolihan's gray eyes lit with amusement. "My sole saving grace is that I can lie down with dogs—and get up without fleas. It doesn't make me pure, but I keep my balance. And so, you see, there's nothing contradictory in my loyalty to Anson and you, Claire, and to Lucille, though don't misunderstand—I didn't always approve of what she did, not only to your family, but to others whose tales don't bear discussion here. Still, I admired the spirit that allowed her to do it. Lucille had spirit, all right, and she deserved her success, but try to imagine what that success meant to her, in the beginning, when for the first time in her life she had some security."

Claire snorted and resumed walking. "She had money up the ying yang is what you mean."

"Up that and everything else, no doubt, but precedent, Claire, precedent—imagine what she must have felt the first time she rolled over in bed and realized that when that old man died, everything she had worked for would go into the grave with him. Lucille is guilty of some undeniably unsavory doings, but she was not motivated by hate, as everyone in your family assumes, but by fear. And you have to wonder how she talked the Senator into leaving her Swallow Lines at all, since he never thought she was anything but brainless and delectable. She was delectable," he added as an afterthought and with a smile.

"You'd never guess it to look at her now."

"No," he said sadly. "She's no longer beautiful."

"But she's still rich, no matter what she says."

"Oh yes, she's rich. But she'll sit in the dark at night to save on the electric bill. She uses little plastic margarine cups for dishes and washes them in cold water. She tabulated her cab fare for a year one night and sold the car the next day. Outsiders look at her and see a mad old hag. A Gucci baglady. I see a brutalized little girl, a frightened, desperate young woman so afraid of poverty that it's sucked her dry, not the money, but the fear of losing it."

"Are you asking me to pity her?" Claire cried. "I don't care if she has her own fingernails for lunch, Hoolihan! How can you ask me to pity a woman who has all that money?"

"It isn't the money. Don't you see?"

Claire answered him coldly. "It is for me."

"Listen." Hoolihan brushed the air in a gesture of dismissal. "I came down here because of something you said in Alfredo's—sorry, something you said last month. I don't ask you to pity Lucille and I don't say she is virtuous, but you accused her of being responsible for Anson's death and she was not guilty of that." He caught himself and shook his head. "Anyway, guilt is all relative, isn't it?"

"Only if your relatives are guilty," Claire contended.

"No, I mean only innocence is absolute and so rare and perishable that I don't even discuss it, but Lucille had nothing to do with Anson's death. In that she told the truth. Anson strangled on his principles."

Suddenly, overcome with fatigue, Claire retreated to the dry sand near the cliffs and they sat down. Before them lay the charred remains of a beach fire, complete with beer cans and a used condom. The October sky was the color of mattress ticking, thick with clouds, the gray sea and gray sky indissoluble at the horizon, where a solitary sailboat braved the certain storm. "It had something to do with Lucille," Claire said stubbornly. "My father may have died of cancer, but he was eaten up inside with—I don't know what—revulsion or loathing, or some kind of monumental disgust killed him and I'm certain it had to do with Lucille."

"That's not true."

"All right then, with Lucille and my grandfather's will. I was there, Hoolihan. I watched my father take thousands of dollars and throw the lot of it into the Pacific. It was money the Senator had left him, and I stood beside him on the Swallow dock and watched while he threw it all away. He was demented, I tell you. He said he did it to free us from the past and then he maundered on about taint and principle and a lot of other bullshit. What did I know of taint? What did I care about the past? I was eighteen. And principle! God, I hate the very sound of that word on men's lips. But the worst of it was, Hoolihan, my father begged me never to curse him for that act and I never did. Not until last month." Claire's shoulders quivered. "I sat across from Lucille and I cursed my own father and I knew then, for certain, that it was all her fault."

"No. You may have watched Anson throw the Senator's money away, but I watched Patrick Ryan lean forward in the gas chamber. I saw his lips move for the last time. It was his dying breath and he used it to curse the judge who sentenced him and the Senator who—"

"Who is Patrick Ryan? What's he got to do with this?"

"Everything. But I'll come to that in a minute. I just want you to understand that Lucille was not implicated in Anson's death. If you want someone to blame for your father's death, you might as well start with me. It might have happened without me, but Anson killed himself in a kind of slow suicide, and I'm the one who handed him the weapon."

"You! What could you do to my father?"

"I told him the truth, Claire. And it killed him." Hoolihan took a charred stick and began to draw intersecting lines in the sand around the shriveled condom. "And once I'd told him the truth, there wasn't a lie I could offer that would have saved him." He added reflectively, "It's the only thing I've ever done that I've been really ashamed of. I can justify everything else."

Claire drew her knees up and held them. "I don't believe you."

"I'm willing to tell you the truth, Claire. It will absolve Lucille, and it won't kill you. You're not made of the same stuff as Anson. You'll get bitter and angry and nasty, but you won't die. But I won't go on if you don't want to hear it."

Claire took a short breath and exhaled the words, "Tell me."

"After the Senator's death, when I became Lucille's legal counsel—and her lover—your father despised me. He was wrong to do so, I think, but then I never let principle interfere with passion, and for your father they were one and the same thing. He dealt with me fairly in the courtroom, scrupulously so, as he did everything else, but our friendship—and it was a friendship, Claire, fledgling perhaps, but bona fide—died under the weight of his disapproval of me and his disgust with Lucille. Eight years passed like that and then one night, out of the blue, he calls me and asks me to meet him for a drink."

"When was that?"

"Just about this time of year. Autumn. September, it was, September 1962. I said I'd be delighted and so I met him at a bar not far from the courthouse. He was already there, I remember, sitting alone in a booth and sipping a brandy. We talked of this and th t, Anson was cordial. I was elated to be back in his good graces. And then, after a few drinks—I had a few, more than a few, Anson kept to his single brandy and his pipe—Anson finally said he had a few questions about the Ryan case he hoped I could clarify since I had been Ryan's attorney."

Claire could picture Anson, sitting in a booth in the dim bar with his pipe and solitary brandy. Of course he would have got there first; he disliked walking into a sea of expectant, anxious faces—too much like the courtroom. Competent, thoughtful, controlled Anson. And yet. To the tune of "Minuet in G", she could remember a barking, bellowing Anson, papers raining to the ground. She glanced at the sailboat before her, pitching on the frothing sea, plunging headlong into the low clouds. She heard the "Minuet in G" halt in mid-air. "Who's Ryan?"

"Patrick Ryan, my dear, was an ambitious attorney. No, that's too modest. He was hungry. Ravenous, never content. Patrick Ryan wanted everything that had been denied him because he was the son of turf-cutting, peat-eating micks. When you're that hungry, money won't suffice, it's power you want, position, and Ryan was well on his way to achieving all of that, but in the meantime, Pat garnered a little side income—and believe me, he needed it—from looking after the affairs of widows. One of his widows was a woman named Sophie Goldstone. One-Strap Sophie, they called her. She was quite wealthy, but she lived in the most grueling and eccentric poverty, not," Hoolihan sighed, "unlike Lucille. In fact, I look after Lucille's affairs in much the same way that Ryan looked after One-Strap's, with the salient difference that Lucille and I go back thirty years and we were in love. Ryan never loved anything or anyone. And as near as I can judge, no one ever loved Sophie Goldstone. No one mourned her, and if it hadn't been for the money, she would have been dumped, buried and forgotten." Hoolihan drew concentric rings around his parallel patterns. "The Ryan case can be summed up easily enough. One-Strap was murdered. Two jailbirds confessed and said that Ryan ordered them to do it. Ryan stood trial. Your father was the judge, and I was the defense attorney. Ryan was found guilty and executed by the state. He was certainly guilty beyond a reasonable doubt, as they say, but it was clear to me when I met your father later at Patrick Ryan's grave that Anson suffered from unreasonable doubts. Still, I wouldn't have guessed him to be tortured for ten years, but then, I'm not made of the same fine fabric as Anson Swallow. When I met him in the bar that night after eight years' enmity, I was eager to regain his friendship and regard, and admittedly, I even had a few drinks before I got to the bar and I was downright drunk by the time we got around to Ryan. I can't even remember Anson's question, some minor inconsistency in the testimony, or—I don't know. Anyway, it doesn't matter what he actually asked me because I rattled off the whole story. Not a confession exactly, but—"

Claire could see them in the darkened, intimate booth: the grave judge, the high-spirited, half-drunk Hoolihan confessing the sins of others to gain absolution for himself. "What did you confess?"

"The truth, of course. Who could it hurt? Ten years had passed. Sophie, Ryan, the Senator and all his cronies were dead. Why, Stone had just died the month before."

"Stone?"

"Lucky's uncle or cousin or whatever he was, Mayor Stone. Slime personified."

"My father never liked the Stones. He couldn't abide sanctimony, and neither can I," she added, wincing still under the hurt Lucky had inflicted.

"Anson was a fastidious man, Claire, but the rest of them couldn't tell decency from dog dung. For years, oh, well back into the twenties or even before, the Senator and his rich cronies had a practice of forming temporary cartels, setting up a dummy board of directors, a nameplate on an office door, someone's mistress stuck in there to answer the phone now and then. They'd go after a particular project, make their money, dissolve overnight and be done. Illegal no doubt, immoral certainly, but none of them ever lost sleep—or money. Anyway, at the end of the war, they called themselves Sparrow Enterprises, the Senator's idea of wit, no doubt. They should have called themselves Vulture Enterprises. That's what they were. By 1943 it was clear to anyone who had a brain to play with that the war would soon end and the city would boom and one of the first major undertakings would have to be a new courthouse. You're too young to remember the old courthouse, but it was built in the 'nineties and should have been torn down after the 'twenty-eight quake, but the Depression scotched all that and they had to make do. But after the war—well, the Vultures, connected as they were throughout the city, certainly knew which pieces of downtown property would be likely locations for a building that big and they started buying them up. They offered a reasonable price and everyone sold out. Everyone except Sophie Goldstone. Sophie was a real slumlord, but she lived in her own slum. The vultures should have guessed that anyone who lived like that wasn't likely to rise to conventional bait. Still, they sent their emissaries to her with one tempting offer after another, but One-Strap went after them, flailing a rake overhead."

"Who told you all this, Hoolihan?"

"My client, of course, the erstwhile Patrick Ryan—though not all at once. Oh no. Patrick Ryan danced a jig around this tale for months. He was besotted with his own power and certain of the protection of men like the Senator. Finally, one day I shook his shoulders and I said, Patrick my lad, they're going to fry you like a clam—can't you see it coming? But even then Ryan couldn't admit to his own stupidity. He'd rather be guilty than stupid and of course, in his case, he was both. If he hadn't been stupid and crass and overconfident, he still would have been guilty, but he wouldn't have got caught. Well, Patrick continued foolhardy until well into the trial and this information, what I'm telling you, what I told Anson, only came out a little at a time, like farts at a funeral. Gradually, Ryan told me how One-Strap had come into his office one day moaning and sniping at the Vultures, how they were pestering her for her land. Well, Patrick was a rising young politico, he had some idea of who Sparrow Enterprises might actually be, and on an educated guess, he called up the Senator and asked if he'd like to have lunch at the Regents Hotel—oh, it was all plush drapes, linen and crystal for Patrick Ryan in those days. Normally, I doubt the Senator would have deigned to lunch with a mick attorney, rising or not, but Patrick probably chirped a little sparrow talk into the phone and the next thing you know, they're at lunch, sawing on their chops, discussing the end of the war and the city's fine prospects, and by the time they get round to dessert, Ryan mentions his client the widow Goldstone. My guess is the Senator wiped the spittle from his lips, but not the gleam from his eye, but he said nothing. Not then. The Senator was too smart for that. He phoned (so there's no record or witness), mentioned in a roundabout way that any effort Ryan might expend to urge his client to sell would meet with approval in certain unnamed quarters." Hoolihan flung his stick into the sea and kicked the condom out of sight.

"This is all very murky, Hoolihan."

"Of course it is. True greed is never naked. It always comes swathed in fulsome phrases and clothed in righteousness and wrapped in solicitude. True greed is ever ready with a thousand good reasons why it operates, and in justice to the Senator, he wasn't alone in his greed. Ryan was greedy too, but Ryan wasn't interested in simple profit. After that call, Ryan dug out One-Strap's financial records and spread them across his desk and stared at them, not seeing the figures at all, seeing his grand future flame off those pages. Mayor? Governor? Senator? Anything was possible given the eternal gratitude and support of Senator Swallow and men like him. Money," Hoolihan scoffed, "could always be found, but this was his opportunity to see his aspirations realized, his thirst for power quenched. And all he had to do was convince Sophie to sign. And sure he was that he could do it—a little charm, a little coaxing, wheedling, that's all."

"But she didn't sign, I take it."

"But, Claire, you miss the finer points of his strategy. Offhandedly, he asked her a couple of times, mentioned it, but he didn't want to alarm One-Strap, and when it was clear she wouldn't sign, he had to retrench. He had her power of attorney, after all, and she was just a witless eccentric who left everything in Pat's hands and he paid her a monthly allowance—and extracted a monthly fee for the privilege of doing so. He went so far as to assume that the old girl would die before any of this could catch up to him, so he drew up the deed and forged her signature, sold to Sparrow Enterprises, at a pittance, I might add, every square foot they wanted."

"If he had her power of attorney, why did he forge her signature?"

"He couldn't risk having his name on the deed, and One-Strap didn't exactly write with a dancing master's hand. It was an easy forgery. A child could have done it. What Pat did with the money, I don't know, but the money was nothing. The land was sold. The Vultures were content. Sophie was ignorant. And suddenly the son of root-grubbing Irish peasants was the grand and golden boy—wined and dined and courted. Mrs. Ryan's little Pat went golfing and yachting and game fishing, to polo matches and society balls with Senator Swallow and all the little Sparrows. He got rich by association and powerful by what amounted to their decree. He thought he'd joined the holy angels, but he was playing with the devil—and time. He might have beaten the devil, but time—" Hoolihan shook his head.

"How long did this go on?"

"Oh, a few years, but then in 1951, they started bulldozing Sophie's land, which, it goes without saying, Sparrow Enterprises sold to the county for probably ten times what they paid for it. Maybe more. And if One-Strap had died that day, Patrick Ryan might well have been a Senator. But she lived and eventually she came banging on Ryan's door and he held her off—don't ask me how—time after time, always hoping, praying, wishing she would die and maybe that's when he got the idea of helping her dying along, but I don't know that for a fact. By the time they started to build that courthouse and even with the kindling she had for brains, One-Strap figured out what had happened to her land and she threatened to go to the police. Patrick Ryan should have told her right then: go have yourself fitted for a shroud, Sophie." Hoolihan rubbed his jaw thoughtfully. "I've always been of the mind that Ryan should have done it himself. Done right, it could have worked, but he left it to those two mothballs, Nelson and Hanratty, and—well, no matter."

"Ryan was guilty. Why should his case nag at my father for ten years?"

"Ah, Claire, you haven't a grain of Anson's purity, have you? Imagine Anson Swallow the day after I had my talk with him, imagine him walking into the courthouse that next day—and every day thereafter—knowing he was walking on the bones of Sophie Goldstone. He could probably hear her bones crunching under foot with every step. He knew his father had made money off those bones and that he himself had inherited that money. At the time, I must say, I didn't make the connection between the extra money Anson got in the will and the Ryan case. But Anson did. He probably made the connection even as I spoke. It wasn't until I started to watch Anson Swallow die before my eyes that I realized what I'd done that night. I tried every lie I could think of to ease his pain, but Anson would have none of it. Finally, your mother threw me out of the house and told me not to come back. Probably she was right. Probably I only made things worse for him, but I knew—if she didn't—why Anson Swallow could not eat. It was more than cancer. Every time someone turned on the gas to fry so much as an egg, Anson smelled that chamber, saw Patrick Ryan lean forward and inhale."

"Why didn't Ryan bring the Senator and the rest of them down with him?"

"That was the very question Anson asked me when I'd finished my drunken confession that night in the bar. I'll tell you what I told him. For one thing, there's wasn't a shred of evidence—other than Ryan's word—to connect him to the Senator, nor, by this date, to connect the Senator to the long-vanished Sparrow Enterprises. It would have been the mick against the mighty. And besides, to implicate the Senator and others would have given Patrick Ryan a motive for murder. No, I went into that court and swore before Anson Swallow, before God and all the angels, that Patrick Ryan was innocent, that he hadn't any reason whatever to see his dear pitiful friend One-Strap Sophie done to death. The innocent lamb, Patrick Ryan. That was my defense."

"But you defended him, knowing he was guilty."

"I defended Lucky Stone, too, didn't I? The crime wasn't murder, of course, but Anson Swallow wouldn't have made distinctions like that, would he? Well, I haven't a particle of Anson's fiber either. Leave guilt to the priests, that's what I say. The law is nothing but a boxing ring where you spar with precedent and put a good face on presentation. You don't worry about guilt or innocence or goodness. They are so relative as to be meaningless, as far as I can see."

"My father thought the law was a scalpel to cut the evil out of society," said Claire quietly.

"Claire, if I hadn't been so bloody drunk that night in the bar, I'd have remembered that of Anson, but all I could think of was that we were friends again, that I was back in Anson's good graces, despite my relationship with Lucille. We walked out of that bar and the last thing I said to him, I laughed and said Patrick Ryan had done the Senator a favor, because if One-Strap had continued to make trouble, the Senator himself would have had her knocked off. And Anson said, yes, that was probably true. If the Senator had been alive, I swear to you, Claire, Anson Swallow would have left me and gone directly to the police and turned in his own father. But the Senator was dead. Ryan was dead. They were all dead. Anson jousted with phantoms."

"And lost." Claire scouted for the sailboat at the horizon, but it had vanished into the rain clouds, bulging like overstuffed pillows.

"Anyway," Hoolihan concluded sadly, "you can see that none of this had anything to do with Lucille."

"I see." But Claire saw what Hoolihan could not: a young woman rising from her lover's bed one morning and coming home that afternoon in disgrace as her mother ordered Hoolihan from the house, a young woman—at that moment—simply the object of scandal and not yet tethered to the shame Anson endured, not connected to that taint unless Anson cast the money—the lies and money—into the Pacific to free himself and his family from the Senator's lies and money, to extricate himself from even the most tenuous complicity with Sophie Goldstone's death or Patrick Ryan's guilt. Patrick Ryan was guilty, but so was everyone else. Anson should have known throwing money into the tidal scum could not save him—could not save any of them—because the money had not undone them in the first place. What had? One-Strap's whimper from the grave? Ryan's final curse as he inhaled? The Senator's venal gift? Or just the collective guilt we share by virtue of our human conduits and connections, our fallible judgment, our persistent misreading of the past? Anson was desperate. Stalked by death and knowing death would win, and desperate (desperate as Claire Stone, desperate as Lucille Swallow) to make some gesture that would ameliorate the irrevocable. Claire saw, as Hoolihan could not, Anson throw the money into the ocean and at the same time wind his daughter into a web of want and desperation that would impel her twenty-three years later to repeat Lucille Cotton's initial transgression: to send Scott to Honolulu, where he was instructed to regard another human being as his job, to have and to hold like a rag doll stuffed with greenbacks. "My father would have despised us all," she said thickly.

"Probably. Or maybe not. Anson could be merciful, but he was so intolerant of any lapse in himself that he couldn't understand, couldn't abide, that tolerance in others. Good deeds, bad motives. Bad deeds, good motives." Hoolihan shrugged. "I respected him above all men, but what Anson didn't know is that the worst wrongs are always perpetrated in the name of love."

When Claire got back to the house, she bolted through the front door and bounded up the stairs to her room, rummaging through the drawer of her bedside table for Albert Smythe's number. The digital clock glowed 6:07 at her. Three hours' difference in their time zones. The middle of the afternoon in Honolulu, but it might yet, she might yet, there might yet—frantically she punched the number into the phone and alternately prayed and cursed as it rang five times before a thin, elderly voice answered. "Mr. Smythe? This is Claire Stone, Scott's mother. Is he there? I have to talk to him. It's important."

"Is Althea ill?"

"Althea! It's got nothing to do with Althea! Let me talk to Scott."

"No trouble, I hope."

"No, I mean yes, I mean no. Please, just let me talk to Scott."

"Scott isn't here right now, but I've certainly enjoyed having him stay with me, Mrs. Stone. He's such an engaging young man, so bright and full of charm and energy. You must be very proud of him."

"Where is he? When will he be back? Where can I reach him?" Hadn't she asked these very questions into the phone at the Emergency Room all those months ago? Scott was n⁻˙ at Stanford then. Scott would never go to Stanford. The cream-colored degree curdled before her eyes.

"Well, to tell the truth, Mrs. Stone. I don't know when he'll be back and I couldn't really say where you could reach him. He's gone to the Big Island for a few days."

"A few days!"

"Well, they just went for the weekend, but it's Tuesday now and they're not back, so I don't—"

"They? Who? Scott and who else?"

"Well, I hate to be the one to tell you, Mrs. Stone, but he went with a girl."

"Which girl? Who?"

"A girl named Christine."

Claire groaned and slumped from the bed to the floor.

"I know it's a shock, Mrs. Stone, but young people do it all the time these days, just go off together without being married or anything. Not even engaged. Where's the romance, I ask you. I'm not even talking about morals. Where's the romance?"

"Not Christine Eckdorf," Claire said weakly.

"Even a nice girl like that. Even on TV these days, young people live together without—"

Claire pressed the phone into the rug, cutting Albert Smythe off altogether. Too late. No chance now to rectify or alter or undo. In loving her son, Claire had betrayed her father. A jury might have made distinctions of degree, but Anson would have judged Claire's conduct in the same light as Patrick Ryan's: motivated by greed, she had sent Scott on a doomed errand, just as Ryan had sent Nelson and Hanratty to do his bidding. Moreover, Claire's sins lay close and parallel to Lucille's. She had equated love with money. At her instigation, Scott had set out to commit a deliberate act of sexual piracy. And yes, cousins could fall in love, cousins could marry, but it had not happened that way; Claire had used Scott and Christine in the same way that Senator Swallow used Patrick Ryan to forward his own ends. Outside, rain pelted the windows as Claire lay down in remorse, her hands dug into her eyes, weeping for the son she had corrupted and the father she had loved. Anson was dead and one cannot plead one's case with the dead; there is no tribunal before which the living may exonerate themselves before the dead. She understood, fathomed at last why Anson Swallow had allowed himself to drift, bobbing toward death like a rudderless sailboat on a windless afternoon. Claire wept for the past and for the future because, like Sophie Goldstone's carcass, Claire's sin could never quite be buried. Scott would come home with his bride and before Claire's eyes would be the inescapable truth: she had become the thing she hated.

iii

Mrs. Stone dropped *The Great Gatsby* in her lap and rested her head against her husband's shoulder, entwining her hand with his. They both wore thick flower leis, and the odor of white ginger and plumeria encircled them in an aromatic wreath. "You think they'll like me?"

Scott kissed the top of Christine's head. "They'll love you. You are the most wonderful person in the world."

The flight attendant came by and refilled their champagne glasses. French champagne here in the first-class cabin, served deferentially. He handed them menu cards. "Well, if I'm going to meet them all in one day, Scott, you ought to tell me who will be there."

"There's nothing much to tell. My family is weird."

"You're not weird."

"No, but they are."

"How weird?"

"Real weird."

"No, I mean, how are they weird?"

"Well, I guess my brothers aren't too weird. Jason likes computers and video games, and Dan wants to be a pilot or play pro baseball. My grandmother lives with us, too. Now, she's weird. She's senile and she knits and talks to herself all day, but she's gentle."

"You couldn't say that of my grandmother."

"She's weird, too."

They laughed and kissed and sipped their champagne. Christine regarded her gold band proudly. Befitting a bride of three weeks, she wore a white cotton dress with a high Victorian collar and a lace inset, which contrasted with her short sleek hair and shocking pink earrings.

"And let's see. My great-aunt Althea lives with us too. She does all the cooking. She's a great cook, but she's really fat."

"We'll never be fat, Scott."

"Never." He nibbled her ear. "And probably my Uncle Bart will be at the party. He looks a lot younger than he is and everyone likes Uncle Bart, but he's pretty boring. Responsible, reliable people are always boring."

"We'll never be boring, either."

"You won't mind staying with my family just for a few days, will you, honeybun? Just till we find a place of our own. There's lots of new apartments east of the freeway."

Christine yawned happily. "I don't care where we live as long as we're together."

"And I'll find a good job soon, too. I know your father offered me a job in Honolulu, but I'm going to prove I can support my wife without help from her parents."

"I don't have to be supported, silly. Besides, we have to go to college. Remember? We promised my parents." She patted the books in her lap, *The Great Gatsby* and an illustrated history of World War II. Christine was a studious girl who conscientiously got acceptable grades by doing everything required of her and studying very hard. Claire's initial assumptions about Christine were correct: save for the zits and braces, Christine Eckdorf had never known a moment's unhappiness nor, up until three weeks ago, given her parents a moment of pain. Her runaway marriage was the only daring thing she'd ever done: such a delicious gamble and so rightly romantic, she relished the thrills of defiance she should have enjoyed at fourteen, when the stakes were not so high. Married or not, her essential character remained intact and she dutifully promised her parents that she would finish college. She had brought *The Great Gatsby* and the illustrated history of World War II on the plane as tokens of that promise. "I knew Daddy and Mama would love you, Scott, once they got to know you. I knew they'd come around once they saw how happy we are. I knew they'd remember what it's like to be young and in love."

Scott nodded and kissed her left hand, remembering the uncomfortable interview he had endured with Christine's father—after the fact—that is, when they had presented themselves as husband and wife at the Eckdorf home, perched high in the blue hills overlooking Honolulu. Scott had removed his earring for the occasion (and never put it back in). Christine's parents had barely absorbed the shock of the runaway marriage before she explained that Scott Stone came from a very good family and they were practically related already.

Lucy Rose ran upstairs weeping, snuffling over what Lucille would say. Randolph insisted on a man-to-man. He led Scott outside to the deck and closed the sliding glass door behind him. The high deck floated like a proud wooden ship on a sea of shower trees below and offered a sterling view of Diamond Head, and it was on this great crater that Scott kept his eyes while Randolph Eckdorf accused him of marrying Christine for her money. Scott swore it wasn't so—and maybe it wasn't. Scott Stone was accustomed to the worship of women, but all the girls in his past seemed hard and sharp and jaded compared to the tender adoration Christine Eckdorf gave him. He had, in fact, fallen in love with her, with the picture of himself he saw reflected in her blue eyes. He told Randolph, however, that he'd fallen in love with her picture. Randolph thought this less romantic than Christine had.

But in the end the Eckdorfs came around. Their daughter's happiness could not be doubted and Scott waxed on them every bit of his artful and accomplished charm and (since Lucille was not there to mention the nasty word *bankruptcy*) the two couples got on splendidly. Lucy Rose and Randolph bankrolled a week-long honeymoon on Maui, this first-class trip to the mainland and gave them a fat check to set up housekeeping, which Scott refused. Out of principle.

Christine put her books on the floor when the flight attendant brought them trays covered in starched white cloths and framed in tiny orchids. Next came glasses of iced shrimp cocktail. "Do you think your parents will be angry with us?" she asked.

"Not at all, I mean, well, my father's pretty wrapped up in his religion. You better be prepared for him, Christine. He'll try to convert you to his church, which isn't even a church at all. They meet in the YMCA gym, but my father's very active in it."

"The gym?"

"No, the church. He's always having meetings at our house with the minister and Emma Duff. I'll bet you anything Emma and her sister Evangeline are there when we arrive. My dad says they're part of our family in Christ. He's weird, all right."

"What else does he do? What's his job?"

Scott chewed thoughtfully. "He's in public service."

"What's your mother like?"

"She's short. I mean, she's one of those little women, but she's not skinny. She's not fat, either. She has light brown hair and dark brown eyes. She can really play the piano. She gives lessons."

Christine pulled a shrimp stem from her lips. "But what's she like? You haven't told me that."

Scott frowned. He knew Claire as he knew everyone else: only in relation to himself. His mother was his staunchest ally, the first of a long line of women to admire, adore and flatter him, but of the intrinsic Claire, Scott knew nothing and had never bothered to flex so much as a morsel of imagination in guessing. He stared at Christine's books on the floor between their feet. "My mother," he said in a stroke of inspiration, "is a combination of Daisy Buchanan and Benitor Mussolino."

At that moment, in a rather Il Duce fashion, Claire was directing her younger sons as they hung a canopy of pink and white crêpe paper over the living room, using the chandelier as a hub. Lucky was on his way to the airport to pick up the newlyweds, and she wanted everything perfect for the family party honoring their arrival. "Yes, that's right. No, don't skimp on it, Jason, there's plenty. Tack it there and toss the roll to Dan." The phone rang and she dug through a pile of presents on the table to find it. She toyed with the huge white ribbon on the most massive present (a microwave oven) as she spoke. "No, I can't spare anyone to come get it. I want that wedding cake delivered as soon as possible."

"There's someone at the back door, Mom," said Jason from his perch on the ladder.

Stuffing her checklist into her jeans and the pencil behind her ear, Claire went to the back door to find Emma and Evangeline sporting decidedly unusual finery: matronly dresses of blue and gray gaberdine. Their clothes were stiff and reeked faintly of mothballs and their feet were already swollen, stuffed as they were into something other than tennis shoes. "We thought you could use some help, so we came early," offered Emma cheerfully.

"Well, actually, I could. Althea's taken care of most of the food and she's in the dining room laying out the buffet, but if you really wanted to help me, Emma, you could go out on the front porch and have a word with Mama. All this activity's unraveled her. You know how rigid she is. She isn't even quite sure who got married. She thinks Jill has finally married whatshisname."

"Don't worry about a thing, Claire. I'll tell Meg how God gave us marriage so's we could fulfill our mortal duties. Oh, and this one's so romantic!" Emma pressed her bony hands to the rhinestone buttons on her bosom. "Just think of Scott going all the way to Honolulu to find the girl of his dreams."

Claire flinched and asked Evangeline to slice oranges for the punchbowl. Althea bustled in with an empty tray. " see you two have decided to change your shirts for once," she said tartly.

"I think both Emma and Evangeline look very pretty," said Claire, quick to their defense. Claire had been unspeakably pleasant to everyone these last three weeks: the goodness of the guilty. Claire was like a child who knows that terrible, just punishment awaits her and she trod softly on everyone's feelings, as if to mollify, placate, soften that certain fate, because when the phone call came, only Dan and Jason evinced surprise that their brother had married. Meg did indeed believe that Jill had finally married whatshisname and mumbled things like: about time. Althea knotted a hanky in her fist, helplessly maundering that she never thought, she never dreamed, she couldn't understand, but Lucky cut all that short by reminding her of her own complicity. And then he turned to Claire, who had sunk into the couch, keeping her eyes on her own wedding ring, which she twisted around her finger. Lucky inquired how Claire intended to tell Bart, and for this Claire had no answer. She still had no answer when, twenty minutes later, the phone rang. It was Bart. Claire did not have to tell him. Lucky did it. And from that day to this, Barton Swallow had neither called nor contacted the family on Jerusalem Road. Claire was just as glad. Her remorse was so overwhelming that she dare not give it words, and no one but Bart would have demanded them from her.

Althea loaded a tray with cocktail napkins emblazoned with silver bells and inscribed CHRISTINE AND SCOTT. She poured pink and white butter mints into leaf-shaped silver dishes. "Oh, there's never been a party in this house before, you know, Claire. The Senator did all the entertaining in town. This was Mother's house." She rubbed a bit of tarnish off the dish. "It's so good to be using Mother's things again."

"It's going to be some shindig," remarked Evangeline, glancing at the stemware and silver and china, the champagne cooling in the sink, the fondue warming on the stove, the colorful pinwheels of cheese and olives. "I guess it would be tacky to ask how you're paying for it."

"It would be tacky," Claire agreed.

Althea's fat face puckered. "I never thought about that. How are you paying for it, Claire?"

"I sold the dining room furniture," she replied flatly. "I was going to tell you when they come to pick it up tomorrow."

The leaf dish clattered to the floor. "But—but—the whole set? The table and buffet and mirror and china cabinet and—"

"Everything."

"But that set's a hundred years old. You had no right to! It was Mother's! It's a priceless antique."

"An antique, yes, but hardly priceless. I got a nice sum for it."

"But—how could you! It wasn't yours to sell!"

Claire bore down on her aunt. "I don't care if I had to sell every sainted stick of your sainted mother's furniture to pay for this party. I'd do it without a second thought. Christine is going to feel wanted here and she's not going to know that we have to count every damn nickel and scrap of bread. We're not going to scrimp today. Whatever happens, Christine is going to remember that we welcomed her into this family, so close up your jaw, Althea. I hated that dining room set anyway. I'm going to move the piano into the dining room so I can give lessons in there without having to worry about the Second Coming interrupting me."

"Amen to that," said Evangeline, concentrically decapitating oranges.

Althea left in a huff, and Claire began to count the champagne glasses. She heard a car pull up. "That'll be the cake delivery," she said, wiping her hands on a dishtowel. She went out the back door and froze to the step. It was not the cake. It was Bart.

Damn Lucky anyway. It was all his fault. Lucky was the one who insisted they send an invitation to Bart and to Lucille as well, for that matter, though Claire didn't worry for a minute that she'd show up. But Bart. Oh, Bart. Claire stood in the fragile sunlight of the November afternoon and awaited Bart's words as if they were the headsman's ax.

"I called Hoolihan. I know everything."

"Everything?" she asked in a tiny twisted voice.

"I heard all about your beggary at that fly-specked Mexican restaurant from Hoolihan. Did you get the idea from Lucille, Claire? Did you think it was okay, that if Lucille could marry for money, so could Scott? How could you do it? And Hoolihan and I both know you did it. We both know that Scott isn't smart enough to think of something like this by himself. He's vile enough, but not that smart. It was your idea to sink Scott's fangs into Christine's throat."

"Scott doesn't have fangs," she replied bravely.

Bart took her arm and pulled her roughly from the porch, opened the back door and propelled her into the kitchen, sat her down at the table, where he faced her. "I want you to tell me how in God's name you could be so depraved."

Claire nodded toward Evangeline.

"I don't give a shit who hears—call in the Fellowship, the butcher, the baker—you might as well tell everyone how you could stoop to something so low and base and cowardly and depraved."

"It's not murder," she said weakly, involuntarily recalling Patrick Ryan.

"It might as well be. Think of what you've done to that girl's life."

Claire knotted her fingers, bent her head and rested her lips against them. Candor was not her forte. "He was all I had to love, Bart. Scott was all I had to love." She shook her head persistently while Bart argued that she had a husband, that she had two other sons. "You don't understand what's happened to us in the six months since Lucky tried to kill himself. You can't know what it's been like for me, living here and worrying all the time. All the time, Bart, not a day goes by without—and no one to talk to, no one who cared about money or the future, especially Scott's future." She continued quickly before Bart could do anything but sneer over Scott's name. "I was wrong, I admit it, but I didn't—it wasn't—it's not depravity, Bart."

"It is."

"But I didn't do it for that." Claire raised her eyes to her brother's bearded face. "I did it for love."

"Do you know how rotten that sounds? You are rotten to the core."

"Please don't, Bart. Please. I do feel bad. I do feel awful, but I'm sure that Scott loves Christine. I'm sure. He wouldn't have married her unless he loved her. I know they're in love. Albert Smythe told me so when I called, and I did call, Bart. I did. I realized how terrible and foolish and what an awful idea it was, but it was too late. Albert Smythe told me they were already in love and I was too late." Claire mopped her eyes with a dishtowel.

"It was an act of bitchery," he said unequivocally. "Bitchery and malice and even Hoolihan—who has a firsthand acquaintance with the queen of bitchery and malice—even Hoolihan is shocked. Even Hoolihan cannot believe that you would do this."

"I didn't do it," she protested. "I just, I only—I know I was wrong, Bart, and I'm going to make it all up to Christine. I am. I'm going to love her like the daughter I never had."

"Oh, Christ. I think I'll puke." He cinched his lips against that possibility and for the first time looked around the kitchen, the gleaming preparation, the colors and textures, the aroma of food jostling with that of flowers, the champagne and canapés lined up like extras awaiting their cue. "Who did you rob to pay for all this? Did you beg Lucille for the money for this, too?"

Claire hung her head.

"She sold the dining room furniture," Evangeline volunteered.

"Oh shut up. Oh, Bart, I'm sure they're in love and I'm sure they're going to be very happy."

"Christine might be in love, but Scott Stone has never loved anyone or anything but himself. This is the most ill-fated union since the dish ran away with the spoon, Claire. Your son is a worthless piece of shit.

He's shallow. He's vain. He's thoughtless and stupid and now, thanks to you, he's downright wicked. He spent his time at Stanford drinking and smoking dope and snorting cocaine with other rich fraternity boys and fucking every girl he could get his hands on—whether they wanted it or not. You didn't have to deal with that girl's father. I did."

"What girl?"

"A girl who went out with your son and was so hysterical afterward that she had to be withdrawn from school for a month and sent home."

"I don't believe it."

"I still have her father's number. Would you like to talk to him?"

Claire brushed her hair from her face. "No."

"Scott is weak and predatory and that's the worst combination there is. The weak always prey upon the strong and I hope for her sake Christine has some strength. She'll need it just to live with that worthless Scott. He'll suck her dry and not just of money. That girl is innocent, but the rest of you just stink with guilt and complicity, and that includes Lucky and Althea as well."

"Lucky didn't do anything."

"That's just it. He closed his eyes and ears and acquiesced to all this and I don't give a shit how holy he is. And Althea! Bitch, bitch, bitch for thirty years, thirty years of blaming Lucille. This was probably Althea's idea in the first place, wasn't it?"

"Sort of," said Claire, happy to share the blame.

"None of it excuses your conduct. I came early today so I'd have the opportunity to tell you that you and I are finished. I'm ashamed to be your brother. I wish I could divorce you. I won't stay away from Mama, just because she's living with you, but I wash my hands of Claire Swallow Stone. God! I never thought I'd say that." Bart's voice trembled, not with anger but with pain. "All my life I have always admired and loved you, but all that's finished. Mama doesn't have to know how I feel, but I want you to make no mistake." His chair screeched back on the floor. "If Father were alive, he'd spit on you." Bart slammed the door on his way out.

Claire buried her head in her arms and wept. Evangeline scooted a chair close by and put her arms around Claire's shoulders, wrapping her in the scent of orange and mothballs and told her not to cry, that Scott and Christine loved each other, that love would triumph and their marriage would be happy. But Claire was still sobbing when the delivery boy knocked at the back door, dwarfed and tottering under the three-tiered wedding cake in his arms.

iv

Christine was prettier than any of her pictures. She was tall and carried herself well (the ballet lessons) and had a lovely smile (the orthodontist's work). She had inherited Lucille's native grace and breathtakingly blue eyes, although she retained many of Lucy Rose's prim gestures. She had the air of a woman who has only just discovered she is beautiful. The family (freshly showered, still smoothing and tugging at their party finery) tumbled over one another on the back porch for a glimpse of the bride, who held Scott's hand and greeted them shyly.

Emma ripped open a bag of rice and filled their cupped hands. "Hooray for Scott and Christine!" she cried. Cascaded with falling rice, the young couple ran into the kitchen and through it, down the long hall and the front entry and into the living room.

Under the swaying canopy of crêpe paper, Lucky opened the champagne and filled the glasses while everyone took turns kissing the bride. Christine smiled at them all. "When Scott told me there would probably be a little family party in San Angelo, I never guessed, I mean, I couldn't have imagined, I mean—you're all so kind. I can't tell you how happy I am to be here and to be part of your family."

"Kiss the bride!" cried Emma.

Scott kissed her, long and sweet, and Lucky handed the champagne around and then raised his glass high. "The Bible says there was a marriage in Cana where Jesus turned water into wine and it was judged a miracle," he began solemnly. "Today we have another marriage and another miracle: I, a man who had no daughters, now have a daughter in Christine. And before this gathering and before God, who is amongst us always, we welcome you, Christine. You may rely on us. The Stones are your family and we will never leave you."

"Is that like leaving no stone unturned," chuckled Emma, "or not leaving one stone upon another?"

"Even so," said Lucky gravely. "For the Bible says, wherefore laying aside all malice and all guile and hypocrisies and envies, and all evil speakings, that we may be as lively stones and build up a spiritual house and so, be a family united. I say unto you, Scott and Christine, you are a chosen generation and we rejoice for and with you."

The bride and groom kissed again. Claire raised her glass with the rest of them, and tiny embers of hope flickered into life: Evangeline

276

was right—love had triumphed. Scott had laid aside all malice and guile and envies; he loved Christine and she loved him. They were in love and they would live happily ever after.

Certainly, they were happy for the moment. The newlyweds, hands still entwined, talked with everyone individually and at once, Bart asking politely after Lucy Rose and Randolph, Scott describing for his brothers the size of the Hawaiian surf, while Althea made discreet inquiries after Albert Smythe. Lucky asked if there was a Fellowship of the New Millenium in Honolulu, and Emma introduced Jesus' name as if commenting on an overachieving nephew. Then Christine declared she'd forgotten all about the presents they'd brought and sent Scott and Dan out to the car, and they returned with two suitcases filled with leis, plumeria and red and white antherium, whose tropical moistness belied the November evening gathering at the windows and the smell of woodsmoke from the crackling fire.

They stacked the wicked antherium on the upright piano and put the leis around their necks while Scott and Christine sat on the floor and opened their presents till the living room was awash in wrapping paper and silver ribbon and oohs and aahs and of course the newlyweds had to kiss after every present and Christine had to show her gold band all around. Even Meg, who sat toying with a single antherium, flapping at its serpent tongue, finally seemed to grasp that Jill had not married whatshisname, that Scott had married Lucy Rose's daughter, and she began to natter on about Lucy Rose's grand wedding and how Claire had caught the bouquet.

Meg's ruminations were cut short by Christine's cry of surprise as she opened the microwave oven. Christine jumped up, then sat down and kissed Scott and then jumped up again and planted a kiss on Lucky's cheek and one on Claire's. "Oh, thank you, Claire—I can call you Claire, can't I? Thank you for everything. Everyone! I can't tell you how happy I am. I've never been so happy. Scott and I are so happy and we'll never forget this wonderful day."

"Praise be!" shouted Emma.

"Isn't that the doorbell?" said Dan. "The front, no less." He got to his feet. "Who can it be?"

"Probably the antique collector," laughed Althea.

But Dan returned to the living room with Hoolihan behind him, and behind Hoolihan stood Lucille, dripping gems from every claw, her thin shoulders hunched under the weight of the jewels around her neck. She leaned on an aluminium cane and wore a pantsuit of yellow and orange that garishly lit her face. Hoolihan's slate-colored sweater underscored his gray hair and the hard gleam in his gray eyes. He sought Claire's face, but she sank to the floor and stared resolutely at her hands.

"Grandma!" Christine flew and embraced Lucille. "Oh, Grandma, you came! I'm so glad! Mama said you'd never speak to me again, but I just knew she was wrong. I knew you'd come."

"I was invited, wasn't I?" Lucille croaked. "Isn't this a family occasion? Aren't I part of the family?" She endured Christine's kiss and then pushed her aside, crossing the room, scattering ribbon and paper with her cane. Hoolihan remained at her elbow as if his physical intervention might be required. "Isn't my name Swallow? One of the dirty, money-grabbing Swallows?"

"Now, Grandma—all that's in the past."

"That's what you think, little Miss Christine Dumbshit Eckdorf Stone."

"Mama told me, Grandma. Scott, too. Scott was honest with me. He told me there was some old bad blood between our families, but this is our chance to make peace, to be friends and let the past be forgotten. Just like Romeo and Juliet."

"Romeo and Juliet died." Lucille advanced toward Althea. "Still fat, aren't you, Althea? Some things never change. And Bart—" She poked her cane at him. "Look, Hoolihan, here's the director of South American trade. I'd fire you in a minute, you know that don't you, Bart? But Hoolihan tells me the board of directors would never stand for it. I should have sent you spinning twenty years ago."

"I'm not implicated in this, Lucille. I knew nothing of it."

"That's true." Hoolihan spoke for the first time.

Lucille grunted. "And here's Meg. Oh yes, I'd know you still, Meg. You know me?" she wobbled closer and thrust her face forward. "It's me, Lucille Swallow."

Meg looked her up and down as if inspecting bad ham. "Do you take me for a fool? Lucille Swallow is a beautiful woman. You have hairs on your chin."

The hairs on Lucille's chin bristled. "Time makes fools of us all. At least I still have my brains, Meg. I hear yours have turned to mulch. I may have lost my looks, but I still have my brains. And my money." She turned to the rest of them. "What little there is of it is still mine." She walked past Emma and Evangeline as if they were doorstops and regarded the awestruck Dan and Jason like fungus. She paused briefly at Lucky to announce that he was a drunk and a crook and too bad he

278

didn't aim right and kill himself. Lucky crumbled under the assault.

Claire longed to go to Lucky, hold and protect him; she commanded her feet to move, but they ignored her. She remained on the floor amongst the wedding paper, her skirt encircling her like an old-fashioned nosegay.

"And then there's Claire. Nasty little Claire. The Senator always said you were willful, spoiled, arrogant, mouthy and a troublemaker. Well, you've really made trouble this time and you'll live to reap it, Claire Swallow. You and that fat virgin," she spat, "cooked up this scheme didn't you? You said to yourselves, Let's take it away from her, let's take from Lucille the one thing she loves in this world."

"I thought you said you still had your money," said Claire with feigned equanimity. "Money's the only thing you care for."

"You waited until I was old and poor," Lucille went on, counter-pointing her clanking jewels. "You thought you'd get me, but you had me all wrong, Althea, all of you. I never hated you. Never. Not until Lucy Rose called me and told me the worst thing I could imagine had happened. I cried—Christine's not dead, is she? And Lucy Rose said, 'no, Mother, no, she's not dead, she's married Scott Stone.' And then I said, 'Not that hunk of meat who works in the doughnut shop?' And Lucy Rose said, 'Right, Mother, that's the one.' And then I told Lucy Rose I'd call her right back after I came down here to San Angelo and murdered you all in your beds, but Hoolihan talked me out of it." She waved her jeweled hand at phantom flies. "But he couldn't talk me out of coming here today."

"Grandma, let me explain—"

But Lucille pushed her, and Christine stumbled; Scott scurried to her aid, caught her in his arms and she buried her face against his shoulder. "No, Christine, you let me explain. You've been used by this family and for one purpose. Mr. Big Dick there married you for one reason. To get his hands on your money—my money. And I came here for one reason—to take you away. You're coming with me, and I'm going to get this marriage annulled and all this foolishness ended."

"Grandma, Scott is my husband and I love him and you're wrong, Grandma. We don't want your money—"

"Not we, sugarplum. He. He wants it bad. And he—" Lucille waggled a finger at Lucky, "—he wants it worse."

"That's a lie," said Lucky.

"And she—" she pointed to Claire, "—she wants it worse than anyone."

"No, Grandma, no. I married Scott for love."

"But he married you for money. Of course he did. Did he tell you his father was bankrupt?"

"What?" Christine murmured.

Bart intervened physically between Christine and her grandmother. "Don't be so hard on her, Lucille. Christine couldn't know any of that, and she shouldn't have to account for it. Christine is not the one who deserves your wrath."

Lucille positively shook with outrage. "I know who deserves my wrath! Don't you tell me about wrath! It was revenge, wasn't it? You—all of you—wanted revenge for thirty years and this was how—"

"It had nothing to do with revenge," Bart interjected. He cast his sister a pitying glance. "It had to do with love."

"And money," Lucille bit back. "Money!" Lucille brushed Bart aside and confronted Christine directly. "I guess Mr. Big Dick there neglected to mention to you anything about money, eh, Christine? I guess he didn't say that his old man was a drunk and a gambler and if it hadn't been for Hoolihan, Lucky Stone would be behind bars with a number on his back. I guess Big Dick didn't tell you that his old man tried to kill himself when the IRS caught up to him."

Hoolihan glanced at Lucky, who had slumped forward as though the stitches in his gut had ripped, his face a tangle of pain and regret and shame. Hoolihan took Lucille's arm as if to draw her back.

Lucille shook him off. "Answer me, Christine. Am I right?"

"No. Yes. No."

"Why do you think they're living in this rotting hulk of a house? This family hasn't got a pot to pee in. They're stone broke, if you'll pardon the pun. Ask them. *Ask them, Christine*."

"No."

"Very well, then. Ask your husband there if he and his mother didn't come begging for money two months ago."

"We didn't beg," Scott said staunchly.

"Ha! I showed him your picture, Christine, and—"

Christine's face lit. "I know that, Grandma. Scott told me how he and his mother went out for lunch with you and he fell in love with my picture."

"Lunch!" she shrieked. "Lunch! They came to beg and I refused and you, my little peach, are what they extracted for my refusal. They expect you to send Mr. Big Dick to Stanford on *my money*!"

Scott held Christine tightly. "I never wanted to go back to Stanford, honey. I never wanted anything till I met you. I turned down that

280

money your father offered us. You know I did. I love you. Only you."

"Bullshit. Get your things, Christine. We're leaving."

"I am not leaving Scott. He is my husband and I love him."

"And he loves your money. Ask him. See if he can deny a straight-forward question."

Christine's face drained, leaving a glimpse of what she would look like if life were unkind to her. She glanced at the stricken expressions of Claire, Althea, Lucky, Bart and even Evangeline, the shock and disbelief buttered over the faces of Dan and Jason, Meg and Emma. Scott looked into the failing fire. "Is it true, Scott?"

"No! Not a word of truth. No. No. No."

"Liar." Lucille's voice curdled with loathing. "Liar."

"It's true that I drank and gambled," Lucky Stone said dryly; he spoke clearly, but to the floor. "The Lord hath punished me with worldly disaster and my family has suffered for my sins. I am like Job. It's true that I am bankrupt. It's true that I tried to kill myself." Lucky knotted his hands and gulped back tears. "But the Lord would not let me die. The Lord hath yet work for me and I will do His bidding." His voice cracked, and he regarded his daughter-in-law with unendurable anguish. "It's true that Hoolihan saved me from prison, but if it had been God's will, I would have gone to prison singing His praises. It would have been just. I was guilty. I'm sorry for the pain I have brought to my family and indirectly, Christine, to—" Lucky looked up and bit his lip "—you. I repent of my sins, but I can't atone for Claire's or Scott's and if God—"

"Works in mysterious ways!" shouted Emma Duff, leaping to her feet and shielding Lucky from Lucille, her arms outflung like the circling beacons of a lighthouse. "And what God hath joined together, let no man put asunder. And no woman either! God's brought them two young people together as part of His Great Plan and don't you think you can just bust in here and undo it! You heard Lucky. From a drunk and a gambler God hath fashioned a good Christian. And whatever you're talking about here, well, all I know is love hath risen from worse ashes than these! You miserable, heathen old woman, look at this boy! He loves this girl! Before you came, we had joy in a house that's been desolate. We had the water turned to wine and we was celebrating the miracle of marriage and if you want to stay and drink to this young couple's health, then stay, but if you come here to pick on Lucky Stone, well, you can just get out!"

"Who is this nut, Christine?"

"Come on, Lucille." Hoolihan suddenly looked very old, his crispness and certainty of purpose wafting from him like smoke from a newly snuffed candle. "It's not up to us anymore."

Lucille planted both her hands on her cane. "Are you coming, Christine?"

Christine squared her shoulders, evoking in those old enough to remember a wisp of her grandmother's headstrong aplomb. "I am a married woman now, Grandma, and I'm going to stay with my husband. I love him and I'm certainly not going to desert him over things that have happened in the past and don't matter to us. I love him." Her voice accelerated with conviction. "And he loves me and we don't care about the past. Oh, Grandma, can't you see? I'm happier than I've ever been, happier than I ever dreamed of being. There's a whole new world of love I never knew existed and I'm just discovering that world. I can't turn back on that! I'm in love! Can't you," she implored, "can't you remember what it's like? Don't you know what it means to be in love?"

Lucille regarded Christine as if she'd spouted Swahili. Lucille had lived with Tom Quinn, with Norris Cotton, with Fremont Ebeneezer Swallow because she was desperate; she had been to bed with more men than she could or cared to count, but she had not loved any of them except perhaps Declan Hoolihan, but Hoolihan had entered her life too late. By then she was too old, by then she knew that the best love can truly offer is loyalty and a friendly set of buttocks in bed at night. Lucille had no idea what it meant to be in love. She had lived her whole life and missed that one untarnished experience: love—alloyed only with dreams and desire—love that, if you are very fortunate, exists for a single finite moment unimpeded by what came before or what comes after.

V

"It's quite a mess," said Lucky. He and Claire sat alone in the kitchen, amidst the carnage of the party, dishes and glasses, scraps of finery, the uneaten food encased in shining foil. Claire was drinking champagne joylessly. The guests had left and the rest of the family had gone upstairs to bed, Meg and Althea and the boys each to their rooms.

Christine and Scott, protesting, took Lucky and Claire's bed at Claire's insistence. Claire finished off one glass and poured another. "This isn't the end of the mess, either," Lucky added.

"No, there's still stuff all over the dining room and the living room and that damned rice and crêpe paper."

"I wasn't referring to that." He put the lid on a fondue pot and put it in the fridge. "I blame myself in a way. I should have put my foot down."

"You should have looked up from your prayers. God's will and God's time." Claire took another drink and stifled a burp. "You've floated like a piece of plankton on God's will."

"What you did was wrong."

"Oh, can it. Save it for Sunday and the YMCA." She opened yet another bottle with a resounding pop and sloshed more champagne into her glass.

"Scott will never go to Stanford. You know that. It wasn't the money at all."

"No, it wasn't the money. It wasn't the money that undid us in the first place. It was something else. Leave me alone, Lucky. Go to bed. I'll clean up."

"You can't clean up the mess you've made, Claire. It's beyond that."

"You're the one who insisted on inviting Lucille, aren't you?"

"It would have happened anyway, sooner or later."

"Yes. You're right. Just leave me alone, will you?"

"I wouldn't blame Christine if she did leave Scott after what happened here today. I don't think she will, though. She's a fine young woman. Better than Scott deserves."

"You're right! You're right! What do you want me to say? Just go away."

"I guess I'll go to bed."

"Go."

"There's a bed up in that turret room, isn't there?"

"There is, but it's covered with twenty years' worth of junk. No one ever goes up there. It's nothing but a storeroom."

"Well, I guess we can sweep the junk aside and sleep there till Scott and Christine find an apartment."

Claire poured herself another drink. "We? Well, I'm flattered— Lucky Stone thinks I'm fit to sleep with."

"You're getting very drunk."

"Right again. You're just a font of wisdom tonight, aren't you,

Lucky? Well, you can take your font and sleep with it elsewhere. It's clear to me that after what's happened here today, you'll never forgive me."

"It's not up to me to forgive you. First you must repent and—"

"Not another word about God! You hear me? Just leave me alone with my withered withins, isn't that what you said—I'm still beautiful without, but not within?"

"There's an extra bed in Dan's room. I guess I could sleep there tonight."

"You can sleep there until your spirit sees fit to commune with my body, Lucky. You can just sleep there until you're ready to make love to me again. Until then, you can sleep wherever you damn please. I always forgave you, didn't I?" she cried. "Not once, not once in all our years together, when you were in trouble, not once when you gambled and drank our money away, did I turn away from you."

"I never said you were disloyal, Claire. But sending Scott to Honolulu—that was unclean."

"Well, you just remember that your unclean wife never once turned away from you, never left you to suffer alone. And you can sleep with that, Lucky Stone!"

"You're drunk."

"I was always there when you needed me. I never—"

"Good night, Claire. I'll see you in the morning."

"Good night. And good riddance." She got up and shut the door after him. "At least he didn't rag on about repentance," she said to her glass as she refilled it. "At least he spared me that."

She finished off the champagne and then went into the dining room with a tray and began picking up the last of the dirtied dishes. From the center of the table she had sold, the uncut wedding cake accused her; it would rot before they could eat it, before anyone had the heart to eat it. She left it where it stood, turned out the light with her elbow and took her tray into the living room to hunt for stray glasses. The crêpe paper canopy sagged, forlorn and bedraggled. She wished she'd never thought of it. She made sure the fire was out and picked up those few glasses lurking beneath the browning leis, paper and tangled ribbon. She stuck the antherium in empty champagne bottles. The wedding presents were stacked haphazardly, and around them she found a few skulking ashtrays, which she dumped into the fireplace. She turned out the living room light, took up her tray and lurched down the long uncarpeted hall toward the glowing kitchen. Silence shrouded her;

November damp penetrated the flaking mortar, and the smell of the sea stalked the old house.

Claire shivered and promised herself that she would drink another bottle of champagne, two if need be. She needed to be wholly and completely drunk. Once drunk, she would not be tempted to beg God's forgiveness or to admit that she would settle for Lucky's forgiveness. For Bart's. Even for Hoolihan's. She would be absolutely and utterly drunk before she mounted the stairs to pull the accumulation of twenty years off the bed and sleep alone in that turret room. Claire stumbled down the long dark hall, cursing the rice that crunched beneath her feet, cursing its crackle, its cackling whisper. *Another wedding. Another bride. Another groom. Another union. A long time ago.*

CHAPTER FOUR

March 1964

Lucy Rose Cotton sat flossing her teeth, her feet tucked up under her bathrobe. In between swipes with the floss she took a drink of brandy from a glass streaked with toothpaste, and every sip she leaned over and put the glass behind the dust ruffle ringing the canopied bed in this, her former room at the Swallow mansion. From the terraces below her window came the sounds of the sixteen-piece orchestra tuning up. "She'll know you took it," Lucy Rose said to her brother. "She'll count up all the bottles and figure one was missing. You know how carefully Mother accounts for everything, and she'll know you took it."

"Nothing I did would surprise her anyway." Jon stared at his own reflection in the oval mirror on the vanity. He scarcely knew the man who wore suspenders, a cummerbund, pants with a satin stripe and a stiff boiled shirt with a pleated front. The man's hair and beard were neatly trimmed. Jon held the brandy bottle by the neck and took a long swig.

"Don't let Mother see you drink like that."

"Oh, you worry too much about Mother."

"How'll I get the brandy off my breath, Jon? I don't want Randolph to think I had to get drunk to get married."

"Haven't you ever had a drink before?"

"Of course. It's just that well, champagne, something light with dinner, maybe. Mother never lets me drink brandy. She says it doesn't look good on a young girl."

"You're supposed to drink it, not wear it. Gargle some Chanel Number Five." Jon pointed to the myriad bottles gleaming on the vanity.

"Mother doesn't let me wear Chanel Number Five. She says it's too sophisticated for a young girl. White Shoulders, that's what I wear."

"Then gargle with some of that. Christ, Lucy Rose, you should be able to do whatever you want. It's your wedding."

"No." Lucy Rose dragged the floss through her teeth. "It's my wedding day, but this is definitely Mother's wedding."

"Then why go through with it?"

"I love Randolph. I do."

"You like him. He's unobjectionable, that's all you can say about him."

"I can say more than that. He's very sweet and kind and nice."

"If you haven't been to bed with a man, you don't know what he is. You have to get into each other's skins, literally, and not just once but a hundred times, day after day, you have to eat and sleep and be bored and angry and crazy together before you can know a person well. And even then—"

"You can't *live* with someone just so you'll know them well enough to get married."

"You can never know someone that well."

"But people have to get married."

"That's a lot of bourgeois bullshit."

"Please, Jon, don't start on all that. You'll confuse me." Her voice trembled.

"All right. It's your wedding day and you deserve to be happy. Here, have some more brandy." He crossed the room and took her glass out from under the dust ruffle, filled it halfway and handed it to her.

"I can't. I shouldn't."

"In another couple of hours you're going to be a married woman and you won't have to worry about what Mother thinks is right for a young girl. You won't be a young girl."

"I'll still be me, won't I?"

"Don't ask me. I'm not the one getting married. Don't cry, Lucy Rose. I'm sorry. I didn't mean to upset you." He pulled a pillowslip off and handed it to her. "Don't you keep any Kleenex in this. . ." He gazed at the white curtains, white vanity and dresser, the turquoise carpeting and complementary Picasso blue-period prints on the wall. Except for the wedding dress, frothing off a bald and eyeless mannequin, this was an exact replica of a young girl's room Lucille had once seen in *House & Garden*. Jon patted his sister's shoulder. "You're

287

going to be very happy. I like Randolph. Really. When I talked with him at the rehearsal dinner last night, I thought he was very—well, what does it matter what anyone thinks as long as you love him?"

"I do love him, Jon. I want to get married. Oh, I know that you think marriage is silly and stupid and I know you didn't even want to come up for my wedding."

"That's not true. I never received the invitation you sent."

"Mother said you wouldn't come at all. I told her, Jon is my only brother and he'll come and give me away on my wedding day, but Mother said you'd never leave Chagrin and Melinda."

"That's a lie."

"And then, when you didn't even answer the invitation I sent—" Her voice quavered and broke.

"I told you, I never got it."

"—that's when I had to beg Hoolihan, Please go find my brother and tell him how important it is that he come and give me away. Please bring Jon back up here for my wedding." Lucy Rose began to sob in earnest, "If you didn't come, Hoolihan would have been the one to give me away and I like Hoolihan a lot, you're wrong about Hoolihan, Jon, he's really a very good man, but I would have been so mortified to have him give me away when everyone knows he and Mother, that they are, that he is—"

"Fucking her brains out, day and night."

"Oh stop! I can't bear to hear that word! It's so aww-ful!"

"Call it whatever you want, then. I'm sorry. I don't seem to be able to say anything right. Oh, Lucy Rose, I want you to be happy and I think Randolph Eckdorf is a very lucky man."

Lucy Rose took another drink and put the glass back under the bed. She wiped her mouth with the back of her manicured hand. "Jon, there's something I have to ask you. I don't want to embarrass you, but you're the only one I can ask. I mean, when we got to this sort of thing in biology class at Miss Proctor's, the teacher just sort of, well anyway, last week I found a book in the Senator's library, but I couldn't understand the charts and I would have asked the doctor, but Mother was with me and I couldn't say anything in front of her."

"I'm not the one to ask."

"Why not?"

"I don't know if it hurts or not."

Lucy Rose flushed coral, but because her mother didn't think dignity becoming on a young girl, she hadn't any to rely on, though she mustered such composure as she could, got off the bed and walked to the window. Below, she could hear the orchestra, although she could not see them for the white marquees drooping in the dampness. Gardeners pulled up the last of the clashing California poppies, and between the terraces, workers strung ropes of tiny fragrant flowers the Eckdorfs had flown over from Honolulu. Fog wreathed the dappled Japanese plum trees and their pink blossoms floated earthward in a gentle wind. "That wasn't my question," she said at last. "It's too late for that question. Randolph and I, well, not a hundred times like you say, but a few times, quite a few after we got engaged, we—don't use that awful word—you promised you wouldn't."

"I didn't promise, but I won't. What are you worried about? I'm happy for you. At least you know what you're getting."

"Well, yes, and Randolph is—and I will talk with him of course, but I think, I mean, before that, I ought to know, or have some idea—"

"Know what, for Christ's sake."

"When is it safe, Jon?"

"What?"

"When is *it* safe?" She toyed with her walnut-sized diamond engagement ring. "I went to the doctor and he gave me these pills and told me to start on them after my next, when my next—but it hasn't—"

"When was it due?" He asked as if this were an overdue library book.

"Last month."

Jon took another swig from the brandy bottle. He paused before swallowing. "Any other symptoms?"

"The book in the Senator's library said something about nausea and I haven't had any of that."

"That's a good sign," he said unconvincingly.

"Pass me the brandy, will you?" She poured some more and bolted it. "Oh, Jon, Mother's going to die!"

"Not unless you tell her. What are you worried about? You're getting married."

"But if it's true, then in seven or eight months everyone will know. Mother will know!"

"Who gives a flying fuck! Sorry. Quit worrying about Mother. It's not her life. It's yours."

"Dum-dum-da-dum!" Lucille burst in to the tune of the wedding march. "I've got it all here—something old, something new—what are you doing here, Jon? You're supposed to be getting ready, not getting drunk."

"I am ready and I am not drunk."

"Pilfering brandy, I see."

Jon studied the label. "This isn't pilfering. It's Rémy Martin."

"I bought that brandy for my guests."

"I'm your guest. I don't live here."

"Neither do I—thank God! What an old tomb this house is, isn't it, Lucy Rose? Living in the Regents' penthouse is so much nicer, but they would have charged me thousands to have the wedding there and the Swallow Foundation had to let me have this old mausoleum for free."

"I have to go to the bathroom," cried Lucy Rose, grabbing the White Shoulders off the vanity on her way out.

Lucille regarded Jon coldly. "I suppose you've been telling Lucy Rose she ought to run off and not go through with this."

"It's not my place to tell Lucy Rose anything. It's not yours, either."

"Don't tell me my place! I'm not your simpering Melinda!"

"There isn't any Melinda."

"Well, that's true, according to Hoolihan."

"What else did he tell you?"

"Just that you've been squatting in the desert, living in a bus with an Armenian and a couple of lesbians. I don't know which is the more disgusting."

"You shouldn't have sent him."

"I didn't. Lucy Rose sent him and he went for her. Believe me, Hoolihan hasn't any love for you, Jon. He thinks you're a misguided twerp and you'll break your mother's heart one day." She assumed the look of an outraged madonna.

"Doesn't he—of all people—know you don't have a heart?"

"At least I have brains and guts, which is more than can be said for you! Here." She picked his bow tie off the vanity and threw it at him. "Put this on and go downstairs and see if you can't be a gentleman for one afternoon. It won't kill you, and I wouldn't care if it did."

ii

The ceremony was to take place in the salon. Beneath the latticed arbor, standing in front of the beveled windows, Lucy Rose Cotton and Randolph Eckdorf would recite their vows. Ropes of orchid, pikake, white ginger and plumeria wove over the lattice and were draped the width of the room. A white carpet ran down the length of the salon up to the arbor, cutting through the five hundred chairs concentrically arranged, each row marked with tall candelabra, tied with ribbons and antherium, whose snaky tongues seemed equally ready to lick or hiss at the guests. For the occasion, Lucille had ordered all the Senator's lugubrious works of art taken down and the Salon repainted pink.

"Tacky," Althea announced to the rest of the family when she returned from her scouting prowl. "But what do you expect from vipers?"

The Swallows and some fifty other guests milled in the foyer, waiting to be seated in the salon. More guests crowded on the wide veranda outside. The ushers were not very efficient and Althea commented on this, too. Althea of course remained in steadfast mourning, but the other Swallow women, like the rest of the guests, were dressed in colors befitting petit fours.

"George wanted to come," Eleanor explained to Meg, "but I thought the sight of this old home would—well, you know." Eleanor strangled her hanky. "Oh look, Meg, there's Mayor Coldwell."

"Ex-mayor," Althea corrected her.

"Hello, Hugh!" Eleanor waved her hanky.

"Stand up straight, Claire," Meg admonished her. "You're never going to be a tall woman, so you might as well stand up straight."

"Jill doesn't hunch," Althea added. "Why can't you be like Jill? And anyway, you look terrible, Claire. What was your temperature this morning?"

"One hundred and three," mumbled Claire.

"Maybe you shouldn't have come at all. It isn't as if you and Lucy Rose are bosom friends."

"For that you need a bosom," quipped Bart.

"Cram it."

"Claire!" Meg cried.

"Sorry."

"I'm not at all surprised you're sick," Althea continued. "Not when you stay out all hours of the night with strange boys and stay home all day playing the piano. If you're not going to college, you should get married."

"Or get a job," said Meg vaguely, frowning and biting her lip.

"What's wrong, Meg dear?"

"Oh, nothing. Just a phone call yesterday from Mr. Stone. Something about our stock rising, or was it falling? I have to call him on Monday. I didn't understand, but it sounded—well, he wasn't reassuring. Anyway, we don't want to think about that until Monday, do we?" Meg beamed at her three daughters. "You are the walking embodiment of the Three D's," she said benignly. "You all look very pretty."

Althea gave Claire a jab in the ribs. "Pretty is as pretty does."

"I checked the forecast and it's a good day for a wedding." Vera pulled her cloche down tighter on her head.

"Hmph. Look at that fog out there. Thick as rice pudding."

"I wasn't speaking of the weather, Althea. I was speaking of the astrological forecast, of course. It is a good day for contracts and unions and Venus—"

A blast from the organ drowned Vera out. The unseen organist began with a Bach fugue that stunned the guests into solemnity, and gradually the ushers guided them to their seats. Claire hunched again, kept her eyes on the parquet floor and inwardly invoked Matthew Mark Luke and Jon Cotton's anarchistic principles, which surely would not permit him to attend anything so barbaric as this wedding. She should have followed her first inclination this morning, when she stuck the thermometer in her coffee and announced she was too ill to go. But when the girls all lined up to follow Bart to the car, there she was: spring coat, layered chiffon dress the color of grenadine, gloves, hair curled and shining on her shoulders.

"We're friends of the bride," said Meg to Randolph's pimpled younger brother.

"We are not," Althea snapped. "We're Swallows."

"We're just seating the guests as they arrive, madam. If you'll follow—"

"I'll take care of these people, Ernest."

Claire looked up at the sound of his voice. For an infinitely split moment, their eyes met like flint and tinder and then Claire looked away and Jon offered his arm to the redoubtable Althea and the rest of the Swallows dutifully followed him down the aisle and they filed past him into their row.

Save for Claire, the Swallows fidgeted and squirmed, ogling the Eckdorfs, who were five rows ahead, but all that could be seen of Eunice Eckdorf was a fleshy dowager's hump and all that could be seen of Ralph Eckdorf was scanty, frayed hair. In the front row on the other side, Lucille sat regally beside Hoolihan, the two of them conferring in undertones. In his cutaway coat, his boutonnière of white ginger and his evident pride in the proceedings, anyone would have guessed Hoolihan to be the father of the bride.

But Claire cared nothing for Hoolihan or Lucille or the Eckdorfs. Her eyes followed Jon as he led people down the white carpeted aisle. He did not look the same. Had he so completely changed in three months? Clean and neat and clipped unto shorn, his face was devoid of zeal, tenderness or intensity; his expression seemed as painted on as his clothes. Unwillingly, Claire remembered the mat of thick hair crushed beneath his starched shirt. Then she watched her nailpolish gleam in the candlelight.

When the first cannonade of the wedding march sounded, all the guests rose in unison and stood on tiptoes to see the six attendants in their blossom pink gowns come down the aisle, followed by the bride on the arm of her brother. Lucy Rose, swathed, veiled, dripping transparent lacy tentacles like a jellyfish, reeked of White Shoulders, but only Jon could hear her small, genteel burp as he led her up the aisle. He relinquished his sister to Randolph Eckdorf and took his seat beside his mother.

The guests sat down and the dreadful ceremony began in earnest. All this public hoopla over what ought to be private and personal and murmured in secret, Claire thought, and look at Lucy Rose up there, mouthing all that crap about love and honor and obey. Obey! Jon was right. A wedding was nothing more than a public humiliation for a girl—why, you might as well get flogged as get married. The bride ought to die of shame to agree to all that—and in public. Only gradually and as the ceremony progressed did Claire realize that it had to be done in public: you had to have all these people remind you for the rest of your life that if you broke your vows, you hadn't just betrayed your spouse, but your mother and father and aunts and cousins and all of them, down to the most tenuous thread of fleshly connection: you hadn't betrayed one individual, but society itself. You got yourself a husband and agreed to play by society's rules. Everyone smiled on brides because brides vindicated society's expectations, affirmed their choices, right down to repeating the same words, the very vows. Horrible. Contemptible. Oh, and so much to be envied—those ordinary pleasures, those conventional dreams, a home and husband.

When the bride and groom kissed, Claire joined the matrons in a gush of weeping, the snap of handbags, the knotting of hankies, the blowing of noses. But Claire wept for herself.

"What's wrong with you?" Bart whispered. "You've been a wreck all day."

"Bug off."

iii

"Just one more, Jon. You *can* smile, can't you dear? You don't want Ralph and Eunice to think you can't smile, do you? Stand right here beside me and Lucy Rose," Lucille cooed. "Now," she turned to the photographer "for Christ's sake, get the picture."

When the photographs were over at last, Lucille shed her demure silk jacket and revealed her magnificent shoulders and the emeralds resting across her collarbones like a chain of lakes. In her iridescent gown she swam upstream against the tide of wedding guests thronged in the dining room, where the Senator's immense portrait frowned down upon the frozen swallow perched on its six-foot column of ice and the lake of Hawaiian orchids at its base. Lucille nodded approvingly at the huge table spread with black caviar and pink prawns and bright wedges of lemon, at the stiff waiters circulating with silver trays of champagne. She checked the salon, where yet more waiters were taking down the chairs and setting up long tables for the formal dinner to be served later. She stopped at the bar and reminded the bartender of her injunctions and went down to the terrace to make sure that the orchestra followed her instructions as well: show tunes and love tunes and no requests (except from the bride or groom). Lucille certainly wasn't going to have any of that yeah yeah yeah crap to be played at a wedding of hers!

Lucille was not the only overdressed individual. Heedless of the fog, the guests spilled into the terraces like schools of spangled fish. Althea took it all in and commented adversely, but only the hapless Eleanor stayed by her side. Vera drifted away to discuss omens and aspects with anyone who would listen, and Meg left to renew acquaintances she had let lapse in the nine months since Anson's death. Claire got cornered by some old cronies of her father's while Jill and Marietta flashed their eyes at a bevy of cute boys and Bart flirted with a couple of glowing bridesmaids, girls Lucy Rose had known at Miss Proctor's.

Lucy Rose and Randolph swept through the five hundred guests like sparklers radiating untarnished hope and happiness, eliciting smiles and laughter and kisses. Hoolihan shook hands and slapped backs and stopped to chat as he escorted his fragile widowed mother toward a chair on the terrace, where she could watch the dancing. Mrs. Hoolihan's eyes were blue and bright as periwinkles and her dentures clacked with unbridled excitement.

Jon fought off whole tribes of stout matrons who pressed his arm and kissed his cheek and said wasn't it just ages. "Your mother says you're doing social work down in the desert," one of them clucked. Two others beamed nearby, all of them wearing thick floral cologne that made Jon dizzy. "I think that's wonderful. Why, a boy with your—your money"—the matron's voice dipped as her eyebrows shot up—"you could do anything and it's just wonderful that you care about the less fortunate."

"I'm an anarchist," he replied tersely.

"Isn't that something like the Peace Corps?"

Jon put his empty champagne glass on the tray of a passing waiter and bolted for the bar, where he ordered a brandy and soda from the bartender.

"I'm sorry sir, I can't serve anything stronger than champagne until after dinner. Mrs. Swallow's orders."

"Shit. Give me some champagne then."

"Yes, sir." He popped a fresh bottle. "What can I get for you, Mr. Hoolihan?"

"A gin and tonic. Light on the tonic."

"How do you rate, Hoolihan?"

"You want a drink, Jon? Get this man a drink."

"But, sir, Mrs. Swallow—"

"Need never know. Get him a drink." He turned to Jon. "Lucille is running this thing like it was the Kremlin and she was Nikita Khrushchev. Control, control, that's her motto." Hoolihan lit a cigarette and watched Jon inhale his brandy. "Of course, you're the one thing she can't control, aren't you? It's because you can't be bought off. I'm impressed with that."

"Thanks for the drink, but I'd be crushed if I thought you liked me."

"Oh, I don't. Don't get me wrong. I'm intrigued, that's all. I'm always intrigued with people who can't compromise or be compromised. They're rare. They're almost extinct, in fact. Judge Swallow was one of those men. The late Judge Swallow. You know his daughter Claire." Hoolihan puffed and watched as Jon's dark eyes narrowed and his mouth pinched. "Strike the remark. We were discussing Judge Swallow. He was like you in many ways, Jon. An absolutely unshakable man, but it's been my experience that people who can't bend will break."

"I'll never bend to my mother's will."

Hoolihan finished his gin and got another. "Has the draft caught up with you yet? Put you in uniform and send you off to defeat communism in the rice paddies?"

"I'll never fight a capitalist war."

"Then you'll rot in prison."

"The prison and the army are just two fists of the same capitalist power structure."

"You ought to go easy on the capitalists. Your mother's one."

"Sit on it and swivel, Hoolihan."

"Will you be heading back to Chagrin tomorrow?"

"None of your damn business."

"They don't call it Chagrin for nothing, do they? The pit of creation, that town. What is it you do there besides teaching workers the meaning of oppression?"

"I fuck trees."

"Bad for your dick," said Hoolihan, moving away.

Jon finished his brandy and couldn't get the bartender to give him another, so he took a glass of champagne and headed back toward the terraces, avoiding as much as possible the gushing girls from Miss Proctor's, Randolph's relatives and well-wishing matrons, but one of the latter managed to snag his arm anyway, cluck, natter and steer him toward the back of a tall man with slick, steel gray hair. "Hugh!" she called out. "Here's someone you must meet."

Hugh Coldwell turned around and behind him, in the milky shadows cast by the fog, Jon saw Claire Swallow, who would not meet his eyes.

"Here he is at last, Hugh, Lucille's boy, Jon, the one who's doing social work down in the desert somewhere. Where did you say?"

"I didn't."

"Well your mother did, a funny name like—"

"I'm Hugh Coldwell, son." Hugh shook hands with a politician's practiced grip. "Oh, and this is Claire Swallow, the judge's daughter and the Senator's—but of course you two have probably been friends since you were babies!"

"We know each other. How are you, Claire?"

"Chagrin!" chirped Mrs. Coldwell. "That was it!"

"Chagrin." Hugh stroked his chin. "I've heard of that. On the news. Some terrible epidemic there recently, wasn't there?"

"Typhoid," said Jon. "They died like flies." Unabashedly, Jon's eyes swept over Claire's body, drank in the sight of her tawny hair, the pain in her dark eyes, the grenadine chiffon reflecting color into her pale face. "Everything died in that epidemic."

"What kind of social work do you do, Jon?" Hugh inquired gravely.

"I'm an anarchist, Hugh. I'm working to bring about the revolution that will be the death knell of elitist, socially useless gatherings like this."

"Oh dear," Mrs. Coldwell tittered. "Oh, listen to what they're playing. 'The Anniversary Waltz' and look, there's the bride and groom dancing. Oh, Hugh, doesn't it just remind you of our wedding? Now, you two young people go on out there and dance. Weddings are really for young people." She took Jon and Claire each by the elbow and drove them into the dancing, snatched their glasses from their hands and flung them into one another's arms.

The music changed to "Someone to Watch Over Me" and amidst the crowding couples, Jon held Claire self-consciously at first and her hand rested primly on his shoulder and then she raised her face to his, so close her lips could have brushed his beard. The kiss they could not effect glowed between them. He pulled her tight, her arm encircled his shoulder and they danced in a crackling electrical silence, though their faces retained the cordial curves required by these occasions.

At last he murmured, "Why did you leave me, Claire?"

"I didn't leave you," she said fiercely. "I left Chagrin. I'm here now. Don't talk about the past."

"Don't ever leave me again."

"Don't talk about the future. Just hold me."

"Oh, I've missed you, babe, been so hungry and desperate for you and needed you and—"

The tune ended and a round of applause followed as most people changed partners, Lucy Rose dancing with Hoolihan, Ralph Eckdorf with Lucille, and Bart gallantly escorted his Aunt Vera to the floor as the band struck up "The September Song" and Jon could once again put his arm around Claire with impunity.

As they jostled amongst the dancers and scraps of conversation, Claire whispered urgently, "I'm dying without you, I love you." And just as Jon replied that he loved her too, Ernest Eckdorf cut in on him and Claire finished the dance with Ernest, listening to his tales of personal glory on the University of Hawaii's swim team. When at last the song ended, Claire excused herself and made her way back toward her Aunt Vera. Her brother asked her to dance as the orchestra took up "Over the Rainbow," but she declined. She searched the crowd for Jon, but he was picketed in blossom pink gowns and he looked beseechingly at her. Claire's shoulders fell.

Vera patted her hand. "There's lots of nice young men here, Claire, and Venus is in the ascendant," she added confidentially. "You might just find a husband here yourself."

"I only want one husband."

"Why, of course you do, dear. One husband is all a girl ever needs."

The music meandered to "Moon River" and Claire held her breath as she watched Jon plow toward her, through waiters and dancers and guests knotted in convivial clumps; she so concentrated on Jon's beautiful, bearded figure that she did not see Hoolihan approaching from the other side. Hoolihan got there first. Jon stopped short; Jill was close by and he asked her to dance and she accepted with a full measure of decency, decorum and dignity, to say nothing of delight.

Hoolihan swept Claire onto the dance floor gracefully. "Do you remember me, Miss Swallow? We met at the university in Jon Cotton's apartment, just about a year—"

"I remember, Mr. Hoolihan," Claire replied coldly.

Hoolihan and Claire were momentarily pushed aside by Lucy Rose, who dashed across the dance floor, fingers pressed to her lips, skirts hitched up as she headed toward the house. "Too much excitement for her," commented Hoolihan. "Excitement and chagrin."

"Chagrin?"

"A figure of speech. You're not still at the university, are you?"

"No."

"What are you doing?"

"I play the piano."

"Of course! Your father had the highest regard for your musical abilities. More than once he said to me you had the makings of a concert pianist. He always hoped you'd study at the Pacific Conservatory, Claire."

"If we're going to be on a first name basis, then you should tell me yours."

"Ah, I'd love to oblige you, but that's a secret between me and my sainted mother over there." He nodded toward a group of old folks in wicker chairs at the terrace edge.

"Your mother's here?"

"Herself. She wouldn't have missed it for the world." The song ended, applause and laughter intermingled, couples dispersed, but Hoolihan held Claire's elbow more tightly than she would have wished and he directed her through the crowd, releasing her only when she stood before Jon Cotton. "You're in my debt for this, Jon," Hoolihan said lightly. "I cannot in conscience monopolize this young lady any further, but if you don't dance with her, someone else will swoop her up. Thank you for your company, Claire." He asked Eunice Eckdorf to dance, and she blushed and lumbered onto the dance floor.

Jon did not dance with Claire. He offered her his arm in an awkward, formal fashion and then, bobbing unobtrusively like driftwood on the tide of Lucille's bounty, they made their way out of these currents, chatting like amicable strangers till they found themselves alone amongst the dwarf armadas of daffodils lining the garden walks, protected by hedges and arbors. "Does your family know about us?" Jon asked in the midst of their feigned enthusiasm for the weather.

"No one knows."

"What did you tell them when you came home from Chagrin?" He entwined her hand with his.

"Sin, chagrin." She shrugged. "They think I'm a fallen woman anyway, so I just took the Fifth Amendment. I figured I ought to have the same rights as a prisoner and not be required to give evidence against myself. The Mourning Glory threatened and nagged and Bart told me I was thoughtless to cause Mama such pain right after Father's death and Jill tried to get it out of me in sisterly confidence, but I just refused to talk. What could they do? They wouldn't throw me out. Mama raged for weeks, but finally she had to quit. Raging isn't ladylike, and anyway, she likes to keep up appearances. She tells everyone I've come back from the university and I think she actually believes it. Sometimes I believe it."

"I have another question. I know it isn't fair and I don't have any claims on you, but have you found someone else, Claire?"

"No claims?" Claire regarded him with alarm. "You'll always have claims on me and I'll always have claims on you. I don't care what the anarchists believe, it's true! Anyway, I don't imagine you've lived like a monk for three months," she added, skirting the issue.

"I slept with Kathleen and Maggot too, if you want to know the truth. The commune has gone to hell. I've left Chagrin for good.

There's nothing to go back to."

"I'm sorry. I know you believed in it."

"I still believe in collective living. That didn't change. The idea didn't die. It's like my loving you, Claire. Nothing will change my loving you. You'll always be mine, no matter who you sleep with."

"There hasn't been anyone else." A grain of truth gleamed at the heart of this lie: Claire had given her body to many men, but no other lover. "I'm empty without you. I never want to lose you again. I want to come with you wherever you go."

"Oh, babe, that's impossible. I'm on the run from the draft and—"

Claire turned on him fiercely. "Oh, don't give me that. You love some bloodless bunch of dogma better than you love me. You always have. You always will."

"Love is a quality, Claire, not a quantity. Not something you divvy up like a pie and say, so much for this and so much for that. It's an infinite quality. Either you love or you don't."

"Damn your absolutes, Jon Cotton." As an elderly couple meandered by, Claire snatched her hand away and sat down on a stone bench dusted with blossoms from the surrounding Japanese plums.

Jon stood beside her, resting his foot on the bench, his body sheltering their words from the wind. He touched her hair. "I came up here because Lucy Rose needed me, but I needed you, wanted you. I almost called you until I realized there wasn't anything I could say that would change the past or alter the future."

"Are you saying that after this wedding, I'm never going to see you again?"

"I can't answer for never. Or always. You know that. You must have known it when you left Chagrin. You were right to leave me, Claire, but I thought I'd die when you did."

"Well, I'm glad you found comfort with Maggot and Kathleen."

"The old Claire. When in doubt, say something wounding."

"Wounding! What have you done to me?" Then she lowered her voice in deference to groups of old people wandering the bricked walks. "What have you done to my life? You're the only man I love or want and you tell me you want and love me and it can never, never happen. I'll never have anything I want. How am I supposed to live? What am I supposed to do? I won't end up like Althea. I won't be an old maid. I want to marry you. I want to take those same ridiculous and humiliating vows Lucy Rose took. I want to be your wife and live with you and have your children and a life like any other and I'll never, never see a bit of it!"

"Oh, Claire, I'd promise you everything Lucy Rose and Randolph promised each other and it wouldn't be untrue, only impossible. Please don't cry." He bent his head to hers. "We'll always love each other. We'll always belong to each other."

"But not together, is that it?" She sniffed and bit her lips. "The spirit but not the flesh?"

"Please don't cry."

But Claire lost her struggle with tears. Claire Swallow did not have a theoretical mind and—without the certainties of flesh—the assurances of an immaterial spirit, an ethereal soul, seemed vacuous and empty and utterly without comfort, even though she knew what flesh could come to, learned that in the church in Chagrin. Nonetheless, for Claire, love without flesh was as alien as the mythical revolution; she could not serve what she could not see or feel or touch. The warmth from Jon's hand seared through the frail chiffon and burned into her shoulder. "I won't live like that," she snapped, shaking his hand off. "I don't give a damn about disembodied love, and I won't spend my life thinking about the past and longing after a spirit lover, do you hear me? I won't do it. I want a future and a man who can give me a life."

"I hope you find him. I envy him."

"Oh, can it. I hate you when you're noble. I wish I'd never met you. I hate you. I hate loving you. Why don't they ever tell you how dangerous love can be? I hate all those ridiculous love songs, all those delusions—"

"I didn't delude you. I—"

"Love did, don't you see?" she cried passionately. "It's not your fault, it's love's. You can never rely on love. Its nothing but a dream, and when you wake up, you've got nothing. Nothing. I wish I never had to feel anything at all."

"You're not that sort of person, Claire. You act on impulse and you never stop to think about the consequences."

"Really, doctor? What's the cure? Lobotomy? Pass the anaesthetic." Claire wiped her tear-smudged hands on the grenadine chiffon, staining it.

Jon reached up and parted the hair at the back of her neck and rested his fingers at the rim of her dress. "I want to kiss you there," he whispered. "The back of your neck always was a mined field. I want to hold you while you shiver, Claire, and I can, we could. Tonight, babe. After the wedding, if you want, if you can get away. We can have tonight." Jon moved his hand quickly when two old gentlemen rounded the corner, colleagues of the late Judge Swallow who tipped their hats to

Claire even though their heads were bare.

She waited till they passed. "How? I'll do anything you ask."

"I can't leave this reception till after Lucy Rose does. I'm supposed to tie cans to the back of their car or some barbaric damn thing. Lucy Rose is counting on me and I won't let her down, but after she and Randolph leave, you and I can get away. I'll take one of my mother's cars. It will please her to be able to add thievery to my list of defects."

"We could go to Jerusalem Road! San Angelos's not that far. There's no one there and the key is under the step at the back and—"

"All right, then meet me down by the garages as soon as Lucy Rose and Randolph have—"

"There you are, Jon!" Ernest Eckdorf tripped down the brick path. "Your mother told me to come find you. They're getting ready to sit down to dinner, and you have to come." Ernest grinned at Claire.

"You go on, Ernest. I'll be there in a minute."

"Lucille said I wasn't to come back without you," he replied firmly. "She sent me to get you and Randolph to get Lucy Rose."

"Where's Lucy Rose?"

"I don't know, sick or something. Anyway, your mother says she can't start without you."

Jon frowned and rose. "Will you please excuse me, Claire. It's been nice talking to you. Maybe I'll see you again."

"I see. Yes." Claire tingled as though enduring delicious voltage. "Yes. Goodbye."

"You have blossoms in your hair, Claire," said Ernest.

"What?"

"From the tree—those pink blossoms have fallen in your hair."

Claire brushed nervously at her hair as Jon and Ernest took their leave of her, headed back up toward the noise and music.

"I'm going to get a date with that Claire Swallow," Ernest confided to Jon. "As long as I'm here, I might as well get a little beaver. She's a hot number. You can always tell girls who will do it."

"Cram it," Jon replied and Ernest fell silent.

iv

At dinner Claire was uncomfortably wedged between two old men, contemporaries of the Senator's, both of them deaf and dyspeptic. They shouted at each other across her and quarreled about the past, extolling other memorable festivities they'd attended in this salon. Across from Claire, Althea poked through her food, as if looking for worms and vipers. Whenever she could, Claire glanced up at the dais, where the wedding party sat, but every time she caught Jon's eye, she also saw Hoolihan looking at her, scrutinizing her as he might evidence he didn't want admitted to court. Claire looked away. *Hurry up, Lucy Rose,* Claire prayed inwardly over her potatoes Anna. *Hurry up and leave so I can have my love for one last*

"Time has not addled my brains!" the old man on her left shouted to his cohort. "I'd remember something like that. I tell you, Senator Swallow never knowingly invited scum like Patrick Ryan to his house! If you don't believe me, ask Miss Swallow." He belched and excused himself to Claire. "I meant your aunt."

"I see." *And I don't care, I only want to escape to San Angelo and be alone with Jon, to—*

"Tell him, Miss Swallow. Tell him the Senator wouldn't have tolerated the presence of Patrick Ryan in this house. Tell him that's a—"

—lie with Jon and hold him, to make time stop stop stop, you old fools—

Claire endured each course as if holding up under torture, until finally the waiter poured the coffee and Lucille rose and announced that the wedding cake was about to be cut—with all due ceremony, including photographs—in the dining room. An infinite waste of time, thought Claire, but she excused herself to escape the wretched old men and her Aunt Althea. With Bart and Meg and Vera, Claire went into the dining room and watched while Lucy Rose and Randolph cut the cake and fed each other *messy business, cake of custom, why are people such slaves to convention, oh, jam that cake in Randolph's jaws and hurry up Lucy Rose.* The waiters then took over, cutting the cake and arranging the dishes on the trays. Claire and her family took theirs and sat together in the salon, where they could watch Althea holding court, arbitrating between two contentious old men.

As if rehearsing for the night ahead, Claire licked the inch-thick frosting from her fork as she sought Jon amongst the crowd, found him talking to a florid matron dressed in buttermint blue. Judging from the look on the woman's face, Jon had just mentioned the inevitable revolution and Claire started to laugh, but caught Hoolihan's piercing gray eyes and looked away. *Hurry up, Lucy Rose. I haven't got any future. I only have*

"The presents are all in the library!" cried Lucille, garnering their attention with the ring of a fork on crystal. "I think Lucy Rose and Randolph should open them while you're all here."

Claire's heart sank with what was surely an audible thud until Lucy Rose mumbled something to her mother and then ran from the salon, the white tentacles of her dress flying out behind her. Lucille laughed nervously. "Well, Lucy Rose says I should thank you all now and she'll write each of you when she returns from her honeymoon."

The music began again and guests wandered down to the terrace, where, despite Lucille's restrictions, the songs were no longer respectably Gershwin. Old folks tapped their feet while the young people danced to Beatles tunes, "I Wanna Hold Your Hand", and "Love Me Do" and "Money". For possibly every guest except Claire Swallow, the tone and tenor of the celebration lifted along with Lucille's other restrictions, and men could at last flock to the bar.

Ernest Eckdorf monopolized Claire for at least half a dozen dances. She didn't even notice his hand splaying over her back, creeping around to her side, untill he finally pulled her to him, crushed her breasts and said they ought to get together after the party.

"Are you mad?" Claire left him on the dance floor and retreated to the house, delighted to see that Lucy Rose had rejoined the guests and was now about to go back upstairs, attended by the six girls in blossom pink. *Hurry up, Lucy Rose.*

"You're looking very lovely, Claire," said Hoolihan, startling her. He smiled and offered her a cigarette, which she declined. "A grand wedding, don't you think?" He lit up and squinted against the smoke.

"All weddings are the same," Claire replied coldly. "Only the people are different."

"So the evidence would suggest." Hoolihan puffed thoughtfully. "I suppose that next we'll be dancing at your wedding."

"I doubt you'd be asked to any wedding of mine. If I were getting married. Which I'm not."

"Pity," he said with a shrug.

"Why do you keep giving me weird looks?" Claire demanded.

Hoolihan chuckled. "Perhaps it's because you percolate suggestive evidence, Miss Swallow." He demurred at the look of affront on her face. "I don't mean in the lewd sense, of course. I meant in the sense of potential. Potentially, I'd say your father was right about you. You have spirit and dash and possibility—barring of course the possibility that your spirit and dash contrive to defeat your potential."

Claire regarded him as if he'd just quoted from the Magna Carta, too confounded even to murmur, "I see". Sensing an argument in the offing that she would not win, she excused herself briskly and left him, made her way toward the bar, looking for Jon; not finding him there, she wandered the house and when she came to the foyer she smiled to see the bridesmaids filing down the staircase, laughing and chattering like an arpeggio scale. Word rippled amongst the guests that the bride and groom were about to leave. *Oh hurry up, Lucy Rose.* Lucy Rose came downstairs in a blue-green traveling suit that made her look bilious. A long rope of pearls gleamed around her neck, and she held her bouquet of stephanotis, white ginger and pink roses like a scepter.

Vera found Claire in the foyer and pushed her toward the salon. "Go on, Claire. All the young girls have to get ready to catch the bouquet. If you catch it, you'll get the next husband."

"I don't want the next husband. I only want Lucy Rose to hurry up."

"That's what I said, dear, hurry up." Vera nudged and urged and finally grabbed Claire's arm and guided her into the salon, where the tables had been pushed back against the walls. Giving Claire one last shove, Vera thrust her into a milling hub of young women in their rustling chiffons and crackling organdies, giggling, expectant, gossiping amongst themselves. Claire forged through this pastel crush toward the back of the room. She would have crawled behind the potted palms if there had been room or time, but Lucy Rose entered and a cheer went up for the bride. Claire kept her arms pinned to her side and her eyes closed in a fit of chagrin until a roar rose from the crowd and her eyes flew open to see the bouquet hurtling like a satellite across the salon, over the shining heads of young women whose faces all turned to watch it sail past them, to Claire. Claire stepped aside rather than catch it, but there was no one behind her and it hit the wall and her hand flew out instinctively and it landed in her arms on the rebound. She instantly found herself wrapped in a skein of well-wishers, pouting girls, and approving matrons, jocular men. It was like being tied to the stake. They all patted her back and pinched her cheek and asked her who the lucky man would be.

V

A caul of evening fog shrouded San Angelo when the car stopped at the back of the Swallow home. Claire found the key taped under the back step and opened the door while Jon got his small suitcase out of the trunk. Claire went in and turned on all four stove burners; their blue-bright flames cheered the kitchen and the smell of gas chased the odor of damp and disuse.

Jon closed the door behind him and took off his tuxedo jacket, and Claire removed her spring coat. Hard grains of rice clacked on the kitchen floor as he hung them on pegs. He looked around the kitchen and smiled. "I've heard so much about this house, I feel like I've lived here all my life."

"I feel like you have, too," said Claire, oddly struck with the notion that she and Jon were not runaway lovers at all, but a middle-aged couple with twenty years of mutual knowledge behind them and another twenty before them, time to enjoy their love and leisure, to take that love and leisure for granted, to mete their lives out by the teaspoonful. "Would you like a cup of tea?"

"Yes," said Jon, succumbing to the same myth and moment. "I would."

Claire put water in the kettle and got the teapot ready as if this were an everyday act. Until the kettle began to shriek, they sat across from each other making small talk, like people who have long shared assumptions. She made the tea and put the cups and pot on the table before them and let it steep without urgency or eagerness. The stove warmed the kitchen and the tea warmed them and they talked about the wedding.

"Think of all the people who could eat the rice wasted at a wedding like that," said Jon at last. "What a stupid custom. Why do they throw rice at weddings?"

"It's got something to do with fertility, I think."

"Barbaric." Jon frowned; when he'd seen his sister dash for the bathroom the second time, his heart fell and though the obvious implication did not seem to dim Lucy Rose's happiness, it had certainly sobered Jon. Claire poured them both some tea, and Jon wrapped his hands around his cup. "Are you still on the pill, Claire, or should I go down to the drugstore and get some rubbers?"

"No."

"I wouldn't be gone ten minutes. I saw a drug store when we—"

306

"Don't." She smiled warily. "I mean, don't ruin the illusion." She laughed and added lightly, "I hope you've got some real clothes in that suitcase. You don't look a thing like yourself in that tuxedo."

Jon snapped at his suspenders and laughed. "I'll never wear one of these monkey suits again. You better get a good look now."

"I will."

He glanced around the spacious, comfortable kitchen. "You can always tell a house where people have been happy. I don't know how, exactly, but you can."

"Yes, Jerusalem Road is more home than any other house. It's a good place for us now. You are my family now."

He took her hand. "We'll always belong to each other like families do, Claire, like we shared the same flesh and blood and heart and soul." He chuckled uncomfortably. "Listen to me—anarchists don't believe in hearts and souls."

Claire did not laugh; she rose and stood beside him and he wrapped his arms around her and pressed his face against her belly. She stroked his hair. "But you believe in flesh and blood. Don't you?" she whispered. "Mine and yours," *and what could be ours, the only thing that will ever be ours apart from this moment.* She felt a deep internal tingling, a tension beyond the merely anticipatory, as though her body were experiencing the historical imperative.

Claire turned her back to Jon and carefully, as if unwrapping a present, he unzipped the grenadine chiffon and it fell from her shoulders. She stepped out of it and put it in his lap. She unhooked her stockings and garter belt and bra and put them in his arms like gifts; she slid her half slip and pants down her hips and the fragile garments lay uneasily in his strong hands. She felt like a postulant, if not quite a novice, about to take irrevocable vows and wished she knew of some prescribed ritual that could properly dignify, solemnize, this moment, wished she could recite a litany to enshrine what was about to happen, but all she could remember was, "Matthew Mark Luke and John, bless the bed that we lie on."

She turned off the stove and took Jon's hand and he followed her out of the kitchen, down the long, dark sea-smelling hall toward the beckoning stairwell and up to the turret room. Jon took off his clothes and got into bed while Claire went to the window, pushed aside the muslin curtain and allowed gray murky light and the quiet respiration of the waves to waft over them and then she got into bed.

"Oh God, it's so good to hold you again, babe." He closed his eyes and ran his hands over her and Claire was flooded with happiness and certainty. "You're sure it's safe, babe?"

"I'm sure." Claire rolled on top of him and her hair spilled into his face and she stroked his head and coaxed from him the one thing she was sure of: she wanted Jon Cotton, wanted him so far up and in her that she would split like a atom, crack asunder like an overripe melon, wanted to feel something of Jon's flesh pulse inside her like she felt him pulsing inside her now, wanted to mingle his flesh with her own and hold it in her arms. Of this she was certain. The future, with its equal certainties of scandal, shame and anguish, lapped like fog at the window, like the sea on the beach, but Claire willfully dismissed it: she intended to hold onto the man she knew she would lose. She wanted something of Jon Cotton to love, not as memory, but as prospect: if not a life together, then a life created together.

CHAPTER FIVE

March 1986

"And one, two! Lift! Lift! And one, two lift and stop. Very good, ladies. That's all. See you on Thursday."

Christine Stone sat down, mopped her face with a towel and tugged at her shocking pink leg warmers. She stretched and breathed deeply. Aerobics was her last class of the day and she was tired, but tingling: now nothing stood between her and the glorious evening she planned. She reached for her toes and smiled to think of the steaks marinating, the zinfandel chilling in the fridge, the tender asparagus she'd especially chosen for tonight's meal. Maybe she'd even use her wedding china and sterling. It was an occasion, after all; she and Scott had not enjoyed a leisurely dinner at home together in a week. Ten days. Longer?

"Pam and I are going out for pizza after we get dressed, Christine," said Patricia, the young woman next to her. "Why don't you come along?"

"I can't tonight. My husband's picking me up." Her blue eyes glowed with anticipation.

"Well, I guess an evening at the Pizza Forum isn't exactly a treat for you anyway."

"Not exactly," Christine agreed with a smile.

"Why don't you have your husband bring you by later and we could all—"

"Not tonight. Besides," she added, lest her plans for the evening seem too obvious, "I have lab reports for biology and a test on Friday in history."

"But this is only Tuesday!"

"I have to study hard for good grades." Christine remained a conscientious student, though she found San Angelo Community College considerably less demanding than the University of Hawaii.

Christine did not shower, just slid her sweats over her leotard and brushed her short hair, applied some lipstick and gathered up her jacket and books to wait for Scott at the appointed place. She didn't want to be late; she had looked forward to this night for a week and a half. Scott had promised. In general, if Christine wanted to spend the whole evening with her husband, she had to sit at one of the long polished picnic tables at the Pizza Forum, nursing an interminable beer while Scott dealt with the bevy of college boys he employed, his regular customers, and the piano player, whom Christine thought an odious drunk.

She said good night to Patricia and Pam and stepped outside, dismayed to find a light, insubstantial rain falling. She walked to the parking lot at the back of the gym and looked for Scott's familiar black Porsche, but he was late. Christine consulted her watch. Maybe she was a little early. She zipped up her jacket against the fog and chill and clutched her books against her chest. A girl she knew from history drove by and asked if she wanted a ride, but Christine explained she was waiting for her husband. Several other cars came by and picked up people waiting at the kerb, students and secretaries just getting off work. She watched a young woman get into a car driven by a young man, lean over and kiss him before they took off. She wondered if the couple were married.

The rain thickened and began to pelt her, but she didn't want to go inside the gym and risk missing Scott. She pulled up her hood and watched the lamps come on and the gauzy rain reflect their light. Headlights spun through the fog and a blue Datsun stopped in front of her and the passenger's door swung open. "Christine!"

She knelt to peer into the car. "Why, Bart! It's you. I'm waiting for Scott."

"No, get in. I'm supposed to pick you up. Scott called Claire's and said he couldn't make it. I'd have been here sooner, but this campus is full of dead ends and all these new buildings look like gyms to me."

Christine shut the car door. The sharp snap seemed to break the neck off her anticipation, and running from her hopes she could all but see blood, the color of zinfandel. Bart grinned at her and pushed a Beethoven sonata into the tape deck. He left the parking lot and pulled onto San Angelo Parkway. At last, she asked, "Did Scott say why he didn't—couldn't come?"

"Something at the Pizza Forum. Business. I don't know. I didn't ask. He just said he couldn't pick you up, and I said I would."

"You don't usually come down here on weekdays."

"No, but Claire went to some meeting of the county association of music teachers, so I thought I'd spend some time with Mama and Althea."

"You don't get along with Claire, do you?"

"I used to."

"I guess it's none of my business. Sorry."

"There's nothing for you to be sorry for! Claire and I go back a long way."

"You blame her for my marriage, don't you?"

"Oh, Christine—"

"You shouldn't, really. I'm very happy and I can't imagine my life without Scott. I'm glad he came to Honolulu, even if—even if, well—Hoolihan always says good things can come of bad motives and vice versa and you should judge by the results rather than the intentions."

"My father would have said just the opposite."

"But they got on famously, didn't they, Hoolihan and your father?"

"I don't know about famously. At the end of my father's life, they got on."

"Hoolihan says Anson Swallow respected the law and himself and every person—guilty or innocent—whoever stood before him. Hoolihan says there isn't a judge on the bench who is his equal."

"He was a rare man, my father." Bart stroked his beard. "Dead now, what, almost twenty-three years, and I still miss him."

"So does Hoolihan. Hoolihan and I talk all the time. He calls me twice a week. He's bringing Grandma around, you see. He says he's sure she'll see me again in a month. In the spring—that's what he really said."

"No one could stay mad at you. Even Lucille." Bart got on the freeway, and they joined the rush of commuters in the rain.

"I've been wondering—when I go to see her, do you think I should insist she see Scott as well? That she accept him?"

311

"Decide when you go to see her. You have good judgment." Bart put on the blinker as they neared the offramp for the shopping center where the Pizza Forum's neon sign percolated cheer, and Christine could see Scott's black Porsche parked in its reserved spot. "Scott asked me to bring you to the Forum."

"Oh no, Bart. Don't." She breathed easier when the blinker went off and they passed the ramp. "I just got out of aerobics and I'd like to go home and shower if you don't mind."

"I'd take you anywhere, Christine. Whenever you want to go to the moon, I'm the one to ask."

"What's that song on the tape? It's really lovely."

"Beethoven's Eleventh Sonata. Some men my age listen to the Beatles to return to their youth, but I always listen to the Eleventh Sonata. There was a time when that was all Claire ever played—and then, as far as I know, she never played it again. But you should have heard her. She was magnificent." Although Bart's relationship with Claire remained unmended, he often found his old affection for his sister creeping back, like a habit he could not altogether break.

The windshield wipers seemed to pick up the beat of the Eleventh Sonata and suddenly the Datsun seemed very safe and warm, insulated from the rain and all grievance and as they drove north, they chatted about Christine's studies and Meg's health, the forthcoming piano recital of Claire's students and the death of one of Althea's ducks. Christine laughed as she told Bart about the duck's Viking funeral. "Althea wore mourning and insisted that Lucky give the funeral oration, and Emma and Evangeline came too, and Bart, you would have laughed yourself silly to see them push the flaming shoe box out to sea. Claire and I could hardly keep a straight face. Then we had to go back to the house and Althea had a funeral reception. For a duck?"

"She probably wanted an excuse to have a drink," he confided. "If she wants a stiff shot, Althea always has to dream up an occasion."

"I could use a stiff shot myself," said Christine as they pulled off the freeway onto Swallow Boulevard and turned toward the ocean. "Have you got time for a drink, Bart?"

"I always have time for you."

He drove to Portofino, the oceanfront condominium complex high on Jerusalem Road where Scott and Christine lived, and once they pulled under the roof of the carport, they lost the rain's cheerful staccato and the Eleventh Sonata finished without accompaniment. They made a dash for the apartment.

Christine threw her books on the sofa and hung up both of their jackets. "What would you like, Bart? We have everything. Neither Scott nor I drink very much, but Scott likes to keep a full bar for company."

"Whiskey and soda?"

"Will you make one for me, too? Light." She showed him where the whiskey was. "I'll just pop in the shower and be right back."

Christine vanished into the bedroom, and Bart wandered around the kitchen and living room area, drink in hand. Digital clocks glowed at him from every corner: on the microwave, the stove, the VCR, the stereo, the TV and radio; none of them quite agreed on the correct time. They weren't the only things that didn't agree in this apartment, he reflected. Christine had chosen the colors—cream and pale mauve and a trim of darker plum—but a decorator named Andre had "done" the place and it had the look of a magazine photograph, testifying to Andre's good taste rather than the individual lives it harbored.

Bart's one other visit here was a celebrative family dinner just after Scott and Christine had moved in, before Christmas. He saw his own housewarming present, a Peruvian tapestry, hanging on the wall and wished—then as now—that he'd given Christine something more personal. On the occasion of that family dinner, Bart had behaved properly. He had not inquired, not even obliquely (nor had anyone else), how Scott had talked Randolph Eckdorf into funding him, or at least underwriting the purchase of the Pizza Forum franchise, or the Porsche for that matter, to say nothing of the condo. Bart suspected that despite their apparent affluence, Scott and Christine Stone hadn't a dime for the parking meter. Bart was not surprised: Lucky Stone had lived cash-poor and credit-rich for twenty years. Lucky now worked for his son, doing the books for Scott's restaurant. The Stones were afloat again. Bart shook his head and wandered to the sliding glass door, where the ocean view was obscured in the rain. The patio furniture showed signs of rust and a half dozen dead plants drooped in their pots. Bart tried not to believe in omens, but the withered mums and wizened marigolds struck him as pitiful just the same. Bart gathered from conversations with Lucky that Scott spent most of his waking hours (and many of Christine's sleeping hours) at the Pizza Forum. Lucky had argued that any new business required that kind of time of a man. Maybe that was so; Bart was not a businessman and he had never been married, but he wondered nonetheless if a new marriage didn't deserve at least as many hours as a new business.

The phone rang twice and he would have picked it up, but Christine must have got it in the bedroom. She came out dressed in amethyst sweats and looking fresh and revived. "That was Scott," she said, picking up her whiskey and soda. "He was worried when we didn't show up at the Forum. The rain and everything. I told him we'd come later. You've never been there, have you?"

"No, but I'd be happy to drive you."

"You'll like it. It's the fastest growing food franchise in the country. It's a wonderful opportunity. Scott is making buckets of money. He's very happy. He loves his work. I'd like to feel that way about my work, and maybe once I get my teaching certificate, I will. Do you love your work so much you can't wait to get to the office?"

"I enjoy my work and I often stay late at the office, but then, I don't have anyone at home now that Mama and Althea are with Claire. Sometimes I would stay late even when they lived with me." He winked. "It wasn't exactly relaxing to face Althea at the end of a long day."

Christine smiled at the confession. "You might need a stiff shot before going home to Althea, but she certainly can cook."

"I've lost fifteen pounds since last June. And a good thing, too!"

"You look fine, Bart. Any woman would be proud to be seen with you."

"Oh, not anymore. Those possibilities have passed me by, I'm afraid."

"You regret not marrying?"

"I can't regret it, exactly." He toyed with the cover of one of her textbooks. "At the time it seemed more a mandate than a choice. But now I don't know. Work is all very well and good, but if you take it to bed with you, you don't sleep."

"Scott can't sleep when he gets off work. He's too keyed up, he says. Sometimes he brings people home with him after the Forum closes. I used to wait up with them, but I have classes and I can't stay up till four talking to Scott's friends."

"What about your friends? Haven't you made friends at the college?"

"Oh yes. Of course. I never bring them home, though. I don't know why, exactly." Christine blushed. "Maybe that means they're not friends, only acquaintances. I don't make friends too easily. I've never really had a best friend—except Scott, of course."

"Of course. Well, you can say this for Scott, he has charm and he'll never lack for friends."

"People love him! I think some of those customers at the Forum keep coming back just to be with Scott. All his employees love him too—the cooks and waiters and that disgusting piano player. He's always half drunk, Bart, and when Scott's not around, he makes rude comments to me."

"Scott should fire him."

"He says I just have to understand Dick, that's his name. He says I have to learn to take a joke."

"If a man made rude remarks to my wife, I'd fire his ass so fast, his head would spin."

"Scott says Dick is a terrific piano player."

"So is Claire, but that doesn't mean she works at the Forum."

"No, but Beethoven isn't exactly the Forum's style. Well, we better finish up. Scott will be expecting me."

"Why don't you let me take you out to dinner and we'll go to the Forum later. You can't eat pizza five nights a week."

"Scott does."

"Then he's a fool! I mean," he added quickly, "he'll get fat."

"Would you like to eat here, Bart? I have everything."

"Let me take you out."

"No, really. It's all ready. It won't take me but a moment to throw the steaks on the Jenn-Aire and cook the asparagus. Say you'll stay. Please. It'll all go to waste otherwise."

"I'll stay."

As Bart set the table and opened the zinfandel, he realized who this meal was for and felt Christine's unstated disappointment keenly. Christine grilled the steaks and cooked the asparagus, which she had already carefully peeled before going to school that morning. He pronounced the dinner as good as anything Althea might have done, and Christine was flattered, relaxed and happy. She gave into fits of giggles as Bart described his childhood struggles with Claire. "I was the Frank Lloyd Wright of the sandcastle set. No, really, Christine, you wouldn't believe some of my architectural drawings for my sandcastles. I used to know a Gothic arch from a crenellated parapet. I'd spend the evening drawing up my plans and then at the beach the next day, I'd get the girls to help build and just as the castle was nearly finished, Claire would inevitably stomp on a moat or flatten a turret. She was a little beast!"

"You must have hated her."

"No, I didn't, actually. Oh, I cried and raged and told on her, of course, but once Mama had sent her back to the house, the beach

315

always seemed empty. Peaceful, but not nearly as fun. And the next day, there she'd be, ready to shore up the battlements again. She's like that. When Claire is at her best, there's something bracing and tonic about her, and I must say, when we got a little older, she quit ruining my sandcastles and we'd sit there on the beach together until the tide had taken the entire castle back. Mama used to try to get us to come back for supper, but Father said we should stay, that it was a good practice to see something to its conclusion. Of course, we learned that if we built the castles further back, we could sit on the beach a lot longer."

The phone rang and Christine excused herself to reach for it. "Yes, I'm coming. I'm having dinner with Bart. We'll be there in a bit. I don't know, pretty soon. Anyway, I can't stay long. I have a lab report and a test on Friday. Yes of course I want to spend time with you, Scott, but I have work too. I know one night isn't going to hurt, but I've spent four of the last five nights at the Forum and—yes, all right. Fine. I'll see you then." She hung up and turned to Bart, embarrassed.

The Pizza Forum was supported in front by six fake pillars and divided inside into two parts separated by a huge, well-lit kitchen. On one side, only soft drinks were served and on the other side patrons could buy beer and wine as well. All the young male cooks, waiters and bartenders wore derbies, bow ties and red garters on their white shirts. Christine waved to the bartender and he scooted to the office to tell Scott his wife was here. Christine led Bart to a special table near the office, where they sat between chunky plaster pillars.

Bart scrutinized the piano player, a scrawny, goateed man who played "Moon River" to a ragtime beat. "If they're going to call it the Forum, maybe Scott should hire someone who can play Italian opera," he observed.

"Here you are at last!" Scott cried, kissing Christine's cheek and shaking Bart's hand. "This is the first time you've been here, isn't it, Bart? Well, what do you think?"

Bart kept his suggestion about Italian opera to himself and replied in pleasant monosyllables while he adjusted to the change in his nephew, whom he had not seen since Christmas. Last year's earring was certainly gone, but Scott wore an inordinate amount of gold—a thick gold watch, a gold ID bracelet, and three gold chains of varying length gleamed at his shirt front, which was unbuttoned awfully low, Bart thought, considering that it was March and still cold. Scott's hair had been permed and his teeth even looked different, as if they'd been capped or bonded; they too gleamed in the Forum's lantern light, along with the gold chains. Scott's eyes were rather puffy, though he was still handsome. The big bodies of the Swallow men ran to fat if not maintained; beer had given Scott the beginnings of a visible paunch.

"What a brilliant guy," said Scott, referring to the waiter who had brought their beers. "He's a whiz on the computer. He'll be a millionaire one day."

"What's he doing working here?" asked Bart.

"Just working till he can sell some of his programs. He's doing computer work for me and we're going to copyright—"

As he listened to Scott talk, Bart realized that everyone at the Forum—whether cook, waiter or regular patron—either had brilliant prospects or a brilliant past. Dick, Scott claimed, used to play piano for Bob Dylan. The head cook was a Princeton dropout who had once dated Brooke Shields. That guy sitting over there was going to be all pro as soon as he got recruited, and another customer was the son-in-law of Exxon's executive chairman. Christine seemed to have heard it all before. She offered nothing, spoke when spoken to and smiled on cue. Bart asked how Lucky was doing as the Forum's bookkeeper and Scott told a funny incident about Lucky's bringing Emma and Evangeline in and the number of beers Evangeline drank. Scott laughed and added, "I've told Dad he can work here as long as he doesn't convert the customers. If everyone went to church on Sunday, I'd go broke!"

"I doubt that. You seem to be doing very well."

"Not only am I doing well, but guess what?" Scott draped his arm around Christine and lowered his voice. "A little rumor has reached me that the Burbank franchise is about to go on the block. Can you imagine what a gold mine that place is? I'd be a fool not to cash in on it."

"But Scott," she remonstrated. "You've only just got this place going and—"

"Think small, stay small. Didn't Benjamin Franklin say that?"

"Benjamin Franklin said, Lie down with dogs, get up with fleas," Bart said dryly.

"I thought Hoolihan made that up," Christine replied, her eyes wide. Then she turned to Scott. "Burbank's way downstate, honey. It's a long way from here."

"That's what planes are for, babycakes." He kissed her ear.

She fidgeted and squirmed away. "I have to be getting home. I have to study. Can I have the keys to the Porsche?"

"Oh stick around awhile, Christine. We're going over to Dick's after we close and—"

"I'll take Christine home," Bart volunteered. "I have to be getting back anyway. It's a long drive to the city."

"I'll go home with Bart, then."

"Oh come on, Christine—"

"No. Really. I must. I'll see you at—" She didn't finish because the Princeton dropout called Scott to the phone.

Bart and Christine drove back to Portofino with only the rain and the windshield wipers counterpointing one another. No sonata. No conversation. He pulled under the carport and turned off the ignition and silence engulfed them. "I'm coming back down on Saturday," he said at last. "Just call me at Claire's if you need a ride. Or anything."

"Thank you." Christine fumbled for her keys.

"If you need anything, you can always call me at home or at the office. You know the number."

"I couldn't impose."

"It's no imposition. Don't think that. I can always whip down here."

"You said it was a long drive."

"It's not, really. I didn't mean it. I just said that so he—because—so that—"

Christine stared resolutely at the dashboard. "When I go to the grocery store"—she coughed and bit her lip—"I see magazines on the rack and they have articles like 'The Other Woman Was His Job' or 'How I Won My Husband Back From His Work', and I leaf through them while I'm in line and sometimes I buy them and bring them home to read. Women write about how they greet their husbands at the door wearing black bras and garter belts, or how they invest in cans of whipped topping so they can lick it off their husbands and not gain weight, but that's ridiculous. Isn't it?" She gave a brittle laugh. "Isn't that funny?"

"It's demeaning. It's disgusting. It's degrading," he said fiercely. "Marriage is supposed to be a partnership. One partner shouldn't have to lick whipped cream off the other just to keep him home."

"That's what I think. And anyway, the articles never tell you how to get him home in the first place." Christine raised her blue eyes to Bart. "Scott loves me, I know he does, but he gets something from the Pizza Forum, from the people there, that I can't give him. I don't even know what it is."

Instinctive courtesy kept Bart from saying that Scott Stone needed an adoring audience, people to fawn over him, court his approbation, that Scott could not recognize peers, but required inferiors, whom he treated with good-natured disdain, or superiors, before whom he no doubt cringed. "Oh, the hell with it," Bart burst out. "I can't stand it, Christine. I can't stand to see the way he treats you. You ought to get rid of him. Leave him. You're young, you're beautiful, you're smart, you have everything in your favor except your jerk husband. Dump him. Everyone makes mistakes when they're young. That's no reason to be shackled to those mistakes for the rest of your life. People don't have to live like that anymore. Cut your losses with Scott and find a man who'll be at home at night when you need him, a man who deserves you."

"You don't think Scott does?"

"Scott's weak. He hasn't an ounce of integrity or responsibility or any notion of justice. Marriage requires these things—oh, I know you think I'm talking through my hat, that I'm old and what do I know, I've never been married."

"I don't think that at all!"

"But I have to say it. Scott never should have married at all, much less someone like you. You're too good for him. You'll never change the way he is. It's his character, don't you see? Not his personality. His personality is what he spreads like butter among all those—those assholes at the Forum, but his character is what you have to live with."

Christine began to cry into her hands.

Bart leaned over and put his arms across her shoulders, his head against her shining hair. "Forgive me, Christine. I spoke out of turn. It's none of my business. Tell me to go to hell and shut up and cram it and whatever else you want and I will, but Christ, I hate to see you suffer."

"I've been so lonely," she said, digging into her purse for a Kleenex. "I'm three thousand miles away from everyone who ever loved me, except Grandma and Hoolihan, and I could never, never let on to them, could I? And Mom and Dad want to come for a visit and I keep putting them off because if they came and saw—well, after the way I ran off, it has to work. It must! And I could never let on to Lucky and Claire. They've been so nice to me, but I get so worn out, Bart, so tired of keeping up appearances." She blew her nose and hurried on. "I have to pretend that yes, I have a husband and a home and an intimate life. Oh yes, I have a lovely home and a man I love, but I can never say—all that's important to my husband is this stinking pizza parlor.

Oh, Bart, I get queasy everytime I go in there. The smell makes me sick. But I'd die of shame before I could admit or let anyone guess. I couldn't. And anyway, I always think, maybe when we get a second car everything will be better, maybe once the Forum gets on its feet everything will be just fine, maybe once it's summer and I don't have to study everything will be terrific, but—"

"It'll never happen. You're too young to be a slave to appearances, to lies. Christine—forgive me if I'm hurting you, but—"

"I need a friend, Bart. I don't make friends at school because I can't let the girls there guess either that my marriage—I have to keep up appearances, even at school, and promise me you won't say any of this to anyone, especially to Lucky and Claire, it would hurt them and—"

"To hell with Lucky and Claire! They've made their choices, haven't they? It's your life that's at stake here. Forget them. God, I'd like to go back to the Forum and grab Scott by his gold chains and rattle his bonded teeth and bring him to his senses, bring him home where he belongs—with you." Bart rubbed his eyes and spent some moments consciously cooling his anger, astonished at his outburst. "Here's what I can do, though," he said finally. "I can be here in an hour and a half anytime you need me. One phone call, that's all it takes. Don't ever think I'm too busy, or any of that. I'm never too busy for you."

Christine tucked her Kleenex back in her purse and smiled at him bravely. "You're a good man, Bart."

"I'll do better than that. I'll come down this Saturday and take you out to lunch and to a matinee. I haven't been to a good movie in—I don't know how long."

"Althea says there hasn't been a good movie since *Casablanca*."

They both laughed, and Bart draped his hand over the steering wheel. "Well, we won't take her with us, then. You go in now and get some rest and I'll call you Friday to find out about your history test."

He walked her to her door, but before she went in, Christine impulsively kissed his cheek and laughed in a way that chimed in his ears as he drove north, a pianissimo counterpoint to the Eleventh Sonata, rumbling through the car.

ii

Clutching her sweater across her cotton blouse, Claire waved goodbye to Justin Moffat from the back step.

"Close that door, Marietta," snapped Meg from the kitchen. "I'm freezing."

"It's May, Mama."

"It's cold."

For this, Claire had no reply. Five miles inland, the sun feebly shone, but defying May's dictates, the beaches and seaside cliffs of San Angelo remained overcoated with a gray chill. Claire turned on all four burners on the stove. "There, that should warm you up, Mama. Would a cup of tea help?"

Claire assumed that the lively dialogue between Meg's knitting needles and the rocking chair meant that she agreed to a cup of tea. The blanket in Meg's lap had grown to immense proportions, colorful random patterns pooling across the floor. Claire eyed it dubiously; when Meg's blanket grew too huge, she was consistently, uncomfortably reminded of a shroud, of certain, irrevocable loss. Claire went to her mother and tenderly tucked the blanket around Meg's knees. Time for Althea to unhook it and roll up the yarn again, Claire thought, filling the kettle. Past time. Claire made a mental note to remind Althea when she returned from her outing with Scott.

At long last, Scott had made good on his promise to take Althea on a personal tour of the Pizza Forum; he had picked her up at four this afternoon and Althea glowed beside him in the black Porsche. For months, Scott had set up numerous dates, and on those occasions, clad in her festive lavender, Althea would be ready, hours in advance, only to be disappointed by a last-minute phone call from Scott. Something had come up. Not today, maybe tomorrow. Not this week. Maybe next. Althea never let on how brutally disappointed she was. Claire's disappointment, equally unstated, went far deeper than a ruined afternoon; Scott had so thoroughly smashed Claire's dreams that she could no longer quite remember what those dreams were save that they had included a Stanford degree, a hope so misplaced that she cringed now even to think of it. No, that terrible day in Alfredo's, both Scott and Lucille had told Claire the truth, and Claire had not heeded either of them. Lucille had said that Anson strangled on principle. Scott had said he wanted to make money. Now he was making money, and clearly, nothing else gave him pleasure. Not Christine, certainly. He treated his wife like an ornament, a pretty artifact, an accoutrement to his gathering wealth. Claire was ashamed of Scott, and her shame festered within her because she could not give it words; not in the darkest of nights could Claire Stone admit how painfully she had misjudged her best-loved son.

Casually, she tossed tea into the pot, listening to the kettle's steady hiss and the needles' rhythmic clack. Other than these sounds and the kitchen clock, the house was unspeakably quiet. Claire wished it were not so, but for the first time in the near year she had lived here, Claire was alone with Meg. Dan's baseball team was in the weekend regional playoffs, and Jason had taken the family car to Sacramento to root, hoot and holler for his brother, San Angelo High's star hitter. Evangeline had driven Lucky and Emma up to the yearly convocation of the Fellowship of the New Millenium, which would last through the weekend. Claire glanced quickly at the calendar and sighed. "Do you know what today is, Mama?"

"Judgment Day?" Meg inquired without looking up. "Veteran's Day? Memorial Day—"

"No, it's May second. Just May second." Claire did not add that a year ago today she had sat helpless with horror in the Emergency Room; she had tried to call Scott at Stanford; she had wept on Bart's shoulder, fearing that Lucky would die. Lucky had lived, but Claire had lost him nonetheless, lost Bart and Scott as well. She was relieved when the kettle screeched and nagged at her, when she could respond to obligation rather than reflection.

"When that little boy is through with his lesson, have him come into the kitchen. I have a question for him."

"Justin's gone home, Mama. No more students today."

"Well you just get him back here, Jill! He didn't get his Lifesaver."

"You can give it to him next week."

Meg's lower lip quivered. "But I'll forget by then."

"I'll remind you," Claire said soothingly. She got out a mug for herself and a cup and saucer for Meg and just then the roar of a powerful car pulling into the driveway filled the kitchen. "Damn that Scott!" Claire cried. "Damn him!"

"So vulgar, dear," Meg clucked.

Claire glanced at the clock and damned her son again. Only five-thirty and he was bringing Althea home. Never mind his promise to take her out to dinner with Christine. Never mind an old lady's eagerness. He was back with a mouthful of excuses and a handful of promises. Damn him. Claire wiped her hands on a dishtowel and stalked outside, ready to do battle, but the car in the driveway was not a black Porsche but a white Mercedes. Claire clutched the banister for support. What did Hoolihan want with her now? What new indignity must she be compelled to face? She squared her narrow shoulders and lifted her chin and regarded the figure rising from the driver's side. A man, but not Hoolihan. Tall, his beard and hair heavily salted with gray, dressed in faded jeans and a denim jacket. He walked across the yard and stopped at the tenderly leafing peach. Matthew Mark Luke and, "Who are you?"

"You know who I am, Claire." Carefully, he approached the porch, mounted the bottom step so that he stood eye to eye with the small woman before him. He smiled. "You've got a little gray, too. I thought you might have stayed the same and only I had changed."

He had changed. There was more of Jon Cotton than there used to be. He was solid, and the added bulk looked good on him. His eyes were clear, though sad, and his face had creased and his fine-grained hands had hardened. Wordlessly, Claire turned and he followed her into the house. He seemed oddly tentative, restrained, or at least he did not fill the room with his old intensity. He draped his denim jacket over the kitchen chair, revealing a brown corduroy shirt with frayed cuffs and collar. He stared at the four blue-flaming burners until Claire went over and turned them off.

The rocking stopped. Meg regarded him resentfully.

"Mama, this is—this is—"

"Jay Coffin," Jon supplied. "Hello, Mrs. Swallow."

"Coffin is a bad name," Meg declared. "You should change it."

"You don't have to worry that she'll recognize you," said Claire. "She wouldn't know if you called yourself Thomas Jefferson."

"I'm sorry to hear that."

"You needn't be. She's not unhappy." Claire poured Meg some tea and placed the cup and saucer on the small table beside her rocker. She asked Jon if he would like some and he nodded in assent. She took the pot and two cups to the table, sat across from him and poured the tea as carefully as if she had rehearsed this small domestic deed and then she remembered that she had rehearsed it: that moment when, belying their youth, they had believed themselves to be a middle-aged couple with time both before and behind them. Now time lay between them.

"This room hasn't changed much," he said, glancing from the herbs in the windowsill to the slumping drainboard and the cracked ceiling overhead. "It's like walking into the past."

"No it isn't," Claire insisted. "It can't be. Why are you here?"

"Here in California or here in this house?"

"Don't quibble with me. I'm not in the mood."

Jon chuckled. "The old Claire."

"I'm not the old Claire. You're driving Hoolihan's car, so it must have something to do with Lucille."

"Hoolihan found me," he sighed. "I don't know how, since I've changed my name twice in the last three years, but he did. I've been salmon fishing and gilnetting up in Washington, Alaska, places like that, but he found me, phoned me one night and convinced me to come back and see my mother before—well, her health has deteriorated badly lately, apparently a lot more since my niece married your son."

"I see." Claire stared into her amber tea. Had Hoolihan betrayed her scurrilous role in that marriage? Certainly Lucille had. "I suppose Lucille said that Scott married Christine for her money."

"Of course. What else would you expect? Money's the only thing my mother understands. She'd never believe they fell in love."

Nothing in Jon's tone was judgmental, and Claire clung to the flotsam of hope. "Your mother was always very mercenary," she replied, trying to sound off-hand.

"She's ruled by money and ruined by it too, judging from the sight of her."

"It's shocking, isn't it?"

"I wouldn't have known her. But then, when she accused me of coming after her money because she was dying, I knew she hadn't fundamentally changed. I'm not sorry I came, even though I know there's no peace possible between us. She is dying, I can see it." He sipped his tea without cooling it and winced. "All she ever wanted was money. That killed her off—inside—a long time ago."

"She might have wanted more than that once," said Claire slowly, remembering Hoolihan's notion of precedents. "She might have done the wrong things for the right reasons. You can't account for what circumstances will do to people," she added, testifying obliquely in her own behalf.

"Well, she says she'll outlive us all and I believe her. She's too mean to die, and if this marriage really has undone her, it's only because she wanted to dictate Christine's life like she dictated Lucy Rose's. She didn't care if Lucy Rose was happy and she doesn't care if Christine is happy." He looked at Claire wistfully, an expression she realized she'd never before seen on his face. "They are happy, aren't they? Christine and your son."

Claire wrapped her hands around her cup for warmth; she thought for a moment before replying that they were newlyweds.

"I suppose that makes Scott my nephew-in-law. Does that make us related, Claire?"

"We were already related," she said dryly.

"Well, I hope I get to meet them before I leave."

"When do you leave?"

"I'm flying back up to Alaska on Monday. I'm staying at Hoolihan's till then."

"You must have forgiven him," Claire said curtly.

Jon smiled. "Hoolihan is really quite a remarkable man. It was his idea that I come to see you today. I wanted to see you, but I thought I ought to call first. Hoolihan said if I called, you'd tell me to stay away. He said you'd be lying." He regarded her closely.

"Hoolihan thinks he knows everything." she contended. "If you had called, I would have—" But Claire did not know what she would have done. Confronted by him here, she scarcely knew what she would do.

"He knew all about us—all those years ago—" Jon glanced at Meg and lowered his voice. "Chagrin. Did you know that?"

"Not until last year. I'm certainly glad I didn't know it at the time."

"I didn't believe him, but he trotted the whole thing out, you working at Petey's, everything. I couldn't believe three-quarters of what he told me."

Claire tensed and the blood drained from her face. "Like what?"

"Like Christine marrying your son. I couldn't believe you had a son that old, that you'd gotten married so young."

Claire was relieved enough to toss her head and retort with some spirit, "I told you what I wanted out of life. Not everyone has the same colossal disdain for marriage that you have."

"I've changed. I have every respect for people who can stay married. Marriage requires a strength of character I guess I just don't have."

"You're divorced?" she asked unwillingly; she had no wish to tread across that vast tundra of empty years between them.

"Never legally. I've lived with several women. One, I stayed with for six or seven years, but I never—well, you're lucky you didn't marry me."

"I married Lucky."

"Yes, and Hoolihan said you had a hell of a time last year, not knowing if he would live or die."

"The doctor saved Lucky's life," replied Claire tartly, "and Hoolihan, in a manner of speaking, saved his ass, and ever since, Lucky's been out saving his own soul." She got up and poured more hot water in the pot and refreshed her mother's cup.

"Where's Althea?" said Meg, startled. "It's very unlike her to run off and not tell me."

"She hasn't run off, Mama. Scott will bring her back after dinner."

"Well, I'm going to lie down, and you tell Marietta to wake me when Althea gets home. I won't sleep anyway." Meg's pink face pouted. "How can I sleep when you girls are running around all night? It's disgusting the way you carry on. Don't you think so, Anson?" she turned directly to Jon. "We gave them every opportunity, Anson. I can't understand it."

"I can't, either," Jon replied gently.

"My father's still alive for her," said Claire after Meg had left them. "She confides in him, asks his advice, scolds him. She ignores death and time."

Jon laid his hand over Claire's. "It would be easy to ignore death and time in this house. To be with you is like—I can see the gas burners lit up and this same teapot and you in your chiffon dress and—"

"That girl doesn't exist," said Claire, though she did not remove her hand.

"Oh, she's still here. She was here once and she'll always be here with a boy in a tuxedo. Can't you hear them? Can't you see them?"

Claire snatched her hand away. "I see a middle-aged man with gray hair who's changed his name twice in three years. I see a middle-aged woman with grown sons and a senile mother, a mountain of debt and a husband who's gone bonkers with religion. And if you weren't such a fool, that's what you'd see, too. You can't go around recreating the past."

"I don't have to recreate it, Claire. I never quit loving you."

"I suppose that any man who could love a revolution that hadn't happened would love a woman he couldn't have."

"I still love the revolution. But I love you more."

"You didn't used to."

"I've changed."

Claire drew a deep quivering breath. "What am I supposed to say, Jon? Better late than never? What do you want from me? Shall I forgive you for leaving me all those years ago or say how thrilled I am that you've continued to love me? What good would it do? Do you want me to tell you that I have always loved you too, thought about you daily? Well, I haven't. I married Lucky and I buried you. I made a life for myself. You made a life for yourself. People live through broken love affairs. They go on." Filled suddenly with unreasoning rage, Claire wanted to smash the cups, the pot, the past, the man before her, the dream she had carried in the form of a child she now despised. She loathed the girl in the grenadine chiffon and the boy in the tuxedo, who (beside or between, or over and through the middle-aged man and woman) laughed while rice clattered to the floor and they pretended to be their middle-aged selves: in middle age, the past changes daily, the present grows more tense and only the future stays static. The girl in the grenadine chiffon did not know that, and Claire hated her for her ignorance. "Let's get out of here," she said, grabbing her coat off the hook. "Let's go for a walk and get away." From what, she did not specify.

Mist chilled their faces and cooled Claire's anger as they wordlessly waded through Althea's garden, where seed packets jacketed short sticks, past the huge artichoke plants, past the quacking ducks, beyond the gate and thick drifting sand to the firm shore, where small waves expired while a flock of gulls eyed their empty hands shrewdly.

"At least you have something to show for your life, some accomplishment," said Jon when their silence grew oppressive. "I'm still a good leftist and I've paid my dues in a hundred jails. I've been beaten and gassed and I've marched and organized and been arrested, jumped bail and gone on, but I've had to leave everything I ever cared about or tried to build. I've lost strikes and causes, deserted friends, left women I cared for—and for what? I'm an outlaw in Yuppieland. How can you talk politics to fitness freaks who don't have a thought outside their own bodies? Nowadays, a draft dodger is someone who shuts a door in a high wind. People like me, we're nothing but living artifacts. They should put us all in the Smithsonian with tags around our necks: Anarchist-Extinctus, c. 1964-1972." He snorted disdainfully. "No, I don't have a single achievement I can point to and say, That's mine. At least you have children."

"That's fact, not an achievement. Motherhood is a bond that's forged only so it can be broken. My sons will always be my sons, but children are finite, temporary. I wish I'd known that earlier," she added.

327

"Yes, but you and Lucky still have each other. You stayed married. That's an accomplishment."

She turned to him and laughed ruefully. "Oh, Jon, you really want to believe that, don't you? You're still committed to absolutes. You must believe that I made all the right choices and you made all the wrong ones. I wish it were true, but it's not and I can't bear that you should insist on framing me in some glowing domestic scene. Don't do it. Lucky is married to a jealous God now. Lucky's repudiated his unconverted past and wants to atone for it. I'm part of that past. I'm not part of his intimate life anymore. I'm not God, after all."

"God is a hard act to follow," Jon conceded.

Claire swooped up some pale stones and tossed them into the water; the gulls took flight. "I've ended up just like you said I would, looking after my mother while she mourns my father."

"People only end up dead, Claire. The grave's the only final resting place. That's why good leftists never commit suicide. They don't believe in rest. They believe in struggle."

"Well, struggle implies resolution, doesn't it? Victory or defeat."

"No, struggle is ongoing."

"Well, maybe you have the strength for it." The wind whipped Claire's hair into her face and she pushed it back with both hands. "But I've only met with defeat. I look back on my life and it's like a dream from which I've just awakened to find myself still Claire Swallow, still playing the piano. I can remember that other life, but only in the pale way you remember dreams. Dreams don't have any substance, no more than a piece of wood that's been cast into the fire and burned up. Smoke and ash," she added, as if both smoke and ash plumed before her.

"You regret the choices you made? The things you did?"

"I can't say," she replied truthfully, since she could not say without revealing her ugly role in the drama of Scott's marriage. "I misread the past," she said flatly. "I regret that."

The cliffs jutted out and the tide came in, forcing Claire and Jon to turn back up the beach, kicking bolts of raveled seaweed from their path. "I misread the past too," Jon confessed. "Or at least I misread history. Is that the same thing? I took myself out of the university and in search of the revolution when the revolution was about to start in the university. I thought it would happen amongst the workers, not the students."

"It never happened at all, did it?"

"Oh, but there was that moment, don't you remember it? May 'sixty-eight, the marches and demonstrations, in 'sixty-nine and 'seventy when people shared commitment and conviction, when they cast off their inherited, conventional pieties. Don't you remember that golden moment? It seemed like all we had to do was seize and shape it."

"You forget, Jon, I had a life of all the conventional pieties—a husband and children. I missed every bit of that. It passed me by."

His shoulders sagged. "It passed us all by, I guess. We seized the moment, but we couldn't hold it. What I thought was the revolution was only a passing fashion. God! I loathe fashion, convention, custom, all those hedges and fences and pickets around human potential."

Her hand grazed Jon's, and rather than endure the old current, Claire folded her arms close against her chest. "Oh, Jon, you didn't just misread history, you misread human nature. People like hedges. They like their lives comfortably picketed. If they were free, they'd be overwhelmed with responsibility for their choices. You can't expect people to leap over time and society and follow you. You wanted too much," she added coldly.

The suffering on his face was unendurable, but Claire resisted the urge to apologize or console him; in twenty-two years, she had forbidden herself to consider the possibility that Jon might return; now he was here and Claire was utterly unprepared, especially since she never expected to pity him. Pity, like debt and gratitude, made Claire uncomfortable.

"I guess I misread the historical imperative," he said at last.

Claire laughed, as much to break the tension as anything else. "How long has it been since I've heard that phrase? I can still see you and Kharabian arguing the historical imperative so passionately in the firelight in Chagrin."

"Kharabian's dead, Claire."

"Dead? Dead!" Claire walked toward the cliffs and sank down, cross-legged in the dry sand. Jon sat close beside her, as if, between their bodies, they protected a sputtering candle. "How? When?"

"He died of a drug overdose in 1970."

"But Kharabian was never into drugs! I mean, a little grass, but—"

"He changed too, I guess. I guess he changed a lot, judging from what Marietta said."

"Marietta! My sister?"

"Hard to believe, isn't it? I met her on a commune in Colorado in 1973. I spent a couple of nights there on my way to—I don't remember

where now. I was talking politics with Marietta and I said that Kharabian had the finest political mind since Kropotkin and that's when she
told me she had known him, that she'd been living with him and a
bunch of others on a commune in New Mexico when he died. He was
thirty-two."

"But Marietta never wrote that she'd met you. I mean, she hardly
wrote at all, but she never—"

"I wasn't Jon Cotton in 1973. I haven't been Jon Cotton since 1964. I
forget who I was in 1973, but it doesn't matter. She wasn't Marietta
Swallow, either. She had changed her name to Neptune. I was in bed
with her when I discovered she was Marietta Swallow," he added uncomfortably. "I might as well tell you that."

"You went to bed with Marietta?"

"No. I went to bed with Neptune. I got up with Marietta." He shook
his head, as though the shock were still fresh. "I didn't ask her anything about you. I couldn't. I would have had to tell her who I was.
Maybe if I'd taken Rick's advice, I'd know who I was from one year to
the next."

"Rick who?"

"Adamson. The doctor from the church in Chagrin. You remember
him?"

The name floated faceless before Claire; she remembered a pair of
Lysol-puckered hands.

"He and I got to be good friends after you left me. He always said I
should forget all this political bullshit and get a medical degree. He said
I had a physician's touch, and if I wanted to serve people, why didn't I
do it with a stethoscope. I told him I didn't want to serve people. I
wanted to serve the revolution." Jon rubbed his deep-set eyes, pinched
the bridge of his high nose. "Now, sometimes, I wonder if maybe I
should have taken his advice. Maybe I could have brought babies into
the world or set the bones of little boys who fell from trees or pumped
the stomachs of people who had despaired of life. I could have been
good at it. But that old saying about paying your money and taking
your choices, it's ass backward, Claire. You make your choices and go
on paying for them." He caught a fistful of sand and let it drain through
his fingers. He added softly, "I haven't any stake in the future, nothing
except a theoretical revolution. I wish I had something real. I wish I'd
married you, Claire, and had children. If we'd had a family, we might
have—"

Claire tuned him out. She hadn't the imaginative wherewithal to consider the concept what if; the subjunctive always confounded her. Claire's abilities lay in the direction of persistent denial, like Hoolihan's defense of Patrick Ryan, but for one moment she was tempted to tell Jon that he had a son. And the next moment she knew she wouldn't. That truth was the one thing still wholly Claire's own and she couldn't part with it. Not now. Not when that son had come to embrace and embody everything his father despised. She thought of Scott and his flashing gold chains and realized that could Lucille be privy to the truth, she might, in her grim, calculating way, understand her grandson, but Scott Stone would have revolted Jon Cotton to his very core. Claire uncoiled her feet and drew away from him. "I couldn't have married you. Young as I was, I must have known that even then. I couldn't have followed you around to more washtub political meetings and anarchist communes. I'm like everyone else. I like hedges and fences. I wanted to be safe."

"Material safety is the refuge of moral cowards," he observed, his low, confessional tone replaced with the ring of certitude.

"You still believe in absolutes, don't you?" Awe and a little envy tinged Claire's voice. "You always will. You're very like my father, you know that, Jon? His principles were absolute and they could be assaulted, but he'd never allow them to be eroded."

"I'll always believe in social justice, even if I don't live to see the revolution, if that's what you mean. I'll never have you, but that doesn't keep me from loving you." He put his arm around her shoulders. "Always."

Claire knew that if Jon kissed her, the old dream would resurrect along with desire, but time had chastened Claire Swallow and she was no longer reckless or heedless of consequences. She rose, dusted the sand from her skirt and offered him her hand.

They walked up the beach, watching dolphins jump and frolic in the sleek waves as a muffled sunset quilted the horizon. Jon put his arm around Claire, and she responded. They kept an even stride, intimacy balanced between them, but they did not speak until they came to the rickety gate, the fledgling garden, the sorry old house. When they reached the porch, Jon pulled her into his embrace.

"I'm not the person you remember," she said before he could kiss her. "I'm someone else altogether. I want you to know that. It's got nothing to do with Lucky or my being married. I can kiss you—I could even go to bed with you—but it can't alter what's happened and we can't go back."

"What's between us hasn't got anything to do with institutions, Claire, or the past or any part of that rot. As long as we're faithful to that love. Say you love me, Claire—"

"I loved you, isn't that enough?" she cried. "Yes, I love you, I always have, but all that rot *has* touched us, changed us, changed me anyway. My love for you persisted in spite of the rot, not because I was above it!"

He raised her chin to kiss her and she lifted herself on tiptoes to meet his lips and as she did, the girl she once was met the woman she had become and the collision was akin to seismic shock; in fact, there was a collision, a crash, close by, the shriek of screaming brakes and a powerful smash from behind the house.

Claire bolted through the front hall and into the kitchen, flung open the back door to see the black Porsche smashed into the peach tree, its front end steaming and hissing, its headlights falling out like bouncing eyeballs. "Scott!" she cried. "Scott!"

Scott thrust open his door, got out and kicked it shut. "Goddamnit!" he bellowed, "God damn that bastard!"

"What happened? Has someone died? Is Althea—" She peered into the car, relieved to see Althea sitting upright and not slumped over. Still shouting obscenities, Scott pushed past his mother and stomped into the kitchen. Claire followed, pleading with him.

"They're here. I know they came here." In one fist, Scott clutched a rumpled piece of notebook paper. "Who the fuck is that?" Scott wagged his clenched fist at Jon, who hovered near the table, looking shocked and expectant, as if he might be called upon to give first aid. Without waiting for an answer, Scott whirled on his mother. "I was doing it all for her. Everything! I did it all for her. Well, she won't get away with this. And him! I'll kill him."

"Who?" Claire implored. "Who are you going to kill?"

"He almost killed me." Althea hobbled into the kitchen. "Thank God for seatbelts. My skull may not mean much to you, Scott, but I like it just as it is."

"Where are they?" Scott wheezed and seethed, his gold chains and gold watch flickering as if they might spontaneously combust. "She can't do this to me."

"Who?" Claire begged, near tears. "Who?"

"Christine," said Althea emphatically, lowering her bulk into Meg's rocker. A smirk perched visibly on her lips. "Who's that?" she nodded toward Jon, who had sunk into a kitchen chair. "You don't look well," she chided him.

332

"Fuck him! What about me! What about my wife! She's left me!"

"Christine has left Scott?" cried Claire.

"Left him for and with Bart," Althea replied smugly.

"Bart!" Claire, too, collapsed at the table, stunned, breathless. "She's gone off with Bart?"

Althea began rocking, her fat hands laced over her thick bosom. "Couldn't you just see it, Claire? Didn't you know Bart's been down here every weekend, taking her out to lunch and to the movies, a walk on the beach, a little talk and laughter."

"I don't—" Claire gasped. "Bart hasn't—I don't see much of Bart when he—I mean, Christine mentioned that she saw a lot of Bart, but—"

"Hmph. You must have been blind," said Althea with obvious relish. "Didn't you ever notice the look in her eyes when she'd talk about Bart?"

"You were in on it, you fat old hag!" Scott approached the rocking chair, oozing menace. "You knew she was fucking around on me—and with that old man."

"Bart is not old," Althea contended, ignoring Scott, concentrating on a bit of lint settled on her shoulder. "He's only forty, and as for the gross vernacular act you allude to"—she gave an imperious sniff—"I don't know and I don't care. I never thought I'd approve of adultery, but I'm happy for both of them. Bart has found a woman worthy of him, and that sweet Christine has a man who loves her. At last. Her husband certainly didn't care about her."

"I loved her," Scott wailed.

"Poop. You never loved anyone but yourself."

Scott brought his fist down on the table, and the cups tumbled and a puddle of tea soaked into the tablecloth and spread. "She can't ruin me like this!"

"She hasn't ruined you," Althea replied. "She's saved herself."

"Can you tell me what happened?" Claire basted the words together with difficulty and addressed them to no one in particular.

"I'll tell you," Althea declared. "Scott took me to the Forum, just as he promised, but of course he didn't have time for his old auntie. He knew better than to bring me home, though. He knew what you'd do to him, Claire, and more's the pity you didn't do it twenty years ago. None of this would—"

"Please, Althea—" Claire glanced from Jon's stricken face to Scott's twisted mask of rage.

"Scott decided to foist me off on Christine. Kept mumbling a lot of twaddle about how long it had been since I'd seen her. I told him, I see Christine twice a week, thank you, when she comes for dinner because her husband—"

"Cut the bullshit—" Scott thrust the crumpled paper in front of his mother and the sepia tea stain engulfed it. "Let's get down to business."

"It's because you were always down to business that you lost that lovely, sweet girl. Who'd ever believe Christine was related to Lucille?"

"What *happened*, Althea?" Claire beseeched her.

"Oh yes. Well, we walk into the condo and Scott calls out Christine's name like he is sucking honey through a straw, all ready to dump the old auntie on the wife, but there isn't any wife." Althea chuckled. "Christine has left with Bart, and I hope they'll be very happy."

"I hope you roast in hell, you fat old hag! You were in on this, weren't you? You wanted to see me fucked over!"

Althea rocked complacently, her face aglow with satisfaction, but she retorted that she never meddled in the affairs of others, especially love affairs.

Reluctantly, Claire picked up the paper; it sogged and fell apart and she had to make out as best she could:

Dear Scott

I have left this on the mirror because I know it is the one place you are sure to look. I am leaving you for good and nothing you can say or do can induce me to come back. I'm not leaving you because of what you've done—or haven't done. I am leaving you because I'm in love. With Barton Swallow and he's in love with me. Happiness is sacred and time is short and I won't go through life tied to a man who doesn't care for me just because I am married to him.

I have already called Hoolihan and he is starting divorce proceedings at once. Of course Grandma will be outraged again, but I don't care and Hoolihan says this is the best news he's heard in years and the best thing I could have done. If you want to contact me, you'll have to go through Hoolihan. Bart and I are leaving for Rio within the week. You can do whatever you want, I don't care. This is my moment and I am taking it.

Christine

"What's happened here?" Meg shuffled in, rubbing her eyes and looking from one anguished face to another.

"You sit here, dear." Althea bustled over and led her to the rocker. "Christine is divorcing Scott, Meg."

"We've never had a divorce in our family."

"She's leaving him for Bart. Isn't that good news?"

"Fuck that news! She can't do this to me. The Burbank deal will fall through, and Randolph won't—he'll—I'll lose—I'll be ruined!"

Althea folded her arms and drew up her multiple chins. "Ruined? Well, we'll soon see what you're made of, won't we? All I can say is that if you're a Swallow, we'll soon know it. And if you're a Stone, you'll sink. Anson never liked the Stones," she added as a final dig.

Claire began to laugh. She held the sogging note in one hand and she leaned back and laughed. Scott's jaw dropped and Althea's aplomb fell before astonishment and Meg looked utterly bewildered. Jon Cotton regarded them all as if the lunacy in this kitchen might be infectious, but Claire saw none of this. She threw her head back and laughed until the tears sprang to her eyes. Until she was weak. And, still laughing, she roused herself out of her chair and went to the phone and dialed.

"Who are you calling?" demanded the dumbfounded Scott.

"I'm calling Bart," Claire replied lightly.

"Good. You tell him, Mom. You tell him he can't get away with it."

"Hello, Bart?"

"Claire?" came the familiar voice, which then retreated into a cold formality. "I can imagine why you're calling."

"No you can't, Bart."

"You know, of course."

"Of course I know! I think it's wonderful!" Claire laughed again and crooned into the phone. "How could I think anything else? I know what that marriage was like for Christine. I have eyes, don't I? I just couldn't say anything, but I knew."

"It just happened, Claire," Bart said defensively. "No one planned it, it just happened."

"No one plans to fall in love—" She glanced at her son and looked away. "When it's right, it happens, and it's right for you and Christine. You deserve happiness."

"You don't think badly of us, then?"

"How could I? I'm glad you found each other and fell in love!"

"I've never felt this way about anyone, Claire. I'm forty years old and I've never really known—"

"You know now!" she cried. "That's all that's important. You're both going to be very happy. I'm sure of it."

Scott intervened, tried to take the phone away from her, but Claire whirled her back to him and cradled the phone tightly against her ear.

"Can you forgive me, Claire, for all those awful things I said six months ago and not speaking and all that terrible—"

"Don't even talk about it, Bart. I don't want to talk about all that rotten past. I'm calling to tell you that I love you both and I don't want either of you to doubt it."

"We're leaving for Rio next week, but—"

"I know. I read Christine's note."

"We'd like to see you before we go. Christine isn't here right now, but she cares for you a lot, Claire."

"And I care for her. Please come by before you leave, and see us."

"I know Mama probably won't be able to grasp all this, but Althea, do you think she can—"

"Don't worry about Althea," she said soothingly. "Althea's overjoyed too. You and Christine are sterling people, and you deserve your happiness."

"All right, we'll see you soon then, Claire." His voice suffused with gentleness. "If you knew what your calling meant to me."

"I know what you mean to me, Bart. You'll give my love to Christine, won't you? I'll see you whenever you get here. We'll—"

Scott accosted her and snatched the receiver from her hands, but not before Claire made her farewells and punched down on the phone, severing the connection. Scott held the dead instrument in his hand and then dropped it and it clattered to the floor. "Do you know what you have just fucking done? Your fucking brother," he explained patiently, as if he were speaking to Meg, "has just run off with my wife. Don't you understand what that means? I'm ruined. I'm your son. You want to see me ruined?"

Claire was not laughing anymore, but neither was she crying. "You are my son and I have loved you better than—better than you know—and I still love you and that doesn't change. But I am ashamed of what you've become, Scott. You haven't any self-respect, only self-love."

"No! I loved Christine! I still love her!"

"Maybe that's true, but it doesn't alter what you've become. Once you got a sniff of that money, you were like an animal in heat. You're blind to everything except money and what money can buy. You're an offense to everything you've been taught."

His face knotted into a vicious scowl. "Everything I've been taught by Dad?" he demanded sarcastically. "All that bullshit Christian stuff or maybe everything I've been taught about cheating and embezzling and—"

"You can just stop right there! I won't hear another word against your father!" From the corner of her eye, Claire caught sight of Jon, who looked wary, as though he might bolt and run for cover, and fleetingly, she realized she had them in the same room—father and son, the son the same age as the father had been when—Claire returned her gaze to Scott: there was a resemblance, but one would have to look for it, to know the relationship beforehand. The high nose perhaps? The forehead? Maybe. But certainly, visibly and in every other way, Scott was a Swallow and in that instant Claire knew what she would probably not live to see: when he was old, Scott would look very much like the Senator.

"And you!" Scott lashed out. "This was all your idea in the first place! I thought you wanted me to be a success."

"What I wanted for you was a future with something you could rely on. You can't rely on money. You ought to know that."

"Me! You're the one who said that money was all I needed and it didn't matter how I got it! You're the one who went begging for money! You're the one who—"

"I was out of my mind." Before Scott could implicate her further, Claire picked up the shredding letter and shoved it at him, pushing him backward with a strength not even Claire guessed she had. "I was out of my mind then," she repeated. "But what's happened since is on your shoulders. If you are ruined, then you better get yourself unruined, but it's your own responsibility."

"Bullshit! It's not my fault Dad drank and gambled and embezzled and lost—"

"Not another word about Lucky! You leave this house and go back to your own home while you still have one and don't you dare come back until you can show some respect for your father and your family. I don't want to lay eyes on you until then."

"Then you'll never see me. Who is there to respect in this mothball family? Grandma's got compost for brains and Althea's a fat old hag and Dad's a religious nut and a sleazo crook and all you can do is give dip-shit piano lessons. You're failures! All of you!"

"Get out of here." Claire marched to the back door and held it open while Meg protested the cold. "Get out and don't come back till you've learned some respect for something besides money."

"Failures," he spat at them collectively.

"Fail and move on," Althea called after him. "That's the family motto. That's what the Senator always said," she added as Scott stumbled down the steps toward his smashed Porsche.

"To hell with the Senator, too," said Claire slamming the door shut.

"I don't think we need go *that* far."

"Oh, admit it, Althea. The Senator ruined people's lives without a second thought. He didn't have any respect for anyone, either. He dirtied up everything he touched."

"I wouldn't say that. Not exactly." Althea went to the fridge and pulled out a head of lettuce, began shredding its leaves like they were dun notices. "The Senator was a dangerous man. You could say that." She gave a forced smile and regarded Jon quizzically.

"I'm Jay Coffin," he offered in an uncertain voice. "I'm an old friend of Claire's."

"I can see that. I mean, you're certainly not a young friend of hers, are you? You look rather shocked by all this. I hope you're not going to faint in my kitchen."

"I'm not shocked, I mean, it's just that I'm not used to—" his voice trailed off.

Claire felt suddenly faint with revelation; she swayed and gripped the table. Of course. That was it and always had been. Jon Cotton relished the clash of historical forces, but he could not endure, he had no resources to absorb the clash of individuals. He was a man of theories, not emotions. The friction, the chafe and scrape of everyday life were not just beneath him, but beyond him. His insistence, in the old days in Chagrin, that Claire accommodate herself to the likes of Maggot and the Schoolbus Seven was not primarily rooted in anarchist principles but in his absolute inability to deal with individuals. Jon could only understand, enjoy, perhaps only tolerate, people in multiples of a hundred. He understood love in that same way; the give and take of ordinary love between a man and a woman was probably unendurable for a man who wanted to uplift, enlighten and convert. Of course he didn't believe in seduction; Claire was the one who had insisted on being seduced, who had insisted on loving and being loved. His confession on the beach came clear and poignant, sad and final as a coda: *he wishes he'd married me and not the leaderless state. He can admit it now, not because he would like to change it, but because he can't possibly change it. Another lost cause. Just like the revolution.* The rock of remembrance that

Claire Stone had carried for twenty-two years shattered in the blast of this recognition, the graves flew open, the ghosts got free, the old questions resolved.

"Now, what I'd recommend for you, Mr. Coffin," Althea went on, "is a little chicken soup with lemon juice, hot as you can stand it. That always soothes shattered nerves. Good for the digestion, too. Of course I can understand why you might be alarmed by all this, and you mustn't think that we ordinarily allow ourselves to have little scenes in front of strangers."

Claire recovered herself and cried, "Little scenes!"

"Our family isn't like that," Althea said stubbornly. "In fact, we rarely have crises at all."

Claire started to laugh all over again. "Oh Lord, Althea! We've had nothing but crises for the past year! Don't you know what today is? Don't you know it was a year ago today Lucky tried to kill himself?"

"Don't remind me," said Althea, giving the head of lettuce a concussive blow.

"Well, I better be going," Jon said hastily, as if another crisis might be brewing. "I have to get Hoolihan's car back to him."

"Hoolihan! I can't imagine that any friend of Claire's could be a friend of Hoolihan's!"

Claire and Jon regarded one another curiously, Claire unwilling to tell the truth, Jon unwilling to lie. When he did not speak, Claire ventured the observation that Hoolihan had proved himself a loyal friend last year in the courtroom.

"He's loyal to Lucille, too," Althea retorted. "Don't forget that."

"Hoolihan," Meg said, picking up her knitting, "is vulgar."

Claire stifled the peal of laughter that rose to her throat. She went to her mother's rocker and knelt, gently wrapping her hands around Meg's; the clacking needles hushed. "Mama, can I have this blanket? The one you're knitting? I need it, Mama."

"It's not finished."

"I don't want it finished. I want it just as it is. Please, Mama."

"Well, of course, Jill." Meg eyed her handiwork critically. "A present for you," she added proudly.

Claire unhooked the colorful blanket from the needles. "A present. Yes. Thank you, Mama."

"What'll she knit now?" Althea asked.

"Something new. Something entirely new. We'll get her some new yarn. It's time."

Hugging that blanket in her arms, Claire walked Jon to the back door as he made his farewells to Althea and Meg, who bade goodbye to Anson. They closed the door and stood on the porch in the misty darkness and Jon framed her face in his hands. "I could call Hoolihan and say I'd be late if you thought we might take that blanket out to the beach, Claire."

Claire reached up and touched his face, carefully, as if to imprint his features on her flesh. "No, I don't think we better. I think we ought to say goodbye. Again, I guess."

"You can say goodbye more than once."

"It doesn't get easier with practice."

Jon kissed her, seized and held her with his old intensity, and Claire gave herself up to the man and moment, tempted to extend that moment and hold that man, but she released him and watched him walk to the gleaming white Mercedes. "I'll be back, Claire," he called. "Count on it."

"I'll be here. I've always been here."

He got in the car and backed out of the driveway and his tail-lights disappeared down Jerusalem Road.

Claire wrapped herself in the unfinished blanket, a small solitary figure on the porch. For a woman who had successively lost each of the men she had placed at the center of her life—father, lover, husband and son—Claire Stone felt oddly elated as she walked around the outside of the old house and out to the beach, elated and free, naked and new as a middle-aged Eve, re-created perhaps, like Lucky, even reborn. The clouds had thickened with nightfall, and if there was a moon, it was lost in the rind of fog that overlaid the sea. Blinking in the distance, Claire saw the rocking light of a solitary sailboat inching northward. She turned and looked back behind her at the cliffs of San Angelo, dotted with condos and expensive homes, their chandeliers glowing high and bright behind glass doors. Nestled between the cliffs, the tall Victorian windows of the Swallow home shone warmly, beckoning. She stood at this, the edge of the known world, and looked out to the Pacific, clutching the blanket, loving it for what it was—not a shroud, but a present of the past. She kept her gaze on the regular and incessant tempo of the waves, and from the fathoms of memory she plumbed the melody of the Eleventh Sonata, timing it internally with the metronomic blink of the sailboat as it disappeared into the fog.